SECOND OPINION

First published in 2011 by MP Publishing Limited
6 Petaluma Blvd. North, Suite B6, Petaluma, CA 94952
12 Strathallan Crescent, Douglas, Isle of Man IM2 4NR

ISBN 978-1-84982-131-5
Second Opinion

1 3 5 7 9 10 8 6 4 2

Book & Cover Design by Maria Smith & Dorothy Carico Smith

Rayner, Claire.
     Second opinion / Claire Rayner.
     p. cm. -- (A Dr. George Barnabas mystery)
     ISBN-13: 978-1-84982-131-5
     ISBN-10: 1-84982-131-3

     1. Women forensic pathologists--Fiction. 2. Infants
--Death--Fiction. 3. Hospitals--Maternity services--
Fiction. 4. Detective and mystery stories. 5. Medical
fiction. 6. Suspense fiction. I. Title. II. Series:
Rayner, Claire. Dr. George Barnabas mystery.

     PR6068.A949S43 2011   823'.914
                       QBI11-600146

A CPI Catalogue for this title is available from the British Library

Claire Rayner

SECOND OPINION

A Dr. George Barnabas Mystery

For Pat Gordon Smith,
*another feisty woman
(and a great daughter-in-law!)*

Acknowledgements

Thanks for advice and information are due to Dr. Trevor Betteridge, Pathologist, Yeovil District Hospital; Detective Chief Inspector Jackie Malton, Metropolitan Police; Dr. Rufus Crompton, Pathologist, St George's Hospital, Tooting; Dr. Hilary Howells, Anesthetist; the British Airport Authority; and are gratefully tendered by the author.

1

The first baby died on the morning of 14 July, or rather, as Sister Lichfield who was a stickler for accuracy wrote in her report, he was found dead in his crib then. It was hard to tell how long he'd been dead; the small body was cold but not stiff, and the eyes were half open. They would have to leave it to the pathologist to decide that, Sister Lichfield said, and busied herself getting the body down to the morgue and doing what she could to comfort the mother.

"Not that I can swear to it that she'll be exactly heartbroken," she confided to her senior staff midwife, Audrey Burke, before she went to the four-bedded bay where the mother had been left to sleep in peace, while her baby had been taken to the nursery for the night because he'd been restless and noisy. "She wasn't what you'd call over the moon about him, was she?"

Audrey, who had delivered Barbara Lennon, had to agree. "Not that you'd expect her to be really, poor thing. Been living on the streets since March, as I understand it, and couldn't be sure who the father was. I dare say she'd have put him up for adoption anyway. All the same, I'm sure she'll be as upset as any other mum would be." Audrey was a sentimental woman who always thought the best of everyone. "Though I have to say she wouldn't hold him when we showed him to her. Didn't even look at him much."

Sister Lichfield proved to be right. Barbara Lennon looked blankly at Sister when she told her of the tragedy, shook her head in some wonderment and just said, "Oh. After all that, an' everythin." Just goes to show, don't it?" And nothing more.

Sister Lichfield made no response to that, merely smiling kindly. She sent the Chaplain to see her and arranged for some bereavement counseling too. Always efficient, there was nothing she would forget for her patients' welfare; having done it she gave the matter no more thought and turned her attention to other more absorbing considerations.

And that was all there was to it, until the end of October when another cot death happened. This time Sister Lichfield was far more rattled, and the whole ward was upset. The news went round like wildfire. Half the mothers burst into immediate tears of fellow-feeling and needed a great deal of comforting and reassuring before they settled again; and of course all the fuss upset the babies who cried noisily all morning while Sister Lichfield, looking crisper than even she usually did, which was very crisp indeed, tried to calm matters down and deal with the parents, who this time were hysterical with grief.

It was understandable. Viv and Angela Chowdary had waited a long time for their first child. It had taken them and half a dozen doctors to achieve the pregnancy, Angela had confided to Sister Lichfield the evening she was admitted with her contractions coming at twenty-minute intervals, so this was a very precious baby.

"Not that they're not all precious, of course," she added hastily as Sister set the fetal scalp monitor in place, making Angela wince slightly but able to smile bravely as well, "but I'm nearly past my sell-by date, let's face it, and there won't be many chances to have another go, will there? Even if Dr. Arundel in the Fertility Clinic'll take me again. So this baby means the moon and stars to us. It's a girl, you know. We had the tests and the amnio and all that—Viv was a bit disappointed at first seeing she's going to be an only one the way things are—I mean, I'm thirty-nine, after all, and—oh!" She caught her breath and looked a little surprised. "That was a big one."

"A very good contraction," Sister said approvingly. "Don't forget your breathing now, dear, the way you learned it. I'll send your husband in, shall I? He's staying, of course?"

"Oh, yes!" Angela said and beamed at her, relaxed again now the contraction had settled, but clearly very excited and happy. "He wouldn't miss a moment of this."

It hadn't been an easy birth. Angela had soon forgotten all she had learned in her prenatal classes, not breathing at all as she should despite Viv's exhortations, and she had bawled a great deal, somewhat to Sister Lichfield's disapproval. She was as modern a midwife as the next, she liked to tell herself, but really she did think privately sometimes that in all this fuss about birthplans and natural childbirth and did-they-or-didn't-they-want-to-be-in-a-birthing-chair-or-under-water, the mothers forgot the virtue of a bit of old-fashioned dignity. Sister Lichfield had trained in the days when a laboring woman was expected to bite her lips and not fuss too much, and certainly not to argue when offered plenty of painkillers to knock her out and shut her up. Sister Lichfield wouldn't have admitted it to her colleagues for the world, but she still preferred the old days when midwives were properly in charge and mothers didn't make such a drama out of it all. A pregnancy, she was fond of saying to her pupils, was after all only a pregnancy. No need to make a career out of it.

But she never let her patients know she felt this way, and was a good caring woman who often remained late on duty to finish a case. In Angela's case, in fact, Sister knew she wouldn't deliver for some time, and went off only to return next morning an hour before her shift was due to see her. And was just in time to deliver the baby who emerged looking bruised and bewildered but seeming well, and when checked over by the pediatric people was charted as indeed being in excellent shape.

The baby, Sister Lichfield thought, showed clearly her grandfather's race—she had soon discovered that Viv Chowdary was the son of an Indian father and Scottish mother—being dark of eyes and with a mass of black hair, and she was very pleased to be told by a now ecstatic Angela that the baby's third name would be Celia, after Sister Lichfield. She smiled and accepted graciously, enjoying the compliment even though it was one she had been paid many times before. This part of East London had a considerable number of Celias aged fifteen and under.

The baby was taken to the nursery to rest, because the birth had been so stormy, though Angela had protested at first, wanting her daughter to be at her side all the time. But she had agreed when Viv had added his own insistence that she should rest and had settled to sleep most of the day away, which wasn't difficult as she was in a single room, while Viv went off to celebrate with his own ecstatic parents and an assortment of brothers and sisters and inlaws of all kinds. Sister Lichfield called Fertility to let them know that another of their successes had duly arrived. Dr. Arundel wasn't there, and wouldn't be back today, she was told, but would come to see her grateful patient first thing tomorrow morning. And the Maternity Ward swung into the daily round of deliveries—a particularly busy one today, in the event—and no one paid much attention to either Angela Chowdary or her baby.

Or not until the late afternoon. Sister Lichfield was about to go off duty, now thoroughly tired after her too early start, when the pupil midwife responsible for Angela's care, a rather anxious girl called Nuala Kennedy, was sent to fetch the baby to her for its first attempt at the breast. It was she who found the baby dead. She ran out into the corridor from the small separate nursery, her eyes almost as wide open as her mouth and shrieking like a steam engine. The noise brought Sister Lichfield into the corridor from her office in her mufti—she'd been changing to go home—together with several of the other nurses and midwives.

"There's something wrong!" the pupil midwife shouted, her face showing real terror.

Sister Lichfield's hand had itched to provide the time-honored remedy for hysteria, but she settled for grasping the girl by the shoulder, hurrying her back into the nursery and closing the door firmly behind her. "Good God, woman, do you want to set the entire ward off? When will you girls learn how to be quiet around the mothers? They burst into tears at the least excuse and then set the rest of them off. Now what is it?"

"The Chowdary baby, Sister," Nuala gibbered. She gulped as sudden tears appeared in her eyes. "I think it's dead—I tried to pick it up and it's sort of floppy and…" She shuddered suddenly, quite uncontrollably. "It's not what I'd expected. Not here in Maternity. I'm sorry to be so—"

But Sister wasn't listening to her. She bent over the cot and looked at the baby. The dark hair looked the same, a thick shock that seemed to grow part way down the side of the face too, but the skin that had been a pleasant sallow pink was now blue and the eyes that had been so bright and wide this morning at the moment of birth stared blankly from beneath unevenly open lids. There was no question that the child was dead. Sister Lichfield felt a stab of regret so deep and so painful she could have joined the young pupil beside her in her tears. But she just stood up straight and snapped, "Who else has been in here today?"

The pupil shook her head miserably. "Don't know, Sister. This is the only baby in here right now and I was told to leave her to rest and…" She gulped again and Sister looked at her briefly and then away, her disdain at the girl's feebleness so visible that the pupil herself winced at the sight of it. But Sister said nothing. She lifted her chin at the glass door through which Audrey was peering, with several of the other staff behind her, and Audrey at once obeyed and came in.

"You people, get on with your work," Sister Lichfield said sharply and turned to Nuala. "You too—go and get yourself some coffee. And don't go near Mrs. Chowdary, whatever you do. Leave her to us. Now, Audrey—"

"Oh, lor'," Audrey said as she looked at the pitiful little creature in the cot. "Another one? How long is it since the last? We haven't lost a baby here for…I can't remember how long. And now two, so close together. It'll cause an uproar upstairs."

"That's the least of my worries," Sister Lichfield said. She looked down at the baby again. "That poor couple. This was the most precious baby…Oh, shit!"

Audrey glanced at her and then away, almost embarrassed. It was unusual in the extreme for Sister Lichfield to indulge in street language. "Yes," she said. "Will you tell her?"

"I'll have to. Oh, blast it all to hell and back." Using her own form of swearing again seemed to strengthen Sister Lichfield and she straightened her shoulders. "I'll get back into uniform, then. Look, tell the staff to keep quiet about this. It'll get out, of course, but if we can contain it for a while it'll help…"

But she was too late. Already all the staff and most of the mothers knew a baby had died, and there was a great deal of noise and running about going on as the mothers wept and demanded an immediate check on their own babies and wanted to know what the baby had died of and was it catching? Audrey set to work to soothe them all and make what reassuring noises she could while Celia Lichfield steeled herself to talk to Angela.

At least, Sister Lichfield thought, her husband was back with her, and at least she was in a single room which helped. But not a lot. At first they stared at her blankly when she told them their daughter had been found dead.

"A cot death, I think," Sister said wretchedly, breaking her own rule about saying anything about diagnoses until she was sure, but needing to say something to these two people who stared at her with uncomprehending eyes and blank faces. "It's something that happens sometimes, I'm afraid. I am so sorry. I can't tell you how sorry. It's a tragedy, a dreadful thing to have happened…"

It was Viv who spoke first. "It's not possible," he said, his voice hoarse. "I saw her this morning. I held her. She was wide awake and looked at me. She knew me. It isn't possible."

"I'm sorry, Mr. Chowdary," Sister said clearly and very directly. She felt her heart sinking even lower. This was going to be particularly difficult. "I'm afraid it's true. I—er—" She thought quickly about how the baby had looked. Tolerable, she decided. "Would you care to come and see her? I'm afraid there can be no doubt, and she looks rather different to the way she did when she was newly born, of course, but—"

Angela stirred for the first time, opened her mouth, and screamed. It was a penetrating, agonized howl and Sister Lichfield felt the skin on the back of her neck crawl. She said, more sharply than she meant, "Now, please, my dear—"

"What have you done to my daughter?" It was Viv who was shouting now, clutching the still shrieking Angela to him and staring at Sister Lichfield over her head with wide eyes, so wide that rims of white could be seen above the iris. "For Christ's sake, what did you *do*?"

It went downhill from there. The parents wept, refused to be comforted, began to scream together and carried on doing so until Angela, given an injection of a sedative, collapsed into dim uncomprehending silence, and Viv, offered brandy by the Registrar in Obstetrics, Didier St Cloud (who had been hurriedly sent for by Audrey to help in the reassurance of the mothers), took it and also lapsed into a stunned and miserable quietness. Which made it possible for Sister Lichfield and her staff at last to reassure all the mothers that this was a rare event, a one-off that could not possibly hurt their babies, and for Didier St Cloud to look at the pathetic little body of Baby Chowdary and pronounce her dead.

"PM as soon as we can fix it," he said. "I'll do the paperwork, shall I? You've got enough on your plate with the mothers." Sister Lichfield looked up at him briefly and nodded. They often fought, she and St Cloud, since he, in her estimation, cherished a great deal too many fancy notions about obstetrics that he pushed on the basis of damn-all evidence, and she, in his eyes, was a fuddy duddy who ought to have been put out to grass years ago; but in this situation they had a lively awareness of each other's worth and were grateful for the mutual support they provided.

"If you would, yes please," she said. "I suppose there'll be no end of a fuss, seeing it was my delivery. I saw no problem, so I didn't call you or Fay Buckland. I didn't think it necessary. I had the child checked by the Ped. team, though. So maybe—"

"It'll be fine," he said, picking up the notes to take them with him to the office he shared with the other registrars so that he could write up his last examination of the infant. "No one can blame you for anything. These things happen. A stormy delivery or a normal one, it makes no odds. If they're going to go in a SIDS, go they will."

"I suppose that's what it is," Sister said a little fretfully. "It couldn't be anything else, could it?"

"Precisely," Didier said and went away. "It couldn't be anything else."

And greatly to Sister Lichfield's relief, the coroner agreed.

The inquest was little more than a formality, and when it was over Angela and Viv Chowdary went drearily home and Sister Lichfield did her best to forget them, though it wasn't easy. The woman who had been so excited and pleased with herself the morning her baby was born looked, by the end of the first week after the birth, twice her age and half her size and grey with misery. Her husband had a remote and chilled air about him and, watching them leave, Audrey murmured to Celia Lichfield, "I wouldn't be surprised to hear he'd dropped her and found himself someone new after a while."

Celia looked at her and frowned. "You're being dramatic again."

"No, this time I'm not. Did you see that man's face when the child was born? It was like someone had lit a bonfire in him. And look at him now. He's the same age as she is, lots of time for him to start again, find someone else to have babies with. She's got a very small chance, after all. Poor cow."

And Sister Lichfield couldn't argue with that. She'd come across similar stories before. She knew, better than most, that there was more to having babies than just long labors and stitches and painful perineums. She could write a book, she sometimes told people, about the things she saw and heard in her Obstetric Unit.

But she didn't write a book. She went back to work and for a while everything went as smoothly as could be wished. The department managed to streamline its systems to get the patients in and out faster, and so pushed up the throughput ("What a horrible word!" Sister Lichfield said to Fay Buckland, the senior consultant on the unit. "Makes it sound like those things they use to clean rifles." "Hush," said Fay Buckland. "They're pull-throughs. And the marketeers'll get you if you talk like that.") and the Finance Department found them some money to upgrade some of their wards a little. "We have to market our Obs department very vigorously, Sister," said Margaret Cotton, who was the Director of Finance for the NHS Trust that the hospital had become the previous April. "Because if we don't the London Implementation Group'll come and close us down. And we wouldn't want that, would we?"

Agreeing sourly that indeed we wouldn't, Sister Lichfield pushed herself harder than ever, not only doing more than her share of deliveries and teaching the pupils and hustling the less experienced of the house officers along so that they learned their business faster, but also spending (wasting, she called it) long hours in meetings with the head of the Family Directorate which covered Obs and Gyno. and Pediatrics as well as Family Planning and the Fertility Clinic, while they tried to sort out their finances and think of what wheezes they could use to lure pregnant mothers away from the more attractive hospitals in proximity to Old East and into their own eager arms. It was more than enough to expunge from her mind all thoughts of the sad Chowdarys and their dead baby.

Until one evening in winter, the first of December, when

it happened again. This time the baby was a boy, a large and bouncing child who had given them no cause for anxiety at all. He had been born after a mere seven-hour labor of great tranquillity to a relaxed and experienced mother, Helen Popodopoulos, who was delivering herself of her third child in the ward while expecting to be treated on a Domino basis; domiciliary care had been given right up to the time of her starting labor, so she had never attended the hospital's antenatal clinic, and she had come into Old East only for her delivery, accompanied by her own district midwife, Ann Powell. Sister Lichfield knew her; indeed Ann Powell had been one of her own trainees long ago, and the hospital (as represented by herself) and the district (as represented by Ann) had long enjoyed a happy relationship. So there was no need for her to have any anxiety about the case. The mother was in excellent hands, and should have gone the morning after she delivered to complete the acronym: domiciliary—in—out.

But she didn't. Because at six a.m. when the night staff went to fetch the baby to take to his mother—the four babies from the bay Helen was in had been relegated to the nursery for the night because two of the mums were particularly tired after difficult deliveries, and the others hadn't in the least minded being assured a night's sleep totally free of the sounds of their crying infants—baby Popodopoulos was dead.

And this time the reaction was very different, because George Postern Barnabas, who had been on holiday when the first baby had died and off sick with an infected injury to her left hand when the second one came down to her morgue, was very much on duty. And there was no way she was going to accept as mere coincidence the occurrence of three cot deaths in Old East within a matter of five months. George knew better than that. And anyway, she was worried.

2

"Nasty to come back to," Sheila said with rich sympathy. "It's awful when babies die. All that wasted promise and the poor mother left with empty arms..."

George grimaced, more irritated than usual by Sheila's sentimentality, but very aware of the fact that she was in general irritated by everything this morning.

The weather was foul, for a start; not cold and brisk, which she could handle easily, but dank with a bone-deadening chill from the river mist which filled the air with the acrid scent of oil and mud and old dead things. Everything she had touched since she got out of bed in her noisy little flat just over the river in Bermondsey had seemed slimy with condensation and sticky with heaven knew what in the way of pollution; and her hand felt heavy and dull and less responsive to the demands she had made on it as she worked on the small body that had been waiting for her in the morgue. Fortunately, it had been her left hand she had accidently stuck with the point of a scalpel during a PM on a vagrant's corpse—a piece of clumsiness over which she was still furious; even thinking about it made her flush with shame—but all the same it slowed her down, even though it was now officially regarded as healed and free from infection, and made her painfully conscious of what she was doing.

At least this morning's PM hadn't been observed by anyone from Ratcliffe Street nick, she thought. It would have been dreadful to have had Rupert Dudley there, looking his usual sardonic and unpleasant self, or one of the younger ones— like Michael Urquhart, who would have been sympathetic and understanding which, in a way, would have been worse than Rupert's sneering gaze. She deliberately didn't think about what it might have been like to have had Gus Hathaway there; he belonged in another part of her mind entirely, and she wouldn't let him intrude where he didn't belong. A thought which she knew was stupid and which therefore made her even more irritable.

And then there was the state of the department when she came back. She'd been off sick for a month, admittedly, but there'd been no need to let the paperwork pile up on her desk so appallingly. Everything looked shabbier and messier than usual, too, and she'd said as much to Sheila, seeing she was the senior technician responsible for efficiency, as soon as she returned. Sheila had bridled and looked offended, then admitted that George was right; things had slipped badly. But what could she, Sheila, do when they refused to replace either Barbara Pratt, the hematological technician, or the junior, Tracy, both of whom had left this summer, and the locum pathologist had been so uninterested in what he was doing? She did her best to keep the work going through but with staffing levels the way they were, how could she, Sheila, be expected to cope? She wasn't a miracle worker, after all, just a humble toiler in the vineyard doing her best with what she had.

And, she had continued, warming to her theme, it wasn't as though it was only in Pathology there were problems with staffing; wasn't the entire fabric of Old East under threat with all the changes the new Trust Board was making? "Counting the bloody paper-clips," she said bitterly. "That's what we're doing. Everything's being cut to ribbons. It's death by a thousand cuts, that's what it is." She said it as though the cliché were a phrase she had newly minted. "There are all those bloody Union meetings all the time and you fall over protesters

and their placards every time you go in and out of the place—
and then to cap it all you come back and have a go at me when
I've done all I could, I swear to you, all anyone possibly could
do, to keep things going properly—"

George had taken a deep breath and stopped listening, while
biting her lip to keep back any comments regarding the amount
of time Sheila might have spent gossiping on the phone—her
most infuriating habit—and said merely that she would talk
to Professor Hunnisett about it. The person who really had
control over staffing, of course, was the Chief Executive
Officer, Matthew Herne, but she knew she'd get short shrift
from him if she asked for more help. The only thing that man
cared about was the rows of figures he spent all his time with;
if she didn't get a clinical ally to help her lean on him, she'd
never get anywhere. Professor Hunnisett, as head of the Clinical
Directorates—these new labels they all had now they were an
NHS Trust were another source of irritation to George—was
the only person she could ask to help her; not that he could be
expected to do all that much. He never did, after all.

She got rid of Sheila by dint of asking for coffee—a request
which sent her off in a huff to complain to Jerry and Jane and
Peter and anyone else in the main lab who would listen that she
wasn't a domestic, for God's sake, the woman could make her
own bloody coffee, before going into the little kitchen to make
it—and settled at her desk.

The paperwork would have to wait; first there was the report
on this post-mortem to do, and she took the cassette Danny
Roscoe, her mortuary porter, had given her after she'd finished
her dictation, and pushed it into her Walkman. It would have to
be typed out so that she could read the notes at her leisure, but
now she wanted to recall what she'd seen and done.

She sat with her eyes closed, slowly rubbing her dull left
hand with her right as she listened, and frowned.

It had seemed to be a cot death. Certainly there were no
signs of any kind to explain the death in any other terms; she

had looked particularly carefully for needle marks and there had been none, and had taken samples for Jerry, her most sensible technician, to check for insulin. She, like every one else in the pathology world, had become particularly watchful for that ever since the fuss last year over the nurse suffering from Munchausen's by Proxy, who'd murdered in-patient children up in Lincolnshire. But she doubted there'd be any; there had been no signs to lead her to suppose anything untoward had been done at all. Inevitably she was left with that most deeply unsatisfactory of diagnoses—Sudden Infant Death Syndrome—to put on the report for the coroner, and she opened her eyes and rewound her tape, glowering as she thought about it. It was as bad as those ghastly historical days, when they had entered things like "Dead of the Flux' or "Succumbed to Melancholy' in cause of death columns in church registers. Positively antediluvian.

She leaned back and rubbed her face, trying to make her left hand feel less heavy, and knew the problem was as much her own mood as anything else. If she kept thinking about her hand, of course it would feel odd. Somatizing, that was what she was doing. She was anxious and pushing her anxieties into her work and thereby into her body. If she hadn't been thinking about her mother that day when she'd done the post-mortem on the vagrant's sadly decomposing body (they'd found him in a pile of dustbins where he had clearly been for almost a week, unnoticed because the street-cleansing work of the local council had been privatized and somehow the collections were "all over the place', as the policeman who brought in the body had told her gloomily), if she hadn't, she repeated inside her head, she wouldn't have let her hand with the scalpel slip. If it hadn't slipped she wouldn't have stuck the back of her other hand and let in the infection that sent it swelling to terrifying proportions and pushed her temperature sky high. And if *that* hadn't happened she wouldn't have had to spend almost a month in the Communicable Disease Ward while they sorted out the causal organism and got rid of the infection. Time she had spent thinking about her mother…

With a sharp gesture she reached for the pile of paperwork and tried to start on it, but it was no use. She still had to decide what to do, for it had been over a month since Aunt Bridget had written, and the sooner she did it, the sooner she'd get her head together.

After a few minutes she pushed the work away and pulled out from her drawer a piece of blank paper. She'd do it in columns the way she usually did when she had a problem to solve. Neatly she ruled a line down the center of the page, then wrote across the top: "EPB. WHAT TO DO."

"ONE', she wrote. She stopped and chewed her pen. After a while she bent her head and wrote firmly: "Ignore A.B."'s letter as nonsense." And then stopped again.

Aunt Bridget, as she had called her since infancy, even though the woman was just her mother's friend and not a relative at all, had never been one to fuss. That was why her mother had loved her and why George herself had quite liked her. So if things were worrying her about Vanny—George's mother—as she had said in her letter, then she was indeed deeply concerned. This wouldn't be a small matter.

"She's not quite as good at caring for herself as she thinks she is," Bridget had written in that strong backwards-leaning script that was so familiar.

> *I can't go into details here and I'm not sure I want to. I just want you to come home and take a look at her. That's all. I've talked to your Uncle Nathaniel and you know what an old bastard he is, and I'm sure you'll forgive me the description for isn't it no more than the plain truth? He said it's none of his af-fair and he has his own problems, and that was that. Though I have to say what the old devil could do is limited, even if he were willing. He's almost seven*

*years older than your ma and I don't have to tell
you her seventieth comes up next January. So, what
are the chances of you coming over to visit with her
for a while? It would please her one hell of a lot, of
course, and it would help me to decide what's best
to do next...*

And apart from some inconsequential chatter about the doings
of some of George's scatter of cousins, most of whom still lived
in New England well away from Upstate New York where
Bridget and Vanny had been contented neighbors and friends
this past forty years, that was all. Not another word about what
it was that worried her. And even when George, anxious about
what little she had said, had phoned her, Bridget had not been
forthcoming.

"Come and see for yourself," was all she would say. "I'm
not the doctor, George. You are. Not that's she's sick, exactly.
I don't mean that. It's just that—well, come and see." And that
had been that, and George, remembering the stubbornness of
the woman, had given up trying.

No, she couldn't ignore Aunt Bridget's letter. So she looked
at her piece of paper again and wrote another line. "Go home
to Buffalo."

She leaned back in her chair and contemplated that. And
then shook her head. It just was not feasible. The job here was
not one she could easily leave for a month or more, not after
such extended sick leave, and there would be little point in
going for a shorter time, surely? Even if she could afford it, and
truth to tell she'd be hard pressed to do so.

It had cost a fortune to get her tiny flat in Bermondsey;
she'd tried to find somewhere in an area still untouched by
the creeping tendrils of gentrification which had invaded the
whole Docklands area, but had had to give that up. No one had
any flat to offer in what she called the ordinary streets. They
were all council tenants or people who had lived in the same

houses for so long no one would get them out till they died, and then the council had a waiting list so long that—No, she'd had to give up that idea, and find herself a flat to buy amongst the smartened-up streets, with their brass carriage lamps and gleaming white paint at which the locals sneered and which made the shopkeepers watch out for the residents so that they could overcharge them. And that had cost money. She'd scraped the bottom of her savings account to get the place, had borrowed to the hilt to furnish it and heaven knew when she'd be out of debt.

So, she was broke and that was the core of her predicament. She couldn't visit Ma, because she daren't take time off for which she wouldn't be paid and she couldn't afford the price of an air ticket anyway.

Again she reached for the piece of paper and this time wrote more slowly: "Get Ma to visit me', and put down her pen and rested her chin in her hand.

She loved her mother dearly—at a distance. When they had shared a home, long ago when her father Oscar Barnabas was still alive, the only thing that had kept them from arguing all the time had been his gentle buffering; he'd told George firmly that he loved his wife and wouldn't let the impetuous young George drive her crazy; he'd told his wife he loved his daughter and wouldn't allow her strong-minded mother to run her life. And they'd listened and managed to live together amiably enough on that basis. But since her father had died— oh, no. There could never be any peace if they lived together.

Face it, woman, George told herself now. You don't want to go to Buffalo because you just don't want to have to live with her. You could get a job there, probably, but you'd rather stay here. And if you can't live with her in Buffalo, having her here will be just as bad.

"I'll ask Bridget too," she said aloud, and then grinned in relief. Of course. She wrote that down on her sheet of paper and then screwed it up and threw it into the waste basket. It had worked again, writing it down, and for the first time that morning she felt better, in control of herself and what was going on around her.

Now she could put her mind to her job. She pulled the paperwork back and started to sort it with swift fingers into piles of urgent, not-so-urgent, and get-someone-else-to-do-it. It only took her half an hour to finish by managing to get a good deal of it on to the someone-else pile (Sheila? Probably. Do her good, she thought with a shaft of malice), leaving herself with some stuff she could get through before the end of the day if she put her mind to it. Which meant she could now go back to the matter of the Popodopoulos baby.

She looked again at the note that had been written on a scrap of paper and attached to the forms that had come with the body. "This is the third infant death we've had in Maternity since the summer? Linked?" The note was typed and unsigned but she assumed it had been written by the registrar who'd verified death, and she riffled through the forms to find out his name. Ah, yes, she thought. Didier St Cloud. A stocky young man with a great deal of untidy fair hair and no hint of a French accent in his speech, even though he had been born and reared in Lyons; she remembered seeing him in the canteen laughing and sitting rather close to one of the prettier young nurses and being told all about him by Hattie Clements, her closest friend among the nursing staff, who was as eager and amused by hospital gossip as was George herself.

"Very bright, according to Audrey Burke. She rather fancies him, I think. She's quite jealous because he's obviously got a thing for Alison Gurney—that's the girl he's talking to—and she knows that Celia Lichfield dislikes him and that makes him even more attractive in her eyes. She can't stand Lichfield though they always seem to get on well together. But then, as Audrey says, you have to try when you're stuck with each other."

None of which, George told herself now sternly, is at all relevant. The thing is, if this is his note and he's right and there've been three sudden infant deaths in Maternity then there is indeed something to worry about. I'll have to ask him if he did attach it to the request form, and why he didn't sign it—because if there's something odd going on, his coyness in being direct about it gets to be significant.

Her spirits lifted suddenly and she found herself whistling softly through her teeth as she left her small office and went to check on the state of things in the labs; it wasn't so bad being here, after all, rotten though the weather was. She'd get Ma over on one of those special tickets that meant she had to go home after a fixed time, so even if they did argue while she and Bridget were staying with her (and it was going to be dreadfully crowded; she only had the one bedroom and they'd have to share, which no doubt they'd fuss about), well, it would only be for a few weeks. And she had an interesting mystery to get herself buried in. Lately, there'd been nothing much to interest anyone.

She stopped outside the door to the main lab and smiled a little wryly. You mean there's been nothing much to interest Gus, she told herself, so you haven't seen much of him and you miss him. Go on, be honest. You miss him.

"I miss the laughs," she said aloud, and then shook her head. It was that of course, but a bit more besides. He really was being very odd in the way he behaved and that itself was a mystery she'd like to solve. There'd been a time, not all that long ago, when he'd been amazingly attentive. Phoning her all the time, dropping into the lab on the flimsiest of excuses, and generally behaving like a really ardent swain. And she'd liked it. Naturally, she wouldn't have let him know that for the world. He was quite conceited enough already, and anyway she still hadn't forgiven him for the way he had behaved back when she had been going around with Toby Bellamy after the business of Richard Oxford's death; he'd actually lied about there being a case they had to go on together just to stop her seeing Toby. And all the time Toby had been at Old East, even long after she and he had rather cooled off each other, Gus had gone on being attentive.

But when Toby had left, a couple of months ago, Gus had started to change. Just as she was getting quite used to the idea of having him around when she wanted him, going out with him when she was in the mood but staying in or going out with other friends when that suited her better, he'd stopped asking her. It had become more and more interesting, and more and more puzzling; and now she had to admit she missed him. Missed the laughs. Missed the fish-and-chip suppers in his restaurant where he was treated like God Almighty by the staff and clearly adored it. Missed having the chance to discuss any complex case they might have.

But the cases they'd become involved with together in the past few months had been very run of the mill: suicides hauled out of the Thames; a few domestic batterings (including one of a woman who had killed her bullying husband, at which George had cheered and Gus had been pugnacious in his condemnation of people who had one set of reactions for men and another for women and where was her sense of justice, for Gawd's sake, all of which had led to a most satisfying argument, which she, she had convinced herself, had won, though he vehemently denied it); and of course the usual crop of stabbings, fights and general mayhem among the young men of Shadwell and its environs.

After all that bread-and-butter work, this case involving three dead babies must surely engage his interest? She pushed open the door of the lab and went in, once more whistling behind her teeth. Of course it would. It had certainly engaged her own. She'd do a bit of checking here in the hospital on her own account and see what she could take to Gus. One thing was sure, though; she wasn't at all happy about dismissing this infant's death as just another cot death tragedy. Three similar deaths in five months did not, in her estimation, seem very likely. So after she got things running again as they should here at the lab, she'd put herself about a bit; and then she made a face as she realized how easily she'd slipped into using one of Gus's familiar phrases. Bloody man, she thought, I'll show him! And felt absurdly elated.

It was an elation which lasted her all through the day and only faded when she had to settle down in front of her phone at nine o'clock that night to call her mother, who should be at home at around four in the afternoon. Or was it now a six-hour time difference? She could never remember.

This call, she thought gloomily as she dialed the fourteen digits that would connect her with her old home, would not be easy. She sat staring at the freshly painted walls of her new flat, listening to the series of single rings in her ear and visualizing the big old parlor at home with its over-stuffed chesterfields and deep loungers and her pa's roll-top desk where the phone stood, seeing her mother coming out of the kitchen through the old swing door to answer it, and when the phone was at last picked up said, in the brightest voice she could, "Ma? So how are you, hon? It's George. How're things?" And settled down to listen.

3

"What note?" Didier St Cloud said and rubbed his nose with the back of his hand. He was in his theater greens and the line of his face mask, which had been tied far too tightly, still marked the bridge of his nose. "I don't know what you mean."

"It was attached to the PM request form," George said patiently. "On the Popodopoulos baby."

"Nasty one that. The mother was in a shocking state, poor thing. The whole family was—awful. But I did no special note about it. Only the normal ones."

"Look, I'll show you," George said and flipped through her file. "If I haven't left it down on my desk, that is—No, here it is. Look." She thrust the path. lab request form across Sister Lichfield's desk and he bent his head to look at it.

"This is the third infant death we've had in Maternity since the summer? Linked?" he read aloud. He shook his head, puzzled. "How could I have written this? It's typed."

George looked around the cluttered office. "Well, there's a typewriter here," and she lifted her chin to indicate the rather battered machine that sat on the small desk on the other side of Sister Lichfield's office. "Some people type everything, and I'm glad of it. It's a damn sight easier to read than their handwriting, I can tell you."

"Well, I guess you're stuck with my awful scribble," Didier said cheerfully. "I'm a technoprat. I could no more type on that than fly. It's electronic, for Gawd's sake, so this is nothing to do with me!" He flicked the note with thumb and finger and pushed it back at her.

"Odd though, isn't it?" George said, stowing the note back in her files. "Don't you think? Someone writing that…"

Didier shrugged. "I don't see why. It's not all that surprising, is it? I mean, we have had three cot deaths up here since—when was it? July. I suppose someone thought they ought to point it out to you, seeing you've been away. If you'd not been off sick, you'd have known about them all, wouldn't you? I dare say someone bright remembered that and typed the note just to make sure you knew. Which rules me out again. I'm not that bright." He grinned disarmingly at her and stretched. "It's the old hospital superstition, isn't it? They say these things always come in threes. And it's sort of true. I've just delivered my third set of twins this month. Not bad, eh?"

"It might be, if they were yours and not the parents'," George said. She got to her feet and turned to the door. "Oh, well, I suppose you're right. It's not important who sent the note. The important thing is to tell the coroner I'm not happy."

Didier St Cloud was on his feet too. "Really? Is there something fishy?"

"Fishier than three in a row?" George asked. "Isn't that fishy enough?"

"I doubt it would be for a coroner," Didier said. "Would it? You'd know that better than me, but I imagine even coroners know that these things just happen sometimes. Like my twins. Like the *parents*" twins. No, what I meant was, is there something fishy about the PM? What did you find?"

"A dead baby," George said with some asperity, "and no more than that, dammit. It's difficult to tell what he died of. Or even when, come to that It's harder to pinpoint these things in infants, of course. It looks like a cot death inasmuch as it doesn't look like anything else, so—"

"So a cot death it is, surely?" Didier said. "Why make a hoohah with the coroner about it?"

George looked at him sharply. "Are you suggesting I let it through on the nod?"

"I suppose so," Didier said. "Why not?"

"Because sudden infant death syndrome isn't a diagnosis of a cause of death. It's an admission of failure to find out what really was the cause. And I'd like to know why you want me just to nod it through. What does it matter to you?"

"Not a thing, personally," Didier said, coming round the desk to reach the office door and lead the way out. "I was just thinking of the parents. It's bad enough their baby died, why make life harder for them by fussing with the coroner so that their funeral has to be delayed? That upsets them as much as the death itself, in my experience."

George opened her mouth to retort that she was as concerned about the parents as he was, but along the corridor a light began to flash over one of the labor suites as a bell started its din overhead. St Cloud lifted his hands in a resigned here-we-go-again gesture and dragged his too-tight mask up over his mouth and nose again. "Gotta go. Can't argue with an urgent uterus," he said. "Well, whatever you do, it's all a damn shame. Me, I don't like dead babies." And he was gone in a long loping run down the corridor, leaving George to snap into the empty air where he had been, "Any more than I do…"

She stood there for a moment or two, undecided, as the Maternity department went on its usual frantic way around her. Babies could be heard bawling from all directions and somewhere down the corridor a laboring woman was letting the world know, in no uncertain terms, that as the contractions became stronger and more enthusiastic she personally had changed her mind about the whole damned business of motherhood and wanted no more to do with it, whilst down in the ward kitchen at the far end of the corridor a bad-tempered ward orderly was banging pots around in a cacophony of resentment and all-round loathing of absolutely everything.

She sighed, and went, glad to escape the smell of the place as much as the noise. She preferred the heavy dead earthiness of her own mortuary to the somewhat sickly reek of scented talcum and disinfectant, laundry, milk and sex which seemed to her to permeate the Maternity Unit's airspace. How anyone could work in so frenetic an atmosphere for hours on end, day after day, was beyond her, she thought as she headed for the staircase and thence the underground walkway which would take her from Red Block through to Green Block and Pediatric Outpatients. She needed a word with one of their people before she finally made up her mind what to do about the death certificate for Baby Popodopoulos.

It wasn't till she'd made her way downstairs and on past Physio. and Occupational Therapy to the Outpatient Department for Green Block that she remembered the Children's new Unit had been opened at last, and swore softly under her breath as she retraced her steps and went the other way through Blue Block to get to the new walkway which had been cut underground to take visitors through.

It was startlingly different here from the rest of the hospital. Old East was an establishment that had grown over many decades "like some sort of wart infestation', as Toby Bellamy had once said (and she remembered him now with a momentary pang of loneliness; it had been fun when he'd been around), and now lay sprawled over a big slice of Shadwell land with such architectural virtues as the original Georgian building might once have claimed hidden by a welter of Nissen huts and Portakabins and other temporary erections which had been there for decades.

The Children's Unit, Barrie Ward, named sycophantically after the creator of Peter Pan in the fond hope that maybe they'd get a bite out of the great man's estate (a vain hope, since all the cash from that source went straight to the Great Ormond Street Children's Hospital, leaving Old East well out in the charity cold), had been decorated with such cheerfulness and enthusiasm that it made George's head spin a little. The corridors that led from Casualty in Blue Block, and from the main entrance to the hospital, were painted in the richest of summery yellows, although virtually every inch of available wall space had been taken up with pictures of such unrelenting cuteness that they made George feel positively Scrooge like.

"But I can't shout 'Disney crap' at the top of my voice, can I?" she had said to Hattie Clements the first time they'd walked through together. "However much I yearn to. All these Bambis and Thumpers and Dumbos! It's enough to make your teeth fall out from being over-sugared."

Now, as she hurried by the gaudy colors and the wide dead eyes of the cartoon characters she asked herself what possible relevance this sort of stuff had to dead babies like the small Popodopoulos corpse, now lying in one of her ice-cold drawers in the mortuary, and what effect it might have on frantic parents coming to see a dying child; and then castigated herself for being so sour. The children probably adored it all and the place was here for them, after all, not for cynical forensic pathologists.

Barrie Ward was, if that were possible, noisier than Maternity had been. Here too children cried, a good deal more loudly and piercingly than the babies over in Maternity, but their din was topped by the joyous shrieks of other children in the playroom, the babble of a TV set from one end of the big central space and the shrill repetition of pop music from a video machine at the other. George recoiled for a moment and then went in search of someone to talk to.

She identified a tall boy of twenty-two or so in battered blue jeans and a much-scribbled-on T-shirt as a nurse by the name badge he wore: Staff Nurse Philip Goss; and stopped to talk to him. He was sitting on the floor surrounded by a group of children and got to his feet quickly as she came up to him. The children bawled at his defection and one tugged at his T-shirt, so the boy picked him up and sat him on one hip, patting his back abstractedly as he lifted his brows at George in query and said, "Morning! Can I help you?"

She was struck, not for the first time, by the tenderness these male nurses seemed able to show to children, not a trait they shared with all that many men, she told herself, and smiled at him. He grinned back.

"I'm not sure. I want to talk to whoever did the pediatric checks on Maternity last—let me see..." She riffled again in her file. "On Wednesday night. Any ideas who it might have been?"

"That's a medical matter, I'm afraid. You'll have to ask one of them—there's Dr. Kydd by the desk. I dare say she'll be able to help. Sorry I can't..." And he hugged the little boy on his hip who was now tugging on a lock of his curly hair with considerable ferocity and shook himself free of the small clutching fingers by dint of tickling the child and making him squeal with laughter. George went on her way towards the desk thinking confused thoughts about the child of three she'd had to post-mortem last month after its father had beaten it to death, and somewhere at the back of her mind considered writing a paper on the social pressures that turned one man into a child-killer and another into a child's nurse of considerable skill and patience. And then dismissed it. Papers had to be scientific if they were to be published and what hard evidence could she marshal to underline her thesis that it isn't the shape of their genitals that make people fit to care for children, but something far more complex? None.

Susan Kydd looked at her sharply as she came up to the desk and that sent all thoughts of writing papers into limbo. Dr. Kydd had a formidable reputation for acerbity, and though George herself had never crossed swords with her, she knew that those who did usually retired battered, leaving Susan Kydd the victor; her name about the place might be Judy, because her large nose and strong curved chin framing a narrow-lipped mouth gave her a strong resemblance to Mr.. Punch's helpmeet,

but a victim she was not. She could be as combative as Mr..
Punch himself, and no one enjoyed upsetting her. And George,
she suddenly realized, was about to ask the sort of questions
that might be construed as critical of Dr. Kydd's staff. She
would have to tread warily.

"Good morning," she said sunnily. "Sorry to barge in. Just
need a few words with someone."

"Oh?" Susan Kydd said. "Who?"

"No idea," George said and smiled as disarmingly as
she could. "Whoever did the routine pediatric checks on the
neonates over on Maternity Wednesday night."

"Wednesday?" Susan leaned over the desk and prodded the
Sister sitting there with her head bent over patients' nursing
records. "Patricia? Any idea who was on Wednesday night
over in Matty?"

"I'll check," Sister said and looked at George and nodded.
"Morning, Dr. Barnabas. Glad to see you looking better. All
OK now?"

"I'm fine, thanks," George said, flexing her left hand
without stopping to think. "It's still a bit numb, but that'll sort
itself out. Some nerve damage, but not too much, glory be. And
it's my left hand, of course."

"What happened to it?" Susan Kydd had gone back to her
own notes but now she looked up, interested. "Needlestick?"

"Scalpel," George admitted and reddened. "I feel such a
bloody fool, but these things happen. Anerobic infection."

"Nasty," Susan said. "Could have been—"

"Well, yes," George said, not wishing to dwell on what
might have happened, knowing perfectly well just how nasty
it might indeed have been. "But I'm fine now and glad to be
back at work."

"Picking up the pieces—misery, isn't it?" Susan said,
grinning and George grinned back, relieved. Clearly the older
woman was in a good humor and there'd be no problems about
her questions. "I remember what it was like when I came back

from Bucharest. I'd only been gone a month but, Christ, you should have seen the mess here!"

Patricia Collinson's face took on a decidedly wooden expression and she said loudly, her head bent over the staff-schedule lists, "Last Wednesday night, Dr. Barnabas? Night before last." She lifted her chin and smiled a touch sharply. "It was you, Dr. Kydd."

"Oh, was it?" Susan nodded. "If you say so. It's so hectic at present I can't remember what I was doing this morning, let alone two days ago. Some sort of problem?" And she looked at George.

"One of the babies you saw that night was a cot death—they found him yesterday morning. I did the PM yesterday and—"

"Cot death?" Susan frowned and her face looked heavy again as the line of her nose and jaw once more took on the shape of a nutcracker. "Let me see if I can remember. There were three that night in the early part and then four more later on. Now, can I recall—yes, a frail pair of twins I wasn't at all happy with, had them sent to SCBU but I know they're all right. I saw them this morning. Coming along nicely. I think they'll do. Oh, and a small-for-dates. I think the mother might have been a cocaine-abuser—no hard evidence, but Sister there seems to think it likely and—"

"Not that one," George said. "This was a fine infant, very healthy as far as the look of the body went. Big child, almost six kilos."

"Eleven pounds?" Patricia said, interested. "Was the mother diabetic?"

George shook her head. "No, we thought of that, I do assure you." Patricia had the grace to redden. "Insulin is one of the things I look for early, especially with a particularly large infant. There's nothing in the mother's history or the accounts of the pregnancy and labor. All very straightforward. Domino delivery—or meant to be—so there were no worries about it at all. Yet the baby died, and frankly I can't find any cause." She stood gnawing her lower lip for a moment, glowering, and then snapped with some sharpness, "I hate using the cot-death label. It's so goddammed unsatisfactory!"

"I do sympathize," Susan said and her face lost its hardness. "It's not so bad when you can find the answers."

"Precisely. So I just wanted a word—"

"To see if I missed something when I did the checks?" Susan didn't sound particularly acid, but George felt herself get pink again.

"Not at all," she said hurriedly. "It was this note." She pulled the PM request form out of her file yet again and showed it to Susan.

Susan stared down at it, read it and then shook her head. "Nothing to do with me," she said. "It couldn't be, could it? The child was a patient in Matty, not my ward. I didn't even know it had died."

"I know. It's a long shot but…" George shook her head. "The registrar, do you know him? Didier St Cloud."

"St Cloud…Oh yes, the one who looks like a dish mop."

George grinned. Susan's own close-cropped grey hair gave her a look of a lavatory brush, in her private opinion. To hear such a judgment on another's appearance from someone as unprepossessing as the Senior Pediatric Consultant was undeniably funny. "Yes. That's the one. He didn't type the note, and I thought…Well'—she shrugged—"I'm not sure what I thought, to tell the truth. So I just decided to come over here and check. I suppose I'll have to ask the nurses and mid-wives on Matty." She shook her head again. "It's odd, isn't it?"

"What? Three cot deaths since the summer? I suppose so," Susan Kydd said.

"Actually, I meant the note," George said. "Let's face it, with a throughput like ours, it's a statistical likelihood we'll have a few cot deaths from time to time. No, it was the fact that someone thought to write this note that I found odd."

"Well, I'm afraid I know nothing about it," Susan said briefly. "And I really have to get on. It's gone eleven and I haven't even been to the SCBU yet. Was there anything else?"

"No, no thanks," George said and stood back to let her pass, and then watched her as she went hurrying away across the big central play area to the door marked "This way to the Special Care Baby Unit." Beside her Patricia Collinson sniffed loudly and lusciously.

"If she makes any more cracks about the place being a mess when she came back from bloody Bucharest I'll murder her, I swear I will," she growled. "Honestly, we'd only been in here a couple of weeks when off she swanned and then Petra Samson went sick and we were short staffed on the nursing side too and what did she expect? But does she make allowances? Does she hell! She never stops niggling—"

"Well, put it down to high standards," George said, uneasy to be the recipient of nursing confidences about another consultant. "She clearly cares a lot about the children."

"No one would argue with that! That was why she took a month's unpaid leave to go to Romania. I just wish she wouldn't nitpick so much about silly little details now she's back, that's all."

"What was she doing in Romania?" George asked, not only to change the tack of the conversation, but also because she was, as always, totally unable to control her passion for news titbits, however miniscule. No one could accuse her of gossiping with nurses about other consultants just because she showed an interest, surely.

"Babies with AIDS," Patricia said and made a face. "We saw this video, you know? Someone had put it together from all the stuff on telly and were using it to raise funds. Now Barrie Ward's finished, the committee that raised the cash was looking around for something to do, and someone brought the video, and Susan saw it. Off she went like a bullet from a gun, looked after some of them and then had to come back. But she goes often now. It's not as bad as it was a couple of years ago, seemingly, but it's still not good." She looked gloomy. "If I know her, she'll be off to Bosnia next to care for kids there and give us hell the minute she gets back because she doesn't like the way we store the request forms for hematology or something."

"You should be proud of her," George said, a touch reprovingly. "It's tough, that sort of work." She too had seen the films of the children of Romania and had wept over them. "I'm not sure I could do it."

"Oh, hell, of course we're proud of her! If we weren't, do you think I'd be complaining like this? It's just that she's such a nitpicker! Everything has to be just so for Judy, and some days she drives me potty. Especially as I'm not the world's best-organized soul." Patricia grinned then. "Forget it, do, Dr. Barnabas. It's been a bad morning. That Dr. Choopani's been on and on at us and—"

"Dr. who?"

"Local GP. Diljeet Choopani. Always on about something. I have to say, when it comes to nitpicking he beats Judy into a cocked hat. He's been trying to admit a child with gastroenteritis all morning and we keep telling him we haven't got an isolation bed and there's no way this side of the millennium we'll take her into a general bed, but will he stop whining?" The phone, as if on cue, rang and she growled, "I'll bet you all I've got to a penny piece this is the old bugger again."

She picked up the phone and fluted, "Barrie Ward, Sister speaking," and then grimaced horribly at George to show she was right. "No, Dr. Choopani. I'm afraid she's not around just now. What?" She listened for some time, her face blank with surprise. "Oh! Well, thank you for letting us know," and hung up. And swore loudly.

"Got the child into Kings, over the river, would you believe!" she said. "Positively gloating, he was. I loathe that man, I really do—"

"Well, I must be on my way," George said quickly, not wanting to listen to another of Patricia Collinson's prolonged whines about her problems—something she was clearly settling down to enjoy—and she picked up her file and moved out of the nurses' station. "Thanks for your help, anyway."

"Sorry we couldn't do more," Patricia said, settling down to her papers again. "Maybe the nurses on Matty'll know whatever it is you want to find out."

"Maybe," George said. "If I get round to asking them. It doesn't really matter that much, I suppose. I was just—well, curious." She looked at her watch. "And I'd better call the coroner, or I'll miss him."

She went, grateful to leave the hubbub of the ward behind. The children had begun to whoop in excitement as the lunch trolleys arrived. There were times, occasionally, when she fretted over the fact that here she was, thirty-six and still childless, let alone husbandless; and others, like this, when she was grateful for the pleasant places in which her lines had fallen, even if they weren't places which included such close relationships.

A thought which, inevitably, reminded her of her conversation last night with her mother. Tomorrow she'd be here, with Aunt Bridget in tow, having arranged a flight just as soon as George had called her. If that wasn't enough to cure her of any yearnings for family life, she told herself gloomily as she made her way back to her laboratory, nothing was.

4

She had no time to think about anything, however, neither her mother nor the matter of the note on Baby Popodopoulos's file, because the lab was in an uproar when she got back to it. An agitated wide-eyed Sheila—who always got immensely excited whenever she had the opportunity—greeted her with an air of great portentousness and told her almost before she'd got inside her office that the mortuary was "positively groaning at the seams with bodies, a ghastly RTA over on the other side of Leman Street and the place is *milling* with police and—"

George sighed, put down her files and reached for her dressing-room key. "I'll see for myself, Sheila," she said repressively. "Who has the PM requests and the notes?"

"Mr. Constant's down there and so's that nice young policeman. You know, the Scottish one and—"

"Right, I'll get on, then," George said firmly and went, cutting off Sheila in mid-flow, clearly to her annoyance. George changed as fast as she could into her greens, tying her hair up tightly in a cap. It was horrid the way the smell of the place clung to her hair if she wasn't careful. She remembered fleetingly how she'd thought a while ago that she preferred the smell of her mortuary to that of the maternity ward, and allowed herself a sardonic sniff at her own stupidity.

The PM room, when she reached it, was indeed in a hubbub. All three of the slabs had occupants and Danny, the mortuary porter, was busy cutting the clothes off them under the beady eye of DC Michael Urquhart from Ratcliffe Street police station, while Harold Constant, the coroner's officer, stood in close colloquy with someone George couldn't quite see, since Constant was a sizeable man whose bulk hid his companion. On the far side of the PM room a young uniformed constable was standing looking a touch pale and anxious. George sighed. The last thing she needed was six foot plus of fainting copper on the floor getting in everyone's way. She went over to him and said cheerfully, "Good morning!" and looked at him closely.

He swiveled his eyes to look back at her. She could see the line of sweat on his upper lip and grinned sympathetically. "Good morning, madam," he said. He was hoarse.

"I'm Dr. Barnabas," she said crisply. "And I think you'd be better off waiting outside. You don't look too wonderful. Smells a bit in here, doesn't it?"

The boy went even paler and closed his eyes for a moment and she said sharply, "Steady! Just lean on the wall and when you feel able, get out—"

"Hey there, Dr. B., you pushin' my officers around again? Ain't you got enough of your own people to bully?"

"I do not bully!" she said wrathfully, turning round, realizing at last to whom Harold Constant had been talking. "And well you know it, Gus! I was in fact showing the guy a bit of sympathy, which is more than you'd do for them. Look at him! He's as green and sweaty as an old cheese. Let him go, for heaven's sake."

"If he's green and sweaty, all the more reason for him to stay," DCI Hathaway said, peering into the young policeman's face. "Are you green and sweaty, Chester? Shame on you! You ought to know better. Stop it at once and settle down."

"Yes, sir," the young policeman said, staring woodenly over Hathaway's head, and George made a sharp noise of irritation through her teeth and turned back to the slabs.

"OK. He's your guy, you bully him your way if you must. But if he keels over don't expect my staff to pick him up. You can do it yourself."

"He wouldn't dare," Gus said amiably. "Would you, Chester? No. Knows better'n to do any faintin' around me. I'd murder him."

"And I'd be glad to give evidence to that effect at your trial and see you well banged up," George snapped and the young policeman began to look a little better, clearly enjoying the sight of Detective Chief Inspector Hathaway getting his share, as he was later to describe the episode to his mates in the canteen at Ratcliffe Street nick. But Hathaway only chuckled, winked at Chester and went back to his talk with Harold Constant, who was looking far from pleased.

"Three in one afternoon," Harold muttered to George as she settled to dealing with the first body. "Sorry to throw it at you in such a rush, but there's some question of one of "em having had a heart attack before the crash and besides we think one of "em's a bloke we want over a bit of naughty with other people's cars. That's why I'm here, o'course. Wouldn't usually hang around a routine RTA, would I? No. Anyway, we have to know as soon as possible, so as to sort out the legalities. There's some problem over the insurance, wouldn't you just know, as well as someone wanting to sue—"

"Which one?" George asked as she pulled on her gloves and again flexed her heavy left hand. This would be her first adult PM since her return and dealing with a sizeable adult body was harder work than an infant's, especially when there was rigor present, as there was in the bodies she now had to deal with. Stiff muscles in the corpse and weak muscles in the operator, she thought at the back of her mind, add up to a hell of a lot of hard work. Oh well, the sooner I find out if I'm up to it the better. Like that young copper learning how to stand throughout a PM without passing out, I suppose. She looked up and caught Gus's eye and he winked at her companionably.

She smiled back involuntarily. Dammit, it is fun to see the old bastard again, she thought. She'd missed the laughs.

It was a long afternoon as she went doggedly through the three cadavers, but at the end of it the answers were clear enough and Harold Constant went off in a much more cheerful frame of mind.

"I'll let "em know, then. The chap in the Rover had the heart attack and that was why he swerved and hit the Nissan head on. That's going to sort out a lot of trouble. The other passenger in the Nissan was all set to sue the survivor of the Rover crash for dangerous driving and she's in no state to cope with anything, poor thing. She's up in intensive care now. Ta, Dr. Barnabas. Helps a lot to have this so clear and so soon."

"My pleasure," she said and turned to go to her shower and change of clothes, but Gus stopped her as the room emptied and Danny stowed away the bodies one by one, ready for the undertakers to collect.

"Here, hang about a bit!" Gus called in an aggrieved tone. "Haven't set eyes on you this past month and there you are slopin' off like I ain't here! Do me a favor!"

"Of course you've seen me!" she said. "You came to visit me in Dagmar Ward."

"Oh, that." He waved a dismissive hand. "You can't count that. You was in that flippin' box and I had to stand outside and shout through the bleedin' glass. That's not visiting someone, is it?"

"It's the only possible way when the patient has an infection that could be nasty," George said. Although she wouldn't admit it to him for the world, she did in fact agree that being shouted at through a double layer of glass was hardly satisfactory communication.

"Well, fair enough. Glad to see you up an' about, anyway. You quite fit again?" He looked at her a little sharply and his voice had a gruff note, and she was touched. That his concern was genuine was undoubted and she smiled at him.

"I'm fine, Gus. Just fine. And you?"

"Oh, me, I'm as chipper as a mouse what's broken through
the larder door. More work'n we know what to do with and half
the force off with ingrowing toenails—"

"Ingrowing—"

"Oh, they've got their bloody doctors to call it flu, but I
know lead swingin' when I see it."

"I'd like to see you with this current flu!" George said.
"You'd be moaning and groaning like a—like a—"

"Yeah, well I haven't got it, so you can't. And you're wrong.
When I'm poorly, take it from me, I'm as good as gold. Give
me a bottle of Scotch and the papers and I'll get better so fast
you won't even miss me. So, any news around the place?"

"News?" She laughed. "I've only been back on duty a day
or so! No time yet to collect all that's going on. When I do,
you'll be the last to know, I promise."

"Mean cow," he said amiably. "Life blood to a copper,
gossip is, and she won't share it."

"I will when it's necessary. Now, can I go and change?"

"Into what? Fairy Fanny on a fir tree?"

"Very funny. Oh, shit!" She lifted both hands in the air and
made fists of them. "I meant to talk to Constant. I bet he's gone."

"Hang on, I'll see if I can catch him for you," Gus said at
once and went, his check overcoat streaming behind him and
his curly hair bouncing in its usual energetic fashion. George
followed him more slowly. It was unlikely Constant was still
around, no need to hurry; but she had been warmed by Gus's
immediate willingness to find him for her. It *was* good to see
him again, and maybe not just for the laughs.

As she reached the door of her changing room, Gus
reappeared at the far end of the corridor with Constant in tow.
The fat man was puffing a little and she thought with a stab
of amusement that Gus, stocky and hard muscled as he was,
looked, at a good four inches shorter, like a particularly self-
important tug pulling a singularly heavy liner and she laughed.

"What's the rush?" Constant was clearly aggrieved. "I have to get back to the office with this stuff urgently, you know."

"Which was why you was dallyin' with Madam Sheila up there and having a nice little natter?" Gus said and Constant threw him a murderous look. "It won't take a mo', will it, Dr. B?"

Now George looked at him murderously. "It's private," she said shortly. But Gus laughed.

"Do me a favor, darlin'! Since when do you have private discussions with old Harold here? Don't make me go jumpin' to any conclusions. I will if you insist on whisperin' sweet nothings into his ear."

George turned her back, knowing from experience when to stop arguing with him, and looked at Constant, who was clearly itching to get away. "It's not much, Harold," she said. "It's the Popodopoulos baby—I'm still not happy about that one. I don't think I can sign the certificate, you know. Will you tell Dr. Porteous and—"

"Oh that's all right," Harold's face had cleared. "That's gone through."

"What?" She frowned. "But I haven't signed! I sent up the preliminary report and—"

"That's right. Cot death, yes? And Dr. Porteous went ahead and settled it all with the parents. They wanted the funeral right away, it's the way they do things in their church, apparently. They wanted to get it over and done with and Dr. Porteous, being such a caring man'—Harold almost smirked—"he agreed. So there's no problem. Can I go now? I really must get back."

"But goddamn it all, I haven't signed—" George began but Harold shook his head.

"Doesn't matter, Dr. Barnabas, you know that. It's up to the coroner to decide, "n't it? And on the basis of your preliminary report he agreed the funeral could go ahead. You haven't discovered something new, have you?" He looked at her sharply. "That'd make a difference, of course, if you had. It'd be a right mess if we had to stop the funeral, of course, but if you say there is something new…"

"No," she said a little unwillingly. "There's nothing to add to what I've already told him. It's just that I'm not comfortable…"

"Oh, well." Harold was clearly relieved as he turned to go. "If that's all, no problems. Better be off. Thanks for all this stuff so quickly, Dr. Barnabas, it's a great help." And he was gone, pounding back along the corridor and panting his way up the stairs to the way out like a self-satisfied hippo.

"And you said nothin' interesting had happened," Gus said reproachfully. "What's all this then?"

"Like I said, nothing," she muttered irritably, turning to go into her dressing room. "No affair of yours, that's for sure. "Bye, Gus. See you around." And she went in and closed the door firmly behind her. Bad enough the coroner had in effect dismissed her; no way was she going to give Gus the chance to do the same.

But when she came out, freshly scented with quantities of shower gel and body cream and her hair still curling damply from its quick shampoo—because she couldn't bear the possibility that despite her precautions her hair might still smell of anything it shouldn't—and went back to her office, there he was, sitting on the edge of her desk and shamelessly reading his way through a pile of her papers.

She snatched them from him and went round to sit down. "Haven't you got a job to go to?" she snapped, glaring at him.

"It's really great," he said admiringly. "The way you learn. Another year or two around me and you'll be talkin' proper English, just like what I do. Yes, I have got a job to go to. I've gone to it. What's this about a baby you wouldn't sign a certificate for that the coroner's shoved through as a natural death?"

"It's none of your—" she began, but he stopped her firmly.

"Listen, Dr. B., I'm not going for that. You taught me good over the Oxford case, you taught me good and proper to pay

attention to your notions. I said Oxford was a natural death and
you said it wasn't. I was wrong, you were right. Now you say
this cot death's suspicious and the coroner doesn't—"

She shook her head. "It's not the same, Gus, honestly.
Last time was—well, that was then. This is—it was a baby in
Maternity, found dead. The only thing that bothered me was
that someone had stuck a note on the PM request form pointing
out this was the third such death there in five months. I didn't
know about the other two on account of being off sick, and
when I tried to find out who'd written the note, I drew a blank.
No one seems to know. I haven't asked everyone, though, and I
dare say someone'll tell me, and it'll all turn out to be nothing.
That was all, really."

She stopped and thought a while, then continued a little
unwillingly. "Except for the fact that this diagnosis of cot
death is one I can't handle. I mean, it's not a diagnosis at all.
It's just a description of what happened, and it gives you no
information on why it happened. And you know me, I can't
stand mysteries…"

"You're telling me," he said with some feeling. "Like I said,
I remember last time. Look, doll, put it on the line. Is this a
dicey one or not? If it is, I'll have to look into it, though I hate
these cases. You have to investigate the parents, and they suffer
hell over it, poor devils."

She looked at him sharply and then smiled. He was a good
old soul, after all was said and done, she thought, using his own
sort of language inside her head. He means kindly.

"I don't know," she said candidly. "I'm possibly just making
dramas where none exist, but there it is—the business niggles
at me."

"Then listen to your niggles," he said, suddenly serious.
"What can you do about them?"

"I'm not sure," she admitted. "I can't repeat the PM to see
if there's anything I missed, though to be really honest, I don't
think I did. It was my first case since getting back, so I was—

well, that bit more aware of what I was doing, you know? I'm always careful, but this one I, like, walked on eggs. Even if I did manage another PM on the body—which I can't get, seeing the funeral's been given the go-ahead—I doubt I'd find anything."

"So this is an academic conversation?" he said. "Just talk for the sake of it?"

"I could dig out the notes of the other two, I suppose," George said, ignoring the little dig.

"The ones the note mentioned?" His voice sharpened. "The mysterious note?"

"Yup. Those."

"Hmm! Will that be easy?"

"Don't know till I try."

"Will you try?"

"I'm not sure…" She knew she was prevaricating and so did he.

"Come off it. You're going to. And when you have, let me know what you've found out, right?"

"Only if it's significant," she said and he shook his head in exasperation.

"Why? Aren't we a team, for Gawd's sake?"

"When it suits you we are. If you prefer to keep me out then you do. Take that matter of the woman who'd been tied up in all those pairs of stockings back in the spring. And the man with the ankle bracelets, and the—"

"They were different," he said loftily. "No medical input needed with them. But if you find there was hanky panky about the way those babies died, why, then—"

"Why, then I'll consider what I want to do about it." She got to her feet. "I have work to do, Gus. How's about you?"

"I like potato chips, moonlight and motor trips, how's about you?" he sang but he got to his feet. "Yeah, I ought to get back. Check all the paperwork on this RTA. I shouldn't ha' been involved at all, really—it's not one for CID, but traffic branch

got their knickers in a twist over some insurance fuss, so there
you go. And there's me with my own work piling up, as the—"

"— man in the livery stables said," she chorused with him.
"Yeah, I know. Time you changed that gag for a new one, Gus,
say one from around 1950. It's getting as high as the livery
stable man's work. Goodbye." She went to the door and held
it open.

"I'm goin', I'm goin." Listen, about tonight…"

"What about tonight?" She waited, her head on one side as,
somewhat uncharacteristically, he hesitated.

"We've done up the Leman Street place all posh—looks a
bit like a shopgirl's dream, to tell you the truth—but the grub's
as good as ever, and we could have a nice tuck-in tonight of
halibut and maybe this time you'd try some of our jellied eels.
They're the best in London and—"

"Nothing in this world or the next will ever get me to eat
jellied eels," George said fervently and he grinned.

"OK, then. Plain old fish and chips it is. You've got basic
good taste, girl, even if you're a bit unadventurous in the
cuisine department. Never mind, I'll make a good foodie of
you yet. Pick you up at around seven-thirty, then? We'll have
a noggin at the Crown and Anchor and then go and tuck in.
Lovely."

"I haven't said I'll go yet!" she protested and this time he
laughed aloud.

"Oh yes you have, ducks," he said. He flicked his forefinger
at his forehead to tip an imaginary hat and went, leaving her
more pleased than irritated—and that of course was irritating
in itself.

5

"The Plaice To Be' in Leman Street was bursting at the seams with people when they got there. It was a raw night with the reek of the river thick and acrid in their nostrils, quite overwhelming the usual diesel stink of the traffic, and she'd been glad of the snug half-hour they'd spent at the Crown and Anchor to start the evening. She had ordered gin and tonic—an English drink she'd learned to prefer to the New York Martinis that had once been her choice—and he had sunk a couple of half-pints of best bitter while they had talked easily and a little lazily of the world news as seen on the TV at the end of the bar, arguing amiably over the rival merits of CNN and the British service, while the chill of the day seeped out of her bones and she began to feel a deep sense of wellbeing. Now, as they reached the brightly lit front of the fish-and-chip shop and restaurant that was the pride of Gus's fleet she felt even more warmed, and that made her feel warm towards him, too.

"It looks great, Gus," she said as they pushed open the door and went in. And indeed it did. The large plate windows were engraved thickly in the old public-house fashion, but only around the edges; passers-by could still see in easily to the great bank of glittering chrome fryers and the bustling staff in their natty blue-and-white outfits with anchors and mermaids embroidered over the left breast. Beyond them in the interior were the tables with their blue-and-white gingham cloths and striped blue-and-white china, and the vast fish tank at the back in which gaudily colored tropical fish swam in aristocratic splendor, clearly unworried by the fate of their humbler cousins who, encased in the crispest of batters, were being slapped down on the tables before hungry eaters. It all looked extremely inviting, and she was happy to tell him so. "You ought to be really proud of it."

"I am," Gus said and beamed as one of the waitresses spotted him and darted over to fuss them to a table bang in the middle of the restaurant. "Wotcha, Kitty. Like the new uniforms, do you?"

"Dead fancy, Guv," the girl said. "Bit snug, mind you," and she wriggled a little as she pulled the tight skirt down over her neat round bottom.

Gus leered. "I'm not daft, girl. I make sure they're so tight so's you won't eat me outa business. And it makes a nice view for the customers, don't it?"

"N't 'e a right MCP, Dr. B.?" the girl said, but without any rancour. "You ought to teach "im better ways."

"I've tried," George said and sat down. "I thought you were at the Watney Street shop, Kitty?"

"I was. But "e's bin and gone and made me manager "ere." She jerked her head at Gus. "Shown a bit o' sense, eh? Well, what'll it be, Guv? The "alibut's a treat and Dave said as how he's got a lovely piece o' turbot if anyone special comes in. You're special, I s'pose, so if that's your fancy—"

"Keep the turbot to sell to the bookies. They've got big money for it. We'll have the "alibut, eh, Dr. B.? Will that suit you?"

"Cor, what a tight wad!" Kitty said and leaned over to rearrange the already perfectly set knives and forks and to swish at the spotless tablecloth with her napkin. "Tell "im you want the turbot, Dr. B."

"I think I will," George said.

The girl grinned at her as Gus threw his eyes up in mock consternation and then said, "And an order of jellied eels, too. The really big ones from Tubby's. Give some to Dr. B.—"

"I won't eat them," George said, grimacing.

"— and a plate o' prawns in case I can't tempt her. Oh, and a bottle of the Sancerre."

Kitty went and Gus watched her appreciatively. George shook her head at him in only partially mocking despair. "You really are an unreconstructed—" she began but he held up both hands in surrender.

"I'm everythin' you ever said or thought a man could be, ducky, so let's not waste our time listin' my faults. All right, then. Do you like the way the place looks?"

"I told you I did."

"Then I'll do it exactly the same way next time."

She raised her brows. "Next time? Are you making all of them glitzy like this?"

"Not all of 'em. The ones over at Bethnal Green—down Cambridge Heath Road and the other one down by Roman Road—I'll leave them alone. The locals like 'em the way they are. But I might open a new one over at Bow. There's a nice little property there, just past Mile End station in Bow Road, that'd make me a good bit o' profit, I reckon. There's a doner kebab place over the road, but that's about it in the way of competition."

"How many places have you got now, Gus?"

He looked away and if she hadn't known him better she'd have thought him rather shy, suddenly.

"Um—nine," he said.

"Nine? That was some business your father left you."

"Oh, he didn't leave 'em all to me!" Gus said, losing his diffidence. "He had six. It was me what started the others."

She set her head to one side and looked at him with genuine curiosity. "I never could quite work it out. Why are you still a policeman? These shops must be worth a lot of money."

"If a villain got me tomorrow, I'd cut up for the best part of a million," he said, and grinned widely, his pride transparent and glittering.

"Why not settle for that? Why work your butt off for what can't be a lot of money, when you could be concentrating on being a sucessful tycoon? You're obviously good at it if you've added another three shops to what you were left—how long ago was it?"

"Four years."

"Yeah. Four years. So why are you—"

"Oh, Dr. B., do stop talkin' a lot of tosh!" he said. "I might as well ask you why you're workin' as a forensic bloody pathologist down here in Shadwell when with your looks and your style you could get yourself some fancy rooms up in Harley Street, set up as a specialist and make more money than you've ever seen, and get half the headaches."

"But there aren't any Harley Street pathologists," she said. "At least not my sort."

"You're dodgin' the point. Purposely, probably, knowin' you. You could be another sort of specialist, couldn't you? If you wanted to? The sort that makes money. But that is the point. You don't want to. You love the job you do, don't you?"

She thought for a moment and then said, "I suppose so. It's complicated, of course, and dealing with some of the new NHS rules, especially about money, is like walking over a wet plowed field in high-heeled shoes, but I suppose it's what I want to do."

"So there you are. I'm the same. I love the job. For me it's the Force or nothing. When the old boy kicked the bucket I thought I'd just sell up what he left and have the cash, but he'd been as crazy about his fish and chips as I am about bein' a copper, so I couldn't do it to him, poor old bugger. He'd ha' come back to haunt me if I had, anyway. So I just run it all in tandem. It's not that tough. Not when you've got girls as good as Kitty." And he leered at the waitress who had arrived with the jellied eels and prawns.

"Yeah, well, that's as maybe," she said amiably. "Listen, Dr. B. you try some of these eels. See? I've took "em out o' the

jelly and set "em on lettuce, like, so they looks nicer. Give it a
go. A drop of vinegar on "em, and you'll see. They've a taste
you'll be sorry you used to miss out on."

"Oh, forget it, Kitty," Gus said as he reached for the vinegar
and liberally doused his own large bowlful of eels, nestling in a
heap of pallid transparent jelly from which George averted her
eyes. "She's not up to takin' chances, this one. I've been tryin'
for ages. Waste of breath."

"Not a bit of it," Kitty said. "You bin shoutin' at her, I dare
say. She'll try "em for me. There you are, Dr. B." She set the
plate in front of her and George looked at it, thinking the small
pieces of silvery fish looked very similar to pickled herring,
which she adored. Maybe they wouldn't be so bad after all—
and it'd be nice to give in to Kitty after having refused Gus's
blandishments for so long.

She picked up her fork and without stopping to worry about
it speared a piece of fish and put it in her mouth, afraid she'd
want to spit it out, but determined to show Gus how wrong he
was about her. And to her surprise found the taste delectable.
She winked at Kitty and ate another piece with genuine relish.

"Watch out for bones," Kitty said. "They're bleedin' sharp.
You can spit "em out—it's all right. Everyone does. Enjoy the
rest. I'll go an' get the "alibut and, yeah, your turbot." And she
laughed at Gus and went.

The rest of their meal went by contentedly as Gus protested
at her willingness to please Kitty by trying the eels after
refusing him and they both enjoyed their fried fish and the
chips, which arrived in a great pile of whispering crispness.
By the time they'd reached the bread-and-butter pudding
(which Gus insisted on ordering even though George knew
she couldn't manage another mouthful and then ate half a
bowlful) they were as contented with each other as if they
had been friends for years, instead of only sometimes edgy
colleagues for barely—she stopped to work it out—eleven
months.

Almost to her own surprise, she said as much. "I feel as though I've been here in Shadwell a hell of a long time," she said. "But it's not even a year yet."

"Good," he said. "That must mean you like it here. And like us."

"Not necessarily." She couldn't help being combative. Not with him. "It could mean that the days drag like eternity and the people drive me bananas."

"Do they? And do we?"

She relaxed and accepted the Irish coffee he'd ordered for her. It tasted remarkably good, if far too rich. "I suppose not."

"So, like I said. Good."

They settled into a silence for a while, until he stirred and leaned forward. His voice dropped and he seemed unusually uncomfortable. "Dr. B….." he said, and then stopped.

"Mmm?" The coffee, following the drinks she'd had in the pub and the Sancerre that had accompanied the fish, was making her agreeably sleepy.

"I wanted to ask you…" Again his voice drifted away and she roused herself and peered at him.

"What's up, Gus? Something bugging you?"

"You could say that. I was just wondering…"

"Well? Spit it out."

"I like you," he said baldly. "You know what I mean?"

"As long as you're not bullshitting, yes. I imagined you didn't find my company totally repellent. Seeing you asked me out tonight."

"Oh, I mean more than that! You don't have to come the silly miss with me, do you? I mean, it's one of the things I like about you. Saying what you think, and all that. Even if you do sometimes go too far."

"Oh?" She began to bristle. "How too far?"

"Well, you know—well-brought-up ladies here in England don't talk the way you do sometimes. Like saying bullshit, just now, and—"

"Like hell they don't!" She was quite awake now. "I don't think you listen to the way ladies—Christ, what a word! Ladies!—I don't think you listen to the way ordinary women talk in this country. You ought to try, instead of just jumping to conclusions about women. You might get a bit of a surprise if you do."

"Wouldn't you just know it!" He sounded disgusted. "Here's me trying to talk sensible and serious to you and what do I get? Another of your naggings about women and the way men like me treat them. Well, I'm here to tell you there's no one who respects women more than I do! And don't you go thinking otherwise!"

"Oh, Gus, you're such a—such—" She was so incensed that her voice caught in her throat and she started to cough. He pushed a glass of water closer to her, leaned over so that his head was very close to hers and banged her back.

"Yeah, I know, MCP. I swear to you, George, that half the time I don't know what you women are on about. I try to talk sense to you about something important and before I can get more than a handful of words out, there you are running your mouth off about men and women. I just don't get it. Are you looking for insults or something?"

"They're easy to find," she retorted. "If you insist on talking about women as though we were all the same, all of us, just— just boobs and bottoms on legs designed for you to trick out in tight skirts so you can gawp at them, then you'll go on not understanding—"

"Tell me what I said!" He almost wailed it.

"Glad to. You said you respect women as if we're all the same—like dogs or something. You said that well-brought-up 'ladies' don't talk the way I do, which is a hell of a line. You said that you don't know what women are on about, which—"

He shook his head at her. "I obviously don't. What should I have said? No, I mean it. Tell me, I want to learn. I've got to learn, for pity's sake. Go on like this and we'll never get anywhere, you and me."

That stopped her, and she blinked at him. "What did you say?"

"Eh?"

"What did—"

"Oh. I said we'll never get anywhere, you and me. And I'd like us to."

"Like us to get—well, where?"

"Oh, somewhere cozy." He grinned suddenly, a great white glimmering grin of sheer wickedness. "Cozy and quiet and comfortable where we'd have plenty of time to have some fun." The grin faded as she sat and stared at him. "Have I done it again? Is it an insult to make a pass at a la—a woman you fancy? I mean like? Oh, shit!"

She couldn't help it. The laughter came bubbling out of her, and after a moment of incomprehension he realized what he'd said and laughed too, until the pair of them were sitting with tears trickling down their cheeks, incoherent and breathless. Kitty, coming back to see if the Guv needed anything more and to prove to him what an excellent choice he'd made when he'd appointed her as manageress, looked at them indulgently and went away again, and one or two people at adjoining tables looked too, laughing in sympathy.

"I'm sorry," he said at length. He took out a massive handkerchief mopped his face and blew his nose loudly. "I didn't mean to go off like that. But it is tricky, George, admit it. There was I trying to chat you up so's you'd know what I was thinkin'—what's the way you'd say it? Yeah, so you'd know where it was comin' from—and all you can do is nag me about the way I talk about women. I can't help what I am, you know! I'm the same as most blokes I know. A bit rough round the edges but pretty good news otherwise. If I promise never to say shit again, and never to complain if you do, will you go out with me? On a regular basis, like?"

She was startled, and couldn't speak for a moment. She knew he liked her, of course she did. He'd made that pretty clear right from the start, after they'd first met when she'd come to Old East eleven months ago, but she'd not seen his liking as anything more than a sort of possessive friendship. He'd never made any sort of physical pass at her, unlike Toby Bellamy…

Mind, he'd been very jealous of Bellamy, she remembered now, but that had blown over and they'd got back on to the old easy footing, laughing a lot, sparring most of the time, but in general comfortable with each other. And now here he was asking her…Asking her what?

"What are you asking me, Gus?" she said. "I'm not sure what you mean by 'going out on a regular basis.' If you explain a bit more, maybe I—"

From behind her there was a sudden crash of glass and she almost leapt out of her seat with shock. She whirled to stare at the origin of the noise, which was now continuing as a confused roar of voices as people shouted and milled about in the front part of the shop where customers had been queueing all evening to buy their fish and chips to take away.

Gus was on his feet and plunging across the restaurant, and George followed him, not sure what else to do. There in the space in front of the fish fryers was a great pile of broken glass, and she could have wept as she realized that one of the beautifully engraved panes had been shattered. But she had no time to regret the loss of beautiful handi-work; in the middle of the wreckage was a heap of bodies, writhing and bawling in a furious fight.

The next few minutes were bedlam as the people from the restaurant came crowding out to see what was happening and the women added their own shrieks to those of the waitresses, and the men jumped into the fray to pull the combatants apart. George, from her position at the very edge of the mêlée, saw that one man was bleeding heavily from a wound on his arm; she thought she saw it pumping and all her medical instincts shoved her into action. She hadn't realized she had joined in until she found herself with the injured man's arm held firmly in one hand as she tried to twist her table napkin—which had still been in her hand when she left the table—into a tourniquet to apply over the blood pumping from his left wrist.

"Hold still," she bawled as the man tried to pull away from her. On his other side one of the fish fryers, a bulky young man with thick arms well covered with freckles and sandy hair, held tightly on to him so that he had to stand still, and she managed to get her tourniquet into place and then lifted the injured arm high above the man's head, almost like a boxer's victorious salute.

"Keep it up like that till the ambulance gets here," she ordered. "That'll need some careful suturing. Is there anyone else who's been hurt?"

By this time the fighting had eased and the heap of bodies had separated into its component parts. Gus was holding a hefty blond boy with a big closely cropped head in a tight one-arm-behind-his-back grip; two of the fish fryers were sitting on another one who looked much the same, dressed, as was Gus's captive, in jeans and aggressively studded black leather jackets. They seemed almost uniformed and George, looking at them and then round the crowd standing peering down at the miscreants with scared faces, caught sight of another in the same sort of clothes sliding away to the door.

"Hey, stop that one!" she shouted, and at once a couple of the men customers turned, saw him and grabbed. There was muffled shouting and some very loud swearing as the fish fryer who had been helping George hold her injured man plunged after the escapee.

They almost got him, but he struggled free just as the police car someone had dialed 999 for arrived, blue lights rotating hysterically and siren whooping, to bring a pair of uniformed policemen into the affray.

From then on it was a matter of moments before it was all over; an ambulance followed the police car within a couple of minutes and George's man, looking dazed now, and with his hand still held up in the air and the other holding a handkerchief to a nose that appeared to be bleeding as well, was scooped up by the paramedics and taken to it. He was a tall man, well muscled, and George thought, looking at him more closely now, Indian or Pakistani. He was well dressed in a casual sort of way, and clearly bewildered by what was happening—until he got to the ambulance, at which point he suddenly seemed to become more aware of what was going on.

He whirled, pulling away from the grip of the paramedics. "Get their names," he bellowed. "Make sure you get them—and every witness you can. I'm going to throw the book at them, I swear to you, I'm going to take them to every court in the land. Unprovoked attack like that, it's disgusting. Unprovoked, no reason at all…Get their names—"

"It's all right, sir," one of the policemen said soothingly. "We'll get all the information there is, you can be sure of that. We'll see you at the hospital, get your statement there. Just go along now, they'll fix you up, Mister—?"

"Doctor," the man snapped through his handkerchief, and as he pulled it away from his face to speak more clearly, George could see that he had a gap in his teeth. Just knocked out now? Probably. She looked down at the floor to see if she could see it. An absurd idea. The floor was a mess of broken glass, blood and spilled fish and chips. If there was a tooth there it certainly couldn't be salvaged.

"All right, doctor," the policeman said even more soothingly. "We'll see you at the hospital, Dr.—?" And he waited invitingly.

"Choopani. Diljeet Choopani," snapped the other, at last climbing into the ambulance to be taken away as the policeman returned gratefully to the cluster of people in the front of the shop.

Gus had his man handcuffed now, as the other policeman bundled the second one to the back of the police car. Its blue light was still rotating on the roof, lifting the whole scene into a lurid facsimile of a discotheque, since there were traffic lights just outside the shop which added their lollipop colors to the mixture. George began to feel a little shaky at the knees as she watched the rest of the proceedings; the two men, now in the car, were being driven off as yet another police car arrived and disgorged a couple of uniformed men who began to shepherd the spectators into the shop to take notes from witnesses.

Gus seemed to have noticed how she felt, because suddenly he was beside her, one hand tightly holding her elbow.

"All right, ducks. You did good there. That fella could have been a goner, bleeding like that."

"Hardly," she said a little sardonically, regaining her equilibrium. "It takes a bit more than that. I just did a bit of first aid. What the hell was all that about?"

"A good question," he said, his voice grim. "We're about to find out. But from all accounts, it was a racist attack. He's a well-known chap, the one they went for. Local GP."

"Of course," she said. "I knew I'd heard his name before."

"We've got two of the blokes who went for him, and there are one or two people here who think they know who the other was. So we'll get "em sorted, you'll see. God, I hate this racist stuff. We've been getting a damned sight too much of it lately. I think—"

She gave him no chance to say anything more. "I think the evening's over, Gus. You stay here and get to work. I know you're dying to, and I'd be the last to stop you. I'll see myself back. See you around."

"Yeah, I'll see you," he said, but he wasn't listening to her. She knew that. His whole attention was focused on The Job. She went back into the restaurant to collect her bag, picking her way over the beautiful broken glass, and then slipped out to go back to her flat.

All the way to the bus stop she thought about the way Dr. Choopani had blazed his rage at the three men who had attacked him and wondered why they'd chosen so public and dangerous a place to do it. They must have realized they'd be caught, surely? Had he provoked them into action in some way? Whatever he'd said and done they'd had no right to behave so, but it would be interesting to know if he'd contributed in any way to what had happened.

She paused before she reached the bus stop that would see her on her way back to her little flat and pondered; it was late, but not that late. After a little more thought, she turned and began to walk rapidly towards Old East. She'd call into Accident and Emergency to see how he was, and maybe find out some of the whys and wherefores. It'd be interesting, she decided, to learn a bit more about him anyway, remembering the way the nurse on Pediatrics had spoken of him this morning.

And of course, thinking about Dr. Choopani was a lot easier than thinking about what Gus had said.

6

A & E was surprisingly quiet when George got there. She had
expected it to be humming with activity as it dealt with the
results of the fracas at Gus's restaurant, but realized, once she
got inside (past the remnants of the anti-NHS Trust picket line,
which had hung about the entrance ever since April when the
new system had started but which was blessedly undermanned
during the evenings) that there had really been only one
casualty; the other men involved had been taken to the police
station and no doubt would be seen by a police surgeon there
if necessary. Dr. Choopani had been the most damaged, and he
was now sitting bolt upright on a couch in one of the cubicles
with the junior casualty officer bending over his wrist.

"Make sure you check the palmar radio-carpal ligament as
well as the nerve supply, the branch of the median nerve to the
thenar muscles passes just under there," he was saying. "I want
a senior man doing this job. I'm not going to be meddled with
by some junior or other. Oh!" He looked up as George came in
through the curtains. "Are you the senior consultant tonight?
I'd rather be seen by one of the men, if you please."

George's brows snapped together. "I am not the consultant
here," she said as smoothly as her anger would let her. "I'm
Old East's consultant pathologist It was I who dealt with you at
the restaurant when you were injured. I came back to see how
you are. I needn't have worried, of course. You're in excellent
hands, none better."

The houseman who had been gingerly exploring the wound on Dr. Choopani's wrist looked at her gratefully and she smiled at him as he tried to look like the sort of surgeon she'd described, rather than the uneasy young one he actually was. "Good evening Dr. Barnabas," he said.

George threw a glance at his name badge, grateful for the new rule that said all hospital staff must wear one. She hadn't the remotest idea who he was, of course; remembering the names of all the junior medical staff was an impossibility. "Good evening, Adam," she said in a voice that made it clear she'd known him for all his professional life, and for some time before that, too, and then looked at Dr. Choopani. "As I say, Dr. Parotsky here is one of our most accomplished surgeons. However, since you're so worried, I'm sure he'll agree to a second opinion, though for my part I'd as soon have Adam than anyone, especially as he's here, and the consultant lives some miles away and will have to be called in. It shouldn't take more than an hour or two, though. Do arrange it, Adam." She looked at the boy who grinned happily. "I'll keep Dr. Choopani company while you dig out Maggy Hill-Sykes."

"Who?" Dr. Choopani said sharply.

"Maggy Hill-Sykes, Dr. Choopani," George said silkily. "Our consultant on Accident and Emergency. I thought you knew all of us by name here! As a local family doctor…"

He glowered at her and then looked at Adam Parotsky. "Can you manage to repair this?"

Adam looked swiftly at George, who laughed easily. "My dear Dr. Choopani, he does a dozen of these a day, don't you, Adam?"

"Er—yes," Adam said.

"Then get on with it," Dr. Choopani snapped. "I haven't all night to sit here, waiting for some woman to—waiting for the consultant to turn out. And make sure someone organizes a skull film." He touched his left eye tenderly. "I might have a fracture of the orbit here."

George leaned over and gently palpated the bony rim of the eye socket. She shook her head. "I doubt it, but if you want a skull X-ray, I'm sure Adam'll fix it Won't you, Adam?"

The boy beamed with sudden euphoria. "I've already ordered it, of course," he said. "Routine after a history like this."

"You see?" George said, nodding at the man on the couch. "I told you you were in excellent hands."

"All right, all right," Choopani snapped. "Let's just get on with it."

Adam disappeared around the curtains to find a nurse to assist him and to get his equipment as George sat down on the end of the couch. "A nasty business," she said.

Choopani glared at her from his good eye. The other had almost closed now. "A singularly obvious remark, if I may say so," he said icily. "It certainly wasn't a nice one."

"I'm sure." George was dripping with sympathy. "Any idea why they attacked you?"

There was a silence and she realized he wasn't going to deign to answer her and she sighed. A tricky man, this. Hard done by and ill treated, of course, but still, not an easy man to deal with. She decided to go in bald-headed. This was not a person who would respond to any sort of softly softly approach.

"Racist," she said loudly. "After you for the color of your skin?"

He looked up at her and now his visible eye was blazing with fury. "What do you think? You sit here in a country that treats its citizens like so much garbage and you ask so stupid a question? Of course it was! What else? These animals, this witless garbage that should be put down and out of the way of decent citizens is allowed to roam the streets and scream its filth at anyone it wants to, and when they hit out and do damage like this, who gives a damn? No one. No one at all!"

She almost recoiled at the venom in his voice and caught her breath. "God, it must be hell for you," she said without stopping to think. He peered up at her.

"Hell? Yes, you could say that. It's hell and a lot more besides. It's particularly hellish when people who one is led to suppose are intelligent—if you're a consultant here you must have something inside your skull—ask asinine questions."

"Ouch," she said. "Look, I know you're angry, Dr. Choopani, but you don't have to kick the cat. I'm actually with you, you know. If I had my way I'd lock up people like the men who attacked you and make their lives as hellish as they make other people's. So try not to attack me."

He looked at her for a long moment, his good eye dripping malevolence, but then slowly leaned back against the pillows and closed his eye, sighing deeply.

There was a long silence before she ventured: "Was there any special reason tonight? Or was it just because you were there—all-purpose malice, as it were?"

He smiled, a chilly grimace, and she studied his face, a pleasant one with high cheekbones, finely shaped lips and an aquiline nose. His skin was fairly dark, like coffee with the minimum amount of cream in it; he must be, she found herself thinking, very good looking when he smiles. Smiles properly, that is.

"It's so silly," he said, still not opening his eyes. "I come of a family who regard those who buy fast food of that sort as the lowest of the low. We have always had servants to cook for us, money, status, yet I come here to work in this slum because I can't get any better job—no one in a high-class practice is interested in me—and I try to fit in, I truly try to fit in. I even go at the end of a late surgery to collect food from a place like that. I will be like the people I care for, I tell myself. I will not be a snob. And what happens? You see what happens."

She bit her lip. Had he stood there oozing disdain for his surroundings, showing in every move he made how low he believed himself to have stooped? If he had, that could have been enough to inflame the sort of youths who were already predisposed to despise those they regarded as aliens. It was an unjustified attack, of course it was. But if he had behaved so…

"Not that I was thinking such things as I waited there," he went on, almost dreamily now. "I was just tired and thinking the food smelled good and looking forward to getting it and going home to get some rest. And suddenly they leap on me."

His good eye opened and he glared at her. "Believe me, I did not provoke. I don't provoke. I understand the smallness of the brains of these people. I understand the immediacy of their responses. I know better than to make any action or to use any facial expression that could be construed as hostile. Yet see what happened. It makes no difference what we do. If we are foreigners in this great country we are despised whatever our status."

She was silent, just sitting, looking at him. And suddenly he grinned a wide smile that made his face light up, for his teeth were very even and white. "And don't think it is possible for you to distance yourself from the matter because you're American. Your country is as bad if not worse."

"I know that," she said. "Do you think I don't? But I've got more goddamned sense than to let the way some idiots behave change the way I behave with individuals. If you treat everyone here the way you treated young Adam Parotsky, then you're going to make a hell of a lot of personal enemies. I'd have thought you have enough of the other kind to be getting on with. You'd be better off being a little more—agreeable, surely?"

He opened his good eye and looked at her with obvious puzzlement "In what way was I disagreeable to—who was it?—Parotsky?"

"You were very rude to him. And to me too. Insisting on seeing a man consultant, for heaven's sake!"

He seemed to be considering that "I make errors from time to time," he announced. "I come from the sort of family that has difficulty in seeing its women as professional persons. Just understand and forgive me."

She laughed. "You're quite something, you know that? Even when you apologize, you come across as a—well—as definitely on the hostile side!"

"It is a problem I seek to overcome," he said calmly. "So, the young doctor you recommend, he takes his time."

"You're not the only patient here, you know," she said. She'd heard the sounds from beyond the curtains that told her other people had arrived in the waiting hall. "He could have been caught up in a greater emergency."

"No doubt," he said, and seemed to go to sleep. She hesitated for a moment but then he opened his eyes again. "I did not, of course, believe your promise that he was a great surgeon. I know a young beginner when I see one. However, I also looked carefully at my own wound. It is a clean one and has happily missed doing damage to any important structures. He will, I dare say, be exceedingly careful. If I am not happy with his work I can insist on someone else doing it again. I tell you this so that you don't think me a complete fool, Dr.—ah—"

"Barnabas," George said. "And no, Dr. Choopani, I don't think you're a fool. I also suspect you're not quite as unpleasant as you make people think you are by your behaviour."

"Unpleasant? I am never unpleasant! I speak directly, perhaps, but never unpleasantly."

"Don't kid yourself," she said firmly. "You can be very unpleasant. You had an argument on the phone with the people in Pediatrics this morning."

He frowned, a movement that made him wince slightly. "Pediatrics?"

"I was there. I heard all about it. You wanted to admit a child with gastroenteritis—"

"They are so silly!" he snapped. "I need a bed for a sick child, they say they cannot take her because they have no isolation bed! Such nonsense! Don't nurses know any more how to prevent the spread of infection? Are they so useless they cannot do the job they are trained for without special wards?

Yes, I complained about this, but I am fair—I am fair! When I managed to get a bed elsewhere I told them so that they would not waste time looking for a bed here at Old East. Yet this does not seem to please them!"

She shook her head slowly as she gazed at him. "You really do have a communication problem, don't you? It was the call you made to tell them you'd got your patient in at Kings that I overheard. They thought you were gloating—that that was why you called."

He was furious. He reared up on the couch so that he was once more sitting bolt upright and stared at her in outrage. "Gloating? Gloating? I would waste my time telephoning to gloat? What do they think I am? An idiot with nothing better to do with my time? I wished only to save them trouble! I don't understand these people."

"Obviously." She got to her feet as the curtains parted and a nurse came in pushing a trolley loaded with surgical equipment, followed by Adam Parotsky. "I'd better go. If there's anything I can do to help, let me know." She stopped at the curtains. "Meanwhile, a word of advice. Don't think everyone understands what it is you mean. They don't."

He made a sound, half sibilant, half barking, that reminded her powerfully of old black-and-white movies about unspeakable villains and impossible heroines, and she grinned at him. To her amazement, he made an effort to smile back.

"I must thank you," he said. It was clearly an effort for him. "You were very quick and saved me much blood loss. I would not have died of it, but it could have been tiresome. I am grateful."

"You're welcome," she said. "Any time," and went.

She got back to her flat at about eleven-thirty, a little surprised to find it wasn't later. It certainly felt as though it had been a very long rime since they'd been sitting there in Leman Street over that wreckage of bread-and-butter pudding while Gus talked to her—about what? Better not to think about that.

He might still be there she decided and, curling up on her sofa, reached for the phone. Worth a try, anyway. Maybe she'd find out a little more about the odd Dr. Choopani, for whom, she had to admit, she had a warmer liking now than she had when she'd first talked to him. Arrogant and proud he might be, but there was no malice in him. He had obviously been reared to be the man he was, and had no insight at all into the effect he might have on other people. It wouldn't hurt to tell Gus that. Or so she told herself.

He was still at the nick, she was told by the switchboard operator, they'd try to find him, please hold on, and hold on she did for what seemed an age until at last he was on the end of the line, sounding tired and a little distracted.

"Mmm?" he said in response to her question. "Oh, yes, we've got them sorted. No one hurt much. The one who ran away we picked up half an hour ago. It was on his behalf they did it, they say."

"How do you mean? On his behalf?"

"He's got a girlfriend lives over the other side of the Watney Road estate. Never goes near her if he can help it, as I understand it, since she had the baby, but very swaggering about it, you know? Anyway, it seems the baby died a couple of weeks ago."

"Died," George said, feeling suddenly horribly sure that she knew exactly what was coming. "What of?"

"Um—cot death, according to our community liaison girl," Gus said. "Yeah, I know. It made me think a bit too."

"Well, we do seem to be having some sort of epidemic. This one wasn't sent to Old East for the PM by any chance?"

"No, it went to—let's see..." There was a rustle of papers in her ear. "Um, St Chad's took it. But really, Dr. B., it's got nothing to do with tonight's events. Or, not really..."

"Not really? You can do better than that."

"Well, it has in a sense, a rather oblique sense. The thing is, the father, this precious father who didn't give a tuppenny damn about his kid while it was alive, takes violent umbrage when it dies and blames the doctor. The mother gave him some story about the doctor seeming to suggest she'd done it—you know how ham-handed some of these doctors can be—"

"I know how ham-handed this one can be," she said feelingly. "Mind you, so can your coppers."

"Not on this patch," he said swiftly. "My people are very carefully trained now on how to deal with parents in cases like these, so mind your—"

"I'm minding, I'm minding," she said. "So that's the story? The grieving father gets his mates and goes after the doctor because they want someone to blame?"

"That's about the size of it. They followed him from his surgery—one of them's singing like a bird, of course, there's always one that does—and jumped him from outside." He took a deep breath. "You've got to hand it to the buggers. Plate glass that thick and they jump through it, would you believe, jump through it! Could have killed themselves and I wish they had, the money it's going to cost to put that glass back, notwithstanding the insurance! The size of the premiums they'll be asking in the future—I tell you, who'd be a businessman?"

"I know a copper who likes it," she said.

"Yeah, well the charm's wearing off. Listen, George, are you OK? If I hadn't been so thrown—and I don't deny I was—I'd have seen you home properly. I'm ashamed to have sent you on your own. And anyway, we hadn't finished talking."

"We have for the present, Gus," she said firmly. "I must go."

"Let's try again tomorrow?" he said. "Eh? What about it? Different place this time. I'll take you down to my 'Sole Provider' by St. Katherine's Dock. What do you say? It's not so posh as the 'Plaice To Be,' mind you, though at least it's got all its bleedin' windows in position."

"Not tomorrow night, Gus," she said and was genuinely sorry. Or at least she thought she was. Talking again in the way he had been might be a bit—well, never mind. Stick to the situation as it was. "My ma and her friend arrive from Buffalo to spend Christmas with me tomorrow. I have to be at Heathrow to meet them at the crack of dawn."

"Bring "em with you," Gus said after a moment. "Glad to meet your mum, I'd be. Maybe she'll help me make some sense out of you."

She ignored that. "They'll be jetlagged. Some other time, Gus."

"Well, all right. If you insist on being such a misery. How about Sunday night?"

"Gus, I'll let you know," she said firmly and almost hung up and then snatched the telephone back. "Hey, Gus?"

"Yeah?"

"Let me know anything interesting about that cot death, will you? Like the PM report. Can you do that?"

He was silent for a moment. "I might. For a consideration."

"What sort of consideration?"

He chuckled and there was a leer in it "I'll let you know." And it was he who hung up first

7

•

Heathrow, as usual, made her feel restless. The ebb and flow of totally self-absorbed people all screwed up into a state of excitement over impending or just completed travel filled the air with the reek of anxiety and she caught it.

She had once thought it might be interesting to set up some research into pheromone levels in airports; was there more fear about or more sexual signallers? Certainly watching people greeting each other and saying goodbye revealed a good deal of high-level sexual tension, she thought now as she pushed her way through the hubbub, past Sock Shops and Knickerboxes and Menzies Bookstalls filled with people eager to spend money on something, anything, with which to assuage their unease, towards the exits out of which the passengers on the overnight plane from Kennedy, New York, would appear.

Please let the plane be on time, she prayed inside her head to a deity in which she did not believe; please let them be reasonably relaxed and not miserable when they get off; please help me keep a control on my tongue if Ma starts saying things that make me mad...

The plane was only fifteen minutes late touching down and by some miracle the passengers cleared the customs hall and began to come out within half an hour. "They're shovin' "em through immigration and customs fast today," confided the cab driver standing at the barrier next to her with his slate marked "Mr. Jabowalski, United and Combined Services Ltd' in large letters. "I'm always glad when people come on this flight. It's never that much of a wait, but today's magic."

He was right; she saw them only a few minutes later, pushing their trolley of luggage, looking a little dazed and uncertain, two white-haired women in the neat clothes and sensible shoes that she remembered so well; she pushed her way forwards to wave furiously and Aunt Bridget's face lit up—her mother still looked rather vague—as she reached them.

The next twenty minutes were a flurry of hugs and chatter and sweating as they got the luggage—rather a lot of it, George noted with a slightly sinking sensation—to the car park. She'd borrowed Hattie Clements's car this morning, since she had no car of her own and had to explain all this to an incredulous Aunt Bridget as she maneuvered her way out of the airport and on to the route that would take her to the M4 and the middle of London.

"No car of your own?" Bridget said, shocked to the core. "How can you possibly not have a car, honey? How do you -?"

"I really don't need one," George said, trying to concentrate on the unfamiliar stick gearbox. She'd only driven the car a couple of times in the past, apart from this morning on the way here. "It's easier to use buses between the hospital and my flat, or walk, and parking's hell in London. Public transport's terrific though. Hattie—the woman who owns this car—hardly uses it for the same reason. Listen, are you OK back there, Ma? Are you comfortable?"

"I'm fine, thank you, sweetheart," Vanny said and smiled at George in the rearview mirror. "Just a bit weary, I guess. It was kind of noisy on the plane, what with the babies and all'

"Tell me about it' Bridget said with great feeling. "Jesus, the way that kid bawled! I thought it'd never stop. I told the mother I had some Valium tablets in my bag and a half of one wouldn't do any harm, give the poor little scrap a bit of peace—as well as the rest of us, though I didn't say that, of course—and you'd have thought I was trying to poison the child! But kids do fine on small doses of the stuff. My niece Mary has to fly her three over to Hawaii all the time and she always knocks them out. That way it's no hassle and the kids don't act cranky for days after they arrive."

"The food on the plane was not good," Vanny announced suddenly. "I have to tell you, George, I am famished, famished and tired. Could we stop for breakfast, please?"

The car was now on the motorway at last, locked in the usual morning rush hour, and George swore under her breath.

"I wish you'd said at the airport I could have got you something there easily. Now, it's not so good. It's a fair way into town and I didn't see any clean eating places on this road." She peered out at the heavy traffic and shook her head. "And I do have to go into the hospital some time today, so I have to... Look, hold on in there and I'll do the best I can to get us home fast. Then I can fix you some breakfast and see you settled before I have to go to work."

"It's not important," Vanny said peaceably. "I just thought... Don't worry, I can wait."

Which of course made George feel deeply guilty for her thoughtlessness. She should have considered the possibility of hunger and offered them food at the airport, however late that would have made her; but there it was, she hadn't. And, she thought gloomily, I might as well get used to feeling this way, guilty and angry and annoyed with Ma about it, and all the rest of it. It's not going to go away.

They were happy passengers, exclaiming over the dear little houses and how odd it felt to be on the wrong side of the road and displaying some surprise that the place looked so—well, like any US city really, apart from the billboards and the shopfronts and, of course, the dear little houses, and she encouraged the chatter and told them all she could to fill them in on local knowledge, even if she wasn't sure of her facts, taking the road south of the river, once they got to town, by going over Westminster Bridge. That way she could point

out some obvious sights, and they cooed happily over Big
Ben and the Houses of Parliament and seemed to perk up a
good deal.

They were a bit dismayed by the flat though they assured
her they were enchanted to be so near to Tower Bridge and to
be able to see it from her kitchen window; they said they didn't
mind sharing a room one little bit, truly they didn't; but she
wasn't fooled. She set about organizing a late breakfast for them
while they unpacked, knowing the coming days were not going
to be easy as they came to terms with living in such cramped
quarters after the comfort of their own big houses. Maybe they
wouldn't stay over Christmas, she thought hopefully, and again
the guilt welled up. How could she be so unkind when they'd
come so far to visit with her? It was shocking.

As a result of that feeling she gushed over them when she
settled them to their breakfast, making a bit of a drama of
squeezing oranges specially for the juice (quite forgetting how
commonplace this was to them both) and chattering cheerfully
of how much better English bagels were than New York ones,
and they sat in increasing gloom as she burbled on, watching
her over the rims of their coffee cups.

"Look, honey," Bridget said at last. "I know I may be
speaking out of turn and so forth, but I have to say, speaking
for myself, that I don't mind one bit if you want us to stay in
a hotel or someplace else. It is tricky for you, seeing you have
your job at the hospital and all…"

George was appalled. She sat down hard and stared at
Bridget. "Oh, but Bridget, the last thing I want to be is—is
unwelcoming. I thought—"

"You're not being unwelcoming," Bridget said, smiling at
her so that her eyes crinkled and disappeared into slits set in
her pouchy toad-like cheeks. She looked so familiar, in a way
George had quite forgotten, that George began to feel better.
"It's just that we know you, your ma and me, and we sorta
got the idea you weren't too sure this would work, this visit. I

know we decided kinda fast to come, but you know me. I do everything in a rush."

"Ma?" George looked at her mother for the first time since her arrival. So far she'd chattered and busied herself so much she'd been able to avoid eye contact "Ma, did you think—"

"Oh, Bridget's got it about right, I guess," her mother said and smiled her long slow smile. "She picks up these things when I don't, you know. She's my good right hand these days. And leg as well." She reached out, touched her friend's hand with one gnarled and beautifully manicured finger and winked at her. "If she thinks it's too much for you having us here, why, we'll go to a nice hotel someplace and be very comfortable. Just as long as we're in the same town for a while, I'll be happy, George. You're looking very well, a shade peaky, maybe, but your eyes are clear so I guess you're happy enough."

"I'm very happy, Ma," George said. She reached out her own hand and Vanny took it and patted it with slow-moving fingers. "And I do want you here. I couldn't pretend I didn't suddenly realize how crowded we're all going to be, but if you can manage, then—"

Bridget had got up and slipped out and George had hardly noticed. She was looking at her mother, noting the way her mouth had sprung railway lines all round the lips into which her pink lipstick had bled a little, and the fine line round the irises of her eyes. Oh, God, she thought. Arcus Senilis. My mother is getting old. So I'm getting old; and a sudden wave of desolation swept over her. She hurled herself forwards and hugged her mother close. Vanny said nothing; she just held George and let her cling and then, when she sat up again, Vanny lifted both her rather shaky hands to pat her hair tidy.

"Ma, I won't hear another word about hotels," George said. Her voice was a little husky. "You're staying here, crowded or not. We'll manage fine."

Bridget came drifting back from the small room she was sharing with Vanny, her face wreathed in smiles. "That's better," she said approvingly, as though she were talking to a backward child. "Now listen, hon. You just leave us be. You go to your work and me and Vanny, we'll take a little nap to get over last night and then when you get home—"

"I'll cook us a great dinner and we'll catch up on all the news," George said, getting to her feet. "Now, is there anything else you need? Towels in the bathroom and—"

"We're just fine," Bridget said. "Off you go. No, leave the dishes. We'll do them. Go on now! We need a bit of space, you know?"

And George laughed and went. It was all she could do under the circumstances. The next few weeks were not going to be at all easy, but she'd manage somehow. And maybe it would turn out that all was well with her mother after all and Bridget had just been fussing. Vanny had seemed tired this morning, of course, but then she would. She'd never been to Europe before, and a long flight across time zones made the youngest and most chipper feel lousy, she told herself as she ran for the bus that would take her over the river to Shadwell. It'll all be OK, I'm sure it will.

She had little time to think about her personal affairs once she got to the hospital. It was almost lunchtime before she reached her office, having had to go in the long way round via the rear entrance in order to avoid the group of protesters at the main entrance, who still bore their battered placards proclaiming "The NHS For The People Not The Market Place', and "Down With Trusts—No Privatization' in spite of the fact that no one in authority paid them any attention at all, and then found she was wanted urgently on a consult in Pediatrics. She muttered under her breath, looking at her cluttered desk, and then shrugged her shoulders and went They wouldn't call her if it wasn't important.

And was that much angrier when she got there and was told what the problem was with a baby that Prudence Jennings, the Pediatric Registrar, had just admitted. "She wants some special blood work done," the nurse at the desk told her. "She's down in the cubicle at the far end."

"Blood work?" George frowned. "Couldn't you have just sent the blood over to me?"

The nurse shrugged. "I said that but she insisted she wanted you to take it yourself. She'll explain, I imagine." She sniffed suddenly, showing her own irritation for the first time. "I've taken blood from younger babies than that one and had no problems. I could have done it easily. I can't imagine why she had to drag you over here. Don't blame me. I wouldn't have bothered you, take it from me." And she looked as self-righteous as only nurses can in such circumstances.

George found Dr. Jennings in the last cubicle, sitting beside a cot in which a small fretful infant lay, rocking its head from side to side. She was staring down at him with a frown between her brows.

"Oh, Dr. Barnabas, it's good of you to come over," she said, glancing at George briefly. "I've got a tricky one here."

"Oh?" George said and looked from the baby to the blood-taking tray that was waiting beside the cot on a locker. "I understand you want some blood work done? Why not just send the blood?"

"That's right' Prudence was still looking at the child and seemed not to have noticed the question. "I made sure they had everything ready. Listen, Dr. Barnabas, how old do you think this child is?"

"Eh?" George, still annoyed and wanting an answer to the question why she'd been brought to the ward to do a job one of the nurses could have handled perfectly well, let alone one of the medical staff, was startled. "How old? I don't know. Isn't it on the notes?"

Prudence shook her head. "No, that's not what I mean! I mean, looking at him, how old would you say he is?"

George looked at the child and then at the doctor, a woman around her own age, red-headed and a little untidy, but clearly good at her job. She'd never have lasted as Susan Kydd's registrar if she weren't Susan was a famous martinet, and had sent any number of young doctors away in a state almost of gibbering fear. Yet here she was, asking such a banal question.

Prudence apparently followed George's train of thought, and gave her a wintry smile. "Indulge me," she said, "then I'll explain."

George shrugged and looked at the child. He was a small-framed infant, she thought, too thin for a baby, and with the deep-set eyes of fever set in large sockets. He had the shrunken look of dehydration also, and she said as much.

"No, it's not that At least, not entirely. He hasn't been vomiting or purging," Prudence said, reaching over into the cot and pulling back the child's cover and clothes. The belly was round and clearly tense and she set one finger on it and pressed gently. The baby's face puckered and he began to cry thinly. Prudence made an odd little hissing sound through her teeth and covered him up. The baby seemed to find the sound soothing. He stopped crying and closed his eyes.

"Go on," she said. "How old?"

"I'm no expert in these things," George said and bit her lip, trying to remember the little time she'd spent in pediatrics. She knew well enough what dead children looked like at various ages; then she had the evidence of epiphyseal development to tell her, and the state of the sutures of the skull. Babies with wide-open soft spots at front and rear of their heads were still very young.

She reached to touch the baby's head but Prudence shook her head and held her hand back. "Just use your eyes," she said. "Please."

George threw a glance at her and then shrugged again. "Oh, well, all right," she said irritably. "Under a year, ten months maybe. And not at all well."

"Try eighteen months," Prudence said. She shook her head. "I've checked the skull sutures, measured the bones and checked the dimensions. If this boy is any younger than eighteen months then I'm a chimpanzee. Yet the mother says he's *eight* months old! It makes no sense to me."

George had forgotten her irritation now and was fascinated. "That is weird!"

"You could call it that. I'm wondering…" She shook her head. "There's no family history, though the mother swears he was breast fed till a few weeks ago, and if she was positive it would account for it—well, I was wondering about HIV. If she's positive and he's been breast fed by her, couldn't he have AIDS? He looks ill enough."

"I suppose it's possible," George said slowly. "What history do the parents give?"

"A shaky one. Makes no sense to me. Born abroad, they say, no problems at birth. No suggestion of any premature closure of skull sutures. I asked them. Just a normal birth, they said. Anyway, they left him here, but only under protest. I said I'd have to do some tests and they could come back later—for two pins I thought she'd just walk out with him. But her husband persuaded her to leave him till the tests were done, so can you get on with them? You can see why I didn't want anyone else taking the blood. I'd have to say what the tests were on the specimen-bottle labels and the way people gossip round here, we'd have a major panic on our hands in no time. AIDS baby in Old East—can't you just see the headlines?"

"Yes," George said and went across the cubicle to wash her hands in the corner basin, "I take your point. OK, you hold him for me, will you? Not that I expect the poor little devil to fight much. He looks too sick."

"Doesn't he just," Prudence murmured, picking up the child who protested only weakly and, with expert fingers, holding him positioned for George's syringe.

They worked in silence though the baby whimpered from time to time, and again Prudence made that odd little sound that seemed to comfort him. When she'd finished George straightened her back and carefully marked the bottles and slipped them into her white coat pocket. "We'd better clean the gear ourselves," she said. "Just in case."

Prudence nodded. "You can leave that to me. I'll be very careful. Urn—you'll send the report to me as soon as possible? I'd like to sort it out before, well, before I go off duty tonight'

George shook her head. "No can do. Some of the HIV work takes rather longer to do. A couple of days or so."

"Not all of it, though?"

"No, not all of it. I can give you some answers tonight' She was suddenly aware of what it was that was making Prudence so edgy, and she laughed. "I've just realized. You want an answer before Miss Kydd gets back. Where is she?"

Prudence grimaced. "Lecturing somewhere. She'll be here tomorrow maybe, the day after for certain. And I have to say— well—yes. You know how she can sneer at you if you get it wrong. I may be way out on this, so I don't want to let Susan know that. If I'm right, of course, it'll be different."

"She'll pat your little head and you'll grow, grow, grow, blossom," George said as she made for the door and Prudence laughed.

"Something like that. Thanks for your help, Dr. Barnabas."

"Call me George, for God's sake," George said and went, hurrying past the nurse sitting at her desk, so that she couldn't ask any awkward questions, though she was clearly poised to do so, and getting back to her lab as fast as she could. It would, as she had told Prudence, take some days before all the results could be collated, but the sooner she started the better.

By the time she'd done the preliminary work and then sorted out the things she should have done that morning, it was well past seven-thirty. She stretched and reached for the phone. Her mother and Bridget must be bored out of their skulls waiting for her, she thought guiltily, dialing her own number. But it rang and rang interminably before she hung up, a thin line between her brows. Where on earth could they be? She'd have to hurry home to see what was happening, and she pulled on her coat and left, painfully aware, yet again, of how complicated it was to have the two of them as house guests. "Oh, God," she said to the yellowish glow in the night sky over the river. "Hurry on January. The sooner Christmas is over and done with and I'm on my own again, the better."

8

They were out when she got home, having left a note in Bridget's familiar back-sloping handwriting. "Back soon, honey, just wanted to check on the neighborhood. Hope you had a good day. We slept like babies, feel much better. B."

That gave her time to make sure the flat was shining clean, and when she looked about at the bright scatter rugs against the crimson carpet and the vivid cushions on the new leather studio couch, on which she herself was having to sleep while they were with her, and the flames from the pretend-log gas fire she had indulged in, trying to see it through their eyes, she was content enough. It was, after all, only a flat in a crowded city—far more crowded than any they had lived in, and that being so, she had no need to feel ashamed. By the time they came back, pink about the nose and ears from the chill, she had supper ready; a rich daube of beef and plenty of vegetables; it was easy to do and had enough red wine in it to make it taste more effortful than it had been, and would, she thought, impress them both.

It didn't They ate little, professing it to be delicious, but too much for their capricious appetites, and she put the remainder in a plastic pot and wondered gloomily whether to dump it now or clutter up the fridge for a week and then put it in the garbage. Again guilt gave way to irritation. Oh, hell, she thought, as she made coffee, this is going to be some lousy Christmas.

They watched TV for a while, both of the old women clearly entranced by the BBC, and George preened a little in the reflected glory; it was as though she personally had contributed to the quality of TV here in her adopted country. Bridget looked at her sideways and laughed.

"Being half Brit suits you," she said. "You even talk like them now, but it sounds cute."

"Cute?" George was aghast. "Me, cute? Heaven forbid! And everyone here knows at once I'm an American. I don't speak at all like they do here."

"You surely do," Bridget said. She yawned and stretched. "May I take a while in the bathroom, honey? I like a long slow tub, you know? But I don't want to hog it."

"No problem," George said uneasily, glancing at her mother. "OK with you, Ma?"

"Fine," her mother said equably. Bridget winked at George in a meaningful manner and went off to lock herself and a remarkable array of creams, powders, soaps and lotions into the bathroom, leaving the two of them to sit in silence as the TV murmured on.

George stirred after a while and said carefully, "Ma?"

Her mother looked at her with a smile. "Yes, honey?"

"Are you enjoying this program?"

"I guess so," Vanny said and glanced back at the screen. "It seems very interesting."

"What is it you like about it?" George said, watching her. There was no sense in ducking the issue any longer, Bridget knew that. That was why she'd gone off to hide in the bathroom. She'd brought Vanny here for a purpose, to show her daughter—to show her what? George had no idea: or tried to pretend to herself that she hadn't...

Vanny looked at her tranquilly. "Why, I'm not quite sure," she said. "You know how it is. You watch these plays and you can never be certain till they're finished whether you liked them or not."

George frowned. It wasn't a play that was showing. It was a fairly commonplace Channel Four documentary of somewhat dour aspect about the history of women, with several of them talking about their past lives which had clearly been far from joyous. Did her mother really think she was watching a play, or was she just not paying attention to the screen? She must still be tired after all, despite the sleep she'd had during the day. Jet lag did strange things to people.

"If you're not all that interested, we could turn it off and just talk," George said and again Vanny produced that sweet peaceable smile.

"If you like." She watched as George reached for the remote control and switched off. The room slipped into a silence broken only by the faint hiss of the gas flames leaping so prettily in the grate, and the distant sounds of traffic beyond the curtained windows.

"How's Uncle Nat, Ma?" she said after a short silence, and her mother looked puzzled for a moment.

"Uncle Nat," she said in a ruminative fashion. "Oh, yes, Uncle Nat," and smiled.

The silence stretched, and George said again, "How is he, Ma?"

"Who, George?"

"Uncle Nat'

"Oh, my, yes, Uncle Nat." Vanny looked thoughtful. "Is he here?"

George began to feel cold. "No, darling, of course not. This is London. How could Uncle Nat be here in London?"

"He lives in Boston," Vanny said with, once more, the ineffable smile.

This time George was suddenly angry. It was so inane a look and she leaned forwards and snapped at her mother: "Ma, what is it with you? Of course he lives in Boston. He aways has!"

"That's right," Vanny agreed. "He always has. He's getting old, I guess. Me too. I'm almost seventy, George, isn't that awful? Almost seventy. I feel seventeen inside, of course.

Still, I'm not so bad as Nat. He'll be seventy-seven soon." She laughed and this time it was like the old days, when Vanny would shoot out spiteful little barbs about her stuffy brother-in-law and make everyone laugh.

George relaxed a little. It was just jet lag, she told herself. That's all. Or is it? Could it be more? She could bear the uncertainty no longer and decided to go in bald-headed.

"Ma, Bridget wrote me that you weren't entirely well. Said she was worried about you. What was she talking about? She didn't say."

Her mother was silent, staring at the flames, and then stirred and looked at George with a wide limpid gaze. "Oh, she's just fussing. You know Bridget. Carries on like the world's going to end on account of there's a fly in the buttermilk."

"No, she doesn't," George said. She leaned over and set her hand on her mother's. It felt dry and cool, and she stroked it gently. "One of the things you like about Bridget is that she doesn't fuss. You couldn't have been friends for so long if she did."

Vanny lifted her chin and glanced at George briefly and then away. And shrugged. "Well, I can't say." Now she sounded a little sulky.

"I think you can," George said, her anxiety fierce once more. "What is it, Ma? Are you having symptoms you haven't told me about? Are you sick in some way?"

Vanny laughed, a sound that rippled with pleasure, and pulled her hand away from George's so that she could clap. "Hey, hey, get my daughter the doctor!" she crowed. "Ain't she somethin'?"

George reddened and protested and then laughed too. "Oh, to hell with it, Ma. I'm not playing doctors with you! This is George, you're Ma, and I want to know why it is that Bridget's getting herself all fired up over you. She is, you know. You'd better tell me. I'll not leave you in peace till you do."

"I could kill Bridget," Vanny said, but there was no malice in her tone. It was almost absent-minded. She sighed sharply, then looked hopefully at George. "I think she thinks I'm getting a bit weak in the attic, you know?"

"How do you mean?" George was sharp.

"I forget things."

"What things?"

"Oh, the date and what I'd planned for supper and so forth."

George lifted her brows. "We all do that'

"And the way home from the store on the corner." Vanny was looking away from her. "The one I've been using this past twenty years or more."

This time it was George who held the silence. Then she said carefully, "How often does that happen?"

Vanny glanced at her with a hint of her old sparkle. "Isn't once often enough for you?"

"I guess so," George said. "Ma, tell me, was it—I mean, were you worried about something? Going over things in your mind and just turned the wrong way without thinking?"

"I wish," Vanny said. "It'd be easier if I could say that. No, I just went the wrong way and didn't know where I was or where I was going. Till Bridget came and found me. I was in the park, down by the bus depot. On a bench."

"Oh, God," George whispered, not realizing she'd spoken aloud until Vanny looked at her.

"Yes," she said softly. "It is a bit scary, hmm? Just a bit."

"Not really." George managed to be bright, dragging herself back from the chill that had touched her. "I mean, it's just one lapse. It doesn't mean that—"

"It does, I think. I've thought for years I wasn't all I might be. Forgetting the names of people I've known all my life, for pity's sake. Forgetting the start of a book before I've finished it and having to go back and back. I barely read any more. It's not worth it. And now this."

"I'll fix for you to see a good doctor," George said.

"Like hell you will," Vanny said with a sweet smile. "What can he do but take money from me? There ain't no pills for Alzheimer's."

"Oh, Ma, you haven't got—"

"Let's be adults, hey, sweetheart?" Vanny said. "I saw your grandmother die this way. I don't need to be told."

Now George could say nothing. She just sat and stared at her mother, feeling her eyes hot and hard in their sockets but, a little to her surprise, tearless. Vanny lifted her head from her contemplation of the flames in the grate and laughed.

"Oh, such a face," she said. "I'm not so bad, honey!"

"That's what I was thinking," George said, and her voice had thickened oddly. "I mean, I can just remember Grandma. She really was—"

"Off her rocker," Vanny said as George hesitated. "Screwball. Crazy lady."

"She was sick," George said. "You don't seem at all like that. And how old was she when…"

Vanny nodded very positively. "That's my thinking too. She was younger than me when she passed on. She'd been that way from the time she was—oh, sixty, I guess. If I'm only just starting to lose my marbles, well, maybe by the time they've all gone, I'll be pushing up daisies anyway. I sure as hell hope so."

And George couldn't argue with her.

But, she thought on Monday morning when she was walking over the bridge to the hospital, it's helped, knowing. I suspected that was what Bridget meant, of course. Why else was I so unwilling to see Ma? I remember Grandma too, and there can be a family pattern in Alzheimer's, let's face it.

She stopped to lean over the rails on the bridge looking upriver towards the City, with the wind coming up from the estuary behind her biting her ears. She pulled her coat up with clumsy gloved fingers and looked at the mist through which the Tower of London pushed its stubby head and tried to get her own head into some sort of order. There'd been no time yesterday to think; they'd spent the day in a fever of sightseeing; but now she was alone and couldn't avoid it any longer.

Ma was right about one thing: if this was Alzheimer's, and her explanation of what her memory was doing made it seem horribly likely, then it was early days yet. She could take her to see a neurologist but she wasn't sure there would be much purpose in that. Not unless she was staying here in London. And Vanny had been adamant about that.

"I'm all American, George. Too old now to be anything else. I like Buffalo and you can't get more down home than that, can you? No, I'll go home and live with Bridget who wants to move in with me anyway. She's more than willing to keep an eye on me, and there'll be enough money to pay for nurses later on if I need them. As long as I die by the time I'm eighty, the money'll hold out."

That had been when George had wept, bitterly, and for a while it had been like long ago when she was small, when her father had been remote and everyone at school had been on her back and she was just too big to fit into her own body and Ma had been her only source of comfort. It had been a good thing really, she thought now, looking down at the water slapping greasily at the bridge's piers as a tug fussed busily past; at least her tears had melted the stiffness between them and by the time Bridget emerged from the bathroom in a miasma of steam and scent they had been sitting companionably chattering as though they'd never been parted. By bedtime they'd all agreed a schedule for the coming weeks and had planned how they were to spend Christmas Day ("It's on me," Bridget had said. "And I won't be talked out of it. I want to go to a real fancy hotel or some such. None of your sweating over a stove here at home. It's more fun putting on the flash and really stepping out') and which theaters they would catch and when and where they'd shop ("Till we drop," said Bridget gleefully) and had said not a word about any future beyond that.

But Bridget had come out of their bedroom just as George was falling asleep, on the pretext of seeking a glass of water, and told George not to fret.

"I'll look after her," she said softly. "She's the dearest friend I have. But I just wanted you should know how the land lay, you understand me? It's not right you shouldn't know. Visit as often as you can and she'll be fine. Don't break away from your career here, honey, I'd say. I thought you should, but now, well, I can see it'd make no nevermind. There'd be no sense in that."

Looking down at the Thames, George wasn't sure. She'd need to do some considerable thinking yet about that. To go back to Buffalo to work and live would be...But no. Bridget had told her not to think about that, and it was wise advice. She wouldn't. And she straightened her back and sighed and set out to complete her journey to the hospital.

Some of the preliminary results on the child in Pediatrics had come through. George lifted her brows as she checked them and decided to go over to the ward to talk to Prudence Jennings. She had a right to know how correct her guess had been. But first George locked the results in the safe. No need for any risks at this stage.

Prudence wasn't in the end cubicle when George got there. Neither was the baby. George frowned as she looked around the room, at the crib which had been stripped of not only its linen but its mattress, and at the piled-up gear in the corner, and went out to find someone who could tell her what was happening.

She found Sister Collinson in her usual place at the nurses' station (I wonder if she ever gives any hands-on care, for pity's sake? George asked herself) and she looked disgusted at George's question.

"Dr. Rajabani dealt with that one. A really nasty gastroenteritis, I gather. I didn't have anything to do with the child and only one of the nurses did. Prue handed the case over to Harry—Dr. Rajabani—and he spent most of the night with it. Told me Prue said the nurses weren't to get involved. So bugger her—and him!—I thought, and we didn't. She went off about midnight, I gather. Harry was here all night and then this morning the parents turned up and took the child away and Harry said to fumigate the room. It needs a new paint-job anyway. So, I've managed to wangle it out of the budget. Harry? Gawd knows where he is. Try the canteen. He's been up all night, after all, and probably went looking for some grub."

George found him at a corner table, a large, good-looking Asian with a darker than average skin and an unusually wide and friendly smile. She'd only seen him a couple of times before; he was, she had gathered, a recent appointment. Now he sat a little slumped over an untouched plate of rather leathery scrambled eggs, and she slid in beside him, her own coffee cup in her hand.

"Harry Rajabani? I'm George Barnabas from Path. I was doing some tests on the baby you specialled last night. How come he's gone? He's a very ill child, you know."

"Of course I know!" he said. "I told them not to take him, but they insisted. I tried to call Prue, but she'd just vanished. I didn't know what to do. They flatly refused to wait till I got it all sorted out. Very nasty they were."

"Nasty?" George opened her eyes wide. "How? And why?"

"Ask—ask the damned hall porter or someone! He knows as much as I do. They—the parents—just turned up, didn't want to hear another word from me or anyone, not the results of the tests Prue had ordered or anything. I told them we'd have some through soon but they just said they had to take the child away and apologised for any trouble. And went! They wouldn't say another word to me about anything."

George frowned. "I'd like to talk to them," she said. "There are things about the tests—"

"I wish I could tell you how much I'd like to talk to them too," Harry said bitterly. "I've got to explain to Prue—even to Miss Kydd, God help me, and I don't fancy that—but if they refuse to co-operate to the point of giving a false address and phone number..."

"What?" George said, blinking.

"I know. It's a very strange thing, is it not? I went to the notes as soon as I failed to get hold of Prue and they started to get the child ready to leave, and I tried to call the GP whose name they'd given but it turned out there was no such GP. So then—trying to be logical, you understand—I rang Directory Enquiries for their phone number. It's a good way of confirming, you know, a sort of double check. And they're not listed! No such address seemingly, and the number they'd given turned out to be a dead line. By the time I had found all this out they'd gone, child and all. So all I can do is wait for Prue and Susan Kydd to get back and hope she will not kill me for this."

"It's not your fault. I'll tell them that if you like."

"Yes please," Harry said promptly. "I very much would like. Miss Kydd does not quite like me anyway, I think. I wasn't appointed by her, you understand, but by the Dean, when she was away, so I'm not her choice." His smooth young face wrinkled a little. "I don't say she objects to my race, but— Well, if you'll support me, I am grateful."

"I will," George promised. "What an odd business." She sighed and got to her feet. "I suppose I might as well forget about it all. Though I'll be curious to know what's going on, if you do find out. Give me a call, will you?"

"Oh, indeed, yes," Harry said fervently. He looked down at his eggs. "I suppose I had better eat this, though it's not too palatable. But it would be better than falling over with a blood sugar on the floor, I imagine."

"Indeed it would," George said. "Bon appétit."

She went back up to her department and, having decided there was nothing more she could do, and therefore that there was no point in wasting any more time over the matter, gave little more thought to the baby with AIDS.

Until his body was found on a patch of waste ground on the other side of Watney Street Market a week later and brought in to her for a post-mortem.

She recognized the infant as soon as she saw him; and also recognized very quickly and without any difficulty that this child hadn't died of his disease. He'd been smothered by the use of a small plastic bag over his head. His face was otherwise pale and unmarked, and there were no signs in the lungs or anywhere else that his death had been deliberately inflicted. If whoever had done the killing had taken the bag away, no one would ever have known it was a murder; as it was there could be no doubt.

So once again, Gus arrived in her mortuary.

9

"Well, well," Gus said with relish. "Here's a pretty kettle o' fish!"

"It's not seemly to be so excited," George said, and he roared with laughter.

"Not seemly? Jesus, where'd you get that sort of talk? Why not?"

"Dead babies aren't funny," she said and bent her head again to her work. The post-mortem was showing nothing she hadn't expected to find, but all the same it had to be done with pernickety attention to detail. This case, she felt at a deeply intuitive level, could turn out to be a very complicated one.

"Whoever said I thought it funny? I just meant it's interesting. And don't come the sensitive little flower with me. I've watched you at work too often, kiddo. You forget they're people too. You get so excited by the details and the search for facts you could as well be chopping up a Martian."

She couldn't deny that, but worked on in silence as Gus watched over her shoulder, his eyes glittering with interest. Then she stretched her back, finished her dictation into the microphone that hung over the table—an expensive new addition to her department—and nodded at Danny to start preparing the closure.

"Well?" Gus demanded. "What have we got there?"

"We've got what you saw," she said. "A baby smothered by a plastic bag over its face."

"Is that enough? I mean the bag wasn't tied at the neck or fixed in any way, was it?"

She shook her head. "It doesn't have to be. The breathing attracts the polythene so that it sticks to the mouth and nostrils. That's all it takes. It'd be a matter of minutes after that. If not less."

"No other signs or symptoms?"

"There can't be symptoms. They're what are reported by living patients, signs are what the clinician can see."

"So spare me the lecture. No other signs apart from smothering, then."

"There weren't even signs of smothering. It doesn't show, as I say. Except for the plastic bag, we'd never have known."

"Oh." he said. "It's like the guy was in a hell of a hurry, and didn't have time to remove the evidence of what he'd done."

"Or didn't care if evidence was there on account of he was so sure he couldn't be found," she said.

"I suppose that's possible. Not likely, but possible," he said, and shook his head. "But no one can be that sure. Just as," he added, with an air of sudden illumination, "it's possible it wasn't a he, but a she."

"Or a they," she said. "These people were—well, odd…"

He quirked his head at her. "You know more than you're telling me," he said accusingly and she sighed.

"I cannot lie, dear sir. I must be like the other little George, one Washington. I did chop down the cherry tree…"

"Stop fitting about and tell'

"This child—I saw it in life."

He opened his eyes wide. "Did you, by God. So tell!"

"Like I said, it's an odd story." And she told him. He listened with narrowed eyes and a face smoothed by concentration.

"Let me recap to make sure I get it right. You were asked to see this child by the—who was it?—registrar, Dr. Jennings. She'd been told by the parents, whom you did not see, that the child was eight months old. She reckoned it was over eighteen months, but very frail and underdeveloped."

"I agreed with her," George said. "I have evidence now. I've had a chance to look at the skull properly and at the epiphyses—"

"Epi-bleedin' what?"

"The places in the long bones where growth occurs. In infants they're large, in adults they've vanished. This child was almost two years old, I'd say, and had the body weight of an infant of less than half its age. It's been consistently underfed all its life."

"OK. So, there's a mystery child, brought in by the parents who make this crazy claim about its age. They're persuaded against their will to leave the child for tests. Have I got that right?"

"According to Prudence, yes. They didn't want to leave it. The mother didn't, that is. The father insisted."

"Right. And then you discover, via this other doctor, what's his name?"

"Harry Rajabani."

"Yeah, him. He finds out that they've given false information for the child's hospital notes. But by the time he discovers this, it's too late. They've vanished, baby and all, and that's the end of it till we find the body on the waste ground, under a pile of old bricks." He frowned sharply. "You should have seen Old Potato Head. He's a layabout lives down there, sells what he picks up to fund his boozing. Pinched the bricks a couple of days ago, seemingly, and left them, then went to get them on account he'd found a buyer and there's this poor little corpse. Really turned him up, that did."

it had been there about forty-eight hours, I'd say. Can't be sure," George said.

Gus nodded. "That fits with what the old boy told us. He'd brought the bricks in over a couple of days, built them into a pile with a space in the middle—he does that to make it easier to load them again afterwards. So someone dumped this baby in just after he'd started his bit of entrepreneuring. Right!" He rubbed his hands and turned to the door, "I have things to do. Where'll I find this Prudence woman? And Harry Thingummy?"

"Pediatrics," she said. "And—er—Gus?"

He stopped at the door. "Yeah?"

"Come back and tell me what's what, will you? I'm interested in this one."

He leered at her. "When aren't you interested? OK, but what's in it for me if I do?"

"You'll find out," she said. "A surprise. Go on, get on with it. I'm busy. Got another of these waiting."

"What, another for me?" He grinned beatifically. "Oh, Dr. B., Dr. B., won't we be spendin' a lot o' time together!"

"Not at all. This one died in his bed and no one found him for a couple of days. No mystery. He was eighty-nine and had a heart, so I'm told. On your way, Gus. Come back later..." And he grinned, flicked his thumb and forefinger at his forehead to mime the tip of a hat, and went.

It was late in the afternoon when he came back. She'd got her paperwork done, sorted out a drama in the hematology lab over a set of prothrombins that someone had mislaid, organized a training session for her junior histology technicians and swallowed three cups of Sheila's over-brewed tea by the time he arrived, and she glowered at him. "So what kept you? Here am I panting to hear—"

"She's yearning to hear my step on the way," he said, holding his hands together at chest level and casting his gaze upwards in a look of ineffable soulfulness. "Be still my beating heart! She cares, oh, lo, she cares—"

"She's busting a gut to know what's the news about this infant," she interrupted, pushing a chair forwards for him. "Do you want some of this tea? It tastes like something Russian wrestlers' jockstraps have been washed in, mind you."

"Oh, great," he said and sat down. "Some of Sheila's real poison? Lead me to it, I'm parched."

She waited as he drank his tea thirstily. She knew by now that there was never any point in trying to hurry Gus. If she nagged he became slower and more and more circuitous. Patience was the only ploy that paid with him.

It did today. "Right," he said cheerfully as he clattered his cup back into its saucer. "What do we have? I'll tell you what we have. A thorough-going mystery, that's what Ain't that nice?"

"Lovely. It's the identity of the parents, I take it?"

"And a bit more besides. There's this Prudence in charge of Pediatrics with a tricky case in, right? She also has to watch her rear, on account of the boss, who is, I gather, a cow of the first water—"

"First cream," murmured George.

"I stand corrected. A boss who is a right lump of rancid old butter when she's crossed, then. So you'd think this Prudence would be extra careful, eh? But not she. She goes buggering off somewhere, leaving her tricky case to the care of a very young and slightly dippy houseman."

"Who says he's dippy?" she said sharply, jumping immediately to another doctor's defense.

"The nurses. They should know. He tends to forget things, seemingly. If there's a mucky place to put his foot, he'll find it. One of Nature's mistakes, they say. Like one or two I've got cluttering up the nick."

"Well, he seems OK to me," she said. "Did his best to find out who the parents were. Had the nous to try to call the GP."

"Yeah, that's interesting, isn't it? Turns out there's not only no such person but no such place—the address the parents gave for themselves, down in Docklands, is one of the new developments that never got finished. Very peculiar, all that So, all right, this young Harry ain't so bad as he's painted. But Prue, now, I'm puzzled by that one."

"Was she supposed to be on duty all night?" George said. "Is that what you mean? That she went off when she should have been on?"

Gus nodded. "It's usual, according to the nurses, for the consultant on call, or the registrar, always to be available. They don't have to be actually there, you understand, just as long as they can be reached fast in an emergency."

George was mystified. "Well, of course. That's normal practice. What's the problem?"

"But this one *didn't* do that. She goes off at around midnight tells the boy Harry to stay on the ward in case of problems—so he bunks down on a chair in the nurses' office—and then vanishes. She wasn't in her room in the residence and she'd left no numbers to reach her where she was. All a bit dicey, eh, when this terrifying boss, who checks every damned thing when she comes back from one of her jaunts abroad, is supposed to be the bane of Madam Prudence's little life? Again according to the nurses."

George frowned. "It is a bit unusual for someone on call for a department to go and not leave contact numbers. What about her bleep? I imagine they tried that?"

"Is the Pope a Catholic?" Gus said and she grimaced.

"Silly question. Sorry." There was a silence and then she said, "Is there any other way you can find out about this child?"

"Do you think I wouldn't have used them by now if there were? Or at least started. No, there isn't Usually if a baby's body's found we check all the maternity units and community midwives as well as the registrar's office for information on births, but this one's difficult. I mean, you said the child was almost two—"

"That's right."

"Even though the mother said eight months."

She was silent again and then said, "What name did they give in the notes?"

"Eh?"

"I know it's a false one, of course, but you know how people are. If they invent names for themselves they sometimes leave clues. Like using the same initials or something like that."

He reached into his breast pocket and pulled out his notebook. It was a messy affair held together by rubber bands, with masses of scrappy pieces of paper tucked into it. He spread the scraps on her desk and picked them over.

"I do remember it was something daft," he said. "Ah! Here we are. Teddy Oberlander. I ask you! If you were going to invent a name would you go for anything as outlandish as that? John Smith might be a bit too obvious, but there's something between that and Teddy Oberlander, surely?"

"It does sound a bit over the top," she said. "I imagine you're checking the Oberlanders in the phone book?"

"Even as we speak," he said gloomily. "But I expect nothing from that. We've had a false address, a false GP, why the hell should we expect a real name?"

"People can do strange things. Well. All right. There's the mystery. What now?"

"We go on plodding." He got to his feet. "It's the way that wins, in the end. Meanwhile, ducks, anything else you might have that could be useful would be warmly welcomed. How about it?"

"What could I possibly have—" She looked up at him and he grinned down at her cheerfully.

"You look a right mess," he said. "Your hair's all over the place."

"Thanks a bunch!" she said and managed, just, not to run one hand over her head to smooth it. The hair dryer hadn't been working properly after the shower she'd taken following the PM and she'd had to leave it to dry by itself. The resultant curly mop, she knew, looked less than businesslike. "Stick to the point."

"I am. I'm being happy in my work. And it helps to look at something nice. Like you in a mess. Very nice. Where was I?"

"Out on your ear any second," she said and stood up too. "Go on, Buster. Scram."

"Oh, I know. Asking you for anything else you might have."

He didn't budge from his place beside her desk. "Like those other cot deaths you were on about."

"The other—?" She sat down again. "Oh, yes."

"What about them? Anything funny there?"

"Just that note," she said. "The one that suggested they were linked in some way. I never did track down who wrote that. But I don't see how they can be connected to this case. It's entirely different."

"Not entirely," He sounded judicious. "It's all babies."

"Work on that basis and you'd link up every death in the hospital and call them crimes because they're all people," she said. "That's crazy."

"Maybe. But when you're stuck with a crazy sort of crime—and you have to admit there is an element of craziness in a case where someone uses a name like Teddy Oberlander as a pseudonym for a baby—then even the craziest notion comes in useful. Or might."

"Well, I can't see—but OK. I take your point. Anyway, I should check on that. I can't deny I sort of pushed it to the back of my mind. I've been a bit—well, I've had things to think about."

She opened her drawer and began to leaf through the papers that had been pushed in there. It was a simple filing system; anything that wasn't urgent got stuck there until she had time to look at it Sometimes, she thought guiltily as she pushed a rather large pile of papers around, it does get a bit behind. I'd better sort this stuff first thing tomorrow.

"Here we are," she said at length. "I managed to get hold of the notes for the other cot deaths there've been. I'll go through them first chance I get and see if there's anything for you." She looked up and caught his quizzical gaze and reddened a little. "I promise I will."

"No hangin' on to 'em to do a bit of your fancy private sleuthin'? You know I don't reckon that."

"You don't mind it when it helps you out," she retorted. "I didn't do so badly over the—"

He sighed. "I know, I know. The Oxford case. You didn't do badly, I admit, except for bloody nearly getting yourself killed while you were doing it and getting me fairly duffed up too. Anyway, promise me on this one."

"I will," she said, a little ungraciously, and then brightened. "On one condition."

"I knew it. The woman's shameless."

"That you get me the background stuff on the baby that got Dr. Choopani beaten up. You said you would, and you never did."

"Oh, come on! Why should there be any connection with that one?"

"Because they're all babies, of course. Remember? It was you who said that."

"I did?" He looked wilfully blank.

"Why should there be any connection between these cot deaths, either?" She tapped her papers. "It cuts both ways, mate."

"OK, OK." He gave in. "Fair dos, I suppose. I'll have to track the papers through the system. The fellas who went for Choopani have been in court, and I'm not sure the paperwork's come back. I'll let you know, then maybe afterwards we can get together and talk it all out. How about that, hey? I thought you were going to bring your Ma and her pal to eat at my place with me. We had a date, didn't we? You never showed."

She made a face. "Sorry about that. I did send a message, though, didn't I? They were too bushed. And anyway..." She hesitated.

"You didn't want 'em to see you're hangin' around with a low life like me?"

"Try not to be any stupider than you were born to be—" she said. "No. Nor is it the other way around, if that's what you're thinking. It's just that—well, Ma's not the healthiest of women."

"She can't be that bad if she got herself here from the USA," he said.

"No, it's not exactly that she can't—Oh, damn. Look, let me talk to them about it, hmm? Then I'll call you and we'll make a plan."

"You're on. I'll send the trawlers out to get the best fish in the North Sea for you. And I'll set the jelliers to work on the eels at once."

She grinned. "OK, just stop crowing, will you? You were right and I was wrong. Jellied eels are human food after all. Now, will you go away, Gus? I have things to do. Like going home to look after my visitors."

He showed a strong disposition to linger. "Are they staying for Christmas?"

"Yes," she said a little firmly. "It's going to be busy."

He nodded. "Then I have an idea for you. No, not now. I can think of a night out for your two old ladies that'll knock "em in the aisles. I'll sort things out and we'll talk about it. It's Friday night I've got in mind for takin' you all out to supper. Call me, hmm? It'll have to be early. Around six, even. But it'll be worth it' This time he did go, with that familiar flick of thumb and forefinger, leaving her to lock up the office at last and get on her own way. But she had to admit she felt better for talking to him. He did cheer the place up so, she told herself. That was all it was. And it would be nice to go out and introduce Bridget and Vanny to fish and chips, Gus style. She felt positively excited at the thought.

10

She took the sets of case notes on the cot-death babies home with her. There was no urgency about going through them for clues for Gus, but she felt it might be useful to have them with her; and in the event she had been wise. Bridget had dragged Vanny round the West End of London and through Knightsbridge and Kensington on a shopping spree that had left the pair of them depleted in more than money. They sat after dinner in a state of semi-exhaustion in her small living room, dozing in front of the flickering TV as it murmured softly in the background and fell asleep almost before they'd finished their coffee, so George was grateful to have something to do which wouldn't disturb them.

She almost fell asleep herself, for there was nothing there she could get hold of. She had ordered up the ward notes from the hospital registry before she left, sending Sheila hotfoot to get them, and though the Chowdary file was only a précis—the main file was signed out to Maternity still—there was enough information for her to work on. Now, as she plodded her way through the accounts of the pregnancies and labors that had produced the infants, she marveled at the detail, even in the Chowdary précis, that the midwives had offered. Every moment of monitoring and the treatment over the long pregnant months and the hours of labor and delivery had been carefully recorded and very monotonous reading it all made.

So did the reports of the post-mortems she had not been there to do herself; they were as straightforward and as unsatisfactory as her own post-mortem report on the Popodopoulos baby had been: no real answer to the question "Why did they die?" She sighed deeply as she pushed the papers back together again and tried to think of where she might go next in her investigation.

Was there anything different about any of these babies? She looked again at the brief notes she'd made while going through the voluminous hospital ones. The first two had weighed around three kilos at birth, but the last one had been bigger. The first two had been around 50 centimeters in length, the third one a couple of inches longer—55 centimeters. She stopped and looked again at her postmortem notes on the Popodopoulos baby. According to her own measurements that child had in fact been 59 centimeters long—a discrepancy of about an inch, and she was hopeful for a moment that she'd found something different that might be useful. But then shook her head. She had measured a dead body stretched out and flaccid. The midwives had measured a newborn live and kicking and with normal muscle tone. The chances of their getting the same measure she had were very slim, and anyway, what did it matter? There was nothing in the relative lengths of the babies that might contribute to their deaths.

All right, she thought, what about their backgrounds? This was even less help than the facts about the babies, for they were so widely disparate that there could be no connection between them. The first infant had been born to a mother who abused both alcohol and, the midwives had suspected, drugs; she had lived a hand-to-mouth existence partly on the streets and had had no antenatal care at all. Her baby had in fact been a prime candidate for a death in the neonatal period.

The other two, however, couldn't have been more different The Chowdary baby had been the result of long months spent under the care of the Fertility Department at Old East and had therefore been particularly precious, while the Popodopoulos baby had been the third child of a healthy happy mother who had had excellent antenatal care on the district and who had no history of any illness or problem that might contribute to her baby's death.

"I could go and talk to them in Fertility, I suppose," she murmured to herself aloud, "see if they can add anything to the Chowdary history," and then as Bridget stirred in her armchair, decided to pack up her work. The two old ladies needed to be woken, provided with their malted milk nightcaps and despatched to bed, and she set about doing that feeling rather like one of the nurses on the wards back at the hospital. She'd never before realized just how agreeable it was to live alone and do just what she wanted when she wanted, without any responsibility for anyone else. Oh, the joys of selfishness, she thought, and went and crouched in front of her mother to coax her awake. I'll never moan about being on my own again...

In the event she couldn't find time to visit the Fertility Clinic until Thursday morning, and then she went directly to the clinic before going to her own department. Once she got herself bogged down in the day's work she would, she knew, once again find it impossible to get away, and she did want to follow this through. The more she thought about it, the more peculiar the whole affair was, and anyway, there was another value in having a case like this to think about. If she got absorbed in this, it made it harder for her to think about her mother and her health and the implications that carried for her own future.

The Fertility Clinic was housed in a small set of rooms on the far side of the Maternity Department; not a very tactful placing, George thought as she pushed open the main door. Patients attending the clinic had to make their way through a corridor that it shared with Maternity, so the sounds of crying babies and even, sometimes, yelling laboring mothers could be heard clearly. She could imagine the distress that might cause to people who were yearning to be parents and failing abysmally.

She said as much to Dr. Julia Arundel, the consultant in charge, when she found her in her office. Julia grimaced.

"I know that perfectly well, George! I've been nagging them till I'm blue for a separate unit, but there isn't a hope in hell at present, if ever. They've cut two of my staff as it is, and when I do ask for more help all I get is a lecture about the budget deficit and GP fund-holders not sending the patients here in large enough numbers, and threats to close me down altogether. I've even thought about talking to those people out there on those demonstrations—by the main entrance, and at A & E, you know?—to see if they realize what they might lose here. I might have to eventually, unless I can get my hands on some more money outside the NHS. I've been chasing supporters and sponsors till I'm blue but there's damn all cash around these days and people are so uncaring anyway. Not enough are willing to even think about how desperately important a unit like this is."

George bit her lip, holding back the thought that had immediately come to her, which was that though she sympathized deeply with the misery of people who couldn't have babies, in a world as crowded as this one and a hospital as poverty-stricken as Old East, perhaps it was understandable that not everyone shared Julia's view. But it wouldn't be politic to say that, so she just contented herself with murmuring vaguely about the generosity of those who had supported the building of the new Children's Unit, Barrie Ward, at which Julia at once snorted and shook her head.

"And where will their future patients come from if my department vanishes for want of a few pounds?" she demanded.

George blinked at that. "Well, the birth rate's still pretty good with people who don't have fertility problems—Maternity seems to be run off its feet these days."

Again Julia displayed her disgust. "Maternity? They could double their throughput if they made the effort and streamlined their service so that I could have a couple more rooms, which I definitely need, but will they put themselves out? Not they! No, I have to go around with my begging bowl to keep a decent service going here. I'm speaking to the Operational Board about it at their next meeting. I need all the help I can get—I hope you'll support me there."

"I'm not on the Board," George said hastily. "I have to run my own budget, of course, but as I'm a single-handed consultant they agreed to let the head of the Investigative Directorate be from Radiology. So Dora Hebden's the Board member for me—you'll have to ask her for help."

"A fat lot of good *she* is," Julia said with a fine scorn. "Got three children and had them like shelling peas, as far as I can gather. Certainly she can't—or won't—see that Fertility *matters*. You see what I mean? It's hell trying to get this department properly funded."

The only way to head her off, George decided, was to go straight to the point. "I wanted to talk to you about a baby you produced—sad case. It died soon after birth, in Maternity. A cot death."

Julia looked blank for a moment and then said, "You must mean the Chowdary child. Yes, terribly sad, that. I had the mother here for—let's see…" She reached into her desk drawer for a notebook and then stopped and looked sharply at George. "Why do you ask?"

"There've been a couple of these neonatal deaths recently," George said. "I just wondered if there could be any connection."

Julia looked surprised. "Connection? Why should there be?"

"I've no idea," George said candidly. "If it hadn't been for a note attached to the request form for the PM on the most recent of them, I might never have given it a thought."

"Note?"

George explained and Julia listened and then nodded in comprehension. "Oh, well, yes. Under the circumstances you better had investigate. Now…" She began to riffle through her notebook. "Here it is. The Chowdarys. She's thirty-nine. He's forty-two. Sperm motility a problem as well as the actual count, but she had an oocyte shortage into the bargain. Or so it seemed. We managed to cause a super ovulation, harvested five ova, used a concentrated specimen of his sperm, did a straightforward in vitro job with two of them—she absorbed one fetus early on but managed to retain the second. A very speedy and satisfactory result. And then it went and died even though it had gone to term." She snapped the notebook closed and sighed. "All very sad, as I say. I never even saw the infant, you know." She sounded a touch aggrieved.

"Oh?"

"No. And that matters to me. I photograph them all, add them to the gallery." She waved a hand at the wall over her desk where pictures of babies, many of them in twinned pairs and a few in triples, were posted. George had noticed it of course. It was unmissable. "But I was away the day this one was born. At a meeting in Wolverhampton—the Society, you know. We need to keep in touch with all the newest techniques and it does mean a lot of meetings. So there it was. Couldn't see the child the day it was born. But they had no reason to think there were any problems, I gather, so no one here was alerted to get a picture." She seemed to brood over that for a while and then went on: "When I got back next day and heard it had died I was most put out, I must say. It was very upsetting. But what could we do? Not a thing."

She threw George an almost shy glance from beneath the thick straight fringe of dark hair streaked with grey which hung over her deeply set brown eyes. It was a look that made her seem a little like a mournful dog of the bloodhound sort. "Though I have written and told her we could try again. Usually after they've had one successful pregnancy and birth they have to be turned away or into the fully paid private sector. I can't afford to tackle them again, even though they do pay something for their care. We're not entirely NHS, you see. We can't be, dammit, the way things are at present. But in this case—well, I told her we'd try again."

"Will she?"

"Will she what?"

"Want to try again? I mean, I can imagine her never wanting even to think about pregnancy and childbirth ever again. I think I'd feel that way."

Julia stared at her with real surprise. "Why should she react like that? We've always explained to all our patients the long odds. They know there can be no promises of success—and do remember she succeeded superbly once. She should be pleased with herself. I'm sure she is. I've only agreed to take her back right away because it seemed so unfortunate to have lost the child. But you really mustn't underestimate my patients, you know. They truly are so sensible and strong and brave and uncomplaining…"

George was startled. That some of her colleagues were obsessive about their chosen speciality, she knew, but she'd never realized that Julia Arundel was one of them. Julia didn't involve herself much in hospital affairs outside her own department, it was true, but had always seemed easygoing enough when George met her in the staff canteen or at the occasional three-line-whip events set up by Professor Hunnisett; yet here she was now, looking like a different kind of animal to a bloodhound entirely. She was positively tigerish in her defense of her patients.

George smiled peaceably. "Well, fair enough, Julia. Anyway, I was just wondering whether there was anything in her history that you thought might have contributed to this infant's death."

Julia shook her head. "Once they get pregnant it's Matty's turn because usually they're perfectly normal. I keep in touch, of course, out of general interest and to get my picture." She looked fondly up at her wall. "They nearly always drop in to see me when they come for the antenatal appointments anyway, and of course bring me their babies to say hello afterwards. But the actual maternity care isn't my bag. I never heard there was anything wrong with the Chowdary child. Have you checked the Maternity Unit?"

"Oh, yes. Of course."

Julia shrugged. "Then it's just one of those things, I suppose. It happens, doesn't it?"

"Yes, it happens. If it hadn't been for that strange little note pointing out that there've been three here—I hadn't realized because I'd been off sick, of course—I might never have given it a second thought."

"Yes, the note...Well, I can see how you're thinking, but I can't help. As I've said, once they conceive, I'm out of it Let me know though what you do find out. I'll be most concerned to hear. Poor Angela Chowdary, she was unlucky. But we know we worked the miracle for her once and there's every reason to assume we can do it again. Do you want me to let you know when we do?"

"Er—yes. Yes, please," George said, well aware of the fact that she wasn't nearly as interested in Angela Chowdary's next baby as she was in her last, and Julia got to her feet briskly and went to the door.

"I will, then. Right now I have to go and check some of the ova we took yesterday. We might be using them for a surrogate mother, you know. We've got a most interesting case: a secretary prepared to donate ova for a boss she enjoys working with. Very generous. If you're interested I could show you what we're doing...?"

"Thanks," George said, "some other time," and escaped, wondering at the back of her mind whether she could ever have been the sort of clinician Julia was. To be that involved with your speciality, she thought a little wistfully, must be very nice. And then had the good sense to laugh at herself, for wasn't she as absorbed in her own cases as Julia was in hers? Why else was she traipsing about the hospital trying to find out why a baby had died? She shook her head at herself and set out to return to her Pathology Department.

***

She stopped as she reached the ground floor of Red Block

and set her foot on the walkway that would take her to the far side of the courtyard and her own unit Behind her, an equal distance away, was the new Pediatric Unit, Barrie Ward, and on an impulse she turned and headed that way. What else there might be to find out about the baby called Oberlander (what a ridiculous choice for a pseudonym, she thought again) she wasn't sure, but it might be useful to have another word with Prudence Jennings. All that faced her on her own desk was a pile of budget pages that had to be pored over to see where she could save a few more pennies out of her outgoings, and that was not a prospect that held out any temptations. The fact that she'd have Dora Hebden breathing down her neck for them at any moment now mattered not a whit She'd deal with that problem when it arose. Right now, she was busy. Busy doing Gus's job, but who was to know that, after all?

As she reached the Disney corridor she heard a sudden shout, followed by a great deal of confused noise coming from the ward at the far end and she quickened her step. Whatever was going on there was clearly not just the usual children's play; there were adult voices raised in anger, and she frowned as someone came out of the big swing doors towards which she was heading, looking back over her shoulder as she came.

"What's going on in there?" George asked. The woman jumped at the sound of her voice and then shifted the big carrier bag she was holding to her other hand, clearly anxious.

"Don't ask me, doctor," she said, George's white coat giving her an instant handle she could use. "I was just visitin' my sister's boy—"e broke his leg down the playground. I'm always on about that place, there's never no supervision there like there should be, and then this man come in and started shouting at one of the doctors—that darkie one, you know? "Im with the teeth, very upset this bloke is, and calling "im every name "e can put his tongue to. For me, I speak as I find and I reckon "e's all right, as Pakis go—nice fella, really. Our Wayne likes him, at any road."

Beyond the double doors the noise increased and behind George there was a thud of feet as one of the uniformed security men came running. George nodded swiftly at the woman with the shopping bag and pushed past her to go into the ward just as the security man arrived.

Harry Rajabani was standing in the middle of the floor in a tangle of toys and picture books as a heavy-set man with a stubbled face and grubby clothes bawled at him at the top of his voice, while the young curly-headed male nurse George had talked to on her last visit to Barrie Ward (she reached into her memory for his name, Philip Goss) held on to him with a clearly iron grip. Harry's face looked as though it had been carved out of polished wood; there was no sign that he was affected by the man's shouting, George thought in some surprise, and then saw the muscles at the side of his face bunched and quivering and knew that he was controlling himself with enormous effort.

"You lousy stinking black bastard, killing my boy, you and your nigger notions, get the fuck out of here and back into the trees you come down from, you bastard! If I'd have known you was putting your filthy black hands on my boy I'd have come down here and put a knife in you, do you hear me? A knife's too good for you, you should be strung up and made to suffer like my boy suffered, you stinking nigger—"

"That's enough," yelled Philip Goss, shaking him by the shoulders. "We know how you feel, Mr. Ritchard, but that doesn't mean you can abuse Dr. Rajabani like that No one's to blame for Kevin dying. We're all so sorry. Please come and let me—"

But the man wasn't to be reasoned with. He was disheveled, and his eyes were bloodshot and bulging. He clearly hadn't shaved for some time and he looked drawn and grey as well as stubbled. His mouth was open and still he shouted his obscenities into Harry's rigid face. At the far side of the room a couple of the nurses, including Sister Collinson, stayed white faced and anxious behind the safe barrier of their desk while beyond the second set of glass-windowed double doors that led into the ward proper George could see other nurses peeping out and hear the voices of the children who were also shouting, some of them shrieking with fear.

The security man pushed past George now with scant ceremony and grabbed the screaming man by his shoulders and whirled him around so that he lost his balance and fell against the stocky uniformed body. He was grabbed then by both arms which were held behind him just as two more security men came thudding along the corridor to get involved too.

"Come along, sir," panted the first of the men, who held on as his colleagues came up and joined in. "We'll sort this out, come with us…" And they had him out of the ward and into the corridor with its absurdly simpering Mickey Mouses and Donald Ducks with smooth professionalism, leaving Philip Goss behind calling after them, "He can't help it—his son just died," and Harry Rajabani standing rock still in the middle of the play area.

A sort of silence descended, even the children beyond seeming to quieten as the nurses who were with them stopped staring and at last shepherded them away, leaving George and Philip Goss to hurry to Harry's side. Sister Collinson came over too, now it was safe to come out from behind her barricade, and sent the other nurses into the ward to help calm the children. George reached Harry's side first She took his arm and, when she felt the rigid muscles there, said without stopping to think, "You'll feel better if you shout."

He shook his head, and slowly the muscles in his arm softened under George's hand, his shoulders slumped, and Philip, moving with commendable speed, pushed a chair behind his knees so that he folded, half collapsing into it, as the power clearly left his legs, leaving them like a jelly.

"That was dreadful," Philip said, crouching at Harry's feet. "But you mustn't take it personally, Harry. He's been hell ever since his kid came in, you know that The man never came to terms with the leukemia diagnosis or with the way he used to treat the child as he was growing up. Once he heard Kevin had told you he—well, that was all part of it. He meant no real harm. It was just the misery and the guilt and—and because you had looked after the boy, and knew his history, you got the brunt of it I'm so sorry. We should have realized he'd go like that..."

"Not your fault, Philip," Harry said, his voice thick and shaky at the same time. "Not your fault, but Christ, it gets to you when they hate you that much!" He rubbed a trembling hand over his face, which was now sweating profusely. "I get used to some of the sideways sort, but that direct hatred...Christ."

"You'd better go off to rest," George said. "You're shocked. Sister Collinson, where is Dr. Kydd? She'll want him to go off, too, I imagine, and—"

Harry looked up at her. "Did you come to see me so soon? A phone call would have done perfectly well. I'm not even absolutely sure—" And then, to his own obvious amazement and discomfiture, his eyes filled with tears which thickened and increased at a great rate, streaking down his face to leave glistening snail tracks behind.

"Come on," Philip said and helped him to his feet. I'll take you to your room to lie down. Sister?"

Sister Collinson nodded. I'll see to it that Dr. Kydd knows. She's down in the far cubicle with the Kennedy child, fixing the dressings on his thigh. There's no way she'll stop till that's completely finished. Nurse Coulter?" She turned to one of the nurses who were still hovering, "Go and tell her Dr. Rajabani's been taken ill and I'll be along in a minute. And Harry—" She turned back to him as Philip, with one arm round Harry protectively, led him to the double doors and the Disney corridor. I'll talk to security about what happens next, don't worry."

And she went bustling back to her desk, leaving George with nothing to do but go back to her own department. Which she did, feeling a great deal worse over what she had seen than she would have thought possible.

11

There was an urgent PM waiting for her when George got back to her department and she realized with considerable guilt that she hadn't switched on her bleep that morning. Sheila was in a scolding mood in consequence.

"If I don't know what you're up to then I can't tell any decent lies, can I?" she said. "I've had Danny nagging from the mortuary, and the phone's been blistering all morning and all I could say was I'd give you messages. It's not right, Dr. B., really it isn't."

"I'm sorry, I'm sorry," George said and slid into her chair. "Who called?"

"Oh, the cardiologists about that graph you did them for their prothrombins—"

"But that's perfect! They can't have any complaints about that, for God's sake!"

"They haven't. They wanted to thank you. He called himself, Mr. Agnew Byford, it was." Sheila preened a little. "Talked to me for quite a while instead."

"Well, that was nice for you." George found it easier now she was sitting. The episode with Harry had left her shaky. "What else?"

"Oh, someone from Fertility. It seems you left a notebook there. I said I'd tell you but then someone said to her—I heard it down the phone—that you'd been seen going to Pediatrics and they'd catch up with you there. Did they?"

"Did who?"

"I don't know—someone from Fertility it was. Didn't say who."

"No." George looked puzzled. "No one from Fertility spoke to me when I got to Barrie Ward. Oh damn." She had reached into her pocket. "If it hadn't been for all that fuss in Pediatrics I'd have realized I'd left it on the desk and gone back to get it on my way here. Will you send one of the juniors for it? I don't like to leave it lying around. Very important stuff in it."

"Then you shouldn't have put it on someone else's desk," Sheila said self-righteously. Then her passion for gossip overcame her. "What happened in Pediatrics?" she demanded. "What fuss?"

Probably because she was still so upset, and needed to get it out of her system, George told her, even though everyone knew that any piece of information given to Sheila Keen always spread itself all over the hospital within a matter of minutes. Not that it was likely to remain a secret; too many other people had been there to see what happened and they'd be sure to talk too.

"There was a man in Pediatrics who shouted racial abuse at Dr. Rajabani," she said. "Attacked him."

Sheila frowned. "Dr. Rajabani?" she said, reaching into her pocket. "Oh. He phoned here too, wanting to talk to you."

"Well, I saw him," George said, "poor devil," and went on to tell Sheila all that had happened. Sheila stood there, her eyes round with interest, and when George had finished, shook her head.

"It's terrible the way people go on around here. It's not just those people who're picketing, you know, there're a few of these racists in among them too. It's all over the place. I've heard them shouting like that in the street, over at the market when I go to get my vegetables. Only the other day it was, a whole lot of them, nasty characters with haircuts like lavatory brushes, yelling the sort of—"

"I know," George said grimly, remembering what had happened at Gus's fish shop. "Me too. I just never thought to hear it at Old East, I suppose."

"I can't see why," Sheila said. "It's the same people who're our patients, after all."

"I suppose so. Anyway, it was horrible."

"I'm sure it was," Sheila was at last sympathetic. "I'll get you some tea." And this time George was glad to have it, over strong though it was as usual.

As she sat and sipped it she was very aware of the little light glowing redly on her phone, a sure sign that Sheila had settled down to spread the word about nasty goings on in Barrie Ward. She ought to be told to stop and get on with her work, but George couldn't face a sulky Sheila for the rest of the day, which she'd have to if she did that, and anyway, it never seemed to make any difference to the amount or high quality of the work she turned out. She just seemed to need to get and pass on gossip the way other people needed to breathe.

George picked up the phone herself to call Gus. She flicked her own line on, dialed and waited. She hadn't found out very much, after all, but it would be comforting to hear those gruff cockney tones in her ear; and she was startled at how bitterly disappointed she was when at last she got through to Ratcliffe Street Station and was told that the Detective Chief Inspector was out, and could she leave a message?

"I'll call back," she said. She cradled the phone, then rested her elbows on the desk and her chin on her hands and thought.

Why was she so upset at what had happened to Harry? Unpleasant people who shouted and spat at staff were far from unusual at Old East. She personally had rarely suffered it, though she knew that sometimes the Accident and Emergency staff got a certain amount of abuse from drunks and druggies; but did they get the real hatred that this man had heaped on Harry's unfortunate head? She doubted it, and thought: I'll talk to Hattie. She'll help me see it more clearly.

But when she phoned Hattie, she too was unavailable, since she was working a different shift this week. "I'll give her a message," promised the distant voice, but George told her not to bother. She'd try again.

She went downstairs to the mortuary to get the PM out of the way. There was little else she could do. Getting down to opening a cadaver would at least occupy her mind.

She finished the PM just before lunch and dictated her report at once, since the coroner's office was in a hurry for it, then went plodding upstairs. The morning's episode had been so very disagreeable that it had drained her of energy. Or filled her with disgust. Whatever it was she was not her usual happy self.

Until she reached her office and found Gus sitting in her chair which he had tilted back on its rear legs in a precarious pose, with the desk in front of him spread with a picnic lunch.

"Wotcha," he said, and brought the chair down to four legs with a little crash that made her tense with expectation of disaster. "I thought we ought to have a conference."

"Oh?" She came over to her desk and indicated with her chin. He made a face at her and got out of her chair, and went and plonked himself down on the one facing it on the other side. "Conference on what?"

"Our case so far. I thought I'd go all New York for you today. I got here some of Bloom's best bagels, and smoked salmon and a bit of cream cheese. Oh, and a nice mild onion from down the market. Mind you, it still made me weep, cuttin' it up. Bit like you, really. Supposed to be sweet and mild, but can still bring the tears to your eyes." George ignored that, so he grinned at her and went on. "The coffee's in that flask there—I didn't feel up to Sheila's brew. It should see us nicely. I've even got a bit of cheesecake to finish up with. How's that, then?"

She looked at it all and raised her eyebrows at him. "Are you trying to stuff me like the rest of the Christmas turkeys? You've got enough here for an army."

"S'right. Me an' you. Get stuck in." He sliced one of the rolls through the middle and shoved it at her together with the tub of cream cheese, and she capitulated. Compared with whatever there would be to offer over at the hospital canteen, this was Lucullan fare.

"You still haven't said what case it is we're supposed to be conferring about." She spread the cheese thickly, added a layer of glistening pink salmon and topped it with one of his rounds of sliced onion. Her mouth began to water at the smell.

"Dead babies, ducky. It's all gettin' to be a case, don't you reckon? I'm not sayin' we've got evidence that all of them are dicey, but there is certainly one that is—the Oberlander one, we'll call it for want of a better label—and the others sort of cluster round like kids round an ice-cream van."

"Not a very nice simile," she said and bit into her bagel, which tasted as good as it looked. She licked an errant smear of cream cheese from her upper lip. "It's bad enough when adults are killed. Much worse when it's babies."

"That's sentimentality of the silliest sort," Gus said and for a moment looked harsh. "I don't care if it's a kid of nine months or an old girl of ninety, a life's a life. No one's got any right to interfere with people like that. I won't have it on my patch. And I won't have anyone ever thinking that I'd put one case in front of another on account of age, or anything else come to that."

She reddened and then nodded. "Fair enough. I apologize."

"So I should think," he said cheerfully. "Get on with it. There's another bagel here waitin' for you."

"Have it for your supper. One's enough for me. Have you got anything new?"

He lifted his chin to indicate the letter rack on the right-hand side of her desk. "On the top there. I've brought in the report on that child Dr. Choopani was attacked over."

"Oh?" She reached for it eagerly and began to read, holding it clear of the desk with one hand so that bagel crumbs couldn't drop on it. He leaned over and poured coffee from the flask while she read, not interrupting her.

"Well," she said at length when she'd put the report back in the rack. "Not much there to get our teeth into."

"That's what I thought. Straightforward enough."

She nodded. "With that sort of heart anomaly the baby could have died any time. As it was, a little bronchitis and there you were. A pity it wasn't diagnosed earlier, mind you, while the child was alive."

"I've talked to him about that," Gus said. "The mother refused to bring the child in for check-ups, seemingly. It was born somewhere outside the patch—he never could find out where because she wouldn't say, and she only fetched it to him to get some sort of certificate she needed for a benefit. He'd never have seen the child at all otherwise, he reckons. Said some nasty things about her, he did, but I have to say they sounded justified to me."

"What sort of nasty things?"

"That she was a neglectful mother, that people smoked around the kid so much it probably hardly ever breathed clean air, and that he thought she abused the kid. Not enough to make a case, you understand, but enough to contribute to an early death."

"Did he say that to anyone else, I wonder?" George said and Gus looked at her sharply.

"Got it in one, haven't you? Seemingly he did. Talked to the Health Visitor who went in to the flat and got a right bollocking for her pains, and also talked to anyone who'd listen to him. He complained a lot about the mother—it was all over the place that the doctor wasn't impressed by her—so I dare say the father's attack on him—"

"Makes a certain amount of sense. Yes, I can see that. He's a rough-tongued fella, Dr. Choopani." She shook her head reminiscently. "I could have sloshed him for ten cents, but for all that I sort of liked the guy. Straight as they come, I'd say, but has one hell of an attitude problem."

"That's much my own feeling. I liked him a lot. Got passionate, he did, about the way we sweep people like this family under the mat and label them the underclass and then it's their kids who suffer." Gus sounded unusually serious. "A few more like him round here wouldn't do us any harm, even if he does get up a few noses while he's doing his job."

"Whose noses in particular?"

"Oh, some of the locals. The ones who're looking for any excuse to get at a black face. You know them. They've been making life tough for all the Asian doctors round here for a couple of months now, one way or another. There's a new branch of one of those extreme right-wing groups been formed. We'll give them a hard ride, and sort it out, I'm sure, but, well, it's unpleasant."

"Tell me about it!" she said with heartfelt fervor. She finished the last bite of her bagel and wiped her fingers on a paper napkin. He had forgotten nothing they might need for the picnic on her desk. "This morning was certainly unpleasant."

"What was?" His voice sharpened.

She told him as succinctly as she could. He listened in silence and then grimaced. "Oh, the hell with it. Now we've got it in here as well, have we? This child who died—was he a local one? I mean, did he come off the patch or was he referred from further away? They are sometimes, aren't they, these leukemia kids?"

"I don't know," she said. "But I can find out. Hang on."

She reached for the phone and dialed the number of Barrie Ward. It was Sister Collinson who answered.

"Hold on," she said in response to George's question and went away. It was a long time before she came back.

"Sorry about the delay—the notes were being typed up by the typing pool. He lived on the Lansbury Estate. Less than ten minutes' walk from here, that is."

"And," George said, with a sudden thought, "who is the GP? I mean, who referred the child here to Old East in the first place?"

There was a whispering sound of pages being turned and then Sister Collinson said, "Oh," in a flat voice. "Him."

"Eh?"

"The one who makes all the fuss all the time. Dr. Choopani."

George, remembering what Dr. Choopani had told her that night in A & E about his last conversation with Sister Collinson, opened her mouth to protest and then thought better of it. She merely thanked her and hung up.

"Like I said, an attitude problem," she told Gus after she'd reported the information. "Even Sister Collinson says harsh things about him because they just don't understand each other. This won't help, I imagine."

"No," he said grimly. "It won't. Unless we're careful, we'll have a whole race riot on our hands, with rent-a-mob turning out just to stir the brew and—Oh, shit, I'd better go and talk to Choopani about this."

"It's not his fault, of course." George got to her feet "What's the point of talking to him?"

"Warn him," Gus said shortly. "If it gets out that this father's blaming another Asian doctor for a child's death and that Choopani sent the child here, can't you just see how it'll be?"

"I suppose so," George said. "Oh, goddamn it. Why do people here have to pick up the nastier things out of America? Race riots, ye gods."

"Yeah. Well, see you tomorrow, OK?"

She stared at him blankly. "Tomorrow?"

He was shrugging on his overcoat. "I told you. Dinner for your old ladies and me and you. About sixish, nice'n early, and then a treat. It's a surprise. I'll be there with the car at half-five. Be ready!"

And he left, leaving her with a pile of smoked salmon, cream cheese and bagels, not to speak of cheesecake, to share out among her lab staff (much to the delight of Jerry Swann who jumped at it as though he hadn't already engulfed a vast quantity of liver and onions and steamed pudding and custard in the hospital canteen) and an uneasy sense of trouble brewing over both Dr. Choopani and Dr. Rajabani.

She went back to her office to deal with the day's inevitable pile-up of paperwork, but she couldn't settle to it. There was something bothering her and she wriggled in her chair as though there were something there that perturbed her physically; and came to the conclusion that it was all due to the unease in her mind following the scene in Barrie Ward that morning. She tried to concentrate.

The day dwindled to the inevitable early darkness of December and she stretched her back and looked gloomily at the pile of paper. It seemed as high on the not-yet-done side as on the completed side and she was annoyed at her own slowness. Why on earth should she let this matter get under her skin so much? After all, hostility from patients wasn't, unfortunately, all that rare. Surely she was overreacting to it?

It's not that, she thought then. It's something else. Something I've forgotten. Something that I ought to have done. That's what's driving me bananas. It's like doing an exam and not being able to dig out of your head the one fact that you know will make the whole answer work. You go trawling your memory and it just won't emerge...

She glowered down at her desk. It was almost half-past five and she ought to leave for home soon; Bridget and her mother had opted today to visit Madame Tussaud's (despite George's carefully worded warnings about the length of the queues and the limited satisfaction available from the displays after all that waiting) and she ought to be there to greet them when they got home. Also, she had to do her Christmas cards tonight; there was only a week to go and already the pressure was on. There were presents to buy and plans to make for all that cookery on Christmas Day, for despite Bridget's offer of a hotel lunch, they were to stay home. Vanny had decided that.

She tried to think again about what it was that was irking her like sand in a shoe, but it still eluded her. She went home at last a little abstracted and irritable, and her irritation was increased when she found a message on her ansaphone from her house guests to the effect that they'd decided to make a real day of it and were staying in town to eat and then go on to a theater. "Leave the key under the doormat, honey!" Bridget carolled cheerfully. "We'll let ourselves in." George knew they were being tactful, giving her space by keeping out of the way, but she actually had been looking forward to seeing them and hearing their reactions to the wax models, and now felt absurdly hard done by.

She left the trout she'd bought lying forlornly in the fridge and dined on toast and cheese and hot tea; it was all she wanted, she told herself, even though in her heart she knew she was being childishly lazy about not making a proper meal, and then settled as best she could to her Christmas cards.

It was when she was plodding through the list of names around the hospital she felt she had to send cards to that she remembered. It was absurd; the memory came bubbling up and burst in her mind like a little firework, and it made her gasp as if it had been.

Harry had wanted to talk to her about something. She could hear his voice as clearly as if he were actually there in front of her fire.

"Did you come to see me so soon? A phone call would have done perfectly well. I'm not even absolutely sure—"

She remembered something else then. Sheila this morning, telling her that Rajabani had called the path, lab to talk to her. George had dismissed that; said she'd seen him. But she hadn't actually spoken to him, had she? Or rather, he hadn't really spoken to her.

She leaned back in her chair and stretched. She felt better now she'd remembered, and after a moment she made an entry in her notebook to call Harry first thing in the morning; and then was able to finish her Christmas cards very quickly indeed, choosing a particularly handsome one to send to Harry. She wasn't sure even that he celebrated Christmas and normally she wouldn't have had him on her card list, which she tried to keep well trimmed and which generally included only fellow consultants, but it seemed the least she could do after the poor chap had been through such a battering; and he would, she thought, like the Victorian reproduction picture full of leaping children. It would help him to remember that whatever the parents did or said it was the patients who really mattered.

12

As they came down into the chill dampness of the street, they saw fairy lights in several of the small trees that had been planted in the miniscule front gardens opposite, and most of the downstairs windows had neat Christmas trees in them, winking their lollipop colors bravely into the darkness. At George's side, Vanny shivered in agreeable anticipation. "I'm really excited," she said, sounding like a child on a holiday. "Such fun to be going somewhere and not know where."

"It'll be a nice surprise, just you see, Mrs. Barnabas," Gus said and bustled her to the car. "Now, let me settle you here, and then we'll see Mrs. Connors in on the other side."

"Now you just stop being so formal, Gus!" Bridget chuckled, and went trotting round the car to the other door. "Just you call us Vanny and Bridget or we'll be really put out. We may be old but we don't have to be treated like we're antiques!"

"I wouldn't dream of doing anything to upset you," Gus cried. "I wasn't being formal so much as polite! But if you want to be pally, well then, I'm your fella. Now then, Vanny, are you settled there? There's a nice rug if you need it."

"Oh," Vanny giggled. "This is just like it was being taken out when I was a girl. A rug, for goodness' sake. Don't you have a heater in this car?"

"Of course I do, but, like I said, I want to take the best care of you. No rug then? Fine. Come on, George, what're you waiting for?" He jerked his head at the door he was now holding open for her and George, scowling at him, went, with what dignity she could, to take her place in the front.

He had, in her opinion, been flirting outrageously with both her guests from the moment he'd arrived. He'd brought a bottle of very cold champagne with him, which he insisted on pouring out in large libations (though he managed unobtrusively not to drink any himself, George noticed with reluctant approval, since he was their driver for the night) and within minutes, it seemed, Bridget and Vanny were giggling like schoolgirls of a particularly silly sort and virtually eating out of his hand.

When he archly refused to tell them where they were going after dinner they launched themselves joyously into a question-and-answer session that would have been regarded as a bit passé at the local nursery school. When he'd told them eventually that they were going to see something he was sure they'd never seen before, Bridget became quite outrageous and decided it was a strip show, and insisted that she was much too young to be exposed to such debauchery. He had assured her seriously that he completely agreed regarding her age and therefore had chosen an entertainment that would bring not a hint of blush to her maiden cheek. It was altogether a sickening display of childishness, as George hissed at him when he carried the used glasses into the kitchen while Bridget and Vanny went to get into their coats and gloves and scarves; at which he laughed and told her she was just jealous. Which had done nothing of course to make her feel any less annoyed.

By the time they were settled at their table at "The Plaice To Be' she felt much less edgy. He had been so genuinely funny as he drove them there, dropping the teasing banter in exchange for a more adult line in jokes, that she too was charmed and she felt a certain proprietorial pride as she listened to the laughter coming from the back seat and basked in the knowledge that the two of them approved wholeheartedly of her friend. If he'd been a bit silly with his baby-talk approach earlier—well, it was forgivable. After all, he had to find his way with strangers somehow.

"You got the repairs done fast!" she said, gazing at the great plate-glass window, which looked as though it had been there for ever, complete with its elaborate engraving of the restaurant's name. "How did you manage that?"

"Policemen have a bit of clout when they're dealin' with villains," he said complacently. "And in my book all builders are villains somewhere along the line, if it's only fiddlin' a bit o' VAT. They know it, they know I know it, I know they know I know it, so they get any jobs I want done done fast and done proper to keep me sweet and out of their hair. Know what I mean? Now, Vanny, Bridget, let me see you through the mysteries of a real English fish-and-chip menu."

He persuaded them to eat jellied eels without any difficulty and they both loved them. He offered them perfectly fried pieces of turbot and they purred like well-fed kittens. He made Kitty tip piles of crisp chips on to their plates until they cried they were filled for the rest of the year, and still ate more. He gave them wine and coffee and melting apple pie and by seven-thirty they were his slaves for life.

George, watching them and especially her mother, was grateful to Gus and ashamed of her earlier irritability. Her mother was brighter and more responsive than she'd been since she'd arrived; her eyes wide and shining, her chatter busy, logical and showing no hint of any of the memory loss and hesitancy that George had thought was now a permanent part of her. She caught Bridget's eye at one point when Vanny was being particularly sparkling in her conversation with Gus and saw that she was almost in tears, she was so happy to see her friend so much like her old self, and George felt her own spirits lift in a great tide of gratitude to Gus that made her want to throw herself at him and hug him. She actually had to tense her muscles to make sure she sat tight pretending to eat her own apple pie, for she was now over-fed herself, to prevent herself from doing so.

Gus looked at his watch and hurried them to their feet just before a quarter to eight, waving at Kitty for coats. Kitty came running and bustled them out, winking at Gus as they went. "It's all right, Guv. Got a parkin' space fixed up for you an' everything they ?ave. Lookin' forward to seeing you, they said. Better get a move on though."

The excitement in the back of the car built to great heights and the questions began again. Was it a comedy they were to see? A musical? A drama? Gus laughed and said only, "Yes!" to all of them and they had to settle for that.

He took them by various circuitous routes to Charing Cross and then slid down beside the river into Villiers Street. He parked close by one of the arches running under the adjoining bridge that carried trains over the river, where a young man was waiting to take his keys from him.

"I'll find her a corner somewhere," he said to Gus. "Don't you worry, Guv. Just take "em in. They're waiting for you."

"The Players Theater," Vanny read breathlessly from a sizeable poster as they were hurried in through the crowded little foyer by Gus, who was behaving, George thought with amusement, rather like a sheepdog. "A play then, Gus?"

"Just you wait and see," he said mysteriously. "Coats. Here, Norah, take "em for my girls, will you? Don't want to keep the Chairman waiting."

George was entranced. It was a small, vividly red establishment filled with illustrations of Victorian and Edwardian entertainments as well as being tricked out in totally believable *fin de siècle* style, and she wanted to linger and look—as, indeed, did the others. But Gus would have none of that.

"Later, later!" he cried, "mustn't be late!" and hurried them into the theater itself. George registered bright soft light, red plush, a great deal of gilt, quantities of painted plaster putti, tables as well as the usual theater seating, a piano lit by a candle where a young man in white tie and tails was playing manfully, and a full house of very noisy people. Gus hurried them into their seats very near the front and reached for the bottle of champagne in an ice bucket that was waiting on the table that stood between their places.

"Got everything laid on in advance for you!" he shouted cheerfully above the hubbub. "Now, here are song sheets. Don't worry, you'll find out when you need "em. Just you pretend that this isn't the 1990s but the 1890s and you'll have the time of your life!"

From then on it was sheer enchantment. The show was a Victorian Music Hall done with great panache and in the true style, with a rotund, doggish and most bibulous Chairman who shouted a lot at noisy customers—who heckled back cheerfully—a lot of community singing with the entire audience knowing not only the words of the songs but also every word of the Chairman's usual repartee, and a number of what George took to be faithfully original acts. There were singers and comics, a couple of duets of singularly soulful songs—at one point she saw her mother's eyes big with tears as she listened to one particularly expressive song about gypsies—and a good deal of cheeky cross-talking between the acts and the Chairman. Bridget laughed uproariously at every sally and by the interval was in a state of complete adoration of Gus.

"This is the most *darling* show I have ever seen, I swear to you," she told him. "If we could have something like this at home, why, they'd knock the doors down night after night to see it! It's wonderful. How come we've never seen anything so good in the US?"

Gus grinned. "It's one thing here, quite another when it's out of its normal setting," he said. "Though I think some of the acts have appeared in Washington at Embassy events for your President. Now, more champagne? There's lots left."

"I daren't," said Bridget happily, holding out her glass for more, and Vanny did too.

"Oh, George," Vanny said. "I haven't heard that song for ever. We had an English teacher from Yorkshire who taught us it when I was just a little thing in Boston." And she began to sing in a sweet if slightly off-key voice, "And she's off with the raggle-taggle gypsies, oh…"

"I don't think I've ever heard it," George said. "But it's pretty."

"It's history too," Gus said. "Did you know that, Vanny? It used to be one of the things people were really scared of, gypsies running off with their children. Especially if they were pretty girl children like the one in this song. Mind you, she was a naughty girl, I'm thinking. Probably thought the gypsy men were more exciting than the milk-and-water types she met at home."

"You've got your songs mixed up," Vanny said reprovingly. "You're thinking of the other gypsy one," and she began to sing: "My mother said I never should, Play with the gypsies in the wood. If I did, she would say, Naughty little girl to disobey…"

Gus grinned. "You go on like that, ducky, and they'll think you're auditioning and have you up on stage. Do you fancy a bit of the old thespian stuff?"

Vanny giggled and bridled and giggled again; then they were off once more with their chattering. George leaned back to relax and let them get on with it. Gus was really being very good, entertaining them so well, she told herself a little sleepily as the sparkle in the champagne settled in her bones to create an agreeable somnolence. He doesn't have to. And her mind slid back to the last time she and he had been at "The Plaice To Be." He had said…Well, what had he said? That he wanted to spend the time with her somewhere cozy and quiet and comfortable to have some fun? And what had she done? Launched herself into one of those damned feminist diatribes that seemed to come to her lips far too easily. Of course there were things that men did that had to be stopped. Men who patronized and ignored everything but boobs and bottoms were men who had to be educated; men who, when it came to women, treated them as though they were just, well, chattels who had to be stamped on. But Gus was not like that. He was far more complicated. He talked as though he were like that; he leered, even, and used language that most people these days thought was dreadful, but he didn't actually behave that way. She knew he didn't patronize her, that he respected her for her intelligence and her personality, but he'd also tried to make it clear he fancied her, using very old-fashioned ways to do it, and she had to admit she liked that. It sent a pleasant little frisson through her to think of Gus fancying her; she looked at him sideways under her lashes and tried to imagine being somewhere cozy and quiet and comfortable with him and "having fun."

He caught her glance and laughed. "You look as though you're having naughty thoughts," he said under the cover of Bridget talking to Vanny. "You know, that contented cat look."

She knew she had reddened and hoped it wouldn't show in this generally ruby environment. "So, you're a clairvoyant now!" she said. "Able to read minds. Well, that'll make it easier for you to sort out the nation's sins, I imagine. Spot them by their thoughts before they even commit the crimes."

"It doesn't work for crime. Only with personal thoughts in ladies—sorry, women—I like," he said and slid a hand across beneath the table and took her knee in a warm grip. "Go on. Tell me I'm guilty of sexual harassment now."

She looked down at his hand and thought for a moment. "No," she said. "I shan't."

"Oh? Why not? Isn't it all wrong in your feminist bible for a man to handle a woman?"

"It's the intent that matters in my book, never mind anyone else's. A hand on my knee right here in the middle of a crowded theater when the interval's almost over offers no way you can go any further than a bit of knee-clasping. So it doesn't matter. Clasp on if you enjoy it'

"Oh, for God's sake!" he said disgustedly, taking his hand away. "You're no fun at all." He winked at her to take the sting from his words and turned back to Vanny and Bridget as the Chairman returned to the stage.

"Hold on to your seat belts, girls. The next few minutes'll be bumpy!"

The Chairman advanced to the front of the stage and after some obviously well-rehearsed ad libs in which the regulars in the audience joined with glee, announced loudly that he was interested in the identity of visitors from abroad. Before they knew what was to happen, Gus had both Bridget and Vanny on their feet accepting a graceful welcome from the Chairman to "these citizens of the revolting colonies' and letting him point out to them that "if it hadn't been for that silly misunderstanding in Boston Harbor, all this could have been yours," another line in which the cognoscenti in the audience joined. All this was followed by various people announcing it was their birthday and being sung to (including a set of rather elderly triplets in the back seats, at whose appearance one of the more drunken members of the audience announced in ringing tones, "They are triplets, sir, because their father stuttered!" a sally which reduced both Vanny and Bridget to helpless tears of laughter) and then the audience settled down again to more singing and clowning. Vanny and Bridget sat in blissful contentment and Gus very deliberately leaned sideways towards George and took her hand and held it warmly between both of his.

"Now I know it don't count as harassment, at least I can enjoy this much," he whispered. And leaned back happily to watch the stage.

It was at the very end of the show, when the whole audience was involved in singing yet again, that George heard the bleeping sound. Gus cursed softly and reached into his breast pocket. George could see the pager he brought out and peered at it over his shoulder just as he hit the bleep-cancel button.

"Call in soonest," it said. "Big one."

The show was almost over now and Gus looked at the pager again and then at his watch and clearly made a decision. He sat tight.

It wasn't till the audience was on its feet and surging for the exits that he murmured in George's ear. "We've got a problem."

"What?"

"I've got to call in, and it's probably a body. My pager said a big one. That's Roop's code for a body, and one there's a problem over at that. Which means it could involve you too. No time to take your old ladies home. Do you mind if we put "em in a cab?"

Bridget, who was close behind Gus, leaned over and said firmly, "I heard that What's the matter? Got to go home separately, have we?"

"Sorry, darling, but yes." Gus was very business-like suddenly. "It looks like it Let me get to the car and phone in. If we have to, George and I will go in my car after we get a cab for you two. Got your door key?"

"No problem," Bridget said crisply. "Jeez, this is the real thing, huh? We go out to this fabulous evening of real English fun with the nicest cop I've ever met in all my life, and I've known a few, one way or another'—she winked at Gus—"when I was younger, you understand. And now just at the right time you have to go and do the business. I tell you, it's fabulous. All we need to really fill in the picture is a rolling London fog and the sound of horses' hooves! Don't fret, hon, just point us to the nearest cab and don't you worry about another thing. We've had a great time and we'll be glad to get back. Our gadding days are long over." She gave a theatrical sigh. "More's the pity."

The crowd had thinned swiftly, many of the audience still clustering in the bars, and they came out into the Arches and turned right to get down to Villiers Street and the car—for which Gus had the key in his hand, since it had been given back to him in the interval together with information about where his car was parked—just as a cab with its light on passed the end. Gus broke into an immediate run to go careering down to catch it, bawling "Taxi!" at the top of his voice.

Bridget tucked her hand into George's elbow and chuckled. "That is one very nice man, George. Hang on to him, honey."

"Don't be silly, Bridget," George said sharply. "He's just a friend. You don't hang on to friends. They just stick."

"Such stuff! He thinks you're the best there is. It shows in every move he makes. You let him go and you are one crazy lady. Ain't she, Vanny?"

Vanny wasn't listening. She had her arm held by Bridget and was trotting along, gazing blissfully into the middle distance and humming. "And I'm away with the raggle-taggle gypsies, oh!" in a rather breathy little voice. Bridget laughed.

"She's had the time of her life. Me too. Now I want bed and so does she. And look at that guy, will you? Caught the cab just like that! He really is the best."

They had reached the end of the Arches and there was Gus with the cab door held open, looking at his watch. Bridget urged Vanny forward and pushed her inside the taxi.

"On your way, you two! I wish I was coming with you. Just you tell me all about it tomorrow, promise?" she cried and waved as Gus closed the door on her.

"The fare's paid," he yelled into the back as the driver engaged gears, "so you've nothing to fret about, OK? Talk to you again soon. Goodnight, sweethearts."

"Goodnight," called Bridget. She waved and the cab turned and went, leaving George staring after it, at her mother. She was still singing, sitting happily beside Bridget, repeating the same words over and over again. She seemed stuck on "raggle-taggle', and the sense of misery descended over George again. She had thought that this evening her mother had been her old self, but she hadn't. That had been a momentary thing. Now she was away again, no longer accessible; and George wanted to weep.

"It's all right, George," Gus murmured. "She's very happy at the moment. And do remember she's sleepy and had a certain amount of champagne, which'll add to it all. She'll be better again tomorrow."

George turned and stared at him in the bright light thrown by the shops and cafés that lined Villiers Street. Passers-by jostled her but she paid no attention to them.

"What?" she said stupidly. "Do you know—"

"Oh, yes, I know," he said. "I remember my old mum, you see. She had it And she was very like your Ma. She doesn't make too many slips, but they're there. I saw them, you see, the forgotten things. It's—well, let it be. Mum's gone now. Better off, if you ask me." He tucked his arm into hers and held it close. "It's all right, sweetheart. You can cope. We all have to when it comes to the crunch, eh? Right now there ain't much of a crunch to face up to so forget it. Leave her to Bridget and come with me. Let's see which sort of big one the nick's got for us."

13

The big one, as he discovered on his car radio when they pulled out from their parking place in John Adam Street, was indeed a dead body, and possibly one that got that way by means of murder.

"In the car park of the Rag and Bottle, Guv." George recognized Sergeant Rupert Dudley's voice even though it was distorted. "Down by the hospital, Asian bloke. Could have been—well, I'll tell you when you get here. We've got the Soco there already and there's not much to see, really. We need some forensic. Shall I let the doctor know, or will you?" George reddened in the darkness. Even on the radio she could hear the note of disdain in Rupert's voice. He didn't like her and never had.

"That's all right, Roop," Gus said. "I'll dig her out. ETA— let me see…" He had reached the end of the street where it joined the Strand and peered up at the "No Right Turn' sign, grinned at George and turned right, screeching across the traffic to do it. "ETA, traffic permitting, fifteen minutes outside, over and out and Roger and all the rest of that stuff."

"There's no justice," George said. "If I did that I'd get pinched as sure as—"

"If you did that you'd be a bleedin' miracle, seein' as you don't have a car," he said. "And if I can't get away with a bit of traffic violation, who can? Have you got your gear with you? Or do we have to stop at the hospital or send someone over there to get your emergency kit, as per usual?"

"No, you do not is the answer to both," George said, patting her big leather shoulder bag. "I've got fed up with having a big kit to send for or have about; I've made up a smaller version which'll do for scene-of-crime operations and I take it everywhere now."

"Like a make-up bag," he said approvingly. "I do like a lady that *is* a lady, never caught without her necessaries."

"Rupert was a bit on the uncommunicative side," she said as he swung the car perilously close to the inside lane, taking the turn into the Aldwych. "Started to say what he thought had happened and then shut up."

"So I should hope," Gus said. "There's too much chatter on the radio anyway. I keep tellin' "em they ought to be more professional."

She laughed. "Oh, I see. That was why you said Roger and over and out and all that stuff. Very professional, I don't think."

"I'm the Guv," Gus said with sublime self-assurance. "I can do what I like. It's them that have to mind their ways. And I don't want important facts blabbed all over the airways for any listenin' villain to pick up. And what Roop said means that it's a nasty one. No accident. Murder even. Why else should he call out Soco? No point in having a scene-of-crime-officer if there ain't no crime, is there?—not that he'd dare stick his neck out and say more'n that, even if I *did* let him chatter like a schoolgirl over the radio. It takes more'n his opinion to decide whether there's been a murder or not. Until you and me gets there there's no one properly qualified to say *what's* happened. Right?"

She was touched by the easy way he included her in his view of the aristocracy of the policeman's working world and smiled at him in the flickering light from outside as they sped down Essex Street, heading for the Embankment. Another few minutes at this rate and they'd be at the Tower of London. He had to be breaking every traffic rule there was, the speed he was going, but his control of the car was total and it responded to him as though it had been a sentient creature.

"Thanks for being so kind to my old dears." she said, and he tutted reprovingly.

"Old dears, forsooth? What a nasty label! They're a smashin' pair of interesting lad—women. You should be ashamed to be so—so *ageist*." And he positively smirked at her in a quick sideways glint before he returned his attention to the road.

"Hell, they were old when I was a kid!" she said. "It's hard not to see them except as forever antiques."

"How old is your mother?"

"Urn—almost seventy. I turned up late in her life."

"Thirty-three or -four she was, then, when you were born. I have got it right, haven't I? You're thirty-six."

She was, to her own surprise, a little nettled. "How'd you know that?"

"I make it my business to know everything there is to know about people I'm interested in. I am right, aren't I?"

"Yes, you're right. What of it?"

"Not a thing. Except that your mum was younger than you are now when you were born, and here you are saying she was old when you were a kid. Think about that."

"Oh, thank you. Thank you so much! Now I do feel good!"

"Serves you right for labeling your mum old. She's old, yeah, but not *old* old, know what I mean?"

"Can we change the subject?" she demanded. "All I wanted to do was say thank you for being so kind and organizing such a great evening for them. If I'd kept my big mouth shut I'd not be feeling so over the hill now."

"Who said you were over the hill?" he said. "I reckon you're the perfect age. Like Brie just as it starts running all over the place and before it gets a bit high. Delicious—Oh, get out of the way, you stupid bugger!" He wrenched on the wheel and pushed his foot down hard to get past an elderly Mini that was toodling happily in the center lane. By the time the Mini had honked like a flight of extremely irritated geese and Gus had flung open his window to make a highly unprofessional gesture out of it as he left the other car far behind, the moment for any response to that was past. Not that she would have found it easy to make one; to be told you were delicious was one thing, but like a cheese? Better not even to think about it.

"Nearly there," he said, as the car swept round into the main road leading down to Shadwell. "The Rag and Bottle. That's the local name for the Flag and Flask, you know, and—"

"Yeah. And Christopher Columbus discovered America," George said. "For God's sake, Gus, it wasn't the locals who renamed it—it was the hospital people! In the old days anesthetics were given by dripping ether on to a piece of cloth held over the patient's nose and mouth and that was called a rag and bottle anesthetic."

"Trust you to know best," he said, pulling the car to a slightly squealing stop beside the cluster of police cars with their blue lights flashing waiting outside the pub. "Come on. Let's get some work done."

Sergeant Dudley detached himself from the untidy group of people standing near the cars and came loping over to him. "Wotcha, Guv. Nice time. Round the back here, in the car park—Oh. Evening, doctor."

"Evening, Roop," George said, knowing how much he hated the diminutive form of his name and delighting in using it; he'd only offered his meagre greeting because she'd pushed herself forward and stared at him challengingly over Gus's shoulder. He glared back at her, then turned away to lead them to the car park.

It lay behind the pub at the end of a curving roughly surfaced private alley. Vividly bright Tilley lamps burned all along the way, set there by the police, and at the far end, where the alley entered the wide graveled car park proper, there was another huddle of people.

It broke apart as Rupert arrived and shouldered his way in; people stepped back to let Gus and George follow in easily. At the center the sprawled body lay.

All George could see at first were the clothes; the legs, the right one bent at a sharp angle that showed clearly there was a fracture there, were covered in dark blue jeans, which even under these circumstances showed as fairly new, and the feet were encased in white trainers of the sort that looked trendy but were, in fact, cheap. George had seen some very like them in Watney Street Market piled hugger-mugger in boxes marked "cut price." There was an equally new-looking anorak in dark red covering the upper part of the torso, and on the back of the head—the corpse was lying face down—a woolly cap of the sort that Rastafarians wore. That alone of the clothes looked old and dirty and was well stained with hair oil.

"Not his own hat, then," Gus said, looking down at the corpse, but making no attempt to touch or move it. "What else?"

"Not a Rastafarian, anyway. Dark, all right, but not West Indian. Come round here, have a look. Asian, I'd say."

Gus moved round to the other side of the corpse, George following him, and bent down. George could see only the back of Gus's head as his bulk obscured the view of the dead face, so she moved round a little more to peer over his shoulder.

And heard herself saying, "Christ!" in a sort of half-shriek as she stared down at the now clearly illuminated face of the dead man.

Gus whirled. "Wotsamatter?" he demanded, grabbing at her arm. "Are you all right? Whatever is it?"

"I—" She swallowed and shook her head. "I know him."

Even Rupert looked interested now. All the people around her stretched their necks and stared as the sergeant said sharply, "Well, that helps. We've not been able to get an ID. Not a damn thing on him with a name. Who is he?"

She stared down at the face. It was badly scratched by the gravel; some of the small stones were actually embedded in the gleaming dark skin, mottling it so that it looked as though he had been afflicted with some nameless skin disease. The eyes were half open and the mouth was lax, showing the perfect teeth very clearly. There could be no doubt who he was.

"He's one of the doctors at the hospital," she said as steadily as she could. "Or was. His name is Harilal Rajabani. Harry to most of us."

By the time George had finished her initial examination and given them permission to move the body to the mortuary at the hospital it was well past midnight. She sat on the low wall at the side of the car park, packing up her gear again. She wasn't aware of being tired, but she yawned suddenly; and not with sleepiness. It was with stress.

It wasn't that she'd known Harry all that well, she told herself as she tried to examine the way she felt. He'd been just one of the dozens of junior doctors who could be described as infesting Old East; but that episode in Barrie Ward had made her very aware of him, and she sighed, this time a deeper and more greedy air-gulping movement as she remembered.

It was because she had been so filled with guilt, that was the problem. That man had hurled the most disgusting abuse she had ever heard at Harry Rajabani and no one had done anything to stop him. They had been as paralysed by the venom he had spat as if it had touched them personally, had been frozen into inaction. And then when she'd discovered the man had behaved so out of grief, it had made it worse. His loss didn't license him to behave appallingly but it did make it virtually impossible for anyone to deal with him. To go to a man whose young son has just died and take him to task for racism? It couldn't be done, could it? She couldn't, in fact, be sure, and she sat on the wall staring into the darkness and tried to get her ideas clear.

Gus had been seeing his men off, checking that the site had been properly sealed from interference and the tarpaulins had been set over the relevant parts of the gravel, and now came crunching towards her. "You OK, ducks? Nasty, that one. Sorry you had to do it, seein' he was a mate."

"I've told you before, Gus," she said wearily as she buckled up her equipment case and slid it into her shoulder bag. "He wasn't a mate. He was a—well, I can't even call him a colleague."

"But you knew him."

"How else could I have identified him? Oh, God, there's a thought. Next of kin. Proper identification."

"We'll worry about that tomorrow." He hooked his hand into her elbow and half led, half urged her towards the exit alley, making a wide curve round the place where the tarpaulins lay. They ducked under the yellow plastic ribbons marked, "Police. Do Not Enter', which flapped mournfully in the night wind coming up from the river, and went down to his car. "Listen, ducks, this isn't the time. It's late, you're tired. You must be— I'm knackered! But if tomorrow you can think of anything relevant—"

"Tell me first what you think happened here," she said abruptly. The anxiety that was gnawing at her couldn't be held back much longer, but it might help if she had some facts.

He peered at her and opened his mouth to say one thing, clearly reconsidered and said something else.

"Well, if you insist, though I'm ready for bed. OK. We think that there was a punch-up of sorts in the pub—well, not to say punch-up. A bit of shouting abuse and insults, pretty normal for the manor. They had a go at this Harry. He started to shout back but then someone pulled him away and he went off in a state. The abusers, according to the barman, went off after him—trouble is he can't be sure how long it was between Harry leaving and these other fellas following. We reckon it had to be pretty close, because they caught up with him there. There's a lavatory by the car park as well as the one inside, which was full of people throwing up, seemingly, at the time all this happened. He must have been going there because he didn't have a car out here. There were only the staff cars when we got here, as you saw."

"I didn't notice," George said.

"Well, take it from us. No customers' cars here at all. OK, so these yobs follow him out, duff him up, and—well, we reckon they knocked him down easy enough and then someone ran over him."

She bit her lip, seeing it clearly in her mind's eye. "More than once, I'd say. Going by the injuries."

"Yeah, so you said. Twice forwards, once back, right?"

"Mmm. It accounts for the way the gravel entered the skin. I have to look in detail in a proper light tomorrow of course, but that was how it looked out here."

"And then they drove off. All of "em. They could be anyone, anywhere." He sounded deeply gloomy. "Gettin' "em won't exactly be easy."

"Didn't anyone in the pub know who they were?"

"They say not. Tomorrow we'll get down to it a bit more thoroughly. At least my fellas had the wit to get the names and addresses of everyone in the place and not just in the bar when it happened. They recognized some of the customers of course—it'd be a poor show if they didn't. I'd want to know the reason why if they couldn't put a name to most of them. That's what knowing your community is all about But there were some who were strangers, and we'll have to chase them. It's never easy, of course. They look after their own in these parts."

"Even if their own are killers?" George asked bitterly. "So much for the good old Cockney warmth and good heart you're always telling me about."

"These people aren't my sort and never you dare say they are," he said sharply and his hand on her elbow tightened. "When I said in these parts I wasn't talking about the ordinary good blokes who live around here, but the bloody publicans. They know which side their lousy beer froths and they don't take no chances. But you watch me tomorrow. I'll find out who it was."

"There's something I have to tell you," she said slowly and he peered down at her.

"Now?"

I'll feel better if I do."

"Then let's have it," and again his hand tightened on her arm, but this time it was a warm and protective grip that helped.

"I'm afraid it might be something—well, listen." She told him as briefly as she could what had happened in Barrie Ward on the day Kevin Ritchard died and above all what Harry had said to her that afternoon.

"When he said it, I paid no attention. It didn't really mean anything. But then I heard afterwards he'd tried to get hold of me, and then he tried again and I wasn't available. I meant to get back to him, really I did. I meant to call him this morning but somehow it slipped my mind and—" She bit her lip again, feeling the tension tighten her throat and knowing that her voice sounded thick and tearful in consequence. "I keep remembering what he said to me, and wondering—could it have had anything to do with what happened here tonight?"

He stood very still, clearly thinking, and then shook his head firmly, but to her gratitude, didn't offer facile reassurance. "Listen, there's no way we can possibly know, is there? It sounds to me, from that story, that this has been another bit of racial aggro. If this bloke—Ritchard?—if Ritchard comes out of Old East and tells some of his mates that he reckons that this Dr. Harry has done for his kid—well." He whistled softly on a long intake of breath. "Can't you see the line-up? They get all tanked up, fill themselves with sentimental claptrap about poor dear kids killed by lousy black doctors—I mean, it's written in stone, ain't it? Out they go looking for him and when they find him they deal with him in their horrible way. It makes more sense than thinking he was killed because there was something somebody didn't want you to know, and that he wanted to tell you. What could there be, after all?"

She nodded. "I know. I realize that I've been telling myself the same thing ever since I got here and recognized him. But the fact remains the idea's there. And it's not so easy to get rid of.

"I'll tell you what," he said. "If it'll help you, want to come with me when I go checking tomorrow? Can you get away?"

She stared at him, startled. "How do you mean, come with you? When you go and investigate this, you mean?"

"If it'll help. Then you'll see for yourself the sorts we're dealing with. It could get nasty—you should see these yobbos when you get them in a corner—but you're a tough cookie, as they say. And I'll be there to take care of you. How about it? Then you can see for yourself that you're not to blame for not finding out what it was this fella wanted to tell you. It was probably just some doctorish thing. I mean, you do have to talk to each other about patients, don't you?"

"Of course," she said, a little distracted, trying to think it through. "I'm not sure—"

"It won't be all that dangerous," he said. "Like I said, I'll be here to take care of you. And it's not as though you weren't a sort of honorary copper, is it? You're an officer of the court, anyway."

"Oh, for heaven's sake, as if I cared about that," she snapped. "And I don't need looking after either. I just wasn't sure if I could spare the time. But why not? After I've done the PM on Harry, though. That has to come first."

"Of course. What time shall I pick you up?"

"Make it about eleven," she said. "And Gus?"

He had started to walk round the car to open it. "Yeah?" He looked at her over the top of the car. He was a bit puffy around the eyes and his curly hair badly needed brushing. He had a smear of mud down one side of his face too. He'd never looked, she thought, so, well, so friendly.

"Thanks," she said. "Really. Thanks a lot'

14

The number of people who found reason to call in at the path, lab the following morning after news of Harry's death was reported on the seven a.m. radio news bulletin was remarkable. Sheila was in a lather of excitement which Jerry, the sardonic senior technician who was her deputy, said was as near as she'd get this year to having a sexual experience, and the rest of the lab staff were agitated as well as excited. "To have one of our own doctors killed in a pub brawl," Sheila said, "is not what you'd expect even at Old East, is it?"

George managed to ignore it all by going down to the mortuary almost as soon as she arrived at the hospital and refusing to emerge for anyone. Even for Professor Hunnisett himself who chose to drop in as "he was passing', an explanation which, as Jerry pointed out, was hardly likely since the lab was tucked in such a distant corner of the hospital that no one ever got to it except by making a distinct effort, a comment which made Sheila smirk, and sent her giggling to the phone to summon George up to see the Professor. But George sent a message back that she had already started on a PM (though she hadn't) and could Professor Hunnisett not speak to her on the phone? He did and burbled something inconsequential about a lecture series shortly to be on offer at the hospital about which he wanted to talk to her, before he could bring himself actually to say what it was he'd come over to her unit for.

"This is a nasty business," he said and coughed noisily, so that she had to hold the handset away from her ear. "One of our housemen—well, it's dreadful! Quite, quite dreadful."

"Yes," George said non-committally and waited.

"It's causing some trouble in the neighborhood, you know."

"Really?" said George and again waited. Professor Hunnisett breathed hard at the other end of the line.

"Some people seem to have got hold of quite the wrong end of the stick," he burst out "I mean, dammit all, I've got these demonstrations going on outside! I ask you! As though it's our fault that he got hurt."

"He's more than hurt," George said. "He's dead."

Professor Hunnisett ignored that "It's the most stupid thing I ever saw. Half of them have got banners shrieking about Trusts and safety for patients and a lot of other irrelevant stuff and then there are these others going on about England for the English, though why they should be there, I really can't—"

George's patience fragmented. "They're the ones who are glad Harry's dead," she said more loudly than she needed to have done, hoping her voice made him wince as much as his coughing had hurt her ears. "The fact that Harry's the one who's been killed by their bloody racism doesn't stop them demonstrating against him. Blaming you for employing him in the first place, I shouldn't wonder."

"Oh, dear," said Professor Hunnisett. "Really? That does make one wonder whether one should reconsider one's employment guidelines. Now we're a Trust and responsible for ourselves more, and having to take local opinion into account..."

"Oh, my God," George said and closed her eyes. "If you'll excuse me, I have a PM to do. Some other time, Professor." And she hung up the phone and stood there shaking. Maybe she'd be out of a job now? Was banging down the phone on the hospital's Dean and Clinical Director a firing offense? She didn't know and didn't, she decided, really care. All that mattered was what had happened to Harry. There was something particularly pitiful about the body now lying waiting for her in her mortuary; lithe, well made, young— he had been, she had discovered from his personal file, just twenty-five, a newly qualified doctor in his first real job—and so vulnerable. He'd needed support and help and no one had given it to him...

She stood and stared at the phone. It's I who failed him, she thought. He wanted to tell me something—maybe about that baby with AIDS? Who knows? All I do know is that if I hadn't gone snooping around asking questions maybe he wouldn't have died.

She shook her head at that and went down the corridor to complete putting on her greens and rubber apron and gloves, ready to start on Harry's corpse. Make your mind up, she told herself sharply. Either Harry was killed by a racist attack, which is what Gus thinks happened, or—well, or what? The way you're thinking you seem to be implying that there's something going on here at Old East that he stumbled on and wanted to tell you about. But why would he want to tell just you? Surely he'd have wanted to tell others, whatever it was. His own boss, perhaps, or at any rate Prudence Jennings? That would be more logical, surely, than choosing me who had nothing to do with his area of work.

Except for that baby, the child who wasn't called Oberlander. She rubbed her nose with the back of one hand, a childish gesture she reverted to whenever she was puzzled and tried to control her thoughts. All this twisting and turning in her mind would get her nowhere. Better to get on with the PM and see what facts there were. Afterwards, with Gus, there'd be time and opportunity to dig deeper for reasons and blame-apportioning.

Danny was ready, looking grim. He too had had his share of people wandering by just "dropping in for a natter' and was as disgusted as she was.

"Makes yer sick, don't it?" he said. "Like, they'd never "eard of the poor bugger till "e gets "isself killed and then all of a sudden they're full of interest. It's like those ghouls what stand at the side of the road gawpin' when there's bin an RTA. Sickenin', I calls it." And he pulled the sheet off Harry's body and offered George the big tissue knife with a flourish, clearly quite unaware of the ghoulishness of his own approach to his job, which he clearly savored deeply.

It was an observation which had the absurd effect of cheering George considerably. She was able to get on with the job in hand without too many qualms, and rapidly forgot that this was Harry Rajabani. It became just a body that needed investigating, and one that posed some mysteries; the sort she liked best.

Harold Constant was there as observer as usual, and so was Michael Urquhart, one of the detective constables on Gus's team, and she nodded at him amiably. She liked Michael, had done ever since the first case they'd worked on together when he'd provided the help that had enabled her to prove to Gus that her ideas were right and that there was a case to be dealt with, and he grinned back. He was inured now to the mortuary and the PM room, no longer blanching as he once had when she set her knife just below a sternum, where the ribs met in the midline, and sent it sweeping down to the pubic bone, opening the abdominal cavity completely. He was just interested.

But the abdominal contents were not all that mattered this morning. It was the surface injuries that told the story of what had happened to Harry most clearly, and she made a careful superficial examination before beginning on the viscera, exploring the skin gingerly and with great delicacy.

"Gravel burns on all exposed skin areas," she dictated. "Hands, lower arms, especially on inner aspects and face, especially right cheek. Petechiae and some larger areas of bruising across the back and shoulders, which make it clear that great pressure was exerted. Some overlapping of the injuries consistent with the body being pressured on three separate passes as would occur if a car passed over three times. Beneath the surface bruising, fractures of the ribs, the pelvis, the spine. Some pulpiness in lung, kidneys query damaged. To check on opening the abdomen. Kidney crushed on right."

The dictation went on for some time, and then she turned her attention to the head and neck for last checks before setting to work with her knife. There was less to see on the back of the head and neck; the thick sleek hair had clearly protected the skull, and anyway there was no indication that the car had actually touched the skull. There was, though, a small bruise just under the occiput, where the head met the spine, and she stored that in her mind before setting to work to open the skull.

The desultory conversation between Michael and Harold ceased as the burr of the electric saw filled the air, and they waited for George to speak again; but she was absorbed in what she was doing, so much so that a frown was creasing between her brows. She was surprised and she looked it.

"Something wrong?" Michael Urquhart was alert; Harold Constant seemed almost asleep and hadn't noticed her reaction.

"Well, yes, in a way," she said slowly and then shook her head. "How does this sound for a scenario? Someone gives him a bit of a wallop on the head—very scientific rather than hard. It knocks him out for a few moments—just a bit of concussion in here—and that is why he's lying down so neatly ready to be run over by a large car."

"If you say so, doctor," Michael Urquhart said. "What about it?"

"Well, maybe I've got my view of the racist mob psychology hopelessly adrift, but I imagined they actually enjoyed the beating-up part. I mean, they really hate their victim, don't they? They aren't interested in doing something to him that's hard to spot. They wouldn't get any kick out of coming on to someone who's all unaware and hitting on the back of the neck in a way that makes his head jerk back and leads to an immediate concussion and unconsciousness so that he wouldn't know what hit him. And they wouldn't get any joy out of running over him with a heavy car to kill him. No real blood to see, no groans of agony, nothing like that."

Michael was looking at her with his head on one side, like an intelligent and hungry bird. "You reckon that's what happened here?"

"I reckon," she said. "Look. It's clear, that bruise. And the edema of the brain. It's all indicative of pre-death concussion and that means probably loss of consciousness. There are no injuries to the arms, apart from the sort of gravel burns that came from being dragged against the ground. No sign he tried to fight off his attackers. The car passed over him three times, twice going forward—see the line of bruises, heavier at this end?—and once backward. There, you see? And he just lay there! He couldn't have been aware of what was going on. And as I say, that doesn't sound to me like a racist attack. What say you?"

"I see what you mean," Michael said. "Is that all the evidence, then?"

"Let's open the belly and see," she said, and this time accepted the big tissue knife from Danny. Again silence filled the room until she began to dictate again, her voice clear and crisp.

"Heart displaced by massive tear to aortic arch and consequent extravasation," she said. "Lungs compressed, and right lung pierced by fractured fourth rib. Spleen crushed. Liver crushed and capsule severely torn by displaced fracture seventh rib. Kidney? crushed and pierced by spinal fracture..."

Her voice went on, listing the horrific injuries, and they listened and shifted their weight from one foot to the other.

When she'd finished she looked at Michael.

"I reckon it's clear, don't you? This had to be quite a different sort of attack from the one first imagined."

"Then say so in your report," Michael said quickly. "It's no good me saying anything. It's got to come from you. I'm supposed to be going straight from here to'—he reached in his pocket to find his notebook and flicked it open—"ninety-nine Laura House on the Lansbury Estate. Flat of a Dave Ritchard. If you could give me the report on this to take with me..."

"I can do better than that," she said. "I can bring it with me. Your guv'nor said I could go along on the investigation this morning. Said to phone him when I was ready and he'd get me picked up. So I might as well come with you, right? Gus—the Guv'll be there, will he?"

"He said he would."

"Fine. Give me a bit longer to finish here. Danny?" She looked over her shoulder at him. "Get Sheila to alert the typists, would you? I want this transcript typed up before I've finished my shower. Tell her to get Marie on it. Stop whatever else she's doing and give it priority. She's the best one we've got."

She worked swiftly now, finishing her dictation and sending Danny off with the tape hot foot; dealing with the final details of the PM, including the closure, unaided.

She was very angry. The confusion of the earlier part of the morning had given way to an icy determination to track down who ever had done this and to catch him so tightly that there'd be no way he could wriggle out of it. She had never been in favor of capital punishment; it had always seemed to her the most bestial of acts to do to murderers the very thing the murderers had themselves done; it wasn't justice, but revenge. Yet this time she wished that this killer could hang. Not because Harry had suffered so much more than others, but because she had seen Harry concerned about sick people, spending all his energy and his working life caring for them. The man had been a doctor, dammit, killed because of some aspect of his medical work, of that she was certain now. And to kill such a one was— and she caught herself as her thoughts went careering away. I sound like policemen do when a fellow copper is killed. Do

I, like them, reserve my greatest concern for my own sort? A disagreeable idea, and she took a deep breath to get back some of her emotional control. It was effective. Even before she walked out of the room she felt better. She had, she was sure, identified something very important about this killing, something that would enable Gus to avoid wasting any time and to seek the real killer as fast as possible. There was no need for him to go haring along the racist-attack path. That was definite. He had to come here, to the hospital, because it was here at Old East that the answers were to be found.

15

In the event she couldn't go with Michael Urquhart to meet Gus at the Ritchards' flat; when she got back upstairs, there was a crisis over a set of blood sugars that Jane had done, and Jerry had checked, which the Diabetes consultant, Dr. Maurice Carvalho, swore had been done wrongly. He had come over to the department himself to make his complaints and George, hurrying to collect her typed-up notes, walked straight in on the uproar.

Dr. Carvalho was a small self-important man with a pronounced belly (which infuriated his patients when he lectured them on dieting and not putting on fat) and a sharp way of speaking which was guaranteed to upset people. Certainly by the time George reached the lab Jane was almost in tears, Jerry was in a towering rage and Sheila was white with barely contained temper.

George looked at them and at once sent the junior technologist scurrying up to her office, where Michael Urquhart was waiting, with a message to go ahead without her; she'd call the nick when she was ready to go and they could call back on her mobile phone to tell her where they'd be. Then she weighed into the blood sugars argument to see what she could do to defuse it.

By the time she had worked out what had happened, which was that one of Dr. Carvalho's nursing staff, a junior working in the Diabetic Clinic for the first time, had carefully attached the blood samples to all the wrong notes by accidentally reversing the case note numbers on the computer and then failing to check on the actual names of the patients, a great deal of energy had been expended, and several more people from the lab's staff had been dragged into the row. By the time all this had been dealt with and Dr. Carvalho had been sent off, after being persuaded to apologize (albeit grudgingly) to the path, lab staff, and the staff had been carefully soothed by George, it was lunchtime.

She hesitated, looked at her desk, which wasn't as badly piled up with work as it might have been and then checked through the labs to see the level of work that was going through. It all seemed containable, she decided; the place wouldn't collapse if she vanished for the afternoon. So she told Sheila she was going out on a case and phoned the Ratcliffe Street police station to find out where Gus was and to instruct them to tell him she intended to join him wherever that happened to be.

Her mobile phone rang about five minutes later. "He said to make it down at the Rag and Bottle," the junior constable reported. "And please will you bring your post-mortem report with you."

"Huh!" George said, nettled, even though the report was actually in her pocket as she spoke. "When does he want his next miracle? Before supper, or will afterwards do?"

The junior constable snickered. "Well, doctor, you know what he's like as well as we do. Enjoy yourself." George hung up crossly. She'd wanted to impress Gus by having her report on the PM all ready for him; to have him demanding it as of right was decidedly annoying.

She walked to the pub, a ten-minute journey through the back alleys which she quite enjoyed, going at a fast rate with her hands thrust deep into her pockets and her shoulders hunched against the cold. There was a smell of Christmas in the air; not the pine needles and freshly cut holly of her childhood but hot chestnuts and potatoes being roasted over battered anthracite burners, and from a food factory somewhere nearby a scent of yeast. I really must make my Christmas plans soon, she thought. It's barely a week away now—

The pub smelled too, but not of Christmas, despite the great swathes of glittering aluminum foil in unappetising shades of poison green, blood-clot purple and electric blue that festooned the bar. It was old cigarette smoke and stale beer with, underlying it, human sweat and urine and sick and she tightened her throat against it and looked around her with distaste.

"If you're looking for the Bill try over the way." The landlord was standing behind the bar looking sour and she nodded at him and ducked out gratefully; she could never get used to the way some English pubs were so pleasant and some so revolting. She peered across the road to where Gus might be, and saw his big shining 1970s Austin Vanden Pias blatantly parked on double yellow lines in front of a pizza parlor.

He greeted her with an expansive wave as she came in and shouted at the man behind the counter, "You can serve it up now, Giovanni!" and grinned at her as she made her way through the crowded tables towards him, very aware of the fact that every other customer was now staring at her with avid interest.

"I told you." The man behind the counter was slapping plates down on the table at which Gus was sitting. "My name's bloody Gary, so stop being so bleedin' funny."

"I'll tell him," Gus said and winked at George. "I've ordered for you. It's the sort you like."

She looked down at the hot crisp pizza that was waiting for her; a classic with olives and anchovies and extra cheese and she thought for a moment of saying she wanted something entirely different, just to annoy him. But of course he had remembered accurately that this was the only sort she liked and she shrugged out of her coat and sat down.

"You get worse instead of better," she said. "Always taking things into your own hands. I mightn't have wanted a pizza at all."

"You'd ha' wanted something," he said, all sweet reason. "This way you're not kept waitin.'"

"Yes," she said. "Yes, well—" And couldn't think of anything else. How was it this wretched man always managed to wrong-foot her? "Thanks then. I suppose it looks—well, OK." It was an ungracious speech but the best she could manage. She began to eat.

The pizza was excellent and he watched her as she dealt with it hungrily, and then laughed. "You are funny, George, old girl," he said. "You try so hard to be dignified with me and it's daft really. I don't give a puppy dog's toss for dignity. Intelligence, now, there's somethin' that really does get to me. I get all hot under the collar and various other places too when people are clever. You're clever—"

"I came here to talk about the case," George said with her mouth full. "Let's do just that, OK? I'm not up to anything more complicated this afternoon."

"I was just bein' thoughtful," he said mildly. "Didn't want to talk about nasties while you were eatin.'" It'd put me off my grub, talking about post-mortem reports and what that bugger Ritchard had to say this morning, but if it doesn't worry you…"

"Tell me about Ritchard, if you must," she said. "Then when I've finished I'll tell you about my report of the PM. Not because it'd spoil my appetite now, but because I need both hands to deal with this." She speared another piece of pizza. "Not that what Ritchard had to say is all that important, frankly."

"Oh, really!" He was sardonic. "So you know in advance, do you, what he had to say?"

"I think I do." She chewed busily, watching him over her rhythmic jaws. "In fact, I'll have a go and tell you what he said. He knew nothing about it, wasn't there, feels you're coming on to him unjustly and—"

He lifted his brows. "Is that so? Well, well. Let me see now." He reached into his breast pocket and hooked out his notebook. "Interview, David Richard Ritchard. His mum and dad must ha' thought they had a sense of humor, poor buggers. David Richard Ritchard, of—well, never mind all that Let's get to the juicy bits. Ah, yes. Here we are."

His accent changed, became the slight whining falling inflexion sound that so many of the patients at Old East used, and she watched him with fascination as his face drooped and somehow he actually became the man she had watched with horror hurling invective at Harry over at Old East. Gus could have been an actor, she thought. He's got the talent. And, sort of, the looks. She remembered a film star of her childhood whom she'd watched with fascination in old black-and-white movies on TV. Edward G. Robinson, she thought and her lips quirked.

"How would you feel if it happened to you, then?" Gus went on. "Ere I am, just me and Kev and a right little villain he was, took after "is mum's side of the family and no error; anyway it's just me and "im and "e gets ill and goes into this "ospital and the next thing I know, they say "e'd got a sorta cancer and then "e's bloody dead. Wouldn't you get mad if you found out that some black bleeder was practising "ow to be a doctor on "im just so as to save the expletive deleted "ealth service a few bob? Wouldn't you be upset if it was your kid that was dead? Yeah, I "ad a go at "im and meant to do more "n' all, and I don't care who knows it. I told some of my mates, they all said the same, "e needs a right seein' to, that doctor and we would "a done it if someone else "adn't done it first. But it wasn't me. Yeah, I was at the Rag and Bottle, it's my local, why shouldn't I be? But I tell you it wasn't me or none of my mates what did it for "im. It was some other bugger and I'd like to shake "im by the hand."

"Did you write all that down?" She was incredulous.

"Most of it. Not all the details, you understand, I like to use my memory an' all. If I was in court givin' this as evidence it wouldn't sound quite like this. But you got the gist of it." He grinned at her. "So you're wrong, you see. Our friend Ritchard was indeed involved."

"No, he wasn't." She pushed away her now empty plate and settled down to explain. "He said he was going to—that he *intended* to do Harry harm. But not that he'd actually done so."

"You're a sweet woman, aren't you? Even believe men like the Ritchards of this world are telling the truth."

"When there's corroborative evidence pointing in the opposite direction, then yes. It's nothing to do with sweetness, everything to do with using a bit of common sense. Now listen."

She reached into her pocket, pulled out her notes, and smoothed them in front of her as Gus crooked a finger at Gary and demanded coffee. "I think I've got a clearer idea of what had happened than you have. You think he was attacked by a mob, right?"

"Something like that," he said, looking at her quizzically. "Are you going to tell me that you've got real evidence he wasn't?"

"I've got some highly indicative material. Listen." She explained as carefully and succinctly as she could. Pointed out how it was clear the car had passed over the body three times and how the direction in which it was traveling each time could be inferred from the pressure on the body at different bruise sites, and then went on to detail the state of the skull.

"If he'd been attacked by a group of people there's no way he'd be as unmarked as he was," she said. "I mean, of course he had marks, but they weren't inflicted by hands or by objects. Only by the ground and by pressure."

He was leaning forwards now, very alert. "You're sure of this?"

"As sure as it's possible to be at this stage. I mean, there's no way I can prove whether he was unconscious or conscious when the car ran over him, but logic says he wasn't. No one'd just lie there and let a great lump of car run over him if he knew what was happening, would he?"

He was in tears after three Scotches and useless by the time he'd had four. Used to be able to hold his booze, old Dave, but this has knocked the stuffing out of him."

Listening, George felt a twinge of sympathy for Dave Ritchard. The way he'd spoken to Harry had been dreadful, of course it had; but in his state of grief, and after growing up in these tight narrow streets where everyone shared the same hostilities and suspicious view of outsiders, especially the sort who could be easily identified by the color of their skins, could he help his attitudes? Not entirely. But then she hardened. Not entirely meant that he could to an extent; and he had threatened Harry, after all. Her conviction that he was not involved with Harry's death began to waver.

"Did you see him leave?" Gus was asking.

The landlord wrinkled his face in an effort of recollection. "It was dead busy last night. Busier than—"

"So you told me before. Listen. Let me help you. Shut your eyes."

"Eh?" The landlord looked like suspicion personified.

"Don't be any dafter than you can help," Gus said impatiently. "Do as you're told and don't argue. Now, shut your eyes. OK. It's getting on for ten o'clock—No, keep them shut. Inside your head you're looking, inside your head. It's last night and you're looking inside your head at what's going on here. See the clock?"

The landlord, standing with his eyes closed and looking absurdly like a devout if overgrown choirboy, much to the delight of some of his customers who were shamelessly watching and listening in, looked surprised. "Yeah, I can see it."

"OK. Now look round your bar. See who's in tonight. Give me the run-down."

The landlord kept his eyes closed and frowned. "Right. Yeah. Well, there's Chalky over there with his dog. I told him before, next time that dog gets stepped on and makes a fuss is the last time it comes in here. Chalky, yeah. And then there's a table of silly bits from the betting shop. It's that Dawn's birthday. Look at "em! Skirts up to their you-know-whats and about as much shame as Old Mother Riley's tomcat. They're chatting up some fellas I don't know. They'll know the girls well enough before the night's out though. You can see they're on to a good thing. Um…"

"You're doing fine," Gus said encouragingly. "Keep it up."

"There's Dave Ritchard and he's got the Garnett fellas with him."

"Brothers?" said Gus.

"No, they're cousins, those two. Come from over Plaistow way. Old mates of Eric Phillips and Les Lincoln. They're there too."

"Ah," said Gus softly. "I know them."

"Dave's nearly paralytic. I'll have to send him off soon. But Eric's looking after him all right. Then there's that Paki, all dressed up and nowhere to go."

"Paki?"

The landlord opened his eyes briefly. "The one that got done," he said and then closed his eyes quickly as Gus opened his mouth to react.

"He's talking to someone," the landlord said. Gus closed his mouth and listened intently. "I can't quite see…"

"You never mentioned Harry talking to anyone before," Gus said.

"You never asked. Anyway, I've only just remembered. Sort of. It's like I'm looking at him…yeah. He's definitely talking. Waving his hands about." The landlord's face suddenly lifted and he opened his eyes wide and stared at Gus. "Here, hang about a bit! This bloke—he's left. I mean, he went out with this other one, the one he was talking to. He went out, following, and there's Dave." He closed his eyes again quickly and stared inside his lids at this memory. "Yeah, there it is! I can really see it, like! Dave Ritchard's sitting there as pissed as a man can be and still alive, not fit to walk as far as I can tell, and your bloke's gone."

He opened his eyes finally. "So, if you were thinking it was Dave went for that bloke, it wasn't, because he was still here after the bloke walked out. And I reckon he still was when that bird what found the Paki came running in here shrieking her head off. I mean, even if he could have gone after him to the car park, he wasn't in no state to walk, take it from me. So, there you are. It's amazing what you can remember when you have to, ain't it?" And he looked at Gus with huge self-satisfaction.

16

"You win," Gus said. "Dave Ritchard's out of it. Not that I won't be keepin' a close eye on him. The way that bloke talked, he's dangerous. I'll see to it that the race relations group here keep an eye on him too."

He stretched and yawned, then settled back into a comfortable posture at his desk. George watched him from her seat in the battered armchair he kept in the corner of his office, listening to the sounds that came from the busy police station beyond his glass door, and felt absurdly happy. A puzzling case, Christmas coming, and Ma here (and for all her irritations and problems she was dear old Ma). George tried not to add in the last and most obvious reason for feeling as she did, that she was with Gus, who was getting more and more important to her. That was a complication to her life she really didn't want to think about too much.

"Can we do a sort of recap?" she said. "Go over what we've got—see where it takes us?"

"If you like."

"Questions first, though. Have you any more on the Oberlander baby?"

"Not a bloody thing." He looked petulant, sticking his lower lip out like a sulky child. "Dammit all, you'd think it'd be easy enough to find out what baby's disappeared from where, wouldn't you? Neighbors are mostly very nosey when it comes to kids and they notice if they vanish, but I've put a check out to every nick in the country, and no one reports any kid like this. There are missing children all right, but no babies. Certainly not any sick ones that look much younger than they are."

"There's a bit more to this one than that," she said. "He had AIDS."

He stared at her. "You didn't tell me that before."

"Wasn't sure. Prudence Jennings was the one who put the idea up. She said she thought he might be HIV positive. I've only just got the last test results through. He was HIV positive but he also had clear evidence of opportunistic disease, so AIDS has to be the diagnosis. Damn." She bit her lip then. "I feel a certain twinge of guilt here. I should have told Prudence Jennings."

"Oh?" He looked puzzled.

"She asked me to do the tests. I did the first ones and went back to tell her, but by then the child had vanished, and she wasn't there herself, either. And after it died and I'd done the PM, the whole case was over and done with—sort of—I didn't go back or try to reach her any other way. I have to admit I didn't think of it. She's entitled to know, though."

"Why?" He looked genuinely interested.

"Well, it's the right thing to do, you know. Colleagues should cooperate. And as I say, it was she who put the idea of HIV infection into my mind in the first place."

"I see." Gus looked judicious. "You know, I think maybe I'll have a word with her too."

"Oh?"

"Well, it's this business of her being away and leaving young Harry when she was supposed to be on call. Maybe there's a link there somewhere."

"With Harry's death?"

"Well, maybe. Let's face it, ducks. We've proved he wasn't killed by a bunch of racist yobs, haven't we? You found out from your PM and I found out from my questioning. That means that someone else killed him. Who? Since he had few if any connections outside the hospital, as far as I can find out from the interviews we've done so far, it has to be someone inside. So why not your Prudence? Maybe there was something going on between them. Maybe she set him up for someone else to lure him to the Rag and Bottle and organized for him to be run over. Maybe Prue herself ran him over."

George shook her head. "Hardly. The landlord at the pub said Harry was talking to a bloke."

"Did he?" Gus said. "Are you sure?"

She blinked. "How do you mean? Didn't he?"

Gus flipped open his notebook. "Let's see, now. Here we are. Um—'He's talking to someone…Waving his hands about.' No, hang on, it's further on. Ah, here we are. 'He's left. I mean, he went out with this other one, the one he was talking to. He went out, following…'" Gus closed his notebook and stowed it back in his pocket. "So there you are. It could have been Prudence, couldn't it?"

"You said you were going to get a description from him. Did you?"

"We did. And it doesn't help. I can remember it—it was in Urquhart's notebook though, because he did the checking on that. I was just listening and looking over his shoulder. Let me see." He closed his eyes, waited a moment and then said, "Jeans. Blue anorak. Trainers. Woolly hat in green and orange stripes pulled down over the ears. Medium height and build. Not very much of anything, really." He opened his eyes again and grinned at her. "See what I mean? It could ha' been a woman, couldn't it? At a pinch."

George was staring at him, fascinated. "You've got an eidetic memory too," she said almost accusingly. "You never told me that!"

"So? You're not the only one! I'll bet there're lots of people can remember like that."

"Shutting their eyes and seeing it all over again, right? The way I do. The way I did when we were doing the Oxford case."

"The way I made the landlord do it. It's not all that difficult, after all. I have to admit I was impressed when you did it, though, so I thought I'd try and see if I could too. And I found out I could. What is it you called it? Eidetic? All I know is I've been practising calling up pictures of what I've seen in my mind and sort of reading them off, and I've managed to show other people—a few of "em—how to do it, too."

She grinned, suddenly elated. "It's great, isn't it? I used to pass most of my exams that way. Sort of call up the memory of my notebooks and look at the pages and read off the answers. Just like a crib."

"I'm not as good at it as you are. I can still remember being gobsmacked by the way you managed to remember everything that had been in that bloke's bathroom cabinet. Amazin." It made me want to be the same."

She laughed. "OK. Is there anything else you can remember now that might help with this recap?"

"Ah! Back to our muttons, eh? Fair enough. Let's see what we've got." He began to tick off on his fingers: "Item, three babies dead of cot deaths in Old East."

She frowned. "Look, I don't want to seem argumentative so early in the proceedings, but what have they got to do with these two murders? They were just cot deaths."

"I don't know," he said. "Like you, I'm bothered by that note someone put on the PM request form—even more bothered by the fact that you can't find out who wrote it. So maybe they were murders. You said yourself it's hard to tell with these infants what they died of. Smothering shows no signs, and—"

"Sometimes it does!"

"Yeah, but it doesn't always. So that's enough to make a mystery, right? They could have been deliberate deaths."

"I suppose so," she said slowly. "But I've got a deep hunch those babies died naturally, somehow. It was just a fluke there were so many—though I have to agree the note's a puzzle."

"OK. So we'll include them in our recap. I put them at the top of the list, not because they're the most important element but because they happened first. Then we have a baby with AIDS fetched into Old East in mysterious circumstances, who disappears and is then found smothered in a plastic bag on a piece of waste ground. I think we're entitled to regard that one as a right oddity."

"Yes," she said gravely. "I won't argue about that one, though we didn't have the definitive AIDS diagnosis till after the PM, of course."

"Don't pick nits. So, where was I?"

"Putting the Oberlander baby on the list."

"Right. Then we have Harry Rajabani's murder. This one really is a bit tricky. I still can't help wanting to think about the racial motive. Not because I'm obsessed," he added hastily, seeing her expression. "But because of the link, tenuous though it is, between the blokes who went for Choopani and bashed in my window while they were at it, and Harry."

"What link?" she demanded. "Just the fact that Choopani and Harry weren't white?"

"The blokes who went for Choopani were the same ones who were Dave Ritchard's mates. Some of them were in the pub with him last night, even though the landlord is adamant they couldn't have got out to the car park to do it while Harry was there. They were in the pub though. And there are one or two other tie-ins. Choopani was the GP who sent Kevin Ritchard to Old East in the first place. Though what Dave was doing on the list of an Asian GP, with his views, Gawd only knows."

"The local GPs run a rota on-call service for each other," George said. "It's cheaper for them than hiring locums when they're off duty. They each take a turn at covering for all each other's calls. It could be that Choopani got to see Kevin that way, and spotted something his own GP missed."

"Fair enough. So there are other links, you see, between Harry and Choopani via Kevin, and between Dave and Choopani's heavies."

"But no links with the Oberlander case and certainly none with my cot deaths."

"I'll grant you," he said handsomely, and sighed.

There was a little silence and then she said, "I think I'm going to talk to Prue. See what happened to her that night, and why she left Harry on his own when she was on call."

He thought for a moment and then nodded. "I think that's a good idea. We will interview her, as I said, but if you can get anything out of her now, on the old girls' network, it'd be handy."

She grimaced. The excitement of hunting down clues and unraveling mysteries was unalloyed pleasure for her, generally speaking, but it did make her uncomfortable to think she might be abusing the fellowship of her medical colleagues as part of her unraveling; and Gus caught her eye and seemed to read her mind.

"It's tough, ducks, but there it is. A murderer is a murderer, even if he or she turns out to be your best and dearest mate. If it's too much for you…"

"No," she said firmly, dismissing her qualms. "That'd be daft. It'll do Prue no harm if she's done nothing wrong. And if she has—well, better we find out. Listen, can you do anything more about the Oberlander baby?"

"We're still trying, like I said, but I have to tell you it's a cold trail. If no one reports a baby missing, and we can't find any evidence of a missing child, then finding out who he was, let alone who killed him or why, is almost impossible."

"As for why," George said. "Could it be because of the AIDS, I wonder?"

He looked puzzled. "Is that a motive for killing a child?"

"Let's think it through. You're a parent and you've got this sick child. And you're HIV positive. You know you are, but you don't want anyone else to know. If the baby shows that he's got the disease…"

"Then that shows you've got it, because he must have got it from someone…"

"Precisely." George leaned forwards eagerly. "And I'll tell you something else. Children don't get HIV infection from their fathers."

"Never?" Gus said. "I think I know the answer, but—"

"You do. The disease is spread by body fluids. The most likely cause for a baby to be HIV positive is via breastfeeding from an infected mother."

"Or from a blood transfusion, I suppose."

"Yes, of course. But if this baby got ill from blood transfusion it's obvious the parents would have taken the child back to the doctor who gave him the transfusion, wouldn't they? Or at least would have told Prue about it when it was brought in to Barrie Ward. And, anyway, in the UK transfusions are safe now. It seems to me to point straight to the parents—well, anyway, the mother. She has to be the one who's HIV positive and who passed the virus on. I mean, look at what they did. They brought the child in under an assumed name because it was ill, took it away in panic when Prue talked about doing tests—maybe she even mentioned HIV? I'll have to ask her—and then the baby turns up dead. Maybe they thought that was the simplest way out, since it was likely to die anyway, sooner or later. And looking at the poor little scrap when I did the PM I'd have said probably sooner. Maybe they just, well, cut their losses?"

"And the mother's secret about her HIV status is still safe." Gus shook his head. "There's a catch in this. Hang on…" He wrinkled his face and stared at her, his eyes glassy with concentration. "It's got to do with film stars, I know it has. The catch…"

George stared back at him and then her own expression became gloomy.

"I've just seen the catch," she said. "If the mother got her HIV infection from a blood transfusion a long time ago, before the baby was born—"

"Before blood was safe in the transfusion service…and I've remembered the link. There was a Hollywood actor that happened to, wasn't there? His wife got HIV from blood, she breastfed and so gave it to their baby. A dreadful business. Do you remember?"

George nodded, eagerly. "That's right. I do remember. And, if this mother, like the Hollywood one, had a transfusion and got the infection, there'd be no need for all the secrecy, would there? No one would be able to point a finger and accuse her of some sort of sexual fling where she picked up the virus." She shook her head in sudden anger. "Not that anyone should ever have to be ashamed of being ill. It's a tragedy that happens to some people, and it's got nothing to do with morality any more than—than heart disease. But there's a lot of ignorance about and maybe this mother—"

"Maybe this mother *didn't* have a transfusion and wants to keep from her husband the fact that she's infected, and maybe she killed the baby to stop him finding out?" Gus stopped, irritable. "Too many maybes. Look, I'll spread my own boys about further. It's facts we need, not guesses. We'll do some checking on sexually transmitted disease clinics and with HIV consultants. See if that way we can find a mother who fits the bill. Meanwhile…"

"Meanwhile, I'll talk to Prue and see what happened there." George got to her feet and stretched. "I'd better get home. Um—see you soon, then."

Gus seemed abstracted, already reaching for his phone, and she thought a little bleakly: He doesn't mind me going.

"Mmm. You do, ducks. And yeah, see you soon. Call me with the news, if any. I'll be here late tonight, and most other nights, I think. There's a lot of routine stuff you have to get through with these murder cases. Like checking the car that ran over Harry. "Night, Dr. B."

"Night," she said and went. There was no elation left now.

At home, she found her mother and Bridget busy in the kitchen.

"We're making supper, darling!" Vanny called. "We found this country market where they had all sorts of nice things. I'm making you the sort of things you used to like a lot."

George, her lips curling delightedly at the thought of the sort of country market they might have found in Shadwell, put her head round the kitchen door. Doubt filled her. The smells that were wreathing the place were indeed familiar and her heart sank.

"Ma! Not, I beg you, candied yams!"

"Why not? You always adored them the way I did them, with the toasted marshmallows on top and all. We got some ham steaks too, and some spinach. No collard greens but spinach comes close."

"It's all a bit Southern style for a Yankee," George said, knowing when she was licked. The dish of yams with marshmallows on top was already in the oven; she could see the topping bubbling and browning through the glass door. "You must have found Watney Street. Lots of Afro-Caribbean stalls there. They have yams and sweet potatoes."

"Indeed we did." Bridget lifted a flushed face from the minute kitchen table where, George now realized, she was putting the last trimmings on a pumpkin pie. "I saw they had pumpkin and I said to Vanny, we'll give her the Thanksgiving dinner she never did have. Just to get her all set up for Christmas. We're making it, you know, honey. All of it. There, doesn't it look good?" She held the pie up on one hand, making the fingers into a sort of five legged stand for it. "Just like the pie Snow White made for the dwarves!"

"It's been a long time since I ate Disney food, Bridget," George said. "And as for Christmas, for heaven's sake, you don't have to—"

"It's all arranged," Bridget said seriously. "We talked to the butcher in the market there and made an order for a dear little turkey, and we've organized to get all the vegetables and everything else. Even the cranberries. One of the stores had them in jars, just like home, would you believe. It's going to be great. Better than a hotel any day."

"I'm sure," George said, surrendering, knowing it would be a waste of energy to argue. "I hope you haven't ordered too much. There'll only be the three of us, after all."

"Not three, darling," Bridget trilled. "Four!"

"Oh?" George lifted her head from the little pile of mail that had been waiting for her, her finger halted in mid-slit of an envelope that looked horribly like one from the taxman. "How d'you reckon that?"

"Well, he was so kind to us, taking us out and all, I just had to do something. I said to Vanny, shall we take him out too, and she said she thought that would be a bit—well, too much, you know? And then she said she knew he had no family, since she'd asked him all about his folks, and there you are!"

"Bridget," George said, her heart sliding down her ribs. "What have you done?"

"Why, I sent a nice invitation to Gus today, to spend Christmas Day with us. I handed it in to the police station—the address was in the phone book—and I'm sure he'll get it safe and sound. If not, well, we can call him. You have the number, I imagine? I do so hope he'll come. I have a feeling he will, though."

"Do you know, Bridget," George said after thinking for a little while, trying to decide what she should do about this, if anything, and failing to reach a conclusion. "Do you know, I rather think so too."

She enjoyed the yams with marshmallow more than she had thought she would. Maybe Christmas wouldn't be so bad after all.

17

Mixing detection with running a busy Path. Department, George told herself at ten to one the following Monday, was the perfect way to drive yourself crazy.

All the morning she'd been working at full throttle, dealing with the routine jobs and a prolonged series of complicated telephone discussions with Harold Constant at the coroner's office about a case over which she would have to be in court early in the New Year, as well as fitting in a PM on an old man who'd keeled over dead in the middle of Leman Street, and all the time she'd been itching to get over to Barrie Ward to talk to Prudence Jennings. She could have talked to her on the phone, it was true, but she was unwilling to do that. There was so much more to be learned from people than just the words they used; their behaviour when they were asked questions, the expressions on their faces as they did it, the way they moved, all of it was relevant. And that wasn't available on a phone.

As the morning had worn on however, it had got easier. Sheila was in a particularly co-operative mood and Jerry and the rest of the senior staff followed her lead.

"Christmas," Jerry said virtuously when George murmured something oblique about how surprisingly agreeable everyone was being this morning. "Season of goodwill and all that crap to all men." He'd snickered then. "And pressies. I'm expecting something really smashing from you, Dr. B., after the way I've worked so hard all this year. If you let me down, who knows what sort of mood I'll be in come the New Year?"

"You'll be lucky," George said. "When do I get the time to go shopping?"

"Try the off license," Sheila said acidly. "Give him a bottle or two of whisky, and he'll follow you anywhere."

George, who had already decided to present her staff with bottles of good port and small Stilton cheeses from Marks and Sparks as Christmas presents, pretended not to have heard that and decided to make the best of her opportunities.

"Well, since you're all feeling so benevolent," she said, "I'll disappear for a while. I have things to do, and if I make an effort I can be back here by three in time for that PM. If I'm a few minutes late, make nice noises at whoever comes from the coroner's office, Sheila, will you? I've already asked Danny to see to it he gives them tea and biscuits."

"Yuk," Sheila said. "How anyone can sit down there in among all those corpses and slurp tea is beyond me. OK, Dr. B. We'll hold the fort." And she put on her long-suffering look as George headed for the door.

She went straight to the Pediatric Department. There were other places she wanted to visit to do some questioning, but it was important to get Prudence Jennings sorted out first. She rehearsed inside her head the questions she would ask as she went scurrying through the Disney corridor and on into the main play area of Barrie, threading her way through clusters of mothers and children who were everywhere. Outpatient Clinic morning, she decided, and hoped that Prue wouldn't be too bogged down in work to spare her some time.

Sister Collinson was in the middle of the room and the tangle of toys and floor cushions, arguing passionately with a small bony woman who had four small children, all of whom looked to be well under six, clustered round her. The two women were almost nose to nose as they hissed and spat their rage at each other and the children watched wide-eyed, as indeed did several other mothers who clearly found the whole exchange highly entertaining.

Philip Goss was standing alongside them with a pile of notes under his arm and it was he who sorted the matter out. He moved smoothly in beside Sister Collinson and said something to the woman which made her jerk her head back and look at him, and then down at one of the children.

He was the smallest, a snotty-nosed child of about two, and he had both hands held to his mouth, chewing something with great concentration. His mother yelped and pulled it away from him. The child began to wail at the top of his voice; the mother shrieked and hurled the thing she'd grabbed from him at Sister Collinson—it was a large plastic syringe—who received it in her eye, and then scooped up the child to slap him hard and bawl that he was a dirty little tyke what ought to know better. The child immediately screamed like a steam engine and Sister Collinson fled, clearly intending to do something about her eye. Philip Goss said something else to the mother who, now thoroughly flustered, headed for the door with her other three children running behind her like demented ducklings and, pushing George out of the way, went. Much to everyone's relief.

There was no more to watch so the room emptied fairly rapidly of the rest of the mothers and children. George stood to one side as they made their way out, glad she hadn't been able to get here till the end of the OP session. To have walked in earlier would have been a total waste of time.

Philip Goss was tidying up with swift economical movements, stacking notes on the desk, sweeping abandoned playthings and comics into boxes and neat piles respectively, and straightening rugs and floor cushions so that in a matter of a few moments, it seemed, the big space was tranquil again.

George came further into the room and shook her head at him in admiration. "Is it always like that here? How do you stand it?"

"Oh, good morning, Dr. Barnabas! Yes, pretty well. But we get them through fairly quickly, as long as the doctors don't mess about too much. And as long as Sister Collinson doesn't get the bit between her teeth." He sighed and shook out the last of the cushions before setting it neatly in place. "She'll never learn not to nag Mrs. Proudie. That woman gets excited and demands the moon and the stars, but it's easy to distract her, fortunately." And he smiled, a small close-lipped lifting of the corners of his mouth, plainly pleased with himself.

George set her head on one side and looked at him sharply. "You could have taken that syringe from the child without any fuss from his mother, couldn't you?" she said.

He laughed. "You noticed? Well, I had to stop them somehow, didn't I? It was worth letting poor old Wayne get clobbered by his mum to stop her bawling at Sister, don't you think? Once you deflect Mrs. P. she usually forgets what it was she was mad about in the first place." He shook his head. "Pity Sister got the thing in her eye, mind you. Still, it'll give her something to complain about to everyone this afternoon. She'll like that."

"You're a bit of a villain, I suspect, Philip Goss." George was beginning to enjoy this young man's refreshing style. "Like to get your own way."

"Doesn't everyone? It's not difficult, you know. A bit of a tweak here, a word in an ear there, and it's amazing what you can achieve. Can I achieve anything for you now?" He gazed at her with his eyebrows raised, looking like a very intelligent robin.

"Hmm," George said. "Now it's my turn to do things your way, is it? OK. I want to talk to Dr. Jennings. Is she about?"

"She was. Should have been here till one, in case of any last minute GP referrals. We have this walk-in facility here for under-fourteens, between nine and one every morning. But she asked Alan Prior to hold the fort for her."

"Who?" George's brow wrinkled. She didn't know anyone of that name at Old East.

"Locum," Philip said. "Brought in to cover for—well, after that business with Dr. Rajabani."

George made a face. "Yes. Stupid of me, I should have realized…well, does he know where she went? I really do need a word with her."

"Ask him." Philip had turned his head to look over his shoulder at the big double doors that led into the main part of the ward. "Alan, here's Dr. Barnabas wanting to talk to Dr. Jennings."

He was, George decided, the most traditionally good-looking man she'd ever seen. Tall, blond, with a lick of glossy hair slipping over a wide forehead and very blue eyes. There was a cleft in the chin and a wide smile produced even deeper clefts in his cheeks. He was, George thought, tailor-made to set half the female hearts in the hospital fluttering and the rest pretending theirs weren't too, and she sighed at the thought. Men who looked like 1950s advertisements for chewing gum or Coca Cola were, in her estimation, totally uninteresting, and it annoyed her that so many silly girls disagreed with her views; but she made herself smile at him in as friendly a way as she could.

"Prue? She went off a little early for lunch. Had to deal with something at her bank, she said. Can I help you? Not that I really know what's going on here yet. If you need something important, then you'll have to ask Phil, he's the one who really runs this ward."

Philip chuckled and made for the desk so that he could start to put away the notes and rest of the impedimenta of the morning's outpatient session. As he passed Alan his hand touched the sleeve of his white coat, and Alan's hand came up and touched his bare arm where it was downy with dark hair under the short sleeve of his nurse's uniform. It was as though they'd whispered to each other, and George thought with a little stir of surprise: The girls might get into a flutter over this one but it won't get them anywhere if they do, and then was annoyed with herself for being surprised. It wasn't unusual that people were gay in hospital circles, any more than it was anywhere else.

"Did she say when she'd be back?" she asked as Philip set to work at the desk. Alan shook his head.

"I didn't ask. But we've a ward round at three. Dr. Kydd's teaching and—"

George said, "Damn!" loudly. "I've got a PM then. Well, will you tell her I wanted a word? Maybe I can come back later. Around six or so, if she's still here."

"I'll get her to let you know," Philip called from the desk. She thanked him and turned to go, but on an impulse of curiosity as the door swung closed behind her she glanced back through the central glass panel.

Alan Prior had gone over to the desk and was standing leaning over it, his head close to Philip's, and they were both laughing in that easy intimate way that lovers do. She nodded her head in self-satisfaction at this confirmation of her diagnosis and then went. It would have to be tonight for Prudence. Right now there were other questions to be asked elsewhere.

She thought about going to the canteen where most people would be at this time of the day and then opted to try a visit to Maternity. It had been quite a long time now since that note had been written and attached to the request form for the PM on baby Popodopoulos, but all the same someone had written it, and someone there might remember something about it if she asked again.

The central corridor of the unit was busy with food trolleys and strolling mothers wrapped in lacy quilted dressing gowns that made them look like galleons on the high seas, and she nodded in friendly response to the frequent "Hello, doctor!" greetings that her white coat earned her as she made her way down the length of it.

There was a totally different atmosphere in Matty, she decided, from any other ward at Old East. Here the patients weren't ill; they were often wildly excited or deeply depressed and sometimes in severe pain but however you looked at it, they were well women. And the babies too, generally speaking, were in good health. So there was much less of the undertow of fear and gloom that could pervade other wards where people were wrestling with diseases that at the very least hampered their lives and at worst might be threatening them. She enjoyed the ambience of Matty and let her shoulders relax a little.

There was no one in the main office and she went down the corridor to peep in through the labor ward door to see if there was someone there she could talk to, but the room was bustling and everyone's attention was obviously fixed on the patient in there. About to deliver, probably, George decided and turned away, disappointed. She'd chosen a bad time to try to do any questioning about a note written more than two weeks ago and long since forgotten by everyone, anyway. Her foray from her own department had been a total waste of time. She had garnered no information for Gus at all. In future, she thought a little dispiritedly, maybe I'd better stick to my last and let him do his job on his own.

She went back down the corridor but as she passed the office door again looked in, almost as an automatic act, and this time there was someone in there. A tall thin girl with a lot of crimped blonde hair springing around her shoulders, wearing a minute scrap of skirt and a tight breast-revealing sweater over long black leggings, had her head bent over the filing cabinet in the corner. George went in quietly and said, "Hello!"

At the sound of her voice the girl jumped as though she'd been bitten, yelping as she turned a long face towards George, a face which despite the lavish amount of make-up on it was clearly an unhappy one. The rather long uneven nose showed pink beneath the thick beige powder, and the eyes were red rimmed with recently shed tears as well as heavily darkened with a black pencil. She stood there staring at George with brimming eyes and shaking hands, and George, all compunction, came and took her by the elbow.

"Oh, honey, I didn't mean to make you jump like that. I'm so sorry if I scared you."

The girl shook her head miserably, and continued to stare at George, her eyes brimming with tears. "I'm sorry to get so—I mean, I'm not usually—It's just that it's all so—Ooh, I'm sorry. "S'all right, really it is…" She sniffed lusciously and dug one hand down her jumper between her magnificent breasts to pull out a grubby handkerchief to blow her nose and dab at her eyes. Even in her distress she remembered her make-up and was careful not to smudge it.

"Whatever's the matter, kiddo?" George was full of sympathy now. She took the girl's hand and led her over to the chair beside the cluttered desk in the corner. The girl didn't resist but went with her, her whole body sagging in a posture of utter dejection. George pushed back the typewriter that stood at the front of the desk to accommodate her own bottom and perched on it so that she could look down at the girl in the chair. She was now frankly crying hard, sniffing into her handkerchief.

"You'd better tell me about it," George said as the girl made no effort to speak. The girl lifted her head and looked up with a face so woebegone it was almost funny, but there was no doubt that the misery was real. George reached forwards and touched the girl's shoulder, which made her face crumple even more.

"Try not to cry, kid," George said hastily. "Or at least, not right now. Tell me what the problem is instead. If I can help…"

The girl shook her head. "I just can't seem to get over it," she said. Her voice was thick and husky at the same time. "I mean, it wasn't like it had been for a long time, you know what I mean? Only about a month, if that, but he was sorta nice, friendly like, and o' course—though my mum didn't think much of it all and I didn't dare tell my dad, the way he is about coloreds—like my sister said he *was* a doctor, after all. But it isn't that. It's just that—oh, it's all so…" And she shook her head miserably and wept more than ever.

"I'm not sure I understand," George said carefully, though she was beginning to think she might have an inkling. "Can you tell me a little more clearly?"

"It wasn't like it wasn't serious," the girl said piteously. "Even if it was only a few weeks. He said as he liked me more'n any girl he'd ever bin with—and like I said, it was the first time I'd bin with—I mean, Gary, he worked down in the electrician's shop but—well, he was *different*."

"Who was different, honey?" George said a little more firmly. "Who are we talking about?"

The girl sniffed, gulped and swallowed. "My boyfriend, Harry. Him what got killed. He was my boyfriend and I didn't think I'd ever be so upset about anything the way I am about him. Oh dear…" And she curled up so that her arms were across her knees, buried her head in them and gave herself to a veritable storm of weeping.

18

George was eventually able to soothe her by dint of much hugging and rocking as the storm of distress flooded itself away until at last the girl was just sitting in a sodden heap and sniffing gently. George gave her a final hug and then gently pushed on her shoulders so that she was sitting upright again.

"It was a dreadful thing to happen," she said. "And I know how you feel, truly I do. I'm—er—trying to find out how it happened, and why."

"There's been no end of talk about the place," the girl said drearily. "People saying he was killed by these racists and others saying he was probably pushing drugs the way that fellow was two years ago—that nurse what they caught with morphine down at the market—and that was why he was killed. I know he wasn't, he wasn't like that. And I couldn't say nothing because he'd made me promise I'd never let on we was going out because—" Again her face crumpled. "He wanted to tell his sister about us first. She lives in Holland and I promised him I wouldn't—and I thought, well he's dead now and I can't just go against what I promised, can I?"

"No," George said gently. "No, you were quite right to keep your word. What's your name? I can't talk to you properly without knowing your name, can I?"

"Cherry." The girl sniffed hard and seemed to get some of her control back. "I'm Cherry Lucas."

"And you work here in Maternity?"

Cherry shook her head. "Not exactly. I'm the secretary over on Fertility. It's sort of part of Maternity and not quite, know what I mean? They're always trying to use our rooms and Dr. Arundel, she always fights back like anything. You'd think our department didn't matter, but it does—it makes so many people happier than they could have been and—well." She stopped. "That's where I work."

"And a very important job it is," George said. "Cherry, if I ask you some questions about Harry, will it upset you?"

The girl looked at her miserably. "No," she said. "It'll make it easier, I think. The worst thing's been not being able to talk about him to anyone. It's like he wasn't ever here and I wasn't here with him, know what I mean? I can't talk to my mum and dad 'cause Mum'll only say good riddance and, like I said, Dad never knew, and my sister, she works over the other side of London and I don't get to see her that much and—it'll be nice to talk about him."

"Good," George said and squeezed the hot damp hand that lay in Cherry's lap. "It might help us to find out what happened to him."

"Was he killed deliberate, then?" Cherry looked up at her with her drowned blue eyes wide and sharp, and George thought, this child is a lot brighter than she may appear. "I didn't really believe it at first, when they all said and it was in the papers and on TV. I thought, just horrible violence, but then I wondered, was he killed deliberate by someone who was just after him, like?"

George hesitated. "Yes," she said at length. "Yes, I think he was. But we don't know why, and that's why I wanted to talk to you. Have you any idea who might have been—well, I suppose I have to say an enemy, though it sounds so dramatic, doesn't it?"

Cherry nodded. "That was the way I was thinking. He was so nice, Harry. So funny and—well, nice. I used to think he was ever so glamorous when I first saw him, just like that lovely actor in LA Law, know the one I mean? He's black and ever so handsome, and he's got a white girlfriend and—well, I used to see him and think, cor…I never thought he'd ask me out. But he did and I told you, I just flipped." Cherry looked dreamily at George and managed a smile. "He was good looking, wasn't he?"

"Very good looking," George said. "And I agree, he did look very like that actor. Was he like him in other ways? Like his character, I mean, getting involved in people's problems and so on?"

Cherry seemed almost to light up. "Oh, yes! I told my sister that, and she said I was just being silly and romantic. She's ever so practical, my sister, and she said getting hitched to a doctor could be the best thing I ever did, but not because of him being so handsome, but because of never being out of work, not like her boyfriend. He's in the printing and you know how things are for them now. She saves money all the time and she's—well, she doesn't think like me. But he was just like that lawyer, only better. Really cared about things. Used to worry about the children in Pediatrics, he did, all the time. He was always telling me about the way some of the parents were and getting all upset. His mum and dad had been really nice to him—they died when he was a kid, and it was his sister reared him—and he said to see the things these parents did to their children just made him so sick. Like that man who had a go at him over on Pediatrics that day. Harry said he was one of the worst. His kid told him—told Harry, that is—that his dad had interfered with him. I mean, how horrible can people be? And then the man threatened Harry and—oh, it's all so dreadful!"

"It is," George said. "Dreadful. Was Harry scared about Dave Ritchard? That was the man's name. Did he say there'd been any other threats?"

Cherry shook her head. "No, he wasn't bothered about him. It was bad at the time he said, but by that evening he'd got over it. Then on Friday I saw him in the canteen. At six o'clock. He said he'd pick me up and we'd go out for a drink or something at around nine. Only he never showed up." The tears began to well up in her eyes again.

"Nine?" George said. "Wasn't that rather late?"

"That's what I said." There was a ghost of indignation in Cherry's voice. "I said, why so late? And he said he had to see someone about something important and I said what, and he said he thought there was something a bit odd going on and I said well, what sort of odd? and he said it could be a really important thing only he had to get his facts right and he'd tell me all about it when he saw me. Only he never showed. I stood outside the medical-school gates, where we said we'd meet, till after half-past nine and then I went home in a real temper. I thought awful things about him and then next morning when I heard—Oh, my God." And once more the tears slid down her cheeks.

Outside in the corridor there was a rattle of trolley wheels as the last lunch waggon made its way out, and somewhere further along voices were raised as the labor ward door opened. George lifted her chin to listen, and then leaned over and took Cherry's hand.

"Cherry, I think we ought to get away from here. We can't talk easily. Have you had any lunch?"

Cherry shook her head.

"Then we'll skip away and get some. Come along."

The girl got to her feet obediently but George frowned and stopped. "Er, Cherry, what were you doing here? In the filing cabinet, I mean?"

"What?" Cherry looked back for a moment. "Oh, it was this file." She reached across and took a buff folder which she'd dropped on top of the cabinet when George had come in. "I thought I ought to tidy Harry's desk. I mean…" She bit her lip. "It'll sound daft, I s'pose, but he wasn't the tidiest of people, know what I mean? And I thought I'd kind of sort things out for him. There was a lot of notes in his room and I thought I'd take them all back quietly so that no one would think bad of him. He was always having people go on at him because he hadn't fetched notes back." The woebegone look had come back. "I don't want people saying anything more about him that's nasty. I already put back all of the pediatric ones. There was just this one for here." She turned back to the filing cabinet. "I'll slip it in now."

"May I see?" George said and reached out a hand. Cherry hesitated.

"What for? I mean, you're not—Which department are you? Are you here in Matty? Because I don't want to get Harry into trouble—"

George shook her head. "No, Cherry. I'm the pathologist here. I'm trying to find out what happened to Harry, remember? Maybe there's something there in those notes that might help. After all, he wasn't part of this department either, was he? He was a Pediatric Houseman, so why should he have Maternity notes in his room?"

"He used to come here a lot," Cherry said. "He told me. It was the best part of the job for him. Looking over the newborns to see they were all right." She looked down at the folder in her hand. "He got really upset when things went wrong for them. I told him he was much too soft for his own good. Not like the other doctors here."

George kept her hand outstretched but still Cherry hesitated. The noise in the corridor increased and George felt an urgency rising in her; it was suddenly very important to her to have those notes. But she said nothing, just looking at Cherry with her brows raised and after what seemed an eternity, but was less than a second or two, Cherry gave them to her.

"Great," George said as casually as she could. "Now some lunch. Come on." And she tucked the notes under her arm and shepherded Cherry out into the corridor.

Further along she could see Sister Lichfield in her labor ward greens talking to her staff midwives and she looked up as they appeared at her door. George waved a hand casually. "Won't stop now, Sister, I'll be back. Just a minor query," she called and began to walk along the corridor towards the exit doors, hoping Sister wouldn't notice Cherry walking in front of her. If she did, she would want to know what the girl was doing in her department, surely, and Cherry would tell her about the notes and Sister Lichfield would demand them back and George wanted to look at them…and then she relaxed her shoulders. This was becoming rather silly. All she had to do was tell Sister she needed the notes, whatever patient they belonged to, and promise to bring them back. And yet, and yet…

She tried to think why she was so concerned and then decided that it was due to over-developed suspicions—which at once took off again, running round and round in her head like the proverbial mice on wheels. Maybe it had been Sister Lichfield herself who had attached that note to the Popodopoulos baby's request form. Maybe it was Sister Lichfield who had something to do with the whole affair. Maybe—

Which was so absurd a thought she laughed aloud as she reached the double doors and followed Cherry through. Cherry looked back at her questioningly and George at once straightened her face and pretended it hadn't been she who had laughed; then took her to the canteen to give her some long-overdue lunch.

It was past two before the girl had pecked her lackluster way through a plate of soup which she swore was all she wanted, because she spent most of the time talking about Harry. That she had a deep need to do so was obvious; the words spilled out in a river and George listened and nodded and said nothing as the girl revealed all too vividly her sad little fantasy; of how she would marry her handsome Harry and leave behind the narrowness of the life she lived in a Rotherhithe council block with parents who did little more than watch TV and complain about the noisy bloody blacks in the next flat all evening, and a sister who though only in her late twenties seemed to be totally absorbed in being middle-aged, planning and penny-pinching and never wanting to do anything else. Certainly she had scant respect for Cherry's aspirations; her approval of Harry had been based solely on the value of his future earning capacity, but she had refused to meet him, "seeing he was colored, you see," Cherry said mournfully. And now the girl was alone again, with her fantasy in tatters, and it was hard to tell for what she mourned most, Harry himself or the plans she had painted around him.

She finished talking at last, her voice trailing away, and glanced at her watch and gasped and fussed at how late it was and how Dr. Arundel'd go mad if she didn't get her dictation typed up before five o'clock. She jumped to her feet, then she looked at George with her eyes once more full of the glitter of tears.

"You've been ever so nice to me," she said. "It was kind. Ta ever so."

George filled up with guilt. For the last half-hour she'd been aching for Cherry to stop talking and to go away so that she could settle down to studying the brown folder, which lay on the bench beside her looking innocuous but seeming to shriek its promise into George's inner ear. And now she was being thanked.

"That's OK, Cherry," she said a little awkwardly. "If you want to talk again, just call me at the path. lab and if I'm not there when you phone, they'll tell me and I'll find you. And meanwhile, I'm truly sorry for your loss." And she held out her hand to offer a consolatory handshake as she'd been taught to do for the bereaved in her childhood.

Cherry straightened her drooping shoulders and seemed to grow a little at that. "Thank you," she said with considerable dignity. "Thank you so much," and turned and went. George watched her and again the guilt rippled in her. Why are we all so bad at understanding what it is people need? she thought.

Just some recognition of her pain was all Cherry had wanted, and all I'm interested in is the puzzle and the fun of the hunt. I should be ashamed.

But common sense moved in. She couldn't be emotionally involved with all the people who were touched by death, even violent death. If she did she would find her own feelings in a permanent state of laceration and that would do no one any good, indeed make her useless. Better to do what she was there to do and concentrate on that.

She looked at her watch, took a large bite of her own neglected sandwich, and picked up the folder.

The tab was clearly written: "Chowdary, Angela." George frowned and spread the contents in front of her on the sticky Formica table.

It was all routine stuff. Angela had been referred from the Fertility Department at six weeks of pregnancy, and there was a précis of her previous treatment. George read through the sheets with their account of the use of Clomid and then of human gonadotrophin. They went on to describe the wearing trek through the tedious processes of IVF; timing the harvesting of the eggs, collecting the specimens from Viv, the husband, attempting the fertilization in vitro—and then at last when the eggs were fertilized their reimplantation. It appeared that there had been no remaining fertilized ova suitable for freezing for a second attempt should the first fail and that only one of the two implanted ova had proceeded to develop.

But Angela had become pregnant, and from then on the notes were a straightforward account of a serene and healthy pregnancy. Angela had sailed through it and enjoyed every stage; until the sad note at the end of the sheet of paper on which the findings of the child's first pediatric examination had been listed, reporting its death.

But that was not all there was in the folder. At the back, under a flap, there were half a dozen sheets of paper. They looked crumpled, as though they'd been thrown away and then rescued, and she smoothed them again as she sat and stared at them.

It was gibberish. Line after line of jumbled letters and symbols and numbers that had no significance at all to her. She closed her eyes for a moment and thought, "Oh, hell! Another code!" and then opened them again to stare at the paper.

The Oxford case, soon after she'd come to Old East, had thrown up a code. Breaking that had been part of the solution of the problem. It was too much to expect, surely, that someone else at Old East should now be using a sort of cryptogram?

She sighed and leaned back in her chair, thinking. Well, was it so odd? When the Oxford business had been sorted out the whole place had hummed with talk about it for months. Every single detail had been picked over, analysed and examined time and time again till each bone gleamed bare and polished. The fact that there had been a code must have been common knowledge. Maybe someone else here at Old East with a secret to hide and at the same time a need to make a record of something had got the idea of creating a code from that gossip?

Well, she thought, looking at the paper again, maybe or maybe not; the fact remains that here in this folder is a whole load of gibberish which might or might not be a code. If it isn't, why is it here? And she frowned as she looked at some of the lines.

OK OHRRFR
    YPG(CPLG OFR$
    £HL$CA, (LOFS y23$GP˝HS
    YF ¼ y1KOK6,

It looked frankly impossible, she told herself gloomily, sliding the papers back into the folder. She glanced at her watch. Half-past two. The PM was waiting to be done at three. Maybe if she went back to Pediatrics now she'd find Prudence Jennings? There was just time and she really did need to know what had happened that night the Oberlander baby was in the

department. Had Prudence's absence contributed in any way
to what had happened later to the child? Had it in any way
contributed to what had happened to Harry? But that was
foolish. She was grabbing for threads in what was a tangle
of major proportions and she really would have to stop being
so absurd. She got to her feet and went purposefully back to
Pediatrics.

This time she was lucky, and found Prudence Jennings. She
was sitting at the ward desk with a pile of notes in front of her,
her head down as she scribbled furiously. There was no one in
the play area at all; obviously everyone was bustling around in
the main ward getting ready for the Grand Round. Prudence
didn't look up as George came over and perched on the desk
beside her.

"I have to talk to you," George said bluntly. "About that
child, Oberlander, so called."

Prudence didn't look up. "I can't stop now. Kydd'll be here
in a minute for the ward round and I couldn't be more behind
with my notes. Some other time…"

"No," George said and was surprised at her own
intransigence. "I've been trying to see you for ages and you're
never around—I never see you about the hospital or anything—
and it's a simple question I have to ask. You went off duty and
left Harry Rajabani on his own when you were on call and
Miss Kydd away. Why? I'm not concerned about the way you
do your job, but I need to know if it had anything to do with the
Oberlander child."

This time Prudence looked up. She was pale and her red
hair looked bedraggled and dull. Her eyes looked red rimmed,
too; not from tears like Cherry, but with fatigue and, George
thought, illness. George frowned at the sight and said sharply,
"Are you OK?"

"No, I'm not," Prudence snapped with a little spurt of energy.
"I'm arse over elbows with work and I can't be interrupted."

"Well, you have been," George said. "Come on. Just tell

me." And she sat tight. There had to be some authority, she was thinking, in being a consultant and dealing with a more junior member of the medical staff.

"Oh, Christ," Prudence said and suddenly looked even whiter. George bent closer. The girl looked dreadful and instinctively George put out one hand to hold on to her, for she seemed about to fall forward with her head on the desk.

"Look, I'm sorry if—"

Prudence's eyes were closed and she was holding both hands tightly clenched against the desk in front of her. "Shut up, will you? I'm at the end of my rope and I can't—" She opened her eyes and stared up at George. "Oh, God, I suppose you'll go on until I tell you. If you tell anyone else I'll—" She took a deep breath. "I was pregnant."

"What?" George stared at her, nonplussed.

"Pregnant, damn you! I wanted to be very much. I was very happy about it. And then that night I started to bleed and—and—oh, sod it. I went home. OK? I didn't want to get any help here—Kydd told me when I started that she wanted total devotion to the job and made it very plain that if I let anything get in the way of it, I'd never get any sort of reference from her. This was—is an important job for me. Get this one out of the way and I can maybe apply for a consultancy in a minor hospital somewhere. I didn't dare let her know I wasn't in perfect health. All right? And that night—"

"Oh, hell!" George said. "I'm sorry. You miscarried."

Prudence stared up at her and said nothing and George made a grimace.

"Look, Kydd or not, you could have seen someone, surely? One of the others here would have helped you. How come your husband'—she glanced down at Prudence's naked left hand and amended it—"your partner didn't insist that you did? To sit it out alone in a state like that...How pregnant were you?"

"I have no partner. He left," Prudence said. "OK? He left when I started the baby. So I daren't lose this job and I daren't lose my reference. I have to earn—I had only two months of this job to go. If I could have hidden it that bit longer I could have made it. I know I could. But I miscarried. At twenty weeks. Oh, God." And she bent her head and George thought for a moment that she was weeping, as Cherry had done. But her eyes were quite dry. They just looked a little redder.

"So that's why you haven't seen me around. I'm doing all I can to cope as best as I can. I've got some retained products, I think. I need a D and C but I daren't go off sick. She'll be off again in a week or two and then I'll be able to—"

"This," George said strongly, "is the most goddamn crazy thing I have ever heard. You can't go on working in a state like that! You need proper care!"

"If you say a word to anyone about this I swear I'll—I'll stop trying. You meddle and I'll be over the edge and gone, I promise you!"

"I'm still going to meddle," George said. "And there's an end of it. And don't worry about Miss Kydd. Tough as she is, she doesn't scare me! Come on!" She slid off the edge of the desk to her feet and, with one firm lift, got Prudence up beside her. "We are going to A & E right now. And it's no use arguing about it."

19

"It's the sort of thing you expect from junior nurses," Hattie said. "Not from doctors! But she's clinically depressed, I suspect. Not thinking straight."

"Tell me something I don't know," George said. "Suicidal, too. Watch her, won't you? Look, need this get out? It's the one thing she was scared of."

"What do you take me for, George?" Hattie said indignantly. "Stop trying to teach your grandmother to suck eggs!"

"Ouch," George said. "Sorry. How can you stop the gossip, then?"

"Oh. Didier'll see her here in A & E instead of one of the A & E housemen. He's great—never says a word he shouldn't. If she needs admission and a D and C, which I strongly suspect she will, we can get her into the branch hospital at Rotherhithe. No one there'll know her and she can go in as plain Miss Jennings. Look, about dealing with Dr. Kydd..."

"Ah, yes," George put down her coffee cup and got to her feet. "I have to get back to my own department now, I've a post-mortem I should have started ten minutes ago. Tell Prudence I'll sort things out with Dr. Kydd. No need for her to worry. And I will, take it from me."

All through the post-mortem, which was a blessedly straightforward job demanding little extra in the way of concentration, Prudence and her problems milled around at the back of George's mind. Getting Dr. Kydd to accept her registrar's right to get sick shouldn't be too difficult, she told herself; what was bothering her was the way that the explanation of Prudence's absence from Barrie Ward the night the Oberlander baby was taken away by its parents effectively closed off any other investigation along those lines. It wasn't, she told herself as she weighed and measured viscera and dictated notes on her findings, that she had actually wanted to find out that Prudence was in some way involved in the death of the baby. It was just that she'd hoped, by finding out what had happened to Prudence that night, to be further along the road to understanding. But she wasn't.

It was maddening, she thought as she showered after finishing the PM. A murder had been done—indeed, two— and the perpetrators had vanished as surely as if they had been vaporized. Two people, merely by using a false name and address, that most corny of tricks, had managed to vanish too; yet there must be some way to track them down, some way of finding out how that baby had died. And why.

She was still thinking hard as she went back to Pediatrics to talk to Dr. Kydd, and it wasn't till she got to Barrie Ward that she gave any real thought to what she would say to her about her absent registrar. And decided to play it as it came. It would all depend on the way Dr. Kydd reacted.

In fact, Susan Kydd was not all that difficult. She was sitting at the nurses' desk in the play space just inside the big double doors, her head down over some notes and clearly oblivious to the noise the children were making as they belted each other with toys and cushions in the middle of the room. There was no sign of Sister Collinson, though Philip Goss was there; George smiled at him and he grinned back cheerfully as she picked her way through the small bouncing creatures who surrounded him.

"Oh, it's you, is it?" Dr. Kydd looked up at her and nodded sharply. "And what might you be doing around here? Do we have some sort of infection problems I don't know about?"

"Oh, I'm involved with a few more things than that!" George said, a little nettled, but thinking fast. Infection? An idea came to her. "I have to come over for consults from time to time."

"I know, I know. It's just that I'm damn near single-handed here and I know I didn't ask for a consult—and I doubt Prior would have the nous to do anything like that without asking me first. Drives me mad, he does. No initiative worth whistling at. So, what can we do for you?"

"It's Dr. Jennings," George said with a casual air, leaning against the desk. "It's my fault she wasn't here when you were ready to do your round this afternoon."

Susan Kydd frowned. "How do you work that out? Collinson told me she'd been taken ill."

"Precisely," George said smoothly. "That's the message I phoned and told her to give you. Thing is, Prue had been throwing up. She had every intention of staying at work, but I happened to notice—I walked into the canteen washroom and saw her, and got out of her what was going on. Diarrhea as well. Not a good idea in pediatric ward staff, you'll grant me."

"I'll grant you," Dr. Kydd said. "It's a bloody nuisance if it gets in here."

"That was what I thought, and what I told her, though she argued and fussed. Didn't want to leave her post and all that stuff, swore her hygiene would be adequate protection. But I'm afraid I pulled rank on her." She smiled widely and disarmingly at Susan. "Made it clear I'd throw every book there was at her unless she came to the lab at once and let me sort out specimens and do some checking. There's been some epidemic diarrhea in the community'—mentally she crossed her fingers, hoping Susan wouldn't check and find out that was a thumping great lie—"and I didn't want to take any chances. So, I've got her incommunicado till I've got my cultures done."

"Hmmph," Kydd said. "Well, nothing I can do about that, is there? Nor can Jennings, poor creature. I knew it had to be something important. She's a good girl, not one to play silly buggers with me or her job. Not like that damned Prior." She shook her head. "I don't know where they get their medical students these days. All I know is that the characters they're turning out for junior jobs are the pits. A few more good girls like Prue are what we need."

"You should tell her that," George said lightly. "It'd cheer her up no end. She's worried you'll be so mad over this that—um—well, that you'll be mad."

"Worried about her reference, is she?" Susan Kydd produced a look of sudden wisdom and knowingness that lifted her face into a semblance of good cheer. "Well, she needn't. Not that I'd tell her that, and nor should you, if you don't mind. Got to keep them up to the mark, these young ones. If you lay on the approval too thick they get lazy. Well, I can't stay gossiping here, I've got work to do if no one else has." And she got to her feet, swept her notes off the desk and with a sharp nod went through the inner doors into the ward.

Behind her Philip Goss laughed softly. "What a woman!" he said. "Tough as they come! Where would we be without her?"

"Hmph," George said, unwilling to discuss a fellow consultant with a nurse, however much she liked him. "So how are things here? Busy?"

"Not too bad," he said. "The usual winter crop of snotty noses and bronchitises—all these smoking mothers don't help—but we could be busier. Got a few empty cots."

"Good." George was heading for the door. "Better than being overworked."

"They'll close them, I dare say," Philip said bitterly, bending to sweep up a child from the floor just as she was about to fall and bang her head on a toy truck loaded with wooden bricks. "Now we're a Trust it seems they spend more time closing beds to save money than trying to keep them open to save lives."

She stopped at the door. "You're not keen on the new regime?"

"Is the Pope a Catholic?"

"It's early days yet, though, isn't it? It might turn out better in the long run. Self-government could mean less waste, a better service, all that stuff."

"It ought to, but what they're doing is trying to cut corners too much. They take on the worst sort of staff, pay them less and less and then wonder why the place is going downhill." He shook his head. "They need to think more about what they're doing. If you want an ace service you've got to have ace people to run it. Can't take on every rag tag and bobtail that turns up wanting a job, can you? But this Trust does—Whoops, come here, you little villain!" and he was gone, almost slithering across the floor in an effort to catch hold of a particularly active child who had decided to beat another less energetic one to a pulp.

George went back to the lab in a thoughtful frame of mind. She had never been particularly political at Old East; all during her first months here when there had been much talk of their application for Trust Status she'd held herself aloof. As an American, albeit one who'd lived and worked in Britain for over ten years, she'd felt she had no right to get involved, although she did admire the NHS she had worked in for so long. It was so generous, she had felt, so patient-centerd compared with the hospitals she had known at home, where the accounts department had equal status and probably greater value than that of the most life-saving of specialities. Now, though, even she couldn't ignore the restlessness that permeated the place as the inevitable cuts forced on to the Old East Board by the new NHS rules and financial structures led to redundancies and cuts in all directions. Her own job had been safe because not only was she a single-handed pathologist; she was also a sort of part-time consultant as far as Old East was concerned. Half her time was paid for by the Forensic Service, and that, she knew, always made her particularly attractive to the Dean and the rest of the senior financial people at the hospital.

But if young nurses like Philip Goss were getting so dispirited it was a bad thing. Perhaps, she told herself as she clattered into her department, hurrying to get out of the bitter December chill, I should talk to someone about this. Tell the Professor, maybe, of the sort of vibes I'm picking up. It can't be good for the place if dedicated nurses are losing their heart.

The light was on in her office and she knew at once why.

"Skiving off again, Gus?" she said as she walked in and he, in his usual perch in her tipped back chair with his feet comfortably propped on her desk, grinned at her above his folded arms.

"O' course. No fun bein' in charge if you can't swing the odd brick." He swung his legs to the floor and got up. "Before you ask, here's your chair, nicely warmed for you. I'll settle over here." He went and dragged the spare chair from its place by the wall, dumping the papers piled on it on the floor. "Anyway, for once I wasn't skivin." I was thinkin.'"

"Careful," she said, riffling through the little pile of messages Sheila had left on her desk. There was nothing urgent and gratefully she tucked them into her "Pending' clip. "You might do yourself a personal—"

"I love it when you speak my language. It shows you really care." He leaned down to look into her face, for her head was still bent over the papers on her desk. "Hey, look at me! I'm talkin' sweet nothin's at you!"

She looked up at him and laughed. "And I never noticed! OK, I'm all ears. So, you're thinking! What about?"

"You," he said promptly. "And me. On a desert island somewhere where the water's a rich, silky blue, and the rum punches are satin on the tongue and the sky's like azure velvet and—"

"Sounds like a robbery in a dress shop," she said. "Start again. What were you thinking about?"

"Why do I try? It's like reciting poetry to a concrete wall.

Woman's got no soul, that's her trouble. OK, here's what I've been thinking. I'm stymied, that's what."

"Stymied?" She lifted her brows at him and settled herself comfortably in her chair. "Now you're speaking my language!"

"All right. In English then. Balked. Halted. Trammeled. Stopped in me bleedin' tracks." He looked at her gloomily. "I'd never have believed it could be such a bugger. Not a thing on the Oberlander baby front. It's like no one anywhere saw a thing, no one anywhere noticed a kid going adrift, no one nowhere—you get the picture. Then there's the car, the one that did for Harry Rajabani. Do you think we can get a lead on that? Can we bloody hell! There's not a garage nor a lock-up this side of the river we haven't checked—and the other side too. We've got as far as we can short of checking every single vehicle in the country for traces on wheels and bumpers, and that's just not possible. And then there's the business of the STD clinics—remember? GUM clinics they call them now. I said we'd check all of them for a mum who might be HIV positive—well, there aren't that many, thank God—at least that are known. And we've been through every sort of hoop we can to check on them and we've got nowhere there, either. So, like I said, stymied. Up the creek without the old proverbial. Now what?"

He gazed at her with an expression of wry gloom on his face but she wasn't beguiled. He really was feeling bad about the situation.

"Not your fault, Gus," she said. "Nor your guys." I'm sure you've done all you can. I'm just as stymied as you. Prudence, remember? Why did she vanish the night the Oberlander parents whipped their child away under Harry's nose?"

He lit up hopefully, and she shook her head. "I told you I'm stymied like you. It's, well—there's a personal reason for her vanishing the way she did. It's a true bill, I've checked it and there's no way she's covering up anything. I'll say just that she was sick, no more. And there's not a hint of anything to tie her into the Oberlander baby's death. So, there you are."

"Nothing, then," he said.

Now she smiled, a long slow stretching of her whole face. "Not entirely nothing, as it happens. Not *entirely.*"

"You've got something." He sounded accusing. "You were going to hide it from me, but you've changed your mind."

"How do you know that?" She was genuinely startled.

He winked. "I told you. I like clever women. And for why? Because I'm a clever bloke. And there was something there in the way you looked…Anyway'—he became practical—"if you'd meant to tell me you'd have done it already. You're not one to wait your turn, not usually."

"Maybe I won't tell you after all."

"Don't be a silly cow," he said amiably. "Now you've started you'll have to finish. It'd drive you potty not to tell me now, and we both know it."

She sighed and reached beneath the pile of notes on her desk—was there a desk anywhere in Old East that wasn't so decorated? she wondered—and pulled out the Chowdary file.

"OK. I have picked up something. I did think of having a go on my own but—well, listen." And she told him at length of her conversation with Cherry Lucas and the finding of the notes, and when she'd finished talking, pulled out the crumpled pieces of paper and pushed them over to him.

He crouched over them like a cat with a freshly caught mouse and almost purred. "A code. Oh, I do love a code! It's sort of classy, know what I mean? Something really to get your head into."

"It's weird, though, isn't it? That there should be another, I mean, after the Oxford case."

He shook his head. "Not that weird. People use private codes all the time. Try reading the Valentine's Day messages in the paper next February. And you ought to see the sort of notes some of my lads make. I have to teach "em to be comprehensible to outsiders, on account of their notebooks are used in evidence. Now, let's look at this one."

He began to read the symbols aloud. "OHRRFR YPG…
Hey, that's a new wrinkle!"

"What is?"

"They're usually letters or numbers or mixed, but I've
never seen one before that uses a half bracket! Hmm. CPLG
OFR$. Blimey, a dollar sign, no less! OFR$ £HL$ CA.
Good, sterling gets a look in., (LOFS y23$GP" "HS. This is
ridiculous, commas, quote marks and all sorts." He sighed.
"How many lines like this are there?" He counted. "Blimey.
It'll take more'n a computer to crack this one."

"That's what I thought. I spent ages over it but gave up."

"Let me take the pages away. Then I can put our boys on it
and you can—"

"No! I want to have a go. There are ways of decoding—I've
heard of decoding books, haven't I? I think so. You can't have
them!"

"Split the difference?" he offered amiably. "Photocopy?
You keep the original, I'll take the copies. Fair dos?"

She thought for a while. "Fair enough. I'll get them copied
tomorrow." She held out her hand and he gave her the sheets,
though clearly unwillingly. "I promise to send them over as
soon as I can."

"Bring them over. Then I get to see you," he said, leering
horribly. "I like seeing you."

"You'll be seeing me all day over Christmas," she said and
suddenly, to her own amazement, went a little pink. "It was
good of you to let the old ladies have their way. They've been
fluttering around like—"

"A brace of daffy hens, I can imagine. But I wasn't letting
them have their own way at all. I wasn't being good either. I
was being bloody sensible. It's the best Christmas offer I've
ever had." He beamed. "I haven't looked forward to Christmas
much for years. I usually spend it on my own or on duty and—"

"You're putting me on!" She looked at him closely. "You're
just trawling for sympathy."

"No, I'm not! If I were, you'd get a better story than that. It's true. Been on my own for—well, it doesn't matter." He was grim now and didn't look at her, shrugging into his coat a little fussily. "Anyway I'm looking forward to Christmas with you three. It'll be a gas. I've been shopping my head off today—and you won't be able to argue on account it's the festive season. Bloody marvellous."

He was at the door now, with his hand on the knob. "I leave you with just one thought."

"Yeah?"

"You say Prue's right out of the running on account of she's sick, was sick that night?"

"Yes."

"And it's a true bill—no chance she's putting it on?"

"None at all."

"Well, OK. But that doesn't mean she mightn't still be involved, does it? She was the one who saw the kid first. She was the one who spotted there was something odd about the child's age."

"So?"

"So, it could all be an elaborate cover-up. It won't be the first time people have tried it on that way. I doubt it'll be the last."

She shook her head firmly, but all the same, a worm of doubt began to wriggle inside somewhere. "I'm sure she's out of it."

"Well, if you say so. But think about it. Let me quote good old Oliver Cromwell to you, if I haven't already—"

"You have," she cried hastily, but it was too late.

"'I beseech you,'" he was intoning. "'In the bowels of Christ, consider it possible you—may—be—mistaken.'"

And he was gone.

20

By the end of the week and Christmas Eve, the hospital seemed to have blossomed into a flurry of balloons and tinsel-trimmed trees and glitter. Sheila and Jerry had put up a tree in the lab, bedecking it with strings of lametta, and already had a festive bottle of sherry and a tin of chocolate digestive biscuits on the go, even though the department still had a great deal of work to get through before the day was out. But they seemed to be working as hard as ever and George prudently said nothing about the biscuit crumbs among the slides. She had to trust them to make sure they did no harm, the place couldn't function otherwise; and her trust wasn't usually misplaced.

In the mortuary Danny, displaying a sublime inability to recognize any incongruity in his actions, had threaded strings of red and green aluminum foil streamers through the handles of the great drawers that held the bodies in the cold room and she had to remonstrate with him. He sulked, of course, but cheered up marginally when she agreed to let him put some holly in the dissection room. No one but hospital people or police ever went there after all; not like the rooms where the bodies were, where it was always possible a relation might have to come to make an identification.

By the time she'd dealt with all that and cleared her morning post, which was blessedly light of any real work though it produced a blizzard of Christmas cards (much to her discomfiture, most of them came from people to whom she'd forgotten to send one of her own) she had time to think about other things.

First she checked again on Prue Jennings and was assured by Hattie Clements she was fine.

"Tucked up in Rotherhithe, just another patient. No one's spotted her as one of our medics at all. Needed a D and C and will probably be able to go home this evening. She's got a mum and dad to go to—I've checked on that—so she'll be all right. Have a good Christmas, George! Doing anything nice? We're having people wandering in and out all through Boxing Day, Sam and I'd love to see you."

"I'll try," she said, "but I've got my ma and a sort of aunt staying."

"Bring them too," Hattie said heartily. "The children'd love to see you, and they like old ladies. Bring anyone you want." George promised she would try and turned her attention to the Chowdary file.

She couldn't keep it here in the path. lab for much longer. It ought to go back to Maternity, and from there eventually to the Registry. She decided the best way to get it back there was via Cherry. She had, after all, some reason to go nosing among the files in the cabinet there in a way that George certainly did not. So she picked it up, put her head round the lab door (pretending not to notice that they had a radio on playing Christmas carols) to tell them they could bleep her if she was needed, and headed for Fertility.

The Maternity Ward, as she cut through it, struck her as being the most ferociously decorated place in the entire hospital. No fewer than three Holy-Family-and-the-Crib scenes had been set up at intervals along the main corridor; there were streamers and paper bells and balls everywhere; and a vast tree just beside the entrance. The place smelled odd with its mixture of disinfectant and milk and pine needles, but not unattractive, and for the first time she felt a lift of the old here-comes-Christmas excitement. Maybe tomorrow with Ma and

Bridget and Gus was going to be fun after all. Getting presents for them all had been a hectic affair, carried out in a couple of desperately busy lunch hours. Sometime this afternoon she had to get the things wrapped to take home for the small tree that she knew Bridget and Vanny were decorating this evening; and she pushed open the door that led into the Fertility Clinic feeling light-hearted and happier than she would have thought possible.

And lost it all when she found Cherry drooping over her desk in the cubby hole that was dignified by the label, "Secretary's Office', next door to Julia Arundel's room. There was no sign of Julia, and only a few dispirited-looking people were sitting on the chairs that lined the narrow corridor, plainly waiting to enter the small room at the far end which was the consulting room. There was a bored-looking nurse checking files on a table at the far end, but she didn't look up as George came into the unit.

"Feeling low again, Cherry?" George said, coming to stand beside the girl, who looked up at her with eyes as red rimmed as they had been the last time she'd seen her.

"It's Christmas," Cherry said. "It wouldn't be so bad if it wasn't Christmas. We was going to the theater on Boxing Night. *Cats*. I was looking forward to it ever so."

"It will get easier," George said and touched her shoulder. "Not at once, but eventually. It helps to think of other things."

"I try to," Cherry said, straightening her back. "It's not easy though—not here. We've been so quiet—running the clinics down a bit, you see. The Board says they've got to make cuts on Matty, and we're part of Matty when it comes to the budget so of course we get the dirty end of the stick." She was obviously quoting her boss. Her voice even became more clipped, like Julia Arundel's. "It's disgusting that so many unhappy people are forced to wait even longer because of bad management by the finance people. They just don't take infertility seriously enough, that's the problem."

"So you haven't as much to do as you'd like."

Cherry nodded. "That's right. Well, I'll start knitting something maybe. That'll help. I could do with a new sweater."

"That's a great idea," George said. "You could do some thick leg-warmers to match—the ones you wear over your tights, you know, and you make the sweater big and baggy and wear it without any trousers or skirt, like a sort of troubadour of old."

Cherry lightened considerably. "Yeah—yeah, that'd be great! I'll do that. In nice strong colors, maybe."

"You could get some of that hand-spun wool they sell in Covent Garden market, in mixed-up colors," George said, watching the girl's eyes kindle with interest. "I was given one like that once, long ago. It was knitted for me."

Vanny had made it, she remembered. She still had it at the bottom of her chest of drawers. It had been a fabulous sweater.

"Oh that's a super idea!" Cherry said and for the first time since George had met her she managed to smile and impulsively George bent over and hugged her.

"You're a great girl, Cherry," she said. "Very brave. Now, listen…" She pulled away as Cherry, pink with gratification, straightened up. "I have the Chowdary file here. It ought to go back, hmm?"

"Oh, yes please!" Cherry said. "I've been worrying about that so much. If someone wanted it and they see it's signed out to Harry—well—I'd hate that. I'll put it back then, shall I?"

George handed it over. "Yes please. But Cherry…" She hesitated. "There was something else in there—those papers you found, remember. With added things on them. They're nothing to do with the file so I've kept them. I doubt there'll be any problems."

"Oh, I'm not worried about that," Cherry said. "I only put them in there because I found them underneath, know what I mean? I just thought maybe—" She stopped. "There were some other bits too."

George sharpened. "There were?"

"Well, sort of. A notebook really. There wasn't much in it. Just a few dates. Oh, and something else…" She reached into the drawer of her desk and fiddled about and then brought out a small notebook. It had a red marbled cover, and was very dog-eared. It looked, George thought, exactly like the sort she used to have at school, when she was very young, for her spell-checks.

"I didn't know what to do with this. It's hard to know if it's important, isn't it?"

George looked inside. The first page had, as Cherry had said, what were obviously dates. 14 Jul., 27 Oct., 1 Dec. After the last of them was a hieroglyph and she peered at it. The handwriting was far from clear, being elongated yet crabbed, and she turned the notebook closer to the light to try to read it.

"His writing was awful," Cherry said fondly. "Just like he was practising to be the sort of doctor who writes bad prescriptions everyone laughs at, I used to tell him. Shall I look? I sort of got used to it."

George held it out and Cherry looked. "Oh, that bit? I tried to read that too. It's all sorts of initials, "n't it? I think it says 'W to PL re PM TH 2.' But I don't know what it means."

George looked at it and frowned, then lifted her chin and stared sightlessly at the far wall, on which a sad calendar hung crookedly against the grimy cream-colored paint. "'W to PL re PM TH 2'" she said aloud. "'W to PL re PM TH 2.'" It almost says something, I know it does. It's important, too and yet…" she frowned and tried to focus on the calendar, more as a way of sharpening her thinking than because she wanted to check any dates, and then it happened.

It was something that had happened only a few times in her life before but when it had, it left her overawed at the way her own mind worked, made her wonder at the sort of synaptic connections that had leapt into action to make the whole thing possible. Twice before it had happened during an examination when a conclusion she desperately needed to illustrate her answer had eluded her, and some minor wording on the page, or some object around the room when she had stared about her in desperation, had triggered her mind; whatever had caused it to happen she was always able to use the information, and it had never been wrong.

This time was like the others. The calendar sitting crookedly on the wall looked back at her announcing its information. Rows of numbers from one to thirty-one. Numbers set in neat columns of seven. Each column headed by a letter, M, T, W, Th, F, S, Su, and she looked again at the notebook, and knew at once what the letters there stood for. "Something to path. lab re post-mortem on Thursday the second of December," she said. "He wrote that note—"

"What?" said Cherry.

"When the request came down for a post-mortem on the Popodopoulos baby, there was a typed note attached to it. It said, "This is the third infant death we've had in Maternity since the summer? Linked?" I've been trying to find out who wrote that note and everyone denies any knowledge of it. But I think that Harry sent it. 'W' means Warning or maybe Word—either would do. Warning to path. lab re post-mortem on Thursday the second of December. Word to path. lab...It certainly fits the date. That was the morning the baby was found dead—the Popodopoulos baby." She was talking as much to herself as to Cherry. "And these dates—they fit the other deaths. The Lennon baby died on 14 July, the Chowdary baby on 27 October, and the Popodopoulos baby on 1 December. I'm sure that was how it was. I'll have to check, but I'm sure I remember."

She turned to the door and then stopped and looked back at Cherry uneasily. "Urn. This is all - I mean, I'm not sure what happened to Harry, Cherry, but I think someone was after him. I think he'd found out something that another person wanted kept secret. And I think it ought to be kept secret still. What do you think?"

As Cherry looked back at her, her smooth brow slowly creased and her eyes sharpened. "You mean someone definitely murdered Harry? And might want to murder anyone else what knows?" she breathed.

George shook her head and spoke in as bracing a tone as she could. "Oh, no! Nothing so dramatic. But I do think there's been something going on here that needs investigating, and it'll be easier to do so if no one knows that I'm checking. And I might need these notes a little longer after all. Could I keep them just a few more days? I promise to bring them back very soon."

Cherry looked doubtful, but George wasn't going to give in on this. She reached for the folder and again tucked it beneath her arm. "I'll bring it back soon," she said again. "Meanwhile, can I trust you to say nothing to anyone outside ourselves about all this? I mean, the notebook and the notes in it and –'

"I'll be as silent as the grave!" Cherry almost declaimed it, her eyes alight with fervor, apparently quite won over by George's determination to keep the Chowdary folder. "Not a word will anyone get out of me."

"No need to be so, well, dramatic, Cherry. Just don't talk about it."

"Don't talk about what?" Julia Arundel had appeared at the door and George turned to smile at her.

"Oh, it's the Christmas parry they're doing in Pediatrics," she lied easily. "I'd like to get involved and I came by Matty to see if 1 could get hold of some stuff to decorate a costume. To amuse the kids, you know? They hadn't anything and they sent me through to Cherry here. Thought she might have some gear. She doesn't, I'm sorry to say." She looked at Cherry and smiled even more brightly. "So, there it is! 1 guess I'll have to try elsewhere. But it's a secret, of course. 1 don't want everyone to know or the surprise'll be gone. I'll tell you, though—1 want to dress up as the Statue of Liberty."

"Such fun!" Julia said, staring at her as though she were quite mad. "I don't get involved with all this stuff myself, but good luck with it. Cherry, could 1 have the files from yesterday afternoon, please? 1 may be able to get the letters to the GPs dictated before lunch."

"Oh, yes, Dr. Arundel," Cherry said with a demure air. She picked up her notebook and hurried out into the corridor. "Right away."

She disappeared after Julia into her adjoining office, turning her head to give George a sketch of a wink as she did so, and George relaxed. There was no need to worry about Julia Arundel, but all the same the less that was known about the way her mind was working the better.

As the door closed behind the two of them she opened the Chowdary file and checked the address. Seventy-five Caspar Street, Bermondsey; not far away at all. She bit her lip as she thought and then, moving purposefully, looked at her watch and made her way back to the path. lab and her outdoor clothes at a swift lope.

The house, when she got there, told her a lot about the Chowdarys. She stood in the street looking up and down as well as at the front of number seventy-five, her hands thrust deep into her pockets. Her bleep was warm against her hand and it comforted her; they could get her back to the hospital quickly if necessary. It was only a fast jog over Tower Bridge and it was odds on she'd be able to find a cab anyway; she pushed away the pangs of guilt about leaving the hospital without just cause when she was on duty and looked again at the house.

The whole street had obviously been gentrified to the utmost. The little working men's cottages that had been built a hundred or more years ago had been emptied of their original tenants, tricked up with heavy oak front doors, brass knockers and carriage lamps and a great deal of pastel paint on the old window frames, and resold, probably at absurdly inflated prices. The windows themselves were filled with glowing white net curtains and expensive cars were parked outside many of the houses; she spotted three BMWs within forty yards as well as a couple of Mercedes.

Number seventy-five looked as prosperous as any of the others; even more so, perhaps, for it had bright window boxes filled with glossy-leaved plants and was clearly the habitation of people who regarded themselves as tasteful in the extreme. She rang the bell, which made an old-fashioned clamor inside the house, with some trepidation. Maybe they wouldn't want to talk to anyone from the hospital where they had been made so unhappy...

The man who answered the door was square and stocky, with a neat moustache over narrow lips. His hair had receded to vanishing point on his crown, but his side hair was rich and thick and dark. He was wearing a cashmere sweater over a silk shirt, expensively cut slacks and leather loafers that looked very comfortable indeed. The smell that came out from the warm interior was of whisky and good cigars and expensive food and she could see beyond him to an expanse of silk wallpaper and thick carpets and pale blonde furniture.

"Can I help you?" His voice was low and pleasant and what she knew the British usually called cultured, which meant he sounded like a Radio Three announcer.

"I'm probably all wrong coming here, Mr. Chowdary," she said. "You are Mr. Chowdary? It's just—I'm Dr. George Barnabas. From Old East."

He stared at her with a smooth face devoid of any expression. "I am Viv Chowdary. Why are you here?"

"I—" She caught her breath, furious with herself. She should have thought this out more carefully. Coming at all had been mad. She began to extemporize a little wildly. "I was thinking about your loss, and it seemed to me, well, it isn't easy at Christmas, is it?"

He looked at her for another several seconds until she thought he was about to close the door in her face and then his look softened. "You are kind. Come in. I'm afraid my wife is out, visiting her mother, but I'm happy to see you. Come in."

The room he took her into was richer and warmer even than she had suspected it would be. The carpet was thick, the sofas deep and soft, the walls lined with books, the ornaments costly. He was very hospitable, offering her drinks, almost embarrassed to give her the tonic water which was all she wanted, and then he sat down in the deep leather armchair on the far side of the fireplace where gas flames leapt convincingly in a pile of artificial logs. He cocked his head on one side. "So. What do you want to say?"

"That I'm sorry your baby died." She wasn't extemporizing now. She meant it. This room was so very tidy, so obviously the habitation of two adults. She could imagine how much they had wanted their baby to fill this slightly arid ambience.

"You are most kind," he said with great dignity. "I appreciate it. I am sure my wife will too, when I speak to her of your visit."

She sat and looked at him for a long moment, with no idea of what to say next, and when the words came out of her mouth, she was almost surprised.

"It wouldn't have been so bad for you if you could have had a photograph," she said. "I wish that had been possible."

He smiled, a small secretive little curving of the rather red lips under the narrow moustache. "Ah, well now. Perhaps I should not tell you this—you are a colleague of Dr. Arundel?"

"Oh no. I mean yes in that we both work at the hospital, but not together. I'm—the—I'm in the laboratories." (I hope he doesn't connect me with post-mortems, she was thinking at the back of her mind. Horrible for him if he does.) "So I don't see much of her. I just know she likes to have pictures of—of all the babies born out of her department and, well, of course, with your baby it just wasn't possible."

He got to his feet and went across the room to a desk in the corner, a modern replica of an old Victorian design with little drawers and shelves all over the high back. He reached into one of the drawers and came back with an envelope.

"I took one," he said. "I was there in the labor ward when they were doing things and our baby was lying there in the scales of the weighing machine, you know, and I took a Polaroid. It's all we have."

He opened the envelope and held out a little square of pasteboard to her. She reached out her hand and took it almost reverently. And found herself looking down on the picture of a baby. Parts of the picture were blurred—clearly the child had been kicking so the legs couldn't be easily seen. But the rest of her was clear and leapt out of the picture at her. She had a cap of short dark hair and dark eyes which stared out serenely from a small round face. The hands and arms were streaked with vernix, the greasy yellowish skin-protection substance babies have in utero, and her face was a little blood-streaked. So, it seemed, was her body; across her chest was a long reddish mark. George looked at it, then said, "She was lovely. Really lovely."

"I know," Viv Chowdary said. "That is what made it so hard. She looks so—so normal. Except for the little mark and they told me that would fade eventually."

"Mark?" George said.

"On her chest. There, you see? I mentioned it to the doctor—what was his name? Like a station on the Paris metro. Oh, I know. St Cloud, Dr. St Cloud. I said to him she has a mark, is it the birth, was she injured? Will it go? And he said, oh, it's a strawberry nevus, it will fade before she is two years old, even sooner. But it never got the chance to fade, did it?"

He took the picture back and looked at it for a long moment, and then put it back tidily in the envelope. "But she was beautiful," he said softly and took the envelope back to the desk.

"Mr. Chowdary," George said and she hoped her voice was sounding normal still. "Why didn't you let Dr. Arundel have a copy of that photo for her wall of successful cases? She told me she was so sorry not to have one."

"But it was not a successful case, was it?" He was all sweet reason. "My baby died."

"Yes, she died." George stood up. "And I offer you my deepest condolences in your trouble." And she held out her hand and shook his as he bent his head courteously and led her to the door.

"I hope—I hope it will be possible for you to have another baby, Mr. Chowdary," she said as they reached the front door and he opened it. The street outside looked bleak and cold, for rain was threatening. "Dr. Arundel said you'd be able to try."

"As to that, who can say? It is in the hands of the Good Lord, but we are thinking, Angela and I. Thank you again." And gently but definitely he urged her forwards and the door closed behind her, leaving her staring down the street with its brassy little carriage lamps and windows winking with Christmas lights. Her head was in a whirl and she was trying hard to understand what had happened.

Because in the PM report on the Chowdary baby there had been no mention of a strawberry nevus on the baby's chest. And surely any pathologist worth the name would have made a note of it?

"I have to check with whoever actually did the job," she said aloud to the street. Because if whoever it was missed that, whatever else might he have missed? Maybe there was something done to that baby that we don't know about? Maybe this baby too, like the Oberlander child, was deliberately killed? As Harry obviously suspected.

A car came round the corner and parked beside the first house. The door opened and a delivery man jumped out. He left his door ajar and the car radio, turned up to top blast, echoed down the street. "The cattle are lowing,"" roared the invisible singers. "The baby awakes…"

George pulled her collar up around her ears and headed north back to Tower Bridge and Old East. Christmas and dead babies. They didn't go together at all.

21

She was woken on Christmas morning by the smell of turkey roasting and lay curled up in the tangle of her duvet letting memory roll over her like a sea fog. The Christmases of her childhood had always started so; her mother would get up in the middle of the night—or so it had seemed to small George— to creep down to the kitchen and start the oven. "Because," she would tell the loudly complaining Oscar, "roasting it slow and easy makes it more toothsome and you'd sure complain if I did it any other way." George had spent every Christmas morning of those long-ago years lying listening to her parents bicker downstairs and smelling turkey cook; or had it been on Thanksgiving? Suddenly she couldn't remember, and didn't want to remember; today would be different, she told herself, however familiar the smells, and she threw back the duvet and padded off to the bathroom to shower and dress. It wasn't much fun having to sleep in her living room, but she was getting used to it.

By the time she had finished dressing, climbing into a new pair of vividly black-and-white striped leggings which made her seem taller than ever in spite of being worn with flat blocked ballet shoes, topping them with a baggy scarlet shirt that she knew made her look particularly good, Bridget had cleared away her bedding and set the studio couch back into its usual be-cushioned state. She'd lit the gas-flame fire, too, and brought in a big crimson poinsettia in a pot and set it on the coffee table where it spread itself wide and glowed gloriously in the dim December morning.

"Happy Christmas, honey," she said, coming to kiss George, her skin soft and papery against George's firm cheek. "We want you really to relax today. Vanny and I are going to do everything, just everything. We're well ahead in the kitchen so you sit down and take it easy."

She reached for the record player and pushed a switch, and the sound of Lalo's "Symphonie Espagnole' seeped into the room. George felt her eyelids prickle. They had taken so much trouble, to the extent of making sure her favorite music was playing; it was very generous and, impulsively, she hugged Bridget.

"And a Happy Christmas to you too, love," she said. "And if you think I'm letting you take over my kitchen then you sure as hell have another think coming. Move over, I'm coming through!" and she led the way into the kitchen with her arm about Bridget's shoulders.

Her mother was standing at the stove, stirring something, and George went over and kissed the back of her neck, which was pink and damp with the heat and concentration on what she was doing.

"Happy Christmas, Ma," she said. "It really has the good old down-home smell in here, it's great!"

"It will be," Vanny said serenely. "As long as you stay outa here and let me get on. Bridget, give George her coffee and juice and that Danish and then come back in here and deal with those potatoes. Gus'll be here in no time and I want to be primped up and ready when he comes."

George tried to protest, but got nowhere. The two of them were far more adamant than she was and wouldn't hear of her doing a thing, and at last she gave in, for they were getting more and more heated over her attempts, and she went and sat curled up on her sofa, with a pile of long neglected BMJs and Lancets beside her; she wasn't working, she assured them both, truly she wasn't. Only reading the funny bits.

The morning drifted away in an increasing kaleidoscope of food smells and heat, and as the warmth built up, she was unable to hold her lids open. They'd gone to bed late the previous night, what with the dressing of the tree (which now looked well worth all their efforts as it shimmered proudly in the darkest corner of the room) and the last weeks had been a strain. Now she could relax the inevitable happened, and she fell asleep.

She awoke with a start, throwing her arms out and flailing widely in her alarm. Gus was standing over her, rubbing one cheek with an aggrieved look on his face.

"Hey," he said. "I only bent over you, for Gawd's sake! Just to see if you was really asleep or just restin' your eyes. You didn't have to do that!"

"Do what?" George said, still dazed.

"Hit me from here to Christmas next year," he said and grinned. "Here's to a Merry Christmas this year, anyway."

He looked, she realized, like a stranger. The familiar crumpled suit and tie and overcoat were gone; in their place he was wearing elegantly cut black trousers and a scarlet cashmere sweater over a very white shirt, which was open at the collar showing thick muscles and a broad strong neck. His hair had been carefully brushed but with no effort at the control it usually had when he was working it curled with great abandonment all over his head, so he looked like a raffish and far too knowing middle-aged cherub.

"Happy Christmas," she said and rubbed her eyes. "I didn't hear you ring."

"I didn't have to. Your ma and Bridget were watching for me from the window and didn't give me time. Bridget was down and had the door open as I walked up the steps." He beamed at her. "Soul mates, ain't we? I always said we had a lot more in common than you'd credit."

"How do you mean?"

"Matching," he said contentedly and patted his scarlet belly. "Red and white and black. Very fetching."

Bridget came bustling in from the kitchen bearing a tray with four of George's best custard glasses on it. Each was filled with a steaming pinky-red concoction and Bridget fussed happily, making them each take one and then calling Vanny, pink and perspiring, from the kitchen to take hers.

"Here's to Christmas and happy times," Bridget proposed and took a heavy draft. "And there's plenty more where this came from."

It was potent and spicy and George coughed. Bridget beamed.

"The real stuff, huh? Drink up and I'll fetch more." And she hurried Vanny away and left them.

"My God," Gus said and sipped his glass carefully, holding the handle between his square fingers with great delicacy. "This is lethal." He raised his voice. "What's in the block-buster, Bridget?"

"My own recipe," Bridget sang from the kitchen, the pride in her voice very clear. "A little red wine and brandy and so forth!"

"And so forth," Gus called back and shook his head. "Half a distillery if you ask me." He sat down on the leather footstool at George's feet, for she had curled herself back into the corner of the sofa. "So, how goes it, George? Did you get straight with all your work before the dreaded holiday descended?"

"Not quite," she admitted. "I had to set aside all the stuff we'd been busy with." She made a face. "I got everything else done though, so at least I'll be able to get right back on it, with a little luck, come next week…"

He lifted his brows. "You don't have to be so nose to grindstone, you know. Not for me. We can manage well enough, if you've—"

She bristled. "Trying to cut me out? I won't have that—"

He sighed with an elaborate show of patience. "Let me finish, let me finish! I was about to say, if you've other things to do, we'll hang on till you're free. Then we can look at that code together."

"Oh," she said, a little mollified, feeling her face go pink. She put it down to the hot punch, which she was sipping steadily, for potent though it was it also tasted marvellous. "Sorry."

"That's a step in the right direction," he said and leaned forwards.

In the kitchen Bridget was chattering as usual and Vanny was singing in a high sweet voice "...off with the raggle-taggle gypsies, oh," and nearer at hand the gas flames hissed and plopped in the fireplace. His face looked remarkably large, she thought with a remote dreaminess. I can see right into his eyes. They've got sort of amber flecks in them. I think this punch is doing odd things to me. My pulse has gone up at least ten points, and she marveled a little at how it was possible to be so objective when she was actually feeling very strange indeed.

He bent a little closer and grinned at her. "I could have put some mistletoe in my hair, but the hell with it," he said softly and put a hand behind her head to bring her closer to him and kissed her.

It really was extraordinary. She was a grown woman and not without experience—if of a rather limited nature lately, since her relationship with Ian Felgate had foundered just before she'd come to Old East—and she would never have thought herself a woman to be knocked sideways simply by being kissed. But this kiss was different; and she emerged breathlessly with a whole range of amazing feelings surging through her and a dazed look on her face.

"Who needs mistletoe?" Gus said even more softly, reaching forward and kissing her once more. To her amazement it was just as exciting this time; and she gave up thinking about it or about anything at all. She just put her arms up and round him, and held on tight and co-operated with all the enthusiasm she could find. Which was considerable.

More by luck than judgment they were apart when Bridget came in again, this time bearing a plateful of home-baked biscuits on to which she had piled turkey liver pâté, and she seemed oblivious to George's red cheeks and Gus's air of self-satisfaction.

"Don't eat too many," she instructed. "Vanny'll just about kill me if you lose your appetite for her turkey and all the fixin's. Not long now. Do we open the presents before lunch or after?"

"Uh—I don't mind." George was flustered and trying hard to hide it. "Whatever everyone else wants to do."

Gus looked across at the tree, beneath which there were now more parcels than ever, and grinned. "Leave "em till after lunch. There's nothing so exciting as making people wait for what they most want." He threw a wicked leer at George which made her snort with laughter. Bridget beamed and nodded.

"Just what I always think. OK, then. The great blowout starts in fifteen minutes!"

Lunch was long and excessive and punctuated by much cracker-pulling, greatly to Vanny and Bridget's amusement.

"We only have these for children's birthday parties," Bridget confided to Gus. "It was real sweet of you to bring them. And such fancy ones!"

"I like to be common," Gus said happily. "The more gold paper and frou-frous the better. Hey, listen to this!" He had unwrapped his motto, and was sitting there, his head crowned with a confection of pink and blue paper that made him look like a drunken cherub now. "Tell me what it means, someone! 'Confucius say, man who steals kisses is not thief when lady helps him to help himself.'"

George threw him a knife-sharp glare and said, "That sounds more like a prawn cracker motto than a Christmas cracker one," which was a feeble sally but the best she could manage. Fortunately both Vanny and Bridget had had enough of the excellent champagne, which Gus had also brought, to fuddle them and make them think this exchange was exquisitely funny, so they laughed immoderately and began to fuss over providing second helpings.

The rest of the afternoon was as agreeable as lunch had been. They washed up in a noisy huddle, then shared out their gifts from the tree and adored each other's choices. Gus had given George a large one-volume history of London which he had had bound in crimson leather and engraved with her name in gilt, a beautiful thing that made her blush for what she now perceived as the banality of her own gift—a pair of leather gloves—but which seemed to please him greatly. And then they settled to the somnolence of an afternoon in which the television murmured softly in the background while the old ladies slept away their natural fatigue after all their efforts and Gus and George talked in a desultory fashion.

Always afterwards she was to remember that afternoon as the turning point in her dealings with Gus. They had started on the wrong foot, right at the beginning, when she was new at Old East and faced with the Oxford case. There had been a confusion of identity that had made her pugnacious in her dealings with him thereafter. They had reached a sort of friendship as the months had gone on and they had worked together over several other cases; but this afternoon—this afternoon was different.

It made them true friends, she realized, the sort who could sit and be comfortable together without actually talking all the time; the sort who could pick up the other's thoughts and join in an elliptical conversation with immediate understanding of what the other meant. It was deeply comfortable and soothing and at the same time exciting, for the friendship carried, as they both now well knew, the promise of something more. Much more.

The afternoon light had dwindled to indigo, until the room was lit only by the flicker of the flames in the grate and the shifting colors of the TV screen, when Vanny woke—or seemed to wake—stared widely at George and sang in her high little voice, "I'm off with the raggle-taggle gypsies, oh!" and immediately fell asleep again. Which made both George and

Gus giggle; and then both realized at the same time that she
hadn't behaved as oddly as they first thought, for the TV was
now showing a resumé of the past decade, and at the point
Vanny had woken had been showing scenes of deprivation and
distress among the children of Bucharest. Especially gypsy
children.

"…these children," the voiceover intoned, "are paying the
horrendous price for the ambitions of the dictator Ceausescu.
Thrown into orphanages to rot, with gypsy children making
a high proportion of the numbers, they rock themselves
interminably in an effort to get some of the stimulation and
comfort they fail to find in the arms of loving parents or carers,
their only hope the possibility of people coming from the
West—mostly America—willing and able to adopt them."

"That's what reminded her of the song," Gus said quietly,
but George shook her head.

"She's been singing it ever since she first heard it at the
Players that night," she whispered, not wanting to wake Vanny
again. There was no risk of waking Bridget, who was snoring
happily, well away. "It was just one of those—"

She stopped suddenly and stared at him and then shook
her head. The notion that had slipped into it was absurd. The
result of too much food and drink and sleepiness. She was
fantasizing. She was melodramatic. And yet—

Gus had opened his mouth to speak but she shook her head
at him and returned her attention to the TV set, having to strain
just a little to hear the commentary, for they had kept the sound
turned low deliberately. The screen now showed scenes of
street-fighting in Romania, and she watched eagerly; but then
the commentary shifted and moved on to another story. The
Gulf War this time. Again she pushed away the absurd notion
that had come into her mind. It *was* absurd, too absurd even to
consider, wasn't it?

Gus was watching her curiously. Then he said quietly,
"You've just had the mother and father of a hunch."

"Hmm?"

"So what was it? Won't you share it?"

She was still lost in her own thoughts and he said again, a little more loudly, "May I know what it is?"

Now she looked at him and her slightly glazed expression cleared and sharpened. "Uh—know what?"

"I said, you just had a sudden idea, right? It walked all over your face like a kid in a field of new snow. The footprints went very deep, lady. So let me share, hmm?"

She stared at him and then bit her lip, torn. He looked back at her, his head cocked. For a moment, she wanted to pour it all out, to build on the afternoon's intimacy, to be really close. But then she caught her breath. Suppose she was wrong? Suppose it was a mad notion born out of a punch and champagne-fuddled imagination? She couldn't bear to display herself in a bad light to him; she really couldn't. And as she thought it, she drew back and some of the warmth faded from his eyes as he saw her do it.

"Not—there's nothing to share," she said lamely.

"Rotten liar." He sounded amiable and light-hearted but she wasn't fooled. She'd hurt his feelings and she leaned forward impulsively from her corner of the couch to put her hand on his shoulder; he was sitting on the hearth rug at her feet and it was easy.

"Yes, you're right. I did have a sudden notion. But it's so—well, ephemeral. Silly really. I'd rather do some checking before I make a fool of myself."

He twisted round and looked up at her, his face almost as close as it had been when he'd kissed her. "You're a soppy ha'porth, you know that? There's nothing you could do that would ever make a fool of you in my eyes. I thought we was proper mates. Shared things."

"Yes…" she said, but drew back again, wanting to respond to him and yet aware of the deep stubborn streak that had always been her downfall exerting its pressure. "I will share it. But just let me check something first. I know I don't have to with you, but, Gus, let me be what I am, for God's sake. Don't try and make me different. I'm stubborn, OK? I like to make sure of my facts before I go and—well, usually I like to make sure," she amended, then grinned. "I've learned to listen to myself, that's the thing. I've gone in half-cocked too often in the past and made a—what is it you call it? A right royal cock-up. Give me a day or two, that's all. Then when I've found out if I'm even half right, I promise I'll tell you. But if I'm making a fool of myself, well at least I won't have to let you know it. Fair enough?"

He looked at her for a long moment and at last nodded. "If that's what you want, ducks. Do it your way. It's not that I want to make you do anything. I'm not that sort, take it from me. You'll find out I'm not. I just like to feel trusted, that there's nothing hidden between me and my friends, know what I mean? It's not nosiness. It's just—just sharing."

"I know," she said. "And I promise you I'll tell you when I've found out a bit more. Please don't take it personally—me needing to do that, I mean."

"No," he said, and turned back to stare at the TV screen which was now full of images of a beauty contest as the report raced on, ten years of hectic living being packed into half an hour of their time. "No. I won't take it personally."

But she knew he had.

22

In a hospital the days after Christmas are dispiriting. The decorations that looked so brave and promising before Christmas Eve are tarnished and tawdry by the day after Boxing Day, and the general air of untidiness upsets the staff—notably the senior nursing staff—more than a little, so they bustle and snap a good deal as they try to get straight again, while at the same time bracing themselves for the flood of new admissions that are always a feature of the post-Christmas return to normality.

This Christmas was the same as all previous Christmases and George found the laboratory an unhappy place to be when she went back to work after the break. Jerry was off sick—"The usual hangover, he only gets rid of it in time for a New Year booze-up so he can be off the first week in January as well, the lazy bastard," Sheila said sourly, and set to work grimly to scrub her department clear of any hint of tinsel and tralala and to drive the rest of the staff mad while she did it. No one was more eager for Christmas the week before 25 December nor so waspish about it the week after than Sheila.

George for her part tucked herself away in her office and, grateful that the day hadn't produced the rash of bodies she had half expected as people succumbed to too much festive jollification, set about preparing her year's end statistics for the Board. Not that she had to do a lot—most of the actual work could be carried out on Sheila's computer—but still there were

documents to be sorted and totals to be collated ready to be fed
into the system. That took her all morning.

At lunchtime, however, she felt reasonably free of Old East
work and could turn her attention back to the two deaths Gus was
investigating. The first thing she did was to pull out the Chowdary
file which she had kept hidden in her top drawer. She'd have to
give the notes back soon; someone surely would notice they
were missing from the Registry and Cherry, she knew, was too
concerned about Harry's posthumous reputation to let them stay
with her for much longer; and anyway she'd promised their swift
return. She had to sort it out now, or lose the chance.

She read with great care the PM report made by her locum.
It wasn't precisely the sort she'd have written herself, of course;
whenever did any doctor think a locum's work good enough?
But it wasn't all that bad. He had clearly been a careful man
and one given to paying due attention to details.

And he had made no mention anywhere of a strawberry nevus
on the body of the Chowdary baby although he'd described
every other aspect of the surface appearance minutely. Surely,
surely, had there been one, he would have noted it? Minor
blemishes though such nevi were, usually fading before a child
was three, it had been there, and he should have mentioned
it. Perhaps she could track him down, see if he remembered?
Where was he working now? She looked at the name at the end
of the report; James Browne. No address and a common name.
She'd have to make enquiries and that could take time—unless
she could get evidence from elsewhere of course.

She made up her mind what to do quite suddenly. She
went into the lab to give Sheila all the material ready for the
computer work she would have to do, and escaped to make her
way over to Cherry's little cubby hole of an office in Fertility.
Please let her be at work this morning, she prayed in a vague
unfocused fashion. Don't let me waste more time. The sooner
I can tell Gus what my idea is, the better. I don't want him
thinking I'm being remote and cool, when it's the last thing I

feel. But that was not a subject she could think about right now. So she refused to. It was not easy, however.

Happily for her peace of mind, Cherry was at work, sitting drooping at her desk and chewing the end of a pencil as she stared at the shabby almost-dead calendar on her wall.

She greeted George in a lacklustre fashion, but cheered up a little when she saw the Chowdary notes that George put down on the desk in front of her.

"Oh, I'm glad to see them," she said. "I was just wondering when you'd fetch them back. I mean, I know you promised, but you know how it is. People forget. I've really got to put them back in the Matty files. They'll come complaining about how untidy Harry was if I don't and I don't want that."

"Nor do I," George said. "I've got all I need from them. Thanks." She hesitated. "Will it be hard to put them back without anyone noticing?"

"Mmm? Oh, not really." She looked at her watch. "I go when I know the office'll be quiet. It's pretty quiet now, I think. Lunchtime, you see."

"Good," George said briskly. "Then let's take them back now, shall we? And Cherry, will you do something for me?"

Cherry looked dubious and George patted her arm. "It's all right. I'm not asking for anything outrageous. It's to save me time. I could track down what I need through the Registry if I had to, but you know how slow they can be. I just want the address of a patient—another one who had a baby who died. Like this one." She tapped Angela's notes.

"Oh, well, I suppose I could," Cherry said doubtfully. "As long as no one's there. If there is someone, I'll have to make an excuse and not even put this file back. But it should be all right around now, like I said. Lunchtime. Will you wait here? Tell me what it is you want and I'll be right back."

"I'll come with you. Then I can keep people out of your hair if necessary." George grinned at her. "Anyway, it's always easier for two people."

Cherry seemed grateful for her company and led the way back towards Maternity, George falling into step beside her. George asked the question more to have something to say than anything else. "Those crumpled sheets of paper, the ones you found under this file in Harry's room, they're odd, aren't they?"

"Odd?"

"Well, just rows of numbers and letters and so forth."

Cherry shrugged. "All this medical stuff looks like that to me," she said. "I thought it was just, you know, medical. Isn't it?" She threw a sharp glance at George who remembered again how astute this girl could be.

"I don't think so," George said. "It's not like anything medical I've ever seen."

"Oh." Cherry frowned. "That's funny. I was sure it was. It's like some other stuff I've seen, anyway."

"What?" Startled, George stopped walking, and made Cherry do the same. "You've seen other pages like this?"

Cherry's forehead wrinkled, "Yeah. Somewhere…"

"Tell me about that," George commanded. "At once! Where? When? Who had the pages? And—"

Cherry shook her head, bewildered by George's vehemence. "I don't know," she said.

"Don't know? How do you mean, don't know?"

Cherry began to walk again and George perforce fell into step beside her. "As I said, I can't remember. I saw some stuff like that somewhere. Just a few lines, not whole pages or anything. I can sort of see them. They were just the same." She squinted at the floor. "But I can't remember where."

Again George brought herself and Cherry to a halt, holding on to her elbow. They were in the last little run of corridor before they reached Maternity proper, and it was empty. Just an expanse of red linoleumed floor and pale green-washed walls with a couple of rather grimy windows to give a little light. And themselves.

"Listen, Cherry," she said with some urgency. "There's a way of remembering and it's important you try. Look at that blank wall, and then close your eyes."

Cherry gaped at her and George shook her head impatiently. "Believe me, this works if you give it a chance. I've seen it work. Just look at the wall. Right? Now close your eyes and look at those pages you remember. See them in your memory. Can you do it?"

Cherry stood with her eyes crunched closed and concentrated. After a moment she said slowly. "Yeah, I sort of can. A little pile of "em. All crumpled up."

"Good," George said urgently. Her pulse had started to pound, she was so excited. "Great. Now, concentrate and let your mind's eye sort of open out. There are the papers. What are they in or on? A table? An in-out tray? You look and tell me."

The girl frowned, still with her eyes closed. "I can't—oh! Yes, I think. Basket. There's a sort of basket-weave alongside one of them."

She opened her eyes and George almost shouted at her to close them again. Cherry looked offended for a moment but obeyed.

"I'm sorry, Cherry. I didn't mean to be nasty. I just need to know. Look again. Tell me what you see."

Again Cherry concentrated and George stood there with her tongue-tip held between her teeth, willing the girl to remember; and then suddenly there was a sound of footsteps, and Cherry's eyelids flew open and George whirled.

Didier St Cloud was coming along the corridor from the Maternity Ward, whistling softly between his teeth. He grinned when he saw them and called cheerfully, "Meeting of the Girls' Club is it? The places you have to go to get a bit of peace in this hospital!"

George could have hit him, she was so furious at the interruption. She glared at him. "Nothing of the sort," she snapped. "I was just asking Cherry for some information."

Didier lifted his brows and said mildly, "Well, sorry, I'm sure. I meant no harm! I often bring people out here if I need to talk quietly. It's just about the only part of Matty where you can be left alone." He stared at her curiously. "No need to get so shirty."

She relaxed, deliberately letting her shoulders slump. "Sorry," she said. "I didn't mean to get so screwed up. It was just that Cherry was trying to remember something I need to know and I think she was almost there." She turned to Cherry hopefully. "Unless you already had remembered?"

Cherry shook her head. "Sorry, Dr. Barnabas, but it's all gone," she said a little mournfully. "It's like I said, I sort of remember seeing—"

"Well, that's all right," George said hastily, suddenly aware of Didier's close interest. "Not important now, we have to get on. So long, Didier." She put her hand on Cherry's elbow as unobtrusively as possible and urged her forward and a few seconds later they were in the main Matty corridor, leaving Didier beyond the double doors which swung closed behind them. George took a deep breath of relief.

"Let's face it, Cherry," she said quietly. "We can't know who might be involved in this, can we? The less we talk the better. We'll try to remember again later. Right now, let's see if there's anyone in the office. If there isn't, what I need is the address of the Popodopoulos family. Can you find it?"

"When was she in here?" Cherry was business-like again.

"It was in the little red notebook," George said and closed her own eyes to summon up a memory of the scribbled dates on the first page. "First of December it was, the day that baby died. So she'd have been admitted on—"

"It won't take a moment on the computer," Cherry said and moved along the corridor with George close behind her, making their way past the usual groups of chattering mothers, some with their babies cradled in the crooks of their arms, trying to be as unnoticed as possible.

The office was empty. Cherry darted in and had the Chowdary file stowed safely back in its place in no time. Then as George looked over her shoulder to check, Cherry slid into the chair behind the rather battered computer on the far table, and began tapping keys.

"How do you spell it?" she asked. "Popo—what?" George rattled off the letters as Cherry hit keys and then peered at her screen. "Just round the corner really. One five three five Lansdowne House, on the Shadwell Estate."

"Fifteen thirty-five," George said, committing it to memory. "Lansdowne House."

"That's it," Cherry said. "Anything else you need?"

"Phone number?" George said hopefully and again Cherry punched keys and then shook her head.

"Not listed. Might be in the phone book."

"I'll go there." George was talking more to herself than to Cherry. "I'll just go right there and not tell them I'm coming. It's worth the risk of there being no one at home."

"You'll probably have a hell of a climb when you get there," Cherry said helpfully. "If it's like most of the blocks of flats around here, the lifts'll be out of order and you'll have to climb up. All fifteen floors."

To George's intense relief, Cherry had been too pessimistic. The lifts were working, but she had to admit it would have been more agreeable perhaps to have climbed the stairs, even though the Popodopoulos family lived so high up. The lift cage stank of old tobacco, cats and human urine and the floor was littered with garbage, while the walls were covered in some remarkably obscene but totally unamusing graffiti. Even the buttons on the call panel were sticky to the touch. Her heart sank as she imagined what lay ahead of her.

But the Popodopoulos flat was warm and welcoming and beautiful. The child who came to the door, a stunningly beautiful boy of about seven, with a head covered in rich black curls and eyes to match, grinned at her when she asked for Mrs. Popodopoulos and went back inside, leaving the door open behind him, which she accepted as an invitation to come in. The narrow hallway inside was carpeted in deep crimson, the walls were hung with so many pictures it was almost impossible to see any wallpaper behind them and it led into a sizeable room that seemed to George to be stuffed with richly polished and plumply upholstered furniture, people who were almost as well upholstered and smells of food so strong they were almost like solids hitting her in the face.

There were five women sitting at the table, all as dark as the boy who had answered the door, and all turned handsome enquiring faces to her as she came in. The boy returned to the TV set he'd been watching with another child and turned up the sound. One of the women, clearly his mother for she shared his particular brand of handsomeness, leaned over and turned the sound down again without for a moment taking her eyes off George. The boy muttered but settled down to watch quietly.

"Yes," Mrs. Popodopoulos said. "Can I help you?"

George went straight in as she had done with Mr. Chowdary. It had worked then. Why not now?

"I'm the pathologist at Old East," she said. "Dr. Barnabas. I'm—I—was most upset when your baby died, Mrs. Popodopoulos," she said. "I offer you my condolences."

The five women were all suddenly very still and silent so that the TV set seemed all at once to be loud. They said nothing and just stared down at the table.

George caught her breath, very aware of Mrs. Popodopoulos's eyes fixed on her. She wanted to glance away to avoid that direct look of—what? Pain was too simple a word. There was depth of loss in her gaze that made the back of George's neck crawl with pity and a sort of shared sensation of misery. But she held her gaze firm and looked at the handsome woman sitting there at her table with her hands crossed on the red plush cloth that covered it.

"Thank you," Mrs. Popodopoulos said at last. "I appreciate that." She bowed her head with dignity and the other women relaxed. One of them put her hand on Mrs. Popodopoulos's shoulder and another started to murmur softly in a sort of comfortable croon.

"I want to do more than that," George said, now emboldened. "I want to find out why your baby died."

"My son died of a cot death," Mrs. Popodopoulos said.

"Who told you that?"

"Ann Powell."

"Ann Powell?"

"My midwife."

"Ah, yes." George shook her head. "I don't deny that was what she was told. It was the only diagnosis I could make. It was my—it was up to me to..." She let the words drift away and knew they understood. One of them shrank back a little, staring at her with huge dark eyes and George tried to see herself through those eyes; a woman who cut up dead babies, who pried into such dreadful matters, what sort of woman was that? She made herself look away from the staring eyes and back at Helen Popodopoulos.

"I don't like that diagnosis," she said. "It isn't—it isn't enough."

Helen stared and seemed for the first time aware that George was still standing in the doorway. She got to her feet with a surge of energy that made them all jump up and start to bustle.

"I am ashamed. I have offered you no chair, no refreshments. Please take off your coat. It's warm in here. And you'll take some coffee, yes? And a little baklava perhaps, or..."

Chattering busily she divested George of her coat, who was glad for it was indeed warm in this crowded room. One of the others went off to the kitchen and returned rapidly with a small cup filled with thick, very hot and very fragrant coffee and a plate of honeyed baklava pastry. George was tempted, but decided not to accept. Talking on such a matter with her mouth full would not be right. The coffee tasted good, however, and she sipped it gratefully as Helen Popodopoulos came to the sofa where she had been ensconced and sat beside her.

"Well, now. You think there was something else I should know about my baby son?"

"I honestly don't know," George set down her cup and saucer on the little table beside the richly upholstered sofa arm. "I can't lie to you, I just can't tell you more. I'm acting on a—I just have a suspicion that all is not as I—we have been led to believe. Mrs. Popo—"

"Call me Helen," the other woman said. She held out a hand and took George's in it. "You are a good woman, doctor. I appreciate your coming here. It was a dreadful loss. I have already two sons, but this one was just as precious, just—" She swallowed and shook her head and her eyes were glittering with tears. But she shed none.

"I'm certain he was. And I pray that one day—well, who knows. But I must ask you, Mrs.—Helen, do you have a photograph of your lost son? I mean, before he died?"

Again the room shivered into stillness, only the sound of the children's TV breaking it. They seemed totally unaware of the conversation of the adults around them and for that George was grateful.

After a long pause Helen said, "My husband was very distressed. Very. A man and his sons—you understand."

"A man and his children? Of course," George said. She shouldn't have made the distinction, not to a grieving woman, but she had been unable to stop herself and Helen looked at her sharply and for a moment her lips curled into a smile.

"Yes, well, you are not, of course, Cypriot. You don't understand our ways. Let me just say, he could not bear the thought of a photograph once our baby was dead. To him it was a sacrilege. A picture of a dead baby."

George felt the plunge of her hopes as a physical thing, a hard thump in her chest and she caught her breath and closed her eyes for a moment to mark her disappointment. When she opened them again Helen was looking at her with a slightly quizzical expression on her face.

"That does not mean to say there is no photograph," she said softly. "I am a Cypriot woman and we women have our own ways and our own friends."

She looked over her shoulder briefly at one of the other women at the table. "Arianna, she took one for me. I wanted it and at that time Kostakis did not mind. He did not have a camera, but Arianna did. And she is, after all, my cousin."

George's mouth was dry with anticipation. "May I see it?"

"Gladly," Helen said. "I trust you, of course, not to mention this to Kostakis, should you ever speak to him."

"Of course not," George said. "If that is what you wish."

"It is what I wish," Helen Popodopoulos said gravely, and nodded at the woman at the table. Arianna got to her feet and went across the room to pick up her leather handbag. She brought it back to George and took out a small envelope, stiffened with cardboard and unmarked.

With slippery fingers George pulled the picture from its folds.

"I took it almost as soon as he was born," Arianna said. Her voice was husky with remembered emotion. "I was so excited. He was such a lovely boy and so—well, you can see. But once he was dead Kostakis wanted it burned up. He did not want ever to see it again, to remember the boy who died before he lived." She looked over her shoulder at the three silent women at the table. "We could not bear that. So we keep it."

George turned the picture over and looked, and the dryness in her mouth increased and her throat constricted too as she concentrated. Because now she knew what had happened to those babies. Of that she was sure. She knew what had happened. Not how or why, but what.

23

"I know what happened," George said. "Not how or why, but what."

There was a long silence at the other end of the phone, and then Gus said carefully, "Was this the notion you had Christmas afternoon? The hunch?"

"You've got it," she said, with a sudden lift of exhilaration. It was good to be able to tell him how she felt, and not to hide anything. "I just wanted to check first."

"You didn't have to," he said. "Believe me, you could have trusted me not to—well, let it be. Just make me a promise."

"Depends what it is." She laughed as she said it.

"Don't play the coquette with me, ducks. It's not your style or mine. Just promise me that in future you'll stop playing secrets. We're a team, ain't we? Just tell me what's going on, no matter what."

She hesitated. "I promise, I'll *try*. Will that do?"

He was silent again and she was alarmed. Had she upset him? Hurt his feelings? It was important to her suddenly that she should never do that. Yet at the same time, she had to hold on to herself, to her freedom to do what she had to do. She held her breath, waiting for his response. And then relaxed when he said, "OK, ducks. I'll settle for that. Can't do anything else, can I? All right, let's get on. Out with it. You say you know what happened. What?"

"The babies. The cot deaths, so called."

"Humph," he said. "You've got evidence?"

She looked down at the photograph on her desk. "I think it's evidence," she said. "If you took me into court and asked me to swear to it on oath, I would."

"Good enough," he said. "I'm on my way."

"Don't you want me to tell you now?" She was startled. In his shoes she couldn't have borne not being told immediately.

"I'd rather look at the evidence at the same time as I hear the words," he said. "Anyway, any excuse to see you…Give me fifteen minutes."

The dialing tone buzzed in her ear, and slowly she recradled the phone, still looking down at the photograph. Perhaps, she thought, she ought not to look at it too often. If she did, she might blur her memory; and she closed her eyes and deliberately summoned up the image of the Popodopoulos baby lying on her dissection table in the mortuary. It took a moment or two, which alarmed her a little, but then it worked, and she could see it all clearly: the table; Danny out of the corner of her memory's eye preparing viscera for the scales; the sound of rain on the roof. She'd forgotten till now that it had been raining that morning. She opened her eyes again, relieved. There was no doubt; she could go into court and swear it, if she had to.

Sheila put her head round her office door to say goodnight, putting on her my-God-I'm-so-exhausted face, even managing to look drawn and white. An excellent actress, Sheila.

"I'll get those oncology slides finally sorted by tomorrow," she said. "And the regional lab said to let you know that the figures for last year's cervical smears are on their way. They're sorry they're later than usual."

"Thank you, Sheila," George said. "Sorry you're so pushed at the moment. I'm not exactly sitting around myself, mind you."

"No," said Sheila tartly. "I'm sure." She withdrew her head leaving George feeling thoroughly irritated and a little guilty. There was no doubt that she did lean a good deal on

Sheila while she rushed around being a detective, which wasn't really part of her job description. But after all, why shouldn't she? It still was work, and she wasn't taking time off the way some hospital consultants did for private practice or the improvement of a golf handicap. And then she felt guilty again, for thinking harsh thoughts about her colleagues. It wasn't easy, she decided, having any sort of conscience when you worked in a hospital.

By the time Gus arrived she'd made a pot of coffee and was sitting waiting at her desk, the photograph carefully stowed back in its envelope. She couldn't resist a little bit of theatricality, she thought, and then was amused with herself. It wouldn't be theatrical to him, dammit; he'd never seen the child with his own eyes so the photograph would mean nothing to him. She took it out of the envelope and propped it up against her phone.

He came in in a flurry of cold air, bringing the smell of the dank December street and the river in with him. She watched with a sense of deep pleasure as he shrugged out of his old overcoat and loosened his tie before delving into the shabby plastic bag he was carrying and bringing out a square white box with a flourish.

"Grodzinski's," he announced with great satisfaction. "Best pâtisserie in the East End. You got the coffee ready? Good girl. Here's the strudel."

He opened the box and put slices of pastry on to the two paper plates which he also fished out of the plastic bag. George laughed as he pushed it in front of her, together with a plastic fork to eat it with.

"You must live in fear of imminent starvation," she said. "Whenever I see you you're fetching food offerings. You filled our fridge with an amazing amount of stuff on Christmas Day. Bridget showed me. It wasn't necessary."

"Shut up and eat up," he said amiably. "O' course it's necessary. A man who neglects his stomach neglects life. As Dr. Johnson once said."

"I doubt he said precisely that." George tried a piece of the strudel as he busied himself with the coffee tray. It was delectable and she ate another forkful as he pushed her coffee in front of her.

"See what I mean? Get the grub right and the rest falls into place. Now, tell me all about it. You can talk with your mouth full, I don't mind."

He started on his own strudel as she finished hers and dropped the paper plate in the waste-paper basket.

"No need. Now, listen. I went to see Mrs. Popodopoulos this afternoon."

"Mrs. Who? Should I know?"

"Huh! Some memory you've got. Hers was the third baby which died. The one I did the post-mortem on. I didn't do the others, remember, because I was off sick."

"I haven't asked." He was all compunction. "How is it?"

"What? Oh." She looked down at her left hand. "It's fine. I forgot about it, so I suppose it's fine. Are you listening?"

He had finished his pastry and was now looking at her with a deliberately soulful expression on his face. "I'd rather be sittin' on your floor beside your sofa while your Ma and Bridget sleep," he said. "That beats talkin.'"

"Shut up and listen."

"OK, OK, I'm listenin." All ears, that's me. So, you went to see the woman whose baby died. Why?"

She made a little face. "It'll sound kinda crazy, but it was partly you taking us to the Players Theater, and partly something that was on TV on Christmas Day."

"You were watching TV?" he said reproachfully. "And here was I thinkin' you were concentratin' on me."

"I told you to shut up about that. Anyway, you remember. Ma woke suddenly and sang a line from that damned 'Raggle-taggle Gypsies' song she'd heard at the Players and there was stuff on the program about the children in Romanian orphanages."

"Yes." His attention had sharpened now; the laughter had gone from him. He was watching her face closely as she talked, and that made her feel a little flustered, but she plowed on.

"Well, it wasn't only that. I have to say I'd been to see the Chowdarys too. She wasn't there, but he was—Viv—and he showed me a photograph of his dead baby. It had been taken at the moment of birth, not when it had died. It was a bit messy, but I thought I saw a nevus on it—a sort of birthmark. It looks a bit like a strawberry and on that picture I thought there was one across the chest. He confirmed it. Said he'd noticed and asked about it but they'd reassured him—anyway, the thing is, there was no mention of any nevus on the PM report. And the locum they had for me, he was a reasonably efficient guy, from his reports."

"Not as good as you'd have been, of course."

"Is your stand-in as good as you when you're away?" she demanded.

"Of course not. Go on. Then what?"

"Then, like I said, I remembered what happened when you took us to the Players Theater."

"What's the Players got to do with the price of eggs or the current crimewave? Apart from that song, that is?"

"It was the song that did it for me. When it so took Ma's fancy. We were talking about it, remember? And you told Ma that it was about children being stolen away by gypsies and she said that was a different one and—anyway, that was what we'd talked about and I suppose it put a worm of a notion into my mind. When Ma woke up in the middle of that TV item, I suddenly saw what had happened to the babies."

"So? Why couldn't you tell me then?"

"Don't start that again, please. I was—oh, silly maybe. It seemed a bit romantic. Far fetched. That was why I went to see Mrs. Popodopoulos this afternoon. I wanted to be sure." She leaned forward and picked up the baby's photograph and gave it to him. "The thing is, that baby there is not the baby I autopsied."

He looked at the photograph and then at her and at the photograph again. He said sharply, "You're sure." It wasn't a question but she treated it as one.

"Yes, I'm sure. I remember checking the notes again, not all that long after I'd done the PM though it feels like ages ago. I noticed an anomaly then, but I dismissed it. The baby was measured when he was born and I measured him too, of course—that is, I measured the baby I autopsied. There was a difference. I put it down to post-mortem changes in muscle tone—quite reasonable—but I was wrong. It was definitely a different baby."

"I'd trust your memory anywhere," he said. "Though whether a court would is another story." He looked up then. "But we're a long way from going to court. The only known crimes we have are the deaths of the Oberlander baby and Harry Rajabani. No one's made any suggestion that there was anything wrong—legally speaking—about these cot deaths, have they?"

"No, but they could be linked with the murders, couldn't they?"

"It's possible." He was silent for a while. "But listen, if you're right and the babies that died here aren't the ones who were born here, what's happened to the other babies? Why was it done? And as you said on the phone, how? I mean, finding dead babies lying around to swap for live ones ain't what you'd call the most likely of scenarios." He shook his head. "I'm trying hard to see any connection with our known cases. This is odd, and needs investigating, I grant you, but I say again, what has it got to do with the murders of the Oberlander baby and Harry?"

"I've a theory," she said. "Not evidence, and I know that matters, but it's the only thing I can think of that makes sense."

"Well?"

"It's an adoption scam."

"What?" He looked as alert as a terrier with its ears up. "Tell me more."

"People who are infertile get desperate. Look what Angela and Viv Chowdary put themselves through to get their baby. Well, if they can't have their own, adoption is the next best thing. And there was a hell of a demand for Romanian babies, I remember, when they first found out what was going on there. I remember TV programs about it."

"Yes," he said slowly. "Yes. You could be right. But how can substituting dead babies for living ones help adopters? Call me dumb, but I just don't see it."

"I'm not sure I do," she said candidly. "All I can think of is that for some reason these babies are being taken from our Matty block to give to adopters and they're getting hold of dead babies to replace them with and cover their tracks. Maybe these Romanian babies are brought here and they're ailing and die and rather than disappoint the people waiting for the babies they do a swap?" She shivered suddenly. "It's the most cruel of things to do. It means, if I'm right, that these three babies are alive and well somewhere, while their real parents are breaking their hearts over their deaths. Well, two of them are at any rate. Not the first one—"

"The first one?"

"She's vanished. Homeless drug abuser, apparently. Walked out of here and seemed unworried not to be taking a baby with her, so Sister Lichfield said. When I asked her."

"Sister—?"

"On Matty. A good soul if a bit on the old-fashioned side." She shook her head. "If I'm right, there has to be someone on that ward who's part of it. I can't see it as being her. She's...It just doesn't gel. You talk to her and you'll see what I mean."

"On what grounds do I talk to her? This is all surmise, George, my love. Just surmise."

"I need more evidence, don't I?" She grimaced in frustrated anger at herself. "When I autopsied that baby I didn't see anything to make me suspect he wasn't what I was told he was. A newborn baby with the umbilical cord still in place—though now I think of it…" She wrinkled her forehead. "I suppose it's possible that the stump was a little more dessicated than it might have been at just twenty-four hours of age." She shook her head. "But that's such a variable feature. I'd defy anyone to handle a baby in the first week of life and say for sure how old it was…The thing that really makes me spit is that I so often take photographs of the bodies when I do the PM. I still have vague plans for a book. But I didn't do one of the Popodopoulos baby—if that's who it was—because I was just back from sick leave, and anyway it was just a cot death and I have lots of other photos to fit in that section of the book when I write it. And of course the locum had no call to take photographs. So the only evidence we have is my memory."

"I wonder," he said. "Won't there be other people who saw this baby alive? Who delivered it?"

"I don't know. I'd have to check, in Matty, I suppose. Or it may be in the notes. But what point would there be in talking to whoever that might be? It's people who've seen both the live baby and the dead one we need."

"That's my point," he said patiently. "Maybe whoever delivered the child also saw the body before it was sent down to the mortuary and may have noticed differences. Though, let's face it'—he looked at the photograph again with a considering stare—"one baby looks very like another, doesn't it? It beats me how anyone can tell "em apart, even their mothers, going by the ones I've seen."

"Which clearly isn't many," she said tartly. "They vary hugely. I've seen babies with flaming red hair and with fair hair and like this one with a great mop of black hair, and I've seen them bald and wrinkled and smooth and—"

"OK, OK!" He shook his head. "Is the fact that this baby has a lot of dark hair significant, do you suppose?"

"Hmm?"

"I mean, were all the babies who died—who were supposed to have died—dark haired? Is that why they were swapped?

Because they looked like the babies brought from Romania? It could be, I suppose—if you're right."

"Of course!" She was most struck by that. "Of course, that has to be the reason! It's all hanging together more and more, isn't it?"

He shook his head. "I know how it feels to get such a huge piece of the jigsaw in, but there are still a hell of a lot of holes, George. We don't know how they did it, if they did it, though we've got a suspicion about why. Well, that we have to prove first. Then we can think about the method they used. If people are bringing babies here from Romania we have to know what routes they use and why the babies die. If that's what's happening. They could be coming from other places—Brazil maybe? I've heard they have a baby export black market."

"I'm sure of it," she said. "Aren't you?"

"No. Not sure," he said. "I have to have proof, you know that. But it's a very nice bit of theory, ducks. I'll grant you that. Look, tomorrow I talk to the maternity people—"

"Hold on," she said. "Won't that start a hare?"

"Eh?"

"If you start sniffing around up there then whoever did whatever they did'll get very nervous and back off. Then you'll never find out anything."

"I suppose so." He looked at her sideways and grinned. "You're volunteering, aren't you?"

"Well, why not? They're sort of used to me. I can think of some logical reason for snooping around that should keep them happy. Though I'll have to be careful. I mean, someone up there has to be involved, don't they? It's a matter of access."

"That's what you have to find out. Maybe other people can get at those babies."

"It's not likely, but as you say, I'll have to find out."

"Have you any ideas about who it might be?"

"Hardly—" she said and then hesitated. He pounced on that immediately.

"Spit it out," he said. "You've got someone in your sights. And you promised no more secrets."

She made a face. "It's Didier. He's a nice guy, friendly and all that, but there's something—I mean he's always there, you know. Whenever I'm talking to people or checking things he sort of bobs up." She brooded for a moment and then said unwillingly, "Though that's kinda crazy. I mean, the man's the Obstetric Registrar. Where else would he spend his time except on Matty? I've really a lot of checking to do, you see. And then there's Sister Lichfield and her staff…It could be any one of a dozen or more of them. The place is seething with midwives and so forth."

"Now you'll find out just what detective work's really about," he said, grinning wickedly. "You've just done the fun bits thus far—codes and so forth—any further forrader with your efforts there, by the way? My fellas are getting precisely nowhere."

She told him what had happened with Cherry. "So I suppose it's a bit 'further forrader,' as you put it," she finished. "If she's seen the same sort of pages somewhere, then that should give us a lead—if she remembers where the somewhere is, of course. I wouldn't be too hopeful though. She's a clever girl but not exactly…Well, I'll try her again."

"Do," he said heartily, then tipped his chair back. "Let's do something else now."

"Something else?"

"Mmm."

"Like talk about the Oberlander baby and Harry and—"

"What I had in mind was nothin' to do with the enquiry at all. Neither enquiry. I've got my fellas all beaverin' away on various things like cars that could have done Harry and checkin' records of birth for the Oberlander child, not that I expect to get much from either piece of work, but it has to be done and until it is there's not a lot else we can do. Not tonight." He leered happily. "But I can think of a lovely way to spend the evenin' while we wait for reports. Come and see my lovely Docklands flat."

She stared at him and then laughed. "Like hell I will. I've got other things to do, if you haven't."

"Like what?"

"Going home to Ma and Bridget. I have house guests, remember? I have to entertain them."

"OK," he said sunnily. "No problem. I'll come and help. They love me, those two." He sounded very pleased with himself; downright smug, in fact. "If I walk in with you they'll be over the moon, right? And then we'll encourage "em to go to bed early on account of they're nice tired old ladies and we can settle to some serious snoggin." God, but I have good ideas! Come on—on your way!"

24

She walked to work the next morning, her hands shoved deep into the pockets of her heavy coat and her chin tucked into her collar, for it was a filthy morning, bitterly cold and dark at the same time. Her breath made a fog in front of her whenever she let her nostrils emerge from the woollen cloth of her coat and her hair was spangled with water drops from the mist as around her people scurried, heads down, for buses and cars. Yet she wouldn't have missed the walk for the world. She was happy in a way she hadn't been for a long time and she chuckled softly at her memories of last night; to think that spending an evening "snogging' as Gus put it, should have so beneficial an effect!

But it had. He had insisted on taking her home (and she couldn't pretend she'd argued all that hard) and the old ladies had of course been entranced to see him and fussed over him most agreeably, sharing a bibulous supper with them and, as he had foretold, going to bed just after nine-thirty, leaving them to the sofa and the firelight.

She began to whistle as she remembered, making a soft hissing sound through her teeth and then was amused again, for it was the sort of breathy whistling Vanny used to make when she was particularly contented, pottering among jam pots in the fall when baskets of fruit were all over the kitchen waiting to be preserved, or busy with the house plants which she so loved.

Her joy slid away a little as she thought of Vanny; she'd shown no signs at all of any memory problems since just before

Christmas, and George had become more and more optimistic; maybe Bridget had been fussing, after all. Vanny was much as she had always been, if a touch more fragile. But this morning she had come wandering into the living room, waking George just before her alarm clock went off, looking waif-like and frightened in her white nightdress.

She had stared at George fixedly in the light of the lamp George had switched on almost in a panic when she'd realized someone was in the room with her, and continued to stare for fully half a minute, which had seemed endless to George in her half-awake state, and then plumped herself down beside her on the sofa-bed and taken a deep tremulous breath.

"It's you, George, isn't it?" she said.

"Ma, of course it's me. Who else should it be?"

"I don't know," Vanny had said with an air of great candor. "I was lying in bed looking at whoever it is in there and I couldn't think what had happened. Not who that was or who I was or why or anything. But if you're here it's OK, I guess."

"Ma!" George had sat up sharply and peered at her mother closely. "What do you mean, whoever it is in there? That's Bridget."

Vanny's face had cleared at once, the lines fading from her forehead and her mouth turning up so that it seemed a light had passed over her. "Bridget? Oh, George, of course it was! Dear old Bridget. And this is London, isn't it? Well, of course it is. I'm here visiting with my daughter with my good friend Bridget to keep me nice company, and I'm a silly old woman and I'm going back to bed. It's a very nice bed. Sleep well, George darling. Good night." And she had gone padding back to the bedroom, leaving George staring after her and feeling slightly sick.

As she'd washed and dressed though, she'd begun to feel a little better. It had been a perfectly natural event, she told herself. Morning disorientation—who hasn't woken up in unfamiliar surroundings and found it difficult to remember in a half-asleep state where they are? Why, George herself had been through such moments and no one had ever suggested she might have Alzheimer's disease...

But when it's happened to me it's been momentary, she'd told her reflection in the mirror. With Ma it lasted a long time. I had to tell her who Bridget was; that's not the way it should be.

But she'd stopped worrying when, later, as she grabbed some juice and coffee and a slice of toast in the kitchen, both Bridget and Vanny, neatly dressing-gowned, had come in, looking a touch woebegone.

"Oh, George," Bridget had said in a failing voice. "It was such fun last night with Gus and all, but don't you ever let me take quite so much wine again so near bedtime. I just don't have the capacity any more. Do you realize there are three empty bottles there on the drainer? And just the four of us emptied them. I can't imagine how you look so bright eyed and bushy tailed when your Ma and I are so droopy we're ashamed."

"Well, I didn't have all that much. Left it to you two and Gus," George had said heartily. "I must go. Have a good day, you two. What are you planning to do?"

"Art galleries," Bridget had said mournfully. "If we're up to it. Never you fret about us, honey. We'll be just fine after a vat or so of black coffee. You go to your hospital now, and I'll make it."

"Bye, Ma," George had bent to kiss her mother's soft cheek, as wrinkled and fragrant as a winter apple. "You all OK now? Not worried any more?"

"Hmm?" Vanny had said, blinking up at her. "What was that, honey?"

"Not worried any more the way you were this morning when you woke up?" George said.

Vanny looked up bemused. "Woke up? Well, of course I did! I'm here now, amn't I? Yes, I woke up. Goodbye dear. Have a nice day." And again she put up her face to be kissed and then trotted over to Bridget's side to help her squeeze oranges in George's special juicer.

No, she told herself now as she hurried over Tower Bridge, feeling the sharp bite of the wind coming up river from the Estuary on her right cheek. I'm fretting over nothing. She just had a dream and went wandering—and had too much wine last night. Didn't she? That was all it was. It wasn't anything to do with being ill.

But she didn't believe herself. Not really.

Any lingering thoughts she might have had about Vanny were banished as she hurried up Garland Street to reach the main entrance of Old East. Often she went up along the High Road to get to the back entrance of her path. lab; today, however, she wanted to pick up some paperwork which had been kept for her at the Medical School Porter's Lodge. But she stopped short as she came within a hundred yards or so of the gates.

For all it was still only a quarter to nine, the street was jammed with people and there was a great honking of horns as vehicles, held back by the crowd, tried to push their way through to the High Road. No one would budge for them, though, and many people were just shouting and jeering back, even at ambulances. The noise really hit George hard now, because she had been so absorbed in her own thoughts she'd paid no attention to it hitherto. There were always noises around this part of London; traffic and street stallholders and kids bawling; now she realized that this noise was of a different order and a rather ugly one.

It was full daylight, though very grey and still with a lot of mist, but she could see clearly; and found herself reading banners and placards which were bobbing and weaving above people's heads.

"FAIR DEALS FOR ALL!" read one written in sweeping red capitals on a black board, and "NO SPECIAL CARE FOR IMMIGRANTS"; yet another shrieked "BEDS FOR LOCAL PEOPLE BEFORE BLOOD BANKS FOR IMMIGRANTS!" Others were more specific still: "NO MORE BLACK FavorITISM!"

and "REPATRIATE THEM NOW!" jostled for space alongside "BLACKS GO HOME!" and "BRITAIN FOR THE BRITISH."

She stood very still, staring. There were other people like herself on the outskirts of the mob, staff arriving at Old East for work, and as she looked around she saw several conferring and then with a shrug turning and going. She caught her breath in anger. They were afraid of passing these damned picket lines and prepared to lose a day's work; but what that could mean to the running of the hospital if enough others did the same seemed not to concern them. She wanted to run after them and castigate them for their cowardice, but knew she was being stupid. Better to find out why the pickets' numbers were so swollen compared to the drooping lack-lustre lines that had been hanging around the place for months, and what the hell had brought them out this icy morning.

She began to push her way through, not caring whom she jostled, and several men—they were mostly men in the crowd—shouted at her and one grabbed at her arm. She turned a glare of such ferocity at him, actually baring her teeth in her fury, that he let go and drew back. Immediately though he recovered his aplomb and shouted after her that she was a scab, a stinkin' nigger-lover, and spat; she felt the gobbet land on her sleeve and wanted to vomit. But she pushed on until she was nearly at the main gates of the hospital.

They were closed and standing in front of them were several uniformed police. She was hugely relieved to see them and called, "Hey, it's me. Dr. Barnabas!" hoping to be plucked out of the hubbub and pulled safely inside; but they couldn't hear her above the chanting and bawling that was filling the air and she had to push forward again.

Someone hit her. She felt the blow on the side of her head and it made her spin round, both arms up and flailing, her fists tightly balled in her thick gloves; and she hit out in retaliation and felt her right fist connect with something yielding. Certainly it gave way before her, then all hell broke loose. She was hit again, harder this time, and felt herself falling though she struggled hard to keep her balance; but the people around her instead of holding her up by their proximity seemed to be pulling away and making space for her to tumble. And she would have done, had a hard hand not clamped itself round her arm and pulled her upright again.

"What do you think you're up to, you daft object?" he growled in her ear and she turned her head and squinted and it was Gus; she took a deep breath, hurled herself at him and held on tight.

She had to argue very calmly and at considerable length to persuade them to let her out of Accident and Emergency. Hattie was particularly adamant that she should stay quietly in one of the recovery rooms and then go home; but at last she managed to convince her and Adam Parotsky, who was on duty this morning, much to her relief (she felt he owed her some support and would therefore agree with her), she was not unduly damaged and well able to work.

"OK, so someone spat at me, but it hit my coat and not me, so I won't catch leprosy or anything from it! I've got a small bruise over one cheek—big deal! But I wasn't knocked out, not for a second, and apart from feeling like the dumbest of dumb clucks for getting involved at all when I ought to have backed off and gone around the other way to my department, I'm just fine. See? Like a rock!" And she held out both hands in front of her to show their steadiness and then quickly dropped them before Hattie and Adam could see the fine tremor that was there.

That she'd been alarmed and considerably shaken by what had happened was undoubted, but once Gus had arrived to pull her out and to bring some order to the chaos in Garland Street she'd begun to recover. Gus had delivered her to A & E, ignoring her protests, and had gone back to the gates to help the rest of the uniformed branch "get it all sorted' as he'd somewhat grimly put it, and she felt fine, eager only to get out of the department and back to the gate to find out what was happening.

But there was no way anyone would let her do that so she had to settle for asking questions, and had agreed to stay where she was for half an hour at any rate, on the understanding that someone would tell her what the hell the row was all about, after all these weeks of such desultory picketing.

It was Hattie who obliged. The department wasn't particularly busy; something George found odd at first, until Hattie explained.

"The people picketing aren't being hurt and apart from you no one's been touched. The usual ambulances and walking wounded can't get through to us so they're diverting to whichever hospital they can get into. So I've plenty of time to look after you."

"I've told you, I don't need looking after," George said, swinging her legs down from the couch where they'd insisted she lie to sit with them dangling over the edge. "I'd kill for some of that poisonous coffee of yours, though."

"Hmm," Hattie said. "Bit of a stimulant...Oh, all right, all right!" she added hastily as she saw the storminess appear in George's expression. "But only one cup. It's almost solid caffeine this morning. I'll fetch some."

"You won't," George said firmly. "I'll drink it in your office like a civilized woman. Come on. You too. Adam."

"If it's all right with Sister," Adam said demurely, looking at Hattie with wide eyes. "I wouldn't want to—er..."

"Isn't it great?" Hattie said, quite unaware of any mockery. "I've managed to train him to behave the way a junior houseman used to behave in the dear old days before the reforms and all this first-name stuff. Oh, come now, Adam! You don't have to be so formal—this time. Later, we'll go back to the good old ways. Right now, do you take your poison black or white?"

They sat in a comfortable huddle in the small cluttered office and George felt better by the moment as she sipped the bitter brew and reveled in it.

"Now tell!" he commanded. "What on earth is going on?"

Hattie sighed. "It's the new Sickle Cell Unit," she said. "You've heard about it?"

"I don't think…Oh, yes, of course. That charity thing?"

"You've got it; that charity thing. One of the local GPs got it going—raised a hundred thousand quid from the local Afro-Caribbean community to set up and run for three years a unit for the treatment of and research into sickle cell anemia. I don't have to tell you that they're the ones who'll use it mostly—which makes it extra good of Dr. Choopani to do the fundraising."

"Why?" Adam asked.

"Because he's Asian, not of African descent," Hattie said acidly. "So he personally isn't at risk of sickle cell. Is he?"

"But he must get a lot of black patients who are."

"Tell me about it!" Hattie grunted. "He's been making a special study of them for years. I make sure that any patient I get in here in a sickle cell crisis is told about him. Slowly all the local cases have ended up on his list. The local GPs persuade them all to go to him. Suits them, suits him."

"What's all this got to do with the row out there this morning?" George said. "Are you telling me that—"

"I'm telling you that the local white population is up in arms. They only know because it was in last night's local rag, that the unit's being opened today by Jeremy Malti—the footballer, you know? I think he's from a Nigerian family—and they're screaming blue murder about preferential treatment for ethnic minorities when all the locals get a bad deal on the NHS. You can sort of understand it, I suppose. They've had to close half of the geriatric unit for lack of money. It just makes no sense to them."

"But you said the unit was funded by a charity appeal!" George said.

"So it is. Try telling them that. The unit's going to be sited here, so as far as they're concerned it's a National Health thing."

"Well, why hasn't someone explained all that to them? Maybe once they understand properly, they'll—"

"Oh, George, for a clever woman you can be awfully slow!" Hattie said irritably. "Of course there've been attempts to explain. The Professor's been out there speaking to them—or at any rate he tried to just after he came back from the BBC, he did the Today program about it—and they made such a row he had to call the police. And the Chief Exec's tried—Matthew Herne—and they laughed in his face. They don't want to be told! It's not just the ordinary locals out there, you know. It's your actual rent-a-mob. People who want to make ructions for their own ends."

"Who?" demanded George. "Who'd want to use a unit that's been set up to help kids who go through hell, even die, for making whatdoyoucallems—ructions?"

"Political factions," Hattie said and when George again demanded, "Who?" just shrugged her shoulders. "This is a difficult part of London, George. We've got all sorts of tub-thumpers stirring up trouble round here: the National Front, new Nazis. It wouldn't surprise me if we found out they were behind all this."

It happened again. George had been thinking only about what had happened this morning; she had not been giving any thought at all to the dead babies or to the two murders she and Gus were investigating; but suddenly another large piece of the jigsaw moved, wriggled and slotted itself neatly into place.

"Tell me again about how the unit was set up, how financed," she said urgently and Hattie stared at her.

"What?"

"I said—I have to know. It could be connected with—Oh, Hattie, if I promise to explain later, will you just answer my questions now?" George begged. Hattie lifted her brows at her vehemence and then nodded.

"OK, if you promise. What was it you wanted? How it all started?" She reached for the middle drawer of her desk and pulled it open. It was a jumble of papers and notebooks and odds and ends of the sort that usually clutter a woman's handbag. She rummaged in it in the same rather embarrassed fashion women with such bags do. "I keep on meaning to sort this bloody mess out, but I've been too hectic—Ah! Here it is! Look, here's the first poster he did. Put it up in my waiting room and asked me to point it out to people. That was last—let me see—summer sometime."

"Who did?"

"Dr. Choopani."

It was a crude piece of work: a black-and-white poster, smudged and crumpled from its time in Hattie's desk drawer. It showed a small black child curled up in a posture of pain while an anxious mother hovered over him. In the background a pair of young black lovers yearned into each other's eyes. The text read:

> Do you care? If you are of African descent you MUST care. Sickle cell anemia and Sickle Cell TRAIT could affect YOU and YOUR CHILDREN. We have to find a CURE for this dreadful problem, but cures take money. HELP US to raise the money we must have to provide RESEARCH. COUNSELING, CARE and ADVICE on your chances of having a sickle cell baby gladly given. ADVICE on helping your child cope if he has a sickle cell crisis. All will be AVAILABLE. Call this number now. And PLEASE GIVE GENEROUSLY!

"It's not a very good poster. Not good at all," Hattie said judiciously. "Bit misleading in some ways—I mean, the genetic counseling bit. Anyway, he knew better than I did and told me so. I have to admit he was right. I said he should do a more professional-looking job but he said that'd make people suspicious and this one would work. And it did. A hundred thousand! I ask you! And he talked Herne and the Professor into letting him have that set of rooms over the Pharmacy at a really low rental and he's got the whole thing up and running. Or almost. He'll have staff in next week, he told me, and the first patient coming through the week after."

"But what's he doing for pathology services?" George said, diverted for a moment from her main purpose. "I've heard nothing about this!"

"I don't think anyone ever thought he'd pull it off, so there hasn't been much talk about it. But he comes in and out of here a fair bit now, to tell me what's happening. I think I'm the only one who's really shown an interest, but then I would. We get the kids in crisis in here, you see. Anyway, he told me he had to have all specialist staff, specially trained. I suppose that includes pathology."

"Hmm," was all George said, then she looked again at the poster. "I wonder."

"Wonder what?"

"Remember he was set on?" George said. "One night at Gus's—at a fish-and-chip shop. You patched him up, Adam." She looked at the young doctor silently sipping at his coffee. "Remember?"

"What?" Adam squinted at her and then nodded. "I remember the chap you helped me handle," he said. "You were great. He was a right—well, he wasn't easy."

"He was Dr. Choopani," George said.

"Oh!" Adam said and went back to his coffee.

Hattie looked interested. "He was beaten up? I didn't know that!"

"You were off duty. I don't suppose you check the names of all the patients who were treated when you aren't here."

"Not unless I have to. Why was he beaten up?"

"Racist attack, he thought. So did I at first and then—Well, he doesn't have an easy personality."

Hattie snorted with laughter. "Easy? Do me a favor! He comes across as the most arrogant bastard who ever breathed. Which is a pity really, because he's a nice fella when you get to know him. It's just his manner. Way he was brought up, I suppose."

"Yes." George was still abstracted. Had her idea any logic? And yet, why not? It would be absurd to think that the hospital had a monopoly of common-sense people on the staff. Couldn't it be that...Yes, she decided, it could. She lifted her chin and looked at Hattie beseechingly.

"Hattie darling, it's imperative, really imperative I go and talk to Gus before that bunch out there have been dispersed. He'll get rid of them if anyone can, I know, and—"

"Well, well!" Hattie said, lifting her brows interrogatively. "Do I hear the voice of an admirer? One who sees Sir Galahad in a copper's helmet? One who—"

"Hattie, shut up. Just listen. I really do have to talk to him. We have a tricky case on and I think I have an idea about a clue. Please, Hattie. You helped me over the Oxford case, you and your Sam. Now be an angel and help again."

Hattie looked uncertain. She'd enjoyed her inside seat in the Oxford affair; knowing what had happened before almost anyone else in the hospital had been great fun. Could it happen again?

"Is this about Harry Rajabani?" she said, setting her head on one side.

"You've got it in one," George said. "I really do have to talk to Gus about it."

Hattie leaned over and looked at her, put a finger on her pulse and pursed her lips. "You're sure you weren't knocked out at all?" she said. "Because if you have even the hint of a head injury—"

"I'm not stupid, Hattie! Of course if I had I'd tell you. Believe me, no. Now let me go, for heaven's sake."

"Well, I suppose I'd better. You'll only drive me bonkers if I don't," Hattie said. She sat and watched George rush out of the department so fast that she almost galloped, then turned to Adam. "Time you were back out there," she said sternly. "High time."

"Yes, Sister," Adam said, all demure and biddable again, and grinned at her and went, leaving Hattie thinking hard alone in her office. There was something she'd just thought of that perhaps she should tell George and her Gus. Well, maybe later. When she had time.

25

By the time George reached the main entrance again, cutting across the courtyard to the ambulance entrance and pushing her way through the curious members of staff who had found excuses to come down from wards and departments all over the hospital to see what was going on, her idea had lost its shaky outlines and become a firm and crystalline conviction. She had to tell Gus, as soon as she possibly could, that the likelihood was that the murderer of Harry Rajabani was out there in that mob. If he had to arrest and question every last one of them, well, so be it; she was quite sure she knew now what had happened to Harry, and why.

Again she used her memory, trying to see the two men side by side: Harry with his classic good looks, the wide warm mouth beneath the proud, sharply defined prow of a nose, the liquid eyes and thick curling lashes that made them seem even more lustrous; and Dr. Choopani, just as patrician in profile, just as handsome in his own much older way...

Her conviction shivered for a moment at that point as she stood in the shadows at the courtyard end of the ambulance entrance and peered through the mass of bodies for some sign of Gus. Dr. Choopani had to be a good thirty-five years older than Harry. He still had his hair admittedly, but it was greyish and sparse compared with Harry's springing close-cut curls. Then her spirits lifted and she assured herself that her hunch did make sense. Wasn't it one of the clichés that racists trotted out all the time, the thing about not being able to tell black people apart? Maybe for some of them it was true. Their hatred of skins darker than their own made them incapable of looking on the owners of them as people like themselves with clear physical differences and appearances; with such an attitude, how could they be expected to see that Harry Rajabani and Dr. Choopani were not in fact really alike at all? She stiffened her shoulders unconsciously as she stiffened her determination that she was right; Harry had been killed by one or some of these thugs now demonstrating against the new unit, confusing him with Dr. Choopani. The Rag and Bottle had been crowded that night and wasn't all that well lit at the best of times. And of course people there drank, which would profoundly affect their responses, never mind their intellect (or what passes for it, she thought waspishly). Someone had thought Harry was the man who had so successfully organized the local Afro-Caribbean community that he had raised a hundred thousand pounds for a special unit to deal with a disease black people suffered; and in their hatred of all such people they had chosen to kill the man who threatened by his actions to save black lives.

It had to be true, she told herself firmly as she began to edge forward through the craning people clotting the mouth of the ambulance entrance; it all fitted so elegantly and the sooner she managed to get Gus to see it the better. The end of the case was in sight. Well, the Rajabani part, if not the Oberlander, at any rate, and she pushed a little harder, impatient to tell Gus so. Unwillingly people made way for her, until at last she was at the front. Now she could see what was happening more clearly and her mouth dried with apprehension.

The crowd had grown even greater as passers-by joined in and there had been reinforcements of the rent-a-mobbers, (as she now assured herself they were) bearing even more banners with racist slogans. In addition, a TV camera crew had arrived; she could see them on the opposite pavement craning to pick up with their camera the thickest part of the crowd where the chanting that filled the air seemed to be most tightly orchestrated.

But orchestrated or not, it was hard to hear what they were actually shouting and she stopped trying to, concentrating instead on looking for Gus. There was no reason why he should be here, of course, she realized. This was a job for the uniformed branch of the police, rather than CID; but for some reason he had arrived this morning and must surely still be around. No policeman, whether he had been detailed to deal with such a fracas or not, would willingly walk away and leave his colleagues to it; certainly not Gus. Anyway, she told herself then, he would never have left without checking on me in A & E and that was a thought that warmed her; even in the middle of all this she found herself grinning for a moment.

She saw Professor Hunnisett pressed against the wall at the side of the ambulance entrance and her grin widened. Clearly he felt he had to be there, but the last thing he wanted now was to be seen; his experience of trying to talk to this mob and being howled down must have terrified him, for he was almost clinging to the greasy old brickwork as he peeped out at the crowd with an expression of almost childlike alarm on his pallid face.

Matthew Herne, on the other hand, was right at the front of the hospital contingent, shouting back at the crowd for all he was worth, his face scarlet with the effort he was putting into his stentorian roars—that were impossible to hear above the din of course—and clearly in a huge rage. He went up several points in her estimation at that moment; whatever else the man was—and he could be very awkward, not to say obstructive, to deal with on many hospital matters—he didn't lack guts. She had to admire that in him.

The line of uniformed police that stood between the hospital contingent and the demonstrators seemed to move and shiver and then tightened again and to her huge relief she saw Gus as he ducked under a constable's arm and appeared on the hospital side of the scene. She shrieked his name at the top of her voice.

How he heard her she couldn't imagine, but he did, lifting his chin like a dog scenting a lead and looking around. When he spotted her his forehead snapped into a deep frown and he loped over, his face like a sky threatening thunder. He took her arm, scowling ferociously.

"What the bleedin' "ell you doin' out "ere?" he said roughly. His street accent had never been stronger and she blinked in some surprise, for he was clearly very angry indeed; this was not one of his jocular protests. "You get out o' this and back to A & E—what the bastards there were thinkin' of to let you sneak out this way—"

"Hey, hey, back off," she protested. "Hattie said I could come and find you. I'm fine. Nothing more than a bruise and a bit of a shaking-up, so cool it, buster! I have to tell you—I know what happened to Harry."

Still scowling, he had left one hand on her arm as though to lead her back to A & E, no matter what she did, and she shook herself free crossly.

"Will you lay off and listen to me, Gus! I'm telling you I know what happened to Harry! They confused him with Choopani—this is all happening because Choopani raised a hundred thousand to start a special unit for sickle cell anemia."

"Sickle-cell what?" He was diverted from his anger at last.

"It's a form of genetic-inherited disease that affects mainly people of African origin. Needs special care and research and all sorts." She spoke as urgently as she could, for the shouting of the mob was unabated and indeed seemed a bit more intense now. "He was the one who set out to save black lives with the unit—and that lot are racists and are dead against it, obviously. They confused Harry with Choopani and that was why they killed Harry. When they assaulted Choopani in your shop it was all part of the same thing—it's got to be, Gus. It's the only thing that makes sense."

He opened his mouth to answer her but there was no time. Behind him there was a sudden shrieking that rose shrilly above the ugly noise and Gus whirled, let go of her arm, and headed for the line of uniformed backs that stood between him and the crowd. He pushed his way through, and George, caught in his wake and with not the least intention of being left behind, hung on to his coat tails.

Somewhere in the middle of the crowd fist-fighting had broken out; people were falling back to give those who were attacking each other more space, while others tried to push forward to be able to join in.

The aggression and hatred were so intense that George could almost smell them; it certainly sent her own adrenalin into overdrive. She felt the rush of fear-tinged excitement in her muscles and all through her to her fingers' ends; and the back of her trained mind threw up a little voice which lectured her on the effects of subliminal pheromonal scents on human behaviour and their role in triggering the "fight/flight' response. But she ignored that, and pushed forward herself to get closer to the center of the action.

A tall wooden placard, bearing this time an anti-racist slogan which shrieked, "Death To All Fascists!" rocked overhead, shuddered and came down, crashing on to heads below. Bellows of rage and pain went up and more people joined in the fighting. Blows were flying, and some people had sticks and other weapons (George caught the glint of knuckle dusters on one burly fist) and the sounds of flesh being hit and squeals of pain and anger increased sharply.

And this was the point at which Gus clearly became hugely angry and he bawled something at the senior uniformed officer behind George, where the line of constables was still trying to prevent any contact between the mob and the hospital. He waved his arm furiously, and the other man shouted something back and all hell broke out. The police line wavered, widened and split into its component men and at the same time, it seemed from nowhere, more policemen with riot shields and truncheons appeared and the next minutes were a complete mêlée.

George was never to know quite what happened next; she was aware of fists flailing and legs kicking and making contact with her, but she felt no pain (though later she found the bruises to prove she should have done), rather a huge exhilaration. Responding at last to her adrenalin, she hit out with her own fists balled tightly inside her thick winter gloves. It was a species of mad game and she felt no more fear than if she had indeed been playing, as well as a sense of delight and complete lack of concern for the welfare of others that the professional part of her mind protested at; but she didn't listen to that either.

Suddenly there was a balaclaved figure next to her. She lifted her head and looked up and the wide blue eyes that glared out at her through the black eyeholes sent a stab of the most primitive terror through her. She hesitated, then reached forward with her hand open wide to push him away, but the figure seized her hand and bent it back against her arm so that her wrist swirled with pain, pain she definitely felt this time. She yelped and pecked her head forward hard, and with the most instinctive move she could ever remember having made, bit the hand that was pushing. The balaclaved figure let go, yelled something unintelligible and went for her again, but once more Gus was there; he grabbed the figure from behind and held on tight, though his captive struggled and went on shouting; and then, out of nowhere it seemed to George, there was someone else beside them. A tall man, panting hard; George felt his breath hot on her cheek. He lifted his hand in which he had a large stout stick and brought it down with a sickeningly loud crack on to the balaclava in spite of the fact that Gus was holding the man by his arms. It was as neat a blow as it could be; the man in Gus's grasp slumped and seemed knocked out, for he remained still, and the other, a quite well-dressed man of about thirty, looked almost startled at the effect of his blow.

"He's a fascist bastard," he gasped in an accent so cultured he could have been a character in a 1950s Ealing film, and he looked from George to Gus. "I thought he was trying to hurt you."

"He was," George shouted back—for there was still a great deal of din, though it was beginning to lessen now. "Thanks a whole lot."

"You didn't have to do that," Gus grunted. "I'm a police officer and I had him in my hands, and—"

"Police?" the tall man said and shook his head. "I'm so sorry! I didn't know that though, did I? I only know that this is the chap who's been organizing these bloody fascists and causing a lot of the aggro round here and I wanted to get him—and help you at the same time, of course," he added hastily. He looked around. The fighting seemed to be contained, the police in control, people were running away, though some were being collected by the uniformed men and shoved into police vans which were arriving, and all around them were broken placards and banners on the ground. "I think I'll hop it too, if you don't mind. Take it from me, though, you've got the leader there."

"Hey," Gus shouted as the man began to slip away. "Don't you bloody dare! You're under arrest for—"

"Some other time, thanks all the same," the man called back. "I have to get to work. You hold on to him! He's trouble!" And he was gone, legging it down the street and dodging through the remnants of the crowd with the ease of long practice.

Gus cursed but held on to the slumped figure in his arms, a burden which had prevented him from grabbing the runaway. George reached out for the man's other arm, helping Gus to deal with the weight of him.

"Good luck to him," she said. "If he's right and this is the ringleader, he's done a great job. He doesn't deserve to be collared for it. There, let's take a look at him."

The man was stirring now, moving his head and his arms in a groggy fashion and seeming better able to stand. Gus shouted over his shoulder at another policeman who came running as George pulled carefully on the fabric at the balaclava's chin, pulling it up over the face to leave the woollen material sitting bundled incongruously on the top of the head.

And caught her breath in cold shock. The face that stared out at her, with swimming eyes and a trickle of blood on the forehead from the blow on the skull, was that of Philip Goss, the male nurse on the Pediatric Unit.

26

By the time they reached the A & E department, the peace of the morning that George had found so comforting earlier when she had shared coffee with Hattie and Adam Parotsky was shattered. The place was a maelstrom of stretchers, people with bloody heads and limbs, and distracted staff trying to impose some sort of order on to the chaos.

Gus, grim-lipped and silent, almost carried Philip Goss there and handed him over to one of the uniformed constables in the waiting area with strict instructions not to let him out of his sight, even if the medical staff tried to separate him from his charge, and told him he'd be within shouting call if he had any problems. And then turned to glare at George.

"Now, Dr. B., what am I to do about you? You lay yourself wide open to Gawd knows what in the shape of injury and then bugger me if you don't go and do it all over again."

"Oh, Gus, do stop being such an old biddy," George said impatiently. "Listen, what—"

"Old biddy!" Gus was affronted. "Because I worry over you and want you to be safe, I'm an old biddy? That's just about the most—"

"Gus, shut up, will you? And listen. That guy—his name's Philip Goss, I know him."

"That hooligan? You *know* him?"

"I tried to explain outside there, but you wouldn't stop! Now, will you shut up and listen so I can explain properly?

Philip Goss is one of the male nurses on the Pediatric Unit. He's a good guy—or at least I thought he was. Great with the kids and very supportive of Harry that day Dave Ritchard went for him. I can't imagine that man who hit him was right—but he seemed so certain, didn't he? And if he is, it just doesn't make sense, though he did once say something…" She frowned, trying to remember, but shook her head. "It's gone. But he said something to me once that could have meant he was a bit devious. "I'll try and remember. The thing is, he's got a friend—I think he's gay. There's a new guy on the medical team in Pediatrics, Alan Prior. I've seen them together. I think—well, all I can think is that he's around here as well—I mean, if he was involved in this demo too, it might be worth talking to him about Philip. Because you can't just take that man's word for it, can you? The man that hit him, I mean, and who said he was the leader of the racist lot."

"You're damned right I can't." Gus sounded very gloomy as he looked about at the crowded waiting room. "Evidence, that's what I need. Not that it should be that difficult to sort out—not now we've got so firm a lead. I've always thought there was some organizational skill in operation somewhere on the pitch. Some of the racist incidents haven't been—well, haphazard enough, know what I mean?"

"I can imagine," she said. "Look, let me have a wander, hmm? I can borrow a white coat, look like some of the A & E staff. See if Prior's here. I've met him so I know what he looks like. Maybe I can get something out of him."

"No!" Gus began to protest, but at that moment the officer in charge of the uniformed police came bustling over to him in a fussy, somewhat self-important manner. "Shit!" Gus said under his breath and composed his face into a semblance of a welcoming expression. "You lookin' for me, Bannen?"

"I certainly am." Chief Inspector Edward Bannen peered closely at Gus. "I want to know why you were here this morning. We got a call from the hospital to cover the incident.

I don't see that CID have any place in a situation that involves public order in this sort of way and—"

"Listen, it's like this, Edward, me old pal." Gus put an arm over the man's shoulders and with a flick of an expressive eyebrow at George led him away to the side of the waiting area. George watched them go and grinned. Poor Gus, she thought, much less in control than he thinks he is. And went in search of first a white coat and then Alan Prior.

She found him sitting with his head in his hands in a cubicle in the minor ops unit, waiting for someone to come and put a couple of stitches in a small split on his forehead. He lifted his head hopefully as George looked round the curtain, as she had with all the other cubicles, and looked at her with his eyes wide and pleading.

"You'll try and get a good cosmetic effect?" he said. "It's not that I'm vain, you know, but scars can be so—"

"I'm not here to stitch you," she said, leaning over him and looking at the wound judiciously. "You could dress that with a butterfly plaster and you wouldn't need stitches at all, you know. If someone said they would stitch it, then it's because of wanting a good cosmetic result. You get slightly wider scars with butterfly dressings."

"I asked for a stitch." He put up one hand and touched the skin near the cut gingerly. "I know you, don't I, from somewhere? Tell me, is it a very big cut? Have you a mirror I could borrow?"

"Sorry, no," George said. "And yes you know me. I mean we've met. I'm George Barnabas, Pathology. I met you with Philip Goss in Pediatrics one afternoon."

"Er—yes," he said. He put his hands back on his lap and ducked his chin down so that he had to look at her from beneath half-lowered lids. "Well—er—I think I remember."

"Doesn't matter if you don't. I remember you." She looked at him thoughtfully. Maybe the blunt way in would be best; even if it weren't, she had little time for more. At any moment someone would come and treat the man and she'd lose her opportunity, and Gus was still fussing about. Once he got away from Bannen he'd be sure to come back, wanting to tuck her up somewhere. She might just as well go for broke.

"Philip Goss—he's a special person in your life?" she said baldly.

Prior blinked but otherwise held her gaze. "Is he?" he said.

"Oh come on! No need to be coy with me. It's legal, so why worry? He's your boyfriend, isn't he?"

"If he is, it's no concern of yours."

"Was it his idea you should come down and get involved in this? Did he warn you you might get hurt?"

Prior flushed suddenly. "He did not! I don't pretend to be anything but what I am, and that's a devout coward. I'm not one for bashing and shoving. I won't go on gay rights marches and I wouldn't have come down here for this if he hadn't said it was going to be peaceful. He told me he'd got the whole thing really tightly organized, there'd be no opposition to us—and wasn't he wrong! He was furious when those communist types turned up."

"Communist?" George murmured. "What an old-fashioned word."

"Well, you know what I mean," Prior said fretfully. "These so-called anti-racists. Stupid creatures—if they'd grown up in South Africa like I did, they'd know better. But Philip had promised me we'd be safe, and I thought wearing those damned woolly helmets'd make it really OK. No one'd recognize us, you see, and we'd be—well, *safe*. But they managed to cut me even through all that wool! Look at this!"

He lifted a black woollen balaclava from his lap and showed it to her. It was exactly like the one Goss had been wearing and her breathing speeded up in excitement at the sight of it. It wasn't precisely proof that Goss had organized all the mayhem—including Harry's death—but it was confirmation of his close involvement. "Some chap hit me with the handle of one of those bloody placards and look at me!" Prior went on complainingly and again he touched his forehead near the cut. "Split my head open!"

"It can happen," she said, not altogether sympathetically. "It doesn't always need a knife."

"Honestly, I could kill that Philip! He had no right to bring me down for this. I'm a doctor, not a bloody politician. He may be all excited over it, but me, I don't want to know."

"Politician, is he?" George said as casually as she could and leaned back against the wall, her hands shoved deep in her white coat pockets to hide any excitement they might betray. "What sort?"

"Oh, I don't know!" Prior said irritably. "He's always going on about something. I can't be sure what side he's on, to tell you the truth. He's very fond of playing what he calls both sides against the middle—plotting to get the things done that he wants done."

"Yes," George said softly. "Yes, of course! That was what he said. He told me that once." She could remember it so vividly now that it was almost as though Goss were standing there in front of her, repeating the words he'd used when she'd told him she thought he was a bit of a villain who liked to get his own way. "Doesn't everyone? It's not difficult, you know. A bit of a tweak here, a word in an ear there, and it's amazing what you can achieve." She'd been joking, but she'd been more accurate than she could have expected.

"Told you, did he? Then why are you quizzing me?" Prior sounded more fretful than ever. "When will they come and do this damned stitching? I want to get out of here and sort myself out. I feel a complete mess. It's the last time I do a locum at this horrible place."

"They're a bit tied up," George said. "A lot of cases out there. Including Philip."

He tilted his head up sharply at that. "What?"

"He got a cut head too, but he was knocked out for a while. Probably a minute or two."

"Good God!" Prior looked horrified. "Don't tell me he's got a skull fracture!"

"I've no idea. It's possible, obviously. I imagine he'll be X-rayed. I'm sorry if I've upset you."

She was genuinely concerned for a moment; however much she now suspected Goss of being the man who had murdered Harry, she was still a doctor, and still responded professionally to the pain and distress of the sick or the injured, even though in this case the injured man was Goss's lover. But he shook his head at her, wincing a little at the discomfort as he did it.

"Not upset, exactly. I mean not about Philip Goss. I've had as much of him as I can take. If he wants to stick his fool head out and get it walloped that's his choice. If he hasn't the wit to keep out of situations where he might get a skull fracture that's his lookout." He shuddered. "I've always had a horror of brain damage. Seen too much of it. I worked in Groote Schuur and some of those kaffirs, after the police sent them to us—well, don't ask! No, what makes me mad is that he lied to me! He told me it'd be safe, a bit of fun, no more, and expected me to—well, it's enough to—" He stopped, clearly lost for words, and George tried not to show her disgust. But she couldn't completely succeed.

"I thought you might be worried about him," she said as lightly as she could. "I had the impression you were close."

"Not now, we aren't," Prior said with deep feeling. "And if he asks you, you can tell him so! Oh, at last!" as a nurse came through the curtains with a suture tray. "I thought you were never going to get here!"

"We're doing all we can to deal with you all. The place is jammed," the nurse said. She looked at George. "Are you all right, Dr. Barnabas? I thought you were injured too."

"I'm fine," George said quickly. "Just fine. Thanks, Dr. Prior," and she escaped.

Outside in the waiting area there was no sign of Gus; clearly Bannen had spirited him away somewhere. George hesitated, uncertain what to do next. Go in search of Goss and question him? That might be tricky. Apart from the fact that he was to be accompanied all the time by a police constable, the man would be listed as a suspected head injury and in need of careful attention. The first adage she'd learned in her neurology had been the famous Hippocratic one: "No head injury is so slight that it may safely be ignored, nor so severe that life should be despaired of", or something of the sort. To question a man in such a condition would hardly be the act of a caring doctor. Yet right now she was being a detective...She grimaced at her own confusion and looked around.

And then stiffened. On the far side of the crowded rows of chairs where patients and their friends and relations (now arriving in considerable numbers as the news got out of what had happened at Old East) sat, she saw the neat erect figure of Dr. Choopani. Immediately she made her way over to him, weaving over outstretched feet and between the rows of seats as quickly as she could.

He greeted her as courteously and as calmly as though they were both strolling peaceably at a vicarage garden tea party. "Good morning, Dr. Barnabas. I trust I see you well."

"I'll get by," she said, touching the bruise on her cheek, which was aching a little. There were other parts of her anatomy that were aching too, but she preferred not to think about those. "What are you doing here?"

He raised his brows. "Where else should I be?" he said. "My new unit is to open today, had you not heard? This is a great day for us!"

She tilted her head to indicate the crowded waiting room behind them. "I had heard something about it," she said with deliberately heavy irony. "Like all those other people here."

"This little fuss'—he waved a dismissive hand—"they will get over it. I have always got over the attacks on me in the past, so I will again. As I told you when we last met and you were so kind to me, these people are garbage and not worthy of attention."

"Oh, you're wrong there, Dr. Choopani," George said softly. "Not that they're not garbage—I wouldn't argue with you on that, though it's one hell of a label to put even on people who foment this sort of trouble—but they are very worthy of attention. Suppose I told you that one man has been killed already because he was mistaken for you?"

He contemplated her seriously for a long moment, his eyes never leaving her face. And then sighed deeply. "My dear Dr. Barnabas, I know that these people are dangerous. I am not sure how you can be certain that someone has been killed as part of an intended attack on me, but even if you are right— though I have to say it sounds unduly dramatic to me—even if you are right, it does not change my opinion. They are not worthy of attention, however dangerous! It means we must be watchful and protect ourselves, that is all. But waste time worrying about them? I would be ashamed! Ah, here is the good Sister Clements. You will excuse me—she is my strong support for my new unit, you know, and I want to speak with her. I hope you will come and see our work when you have time? It is a small beginning but we will grow!" And he bent his head politely and slipped away towards the far side of the waiting area where Hattie was in close colloquy with, George saw with a lift of her spirits, Gus.

What happened then was surprising, not because of its suddenness, but because it seemed to George to happen so slowly, almost like a film that had been deliberately run at half speed.

As Dr. Choopani made his dignified way across the waiting hall, stepping over people's legs with a sort of fine disdain that George could see offended some of them—for people hurled ugly looks after him and some muttered as he passed—one of the cubicles on the far side was opened with a rattle of curtain rings and an empty trolley was pushed in. By the time Dr. Choopani was halfway across the crowded space, the now loaded trolley was on its way out again. George couldn't quite see who was on it at first. She just saw a nurse at the head end with a saline bag held high in the air, attached to the IV line on the patient's left arm, and a young police constable hovering behind her, rather out of reach of the trolley. There was a sizeable bandage over the head of the patient so the identity was not clear, although the presence of the policeman George found very suggestive.

Slowly the trolley came forward. It was being maneuvered a little awkwardly by the porter at the foot end, a very young man who looked to George to be a comparative newcomer to the job, for he was clearly inexperienced in the handling of the cumbersome thing. Dr. Choopani went on his majestic way, like a liner quite oblivious of the lesser craft fussing around beneath his bows, and reached the side of the trolley just as it was brought round so that the foot pointed in the direction of the doors that led out to X-ray and the wards.

George worked out without thinking consciously about it that the man was Goss, on his way for further investigations and therefore out of her reach for any sort of questioning. She was about to turn her attention back to Gus and to follow Dr. Choopani in his direction, when the figure on the trolley seemed to rear up, like a whale emerging from deep salt water, slowly and yet forcefully, and with a sort of native elegance.

"You bastard!" The voice was shrill and thick at the same time and George was startled. She moved without realizing she had, rushing across the floor with scant regard for the people in her way.

"You bastard!" the man on the trolley screamed again, and now George could see clearly that it was Goss, as she had suspected.

Goss looked wildly round and glared at the nurse beside him, who was as young and as inexperienced as the porter at the foot of the trolley—and indeed, the young policeman too—and seeming, like him, to be frozen into inaction by surprise at the behaviour of their patient. Goss looked down at his arm and the IV line going into it, reached with his other hand to yank it out, and then pulled on the other end; the nurse started at the tug and let go of the saline bag which Goss took in both hands and hurled with all his strength at Dr. Choopani's head, just a matter of feet away from him. It hit him foursquare and burst. Choopani stood there with saline dripping down his face, and his hair flattened by it; but he made no sign of being affected, staring back at Goss with cold control.

"You and your fucking blacks and their money, saving their shitty lives; dying's too good for them, you stinking lousy bastard—"

It was amazing. George stood there, as frozen as the young nurse beside Goss and indeed as virtually everyone else in the big waiting area, as he went on shrieking and raving and shrieking again, his language becoming ever more ugly and furious.

Once again George's professional mind took over and began to lecture her about the sort of personality changes and loss of inhibition that could occur in certain sorts of brain injury. Goss was now completely without inhibition; his scheming and tweaking and words-in-ears were vanished skills. All he could do was let out all his rage and hatred in a great sickening tide of bile. She shuddered and put her hands up to her ears to block it out, it was so horrible.

Others had begun to move too: Hattie running across the big space to take over from the young nurse and settle Goss down again; Gus joining her and the constable; other nurses and some of the casualty doctors coming to deal with the waiting patients who had been upset and were whimpering in consequence. George too made an effort and hurried over to the trolley where Goss lay panting and staring wide-eyed at the ceiling over his head. He went on mouthing words, but now at least he was doing it silently.

"Oh, lor," Hattie gasped as George came up beside her to help tighten the restraints she was applying from the sides of the trolley to hold Goss safely in place. "Oh, lor! It's like those parsons who start to swear when they're coming round from anesthetics—Thanks, George, I think we've got him now. Listen, Nurse Patterson, you take him, will you? Warn them he's a handful, but we must get him there. They'll do X-rays when he's in the ward. Neurology Three, that's right. Fast as you can."

Hattie watched him go as the waiting room slowly settled to its usual dull roar and someone led the still silent Dr. Choopani away to dry him. "Oh, George, I am sorry," she said, turning a woebegone face to her. "I remembered after you'd gone this morning—earlier, you know?—I remembered that Goss had once said to me that he thought what Dr. Choopani was doing was asking for trouble with the local white people, and he shouldn't be allowed to do it. I thought then it was an odd thing for a nurse to say, especially one who was so busy with others' affairs and the Union and so forth and always going on about ethics. I thought it was the sort of way people who hate blacks talk, but he's supposed to be a champion of equal rights. And I meant to tell you..."

27

"I don't see who else could be the killer," George said again. "He's the one with the best motive we've got, isn't he?"

"You're trying too hard," Gus said. "And you're adding two and two together to make into seventeen. First of all, you want to believe that because Goss is a raving racist, he'd decide to kill Choopani just because he wanted to start this unit for a disease only black people get, and then you want to believe that he mixed up the two men—Choopani and Harry—and killed the wrong one. But that's one hell of a mix-up, George. Choopani's a man in his forties and not particularly good to look at. Harry Rajabani was well under thirty and no end of an oil painting into the bargain—and a man Goss worked with every day!"

"Harry was wearing a woolly Rastafarian hat when he was killed. Everyone looks the same in those things. Goss must have seen him and thought he was Choopani and—"

Again Gus shook his head. "Sorry! Too many maybes, ducks. More coffee?"

She made a face. "If I drink any more I'll be awash. You too. You'll start to twang like a harp if you have any more. You drink too much coffee for your own good, anyway."

He stretched back in his chair. "Oh, she cares for me after all!" he told the ceiling in thrilling tones. "Worryin' about my health now! It's a good sign. She loves me, she loves me not, she loves me—"

"Shut up, Gus," George said, but she was abstracted and sat there staring down at her hands on her desk, frowning and trying to think. They had come back to her office once the hubbub in A & E had died down and the walking wounded had been sent on their way (some of them via the police station, where statements were to be taken and charges made regarding the demo) and the more severely injured admitted to the hospital, Goss among them.

She sighed and shook her head. "You realize the man's in a bad way? They reckon he's bleeding fairly copiously into the skull and that's what's causing the symptoms—the shouting and loss of inhibition among them. They'll be coming out of theater with him in an hour or so." She twisted her wrist to squint at her watch. "And he'll be in intensive care for some time after that. But we've got to talk to him, find out where he was that night and what he was doing and—"

"Marvellous, 'n't it?" Gus said to the ceiling. "Give her an inch and she's bloody off like Mick the Miller. She'll be wantin' my pension next as well as my bleedin' job."

"Are you saying I'm getting too involved in this case?" she demanded pugnaciously, sitting up very straight.

"Yup."

"Oh." She was nonplussed for a moment but then regained her equanimity. "Well too bad, buddy. Too damn bad. I'm in and I'll go on being in whether you like it or not."

"I love it," he said and grinned at her. "I was just tryin' to make the point that interviewin' suspects is something policemen are supposed to do. I don't cut up bodies, you don't talk to suspects. It's tidier that way."

"I've been very useful talking to suspects," she said. "If I hadn't talked to Prue I wouldn't have met and talked to Goss and I wouldn't have known Harry and—"

"Yeah, yeah, you're the best in the world." He leaned over the desk and very deliberately gave her a loud, smacking kiss. "Where'd I be without you?"

"I hate to think," she said, not displeased. "So now what?"

He sighed and got to his feet. "I have to leave you, my love, my own. Cor, get me! I'll be singin' to you next. I've got to get back to the nick, see what's happenin' there. I've got as many men as I can spare diggin' out all they can about adoption and agencies and babies—Gawd knows what they'll find. It's like looking for a sweet-tempered pathologist. And I've got all this new stuff to handle. I'll have to look into Goss's background, find some of his associates, ask a few questions—if you don't mind, that is?"

She laughed. "Tell you what. Go and talk to Alan Prior."

"Who?"

"He's a doctor here, had a sort of affair with Goss. I gather it's over—Prior wasn't best pleased at having his manly beauty damaged in Goss's demo, which he only went on to please Goss, though he probably shares his racist views. He's a thoroughly unreconstructed South African. I think you'll get a lot of stuff out of him." She told him all that Alan Prior had told her in A & E and he listened appreciatively.

"Well done, oh good and faithful servant," he said. "I'll talk to him and a few others here while I'm at it. If Goss has really been organizing round the hospital there'll be someone willing to talk. There usually is. As for you…"

"What about me? I've got ideas of my own about what I can do."

"That's what worries me." He was serious suddenly. "Don't take risks, George. Remember what happened last time when you set yourself up. I don't want you gettin' crazy notions like that again."

"I won't," she said. "I like my own skin far too well. I'm not one of your over-brave types, take it from me."

"But you are, you fool," he said and this time came around the desk to kiss her and did so very thoroughly. "Mmm. Like I said, really ripe Brie at its best, that's you. I could eat you on toast without any butter. Do take care, George. If there's anyone you've got any notions about, tell me, and I'll—"

"Yes," she said extricating herself and feeling a little flustered. Ridiculous at her age to be so thrown by a kiss. Still he really was—She shook her head and was stern with herself. "I'll tell you, Gus. Now get out of here and let me get some of my other work done."

"Make sure you get them to check you over again in A & E," he said. "I don't like the look of that bruise." He touched her face gently. She liked that.

"You should see the other bruises I've got," she said lightly. "I checked in the loo. There's one on my bottom that'd light up the world."

"I'd love to." He produced one of his most lascivious grins. "Just give me the chance."

"Some other time…" She pushed him gently and this time he went, shrugging into his coat. "I'll call you."

"No you won't," he said as he reached the door. "I'll come round to your place tonight—to see the old ladies. I miss "em dreadfully if I don't see them most days." And he flicked his thumb and forefinger at his invisible hat brim and went.

By mid afternoon she'd caught up with the paperwork that was waiting by dint of sending Jerry over to the canteen to fetch her a pot of yogurt and an apple for her lunch and working as she ate, keeping her head down over her desk and refusing to allow thoughts of either Gus or the case they were on to intrude. It was fairly easy to exclude thoughts on the case; keeping the image of Gus at bay was not so simple.

She could still smell the scent of his aftershave on her cheeks, left there when he'd kissed her, and it stirred her in a way that she found startling. She'd fancied men before, of course she had; indeed had to admit that one of her major problems was a distinct susceptibility to attractive men. She had had her share of lovers too. This one, though, was different. He was funny and serious at the same time, clever and surprising and energetic, but above all different, and she sat and stared unseeing at a PM report for a little while, thinking how very different indeed he was from any other man with whom she'd ever had a relationship. Different because of the obvious things, like his background, his speech, his tastes, but above all in his treatment of her. There were none of the usual tricks men used to get a woman into bed. Indeed, they'd gone no further than what he called snogging—which was tender and amusing and hugely enjoyable, she found, if not entirely satisfying, but that in itself added to her delight in him. He was teaching her the pleasures of delay, the joys of yearning and needing and having to wait. She was just reaching the stage where she wanted to get into bed with him so much that if he didn't drag her there soon she'd drag him.

Then she shook her head at herself and tried to work. This time she managed it, and at three o'clock stretched, looked at her watch and decided to take a stroll around the hospital.

"I want to see what's going on, Sheila. There's been a lot of action here today and I want to follow it up. So you be sure to stay here till I get back, OK? I'll be here in plenty of time for you to get away as usual." And she went quickly, leaving Sheila staring resentfully after her because she had intended to do exactly the same thing herself until George had pipped her at the post.

George started her tour at the new Sickle Cell Anemia Unit, finding with difficulty the almost hidden staircase that led to the set of rooms over the Pharmacy which Professor Hunnisett had provided for it. It was modestly signposted but she was amused when she saw the plaque at the foot of the staircase, which had, she assumed, been unveiled this morning by the footballer who had performed the opening ceremony.

"This Plaque commemorates the opening of the First Choopani Unit for Sickle Cell Anemia..." she read and her lips twisted with laughter. First of all because of the wholly typical Choopani-ish self-confidence of the "First', and secondly because he hadn't been able to resist the personal glory of using his own name. And then she chided herself as she climbed the stairs. That attitude was too British by half, she thought pushing open the door at the top. I've been here too long if I'm starting to think it's not perfectly reasonable for a man who's worked his butt off to raise some money for a public service project to have his name on it. He would at home in the States, so why not here?

The smell of new paint was pervasive and she sneezed loudly. A round-faced Jamaican nurse put her head out of a door. "Did you want somethin'?"

"Hi," George said. "I'm Dr. Barnabas, pathologist here. I couldn't come this morning, so I thought I'd kinda have a look round now. Is that all right?"

"Fine by me," the nurse said. "Glad to show you—or would you rather Dr. Choopani did?"

"He's still here?" George was surprised. She'd have thought he'd have gone long since.

The girl grinned. "Well o' course "e is! It's "is unit, "n't it?" She had a broad cockney accent, much broader than Gus's, and George warmed to her.

"I think it's the patients' unit," she murmured. "If you ask him, he'll tell you that, I'm sure."

"Wanna bet?" the nurse said and pushed at a door at the end of the corridor. "You jus' go and ask "im. "E's in "is office, I got stuff to do "ere."

Dr. Choopani was sitting at a large and elaborate desk, on a leather chair that was so new it was shiny. There was another large leather chair facing the desk and the walls bore pictures of various kinds, many of them of Dr. Choopani himself in various clearly important public activities with clearly important public persons.

He looked up at her when she came in and showed no surprise at all. "Good afternoon, Dr. Barnabas. I am pleased to see you visiting us."

"No patients yet?" George came in and looked around curiously. "This is all rather lavish!"

"No, there are no patients till tomorrow when we have the first official clinic, and this office I have paid for out of my own pocket since I care a great deal for comfortable surroundings when I work. It does not come from the fund."

"I didn't mean to suggest it did," George said. "I—"

"Whether you did or not, that is the case." He got to his feet and came round the desk. "Now I will show you round the unit."

He did, lecturing her at length about sickle cell anemia, the way it was passed through the generations, the effects of a sickle cell trait on a family, the horrors of a sickle cell crisis and a great many more things about which she was already well informed. She tried at first to tell him that she had all this at her fingers' ends and really didn't need to be lectured like a first-year nursing student, but he ignored that and continued with his learned dissertation as though she hadn't spoken. He was patronizing and irritating beyond measure but there was absolutely no doubt in her mind of his probity and his genuine interest in what he was doing. Here was a man who was exactly what he seemed, she told herself as she trailed obediently from room to room admiring as best she could consulting room couches, microscopes, charts and the other normal impedimenta of a clinical unit. There was no guile about him, which was what made him so difficult to like—he made no effort to present himself as an attractive modest person. He was pleased with his achievements—as he had the right to be—and saw no need to hide his pleasure. He didn't care that everyone around him would be driven to distraction by that degree of self-satisfaction. But for all that, she thought, he had achieved a great deal. This unit was a good one—or promised to be—and his efforts would do a lot of good for a lot of people. But by the time she escaped, almost running down the staircase to the plaque at the bottom, she was certain that there was nothing to discover from talking further to Dr. Choopani about the murder of Harry Rajabani or of the Oberlander baby. If he had known anything he would, she was sure, have told her by now. It was his nature to do so.

She stopped at the foot of the stairs for a moment. Around her it was deep dusk; the days might be lengthening towards the spring as the New Year hovered in the wings, but there was small sign yet of that; darkness and dampness were everywhere and she shivered. She drew her flimsy white coat a little closer as though it might provide warmth.

She was still standing there, uncertain where to go next, when someone coming out of the Pharmacy door beside the staircase bumped into her in the gloom. She stepped back and said, "Sorry!" quickly as though it had been her fault, but then, aware that it had not been, protested in a squawk.

"So sorry!" a voice said breathlessly. "I didn't see you there—Oh, it's you, Dr. Barnabas!"

George peered and saw the other's face and then laughed. "Cherry! I thought you were someone who was after me for the crumbs at the bottom of my pockets. It's all a mugger'd get! What are you doing here?"

"I had to pick up something for Dr. Arundel from the Pharmacy. How are you, Dr. Barnabas? Did you have a nice Christmas?"

"Not bad," George said, not wanting to sound too enthusiastic about it, remembering how much Cherry had dreaded the holiday. "Was yours as bad as you feared?"

"Worse," Cherry said, and lapsed into silence. She was walking away now, towards Red Block, and George went along with her, not caring much where she ended up. She was just prowling for news, after all. And now she thought of it, there was something she could talk to this girl about.

"Well, it's over now, or nearly," she said as cheerfully as she could. "Just New Year's Eve to get through and then we can look forward to a bit of summer sunshine."

"Yes," Cherry said without enthusiasm.

"And I hope we can get this case solved soon, too. It would be marvellous if we could get it out of the way before the New Year, wouldn't it?"

Cherry looked at her over her shoulder. They were now in the better-lit part of the courtyard, and George could see how dark were the shadows under her eyes and on her temples, and felt a deep stab of pity for her. She was indeed wretchedly miserable.

"There's only a couple of days now," she said drearily. "You couldn't."

"You never know," George said stoutly. "This morning at the demo—you heard about that?"

"Of course, everyone did. There was no end of a row, wasn't there?"

"There was indeed—but it also gave us a strong lead to who might have been Harry's killer."

Cherry shook her head. "Is that supposed to make me feel better?"

George was taken a little aback. "Doesn't it?"

Cherry shook her head again, more definitely this time. "It don't make a ha'porth of difference. Why should it?"

"I'm not sure..." George said and thought for a while. "Except that maybe justice, you know and—"

"Revenge," Cherry said and her voice was sardonic. "Much good that'd do Harry. I don't give a damn now who killed Harry. It's enough someone did. Chasing someone to kill them wouldn't make it any better, would it?"

"We don't kill murderers any more, Cherry. But we do have to catch them."

"Why?"

"To stop them doing it again!"

"I suppose."

"And to find out how and why they did it and—"

"You make it sound like a crossword puzzle," Cherry said,

pushing open the door to Red Block and standing back. "But what good'll it do me if I do find out? I'd still not have Harry."

"Cherry," George said. "I think you need help."

"Eh?"

"You're depressed. You're entitled to be, of course you are. But you can be helped. Talking to someone about it, a counsellor—"

"I don't want a counsellor," Cherry said with huge scorn. "I hear the one up in our department and how she bleats on at these people. Counseling doesn't do anything for you if what you want is a baby. And it won't do anything for me when what I want is my Harry back." Tears collected in her eyes and began to run down her cheeks unchecked. She made no grimaces, showed none of the pain of weeping. She just let the tears roll.

George looked at her, nonplussed, and then did the only thing she could think of doing; she opened her arms and let Cherry creep into them, and she held her close, and let the wave of weeping end itself naturally when it was ready to. Then Cherry straightened her back, nodded, mopped her face and turned to continue her journey back to her department as though nothing had happened. And George followed her lead and went with her. There seemed little else she could do.

28

Sometimes, George was to think later, circumstances conspired for you rather than against you. That was what happened that dull December afternoon in Maternity. As she and Cherry came into the department, they could hear the sound of the television blaring out; the BBC was showing a blockbuster holiday-time movie and George could see all the mothers who were still in the ward (despite the usual heroic efforts to discharge many of the hospital's patients for Christmas) collected in one bay, sitting on their beds and armchairs that had been dragged in, watching it. They had their babies on their laps and a couple were feeding them. They looked contented and happy. It was a pleasant sight, George thought. The staff who were on duty were there too, and all of them, patients and staff alike, were sharing the last of the Christmas chocolate biscuits and drinking cream sherry from plastic cups. George could smell the sweetness of them both as soon as she and Cherry pushed open the double doors.

It was evidently one of those rare days when a lull had hit the department and there were no laboring mothers at all. The door of the labor suite stood open and the lights were out, a rare enough event, and though there were some obviously pre-natal women amongst those watching the James Bond movie with such absorption, there was no suggestion that they were about to give birth. Everyone was relaxed, contented and quite unaware that anyone had come into the ward.

"Nice for them," Cherry said as they walked down the corridor towards the Fertility Unit. "Must make a change from always rushing round the way they usually have to." They were passing the office door as she said it and almost automatically she turned her head and glanced in. "Even Sister's watching that film—"

They were in fact past the office door when Cherry stopped short so suddenly she made George stumble, for she was immediately beside her.

"Blimey!" Cherry said and stared straight ahead.

"What on earth's the matter?" George had to speak up, for the TV sound was turned very high and the chatter of onscreen guns and the swoop of dramatic music filled the air with its ersatz excitement. Whether it was the film or Cherry's behaviour or even a moment of premonition, George would never know, but the flesh on the back of her neck seemed to creep.

"It's that thing you did, making me stare at the wall," Cherry said, still standing motionless.

"Staring at—oh, yes," George said and nodded. "When I was trying to help you remember." Her attention sharpened even more. "What's happened, Cherry? What have you remembered?"

"A basket weave." Cherry nodded at her suddenly, a very affirmative movement. "I said I could see a basket weave and the crumpled pages which had that sort of writing on—a sort of code you said it was."

"Well?" George was almost on tiptoes, she was so tense.

"I just saw it."

"What?"

"The basket weave."

"Where?"

"In here. Sister's office."

They both stood very still for a moment, looking at each other and then, slowly, Cherry turned and retraced her steps, with George following close behind. She stopped at the door of Sister's office and stood there, peering in.

Behind them, obliquely across the central corridor, the soft Scottish accent of Sean Connery chatting up one of his luscious heroines seemed to be absorbing every spectator. Certainly no one turned to look or seemed to be aware that the two of them were standing there in the corridor.

"See?" Cherry said softly. "Over there." And she jerked her chin towards the back of the office.

George looked. Cherry had indicated the battered old table against the wall with its overflow of papers from Sister's desk, which was in the middle of the room. There was a rather battered old Olympia typewriter on it. Beside it there was a stack of flimsy metal trays built up into a tower, each tray held six inches above the other by spindly legs set in the corners. The upper trays were filled with more papers which showed clearly through the mesh of which the trays were made.

"See," Cherry said again. "Basket weave."

George squinted and understood. When Cherry had first used the term she had imagined something made of cane or bamboo or straw, rather like a hat; now she saw that the metal wire of which the trays were made was plaited together in the classic one-over-one-under style used for making so many fabrics out of fibres. She said, "Of course!" loudly and turned to Cherry excitedly.

Cherry had glanced over her shoulder at the bay where everyone was watching TV, alarmed that the loudness of George's voice might have attracted them, but still no one paid any attention and she relaxed a little.

"I shouldn't really go in here unless I've got files or something, Sister gets mad."

"Well, I'm here and I'll say you did nothing you shouldn't," George said, her voice lowered again. "Come on." And she set a hand in the small of Cherry's back and pushed firmly.

Once inside they couldn't be seen from the TV bay and they

both relaxed. Cherry hurried to the rack of trays on the table and began to riffle through the papers in the top one.

"Is that what you saw when you saw the basket weave in your memory?" George said. "Stacked papers like that?"

Cherry stopped in the act of lifting a pile of papers and stood still. She thought for a long moment and then deliberately let them go.

"No," she said. "No, it wasn't. They were sort of—crumpled. Oh, damn. I wish I could remember properly."

"We need to help you concentrate," George said. "Sit down and let's think."

Obediently Cherry sat down on the chair that was in front of the typewriter.

"Close your eyes," George commanded and again Cherry obeyed.

"Look at the memory. Build it up in your mind and look at it."

Cherry closed her eyes and visibly concentrated. There was a tense silence and then sadly she shook her head and opened her eyes again.

"It's no good," she said. "It's gone. All I can see now is the trays the way they are'—she jerked her head at them—"Full of tidy papers. But I know that isn't what I saw last time."

She sighed and swung irritably in the swivel chair. "I wish I could remember! It's so silly." She sat with her back to George now, staring down at the typewriter keyboard and George came to stand beside her and put a hand on her shoulder.

"It can't be helped, Cherry. It was only a try anyway. Don't feel bad about it." It seemed to George very important now to reassure this unhappy child that she had done no wrong in being unable to remember where she had seen those coded sheets of paper; she was unhappy enough in her bereavement. To add to her burdens wouldn't help at all.

Cherry was fiddling now, her fingers tapping on the side of the typewriter keyboard in irritation. She was still looking very doleful and again George tried to comfort her.

"It's all right, Cherry, really it is. I'm sure we'll find another way to sort this out. Don't fret over it. Come on, we'd better get out of here. That movie can't go on for ever."

Cherry had begun to twitch at one of the controls on the righthand side of the machine; a slide marker that went up and down. Like a fretful child she seemed to find some comfort in the repetitive movements, so George brought her own hand down over Cherry's shoulder to set it on the restless fingers and still them.

"Come on, Cherry," she said coaxingly. "Put that back the way it was so no one notices we were here, and we'll get on our way."

"What?" Cherry said abstractedly and looked at her hand, for the first time seeming aware that she had been fidgeting at all. "What's that?"

"I said, put that slide bit back where it was and we'll go."

"Back where it…" Cherry said and peered at the machine more closely. And then to George's dismay her shoulders began to shake. George sighed softly and bent over her, ready to comfort her again as she dissolved into further tears.

But she wasn't crying; she was laughing. George looked at her closely in some surprise and she had to admit a little irritation. "Cherry, for heaven's sake, let's have a bit less of this and get on our way."

"But I know what it is!" Cherry said and turned a face to her that was wreathed in a smile. She looked like a different person; alert and alive and very very pretty, and George caught her breath, for she saw just what it was that had so captivated Harry Rajabani.

"What do you mean?" she said and then straightened her back, hope lifting in her. "Have you remembered where you saw the papers?"

"I don't need the papers!" Cherry said, grinning delightedly. "I can show you exactly how that code, or whatever it is, works! It's not a code at all, I mean, not really, though I can see how it could be used like one."

George frowned, completely at sea. "What are you talking about, Cherry?"

"I'll show you—" She reached for a sheet of paper from the half-open drawer beside her and moved towards the machine as though to set it in, and then stopped and looked over her shoulder.

"I can't show you here," she said. "They'll hear me typing and Sister'll come in and—I know. Just you wait a minute. I'll sort it out," and to George's amazement she was up on her feet and running out of the office as lightly as a child called to fetch ice cream.

George followed her, and saw her stop at the door to the bay where the watchers were still happily wrapped up in their fantasy world, straighten her shoulders, and then slip in and go straight over to Sister Lichfield. Cherry bent and murmured into her ear and Sister listened, looked briefly over her shoulder at George, made a face and then nodded.

"All right," she said. "As long as you do bring it right back."

"Oh, I will," Cherry said. She smiled widely and escaped back to the office.

Sister looked at George and nodded. "Glad to be of help, doctor," she said, and then turned back to look at the TV screen as the sound of a sudden squealing of brakes was greeted by laughter from all the patients and other staff who had paid no attention at all to the little flurry of activity.

George said, "Thank you," mechanically to Sister's back and turned to go back into the office only to meet Cherry coming out. She was clutching the heavy typewriter in her arms, and she muttered at George, "You go ahead and open the doors. I'll be fine. I only need it for a bit—but do be quick! It's ever so heavy."

They reached the little cubby hole that was Cherry's office just in time. Cherry, red in the face with the effort, almost dropped the machine on her desk once George had pushed the word processor keyboard and screen there well to the back out of the way. Cherry let out a puff of exhausted breath. "Blimey, that thing's a lump!" she said.

"Why on earth bring it here?" George asked. "What's the— oh, silly question. To use it, of course."

"Of course! I told Sister mine got broken and you had an urgent report Dr. Arundel needed and no typist on duty on account of Christmas, and she said all right. Mustn't keep it too long, though. Now, let's see."

She began to fiddle at the side of the machine, looking for the flex, plugged it in and switched the power on.

"Now," she said, and sat down at the keyboard with a little flourish like a stage magician about to pull a dove out of a hat. "Just you watch."

She took a piece of paper from her own drawer, put it in the machine and then turned her attention to the slide at the right-hand side with which she had been fidgeting. "Look at this, will you, Dr. Barnabas?"

George looked. On the left hand of the slide there was a column of figures and letters. The bottom one was 10, the one above it 12 and the one above that 15. At the top of the column were the letters PS.

Cherry moved the slide so that it stood alongside PS. "That means proportional spacing. It's something to do with getting the letters all the same size, apparently. I've never found out how it works, on account of no one ever asked for the proportional spacing. You need a special daisy wheel for it, anyway. But just you watch what happens when you use it." And she began to type.

George stood there and watched her fingers. Cherry did not type quickly, but with a certain deliberation. As she hit each key, George could see which one it was; and realized almost at once that it was the basic phrase that offered every letter of the alphabet: "the quick brown fox jumps over the lazy white dog."

But that was not what appeared on the white paper. She stood there fascinated and saw the symbols appear:

ACH >@L, (¼ GF£R UF. E@"]S F[HG ACH
OPZ& £CLAH YF$

"Good God!" she said blankly.

Cherry leaned back in her chair and spread her hands wide
to display what she had done. "You see? It's one of those things
that happens with these machines. I used to have one, but Dr.
Arundel got me that word processor. You see? But I had one
of these ages ago and it happened to me a few times when I
hit the slide by accident. It can happen—it's awful on a word
processor or a computer if you hit the wrong key, mind. You
can make terrific mistakes."

"Like getting blood sugar readings matched to the wrong
patient's name," George said with a combined flash of insight
and memory.

"What?"

"Oh, something that happened in the Diabetic Clinic a while
ago—it was a computer error."

"Well, there you are then." Cherry looked very pleased
with herself. "Like this, eh? This is a typing error, though, not
a computer one. I used to make them a lot. I used to type a
page—well some of a page—in the days when I still wasn't a
very good typist and I looked at the keyboard more'n I looked
at the page, you know? And I used to get so bothered! I'd pull
the pages out and crumple them up and chuck them in the
bottom of my tray and try again. That's what I think I must
have remembered—seeing my crumpled up pages chucked in
the tray. Once I knew what did it, of course, I never had the
problem no more."

She pushed the slide down again till it was opposite 12 and
again typed: "the quick brown fox jumps over the lazy white
dog'; and this time the letters appeared exactly as they should.

"Someone else discovered this and used it," George said,
with absolute certainty. "They made the same mistake and saw

how useful it could be and just typed what they wanted to keep, but to keep secretly, and it came out like this and they thought no one'd ever work out what it was. All they had to do was change the letters back to read it."

"I reckon!" said a jubilant Cherry. "Well, did I get it right or did I?"

George leaned over and hugged her, and Cherry, after a moment's tension, hugged her back.

"You was right, you know," she said when she'd extracted herself. She looked up at George with a little grimace. "It does help."

"Pardon me?" George was puzzled.

"Doing a crossword puzzle. I said before I didn't care who killed Harry. That finding out who it was and all that would just be a sort of revenge. But it's not true, is it?"

"I don't think so," George said. "No. It isn't. Getting the truth about something mayn't change what happened, but it does help you. It's why I do the job I do, I think. Needing to find out things. I can't bear mysteries. At least—" She stopped to think, then went on with some embarrassment. "I have to be honest, I love them really. As long as they're solvable. I enjoy the business of sorting out the tangles. I'm the sort who'd take a plate of spaghetti and try to arrange every strand neatly if I could. There's real satisfaction in untangling things, I guess. I might lose sight sometimes of what it means to the people inside the mystery, though. People like you. I'm sorry if—"

"You don't have to apologize for nothing!" Cherry said strongly. "I told you, I felt better sorting that out than I could have ever thought I could. Thanks for helping me, Dr. Barnabas. You've been good to me. I'm ever so grateful."

"No need," George said gruffly, as embarrassed as if she'd been English through and through. "No need at all. Listen, Cherry, I need a bit more help. Will you type some more of that stuff for me? I need, oh, several rows with lots of space underneath. Then underneath, type the letters the way they should be OK? Then I'll sit down with those sheets of paper I've got and it shouldn't take too long to work out what's really on them."

"Sure," Cherry said, and seemed a little embarrassed herself and glad to have something practical to do, and she set to work to provide precisely what George had asked for. A few minutes later, George had in front of her a sheet of paper on which had been typed several times:

> ACH >@L, (¼ GF£R UF. E@"]S F[HG ACH
> OPZ £CLAH YF$K
>
> THE QUICK BROWN FOX JUMPS OVER
> THE LAZY WHITE DOG.

"Look at the bottom," Cherry said. "I've done it different there. It'll make it easier for you."

George looked again and smiled widely. "I should have thought of that," she said and looked at it appreciatively:

> P ¼, YHU$CLE(0"RF]>GSA@[£. &ZK y-,
> 1340562
>
> ABCDEFGHIJKLMNOPQRSTUVWXYZ.
> 1234567890

"The spacing's different so you'll have to be careful," Cherry said. "But I reckon you should manage all right. Shall I help you? With the code? I mean, doing the pages you've got?"

George bit her lip and frowned. "I don't know," she said candidly. "Oh, hell, that sounds awful, doesn't it? But this is a murder enquiry and—"

Cherry looked stricken and George put out a hand to reassure her. "It's all right, Cherry. No one thinks for a moment that you had anything to do with anything you shouldn't, if that's what you're thinking. It's just that—it's police work, you see. I'd be glad of help, to tell the truth, but I can't let you—"

"Oh," Cherry said. "I didn't realize you were part of the police."

George looked at her for a long moment and then grimaced. "Ouch. Well, OK, not directly, I suppose. Not the police. But I am part of the machinery of investigation. It's normal for me to be part of the job police do. I don't mean to suggest that you were in any way—"

"It's all right," Cherry said. She was beginning to lose the sparkle that the typewriter episode had given her, drooping again like a plant starved of light and water. "It doesn't matter, after all."

"But it does," George said softly and put out a hand to pull Cherry to her feet. "Come on. Time to take that machine back. I'll carry it this time." After a long silent moment Cherry looked up at her, nodded and got to her feet. She looked depressed again now, but at least, George told herself as she humped the heavy machine into her arms ready for the trek back to Maternity, it's helped her a bit to be involved this far, even if I can't let her help me with the deciphering. Maybe I'm being too careful; and for a moment she considered telling Cherry it was all right, after all, she could be involved, but then hardened her resolve. All her instincts were to keep any information she might garner for Gus before letting anyone else in on it, and she trusted her instincts. It was an odd business, she mused, investigating a murder when you had to worry about the bereaved as well as the corpse.

29

George walked over to the police station via Wapping High Street, stopping on the way at the "Golden Palace' where Lee Ho Chin, one of the regular patients in Mr. Agnew Byford's cardiology clinic offered special deals to the staff of Old East. It was her turn, she decided, to take food to Gus; high time she showed him he wasn't the only one who remembered to look after the inner man and woman. Her lips quirked as the phrase came into her mind; it had been used by the Chairman at the Players Theater that night, announcing the interval and time for refreshment for said inner residents, and she had a silly vision of a small version of herself, sitting somewhere inside her belly, looking up hopefully for what might be offered from above. It was amusing now to imagine a small Gus, sitting gloomy with hunger, waiting for something to make him feel better, and her step quickened as she saw the soft glow of light from the stained windows of Lee Ho Chin's restaurant.

She sat and waited for her order as Lee, friendly and communicative but almost impossible to comprehend, chattered busily at her, and went on her way with her little carrier bag full of aluminum containers and a hot egg roll wrapped in a paper napkin, which Lee had pushed into her hand as she left. ("To keep you warm as you go," he insisted. "Good luck for good lady.") She ate it as she made her way through the icy streets. There were Christmas trees in the windows she passed, looking as bedraggled to her eyes as the ones in the hospital now that Christmas was over, but that sight didn't depress her as it usually did. She was on her way to see Gus and that was an exhilarating thought.

She found him in his office, alone in the middle of the big department with its huddles of cluttered desks and battered wall charts and scattered files, and stood for a moment looking at him from the far doorway of the empty main room, which usually was occupied by the other members of the plainclothes division, and tried to analyse how she felt about what she was looking at. It was difficult. He looked endearingly crumpled, with his shirt sleeves pushed up above his elbows to show strong rather hairy forearms, and his hair was untidy, but at the same time he looked strong and reliable. She sighed. Better not to think too much at all about him. Just enjoy the way things were and wait and see.

"Egg rolls," she announced as she marched into his office. "And chicken chop suey, and chopped prawn balls. Oh, and some noodles and a few prawn crackers."

"Wot, no sweet and sour?" he said, not lifting his head from his work. "No won ton? What sort of a nosh-up d'you call that? We'd ha' done better with some stuff from Leman Street. Nice bit o' haddock, maybe? But that'll do." He pushed his work away and stretched. "Beer with it, or a drop o' tea?"

"Beer, you ungrateful lug," she said, beginning to unload her bag on to his desk. "You don't deserve anything. When you feed me, don't I show a decent gratitude? Don't I make it clear how much I appreciate your thoughtfulness? Don't I—"

"No you do not," he said. "That's why I don't. Hey, listen, what's this? No chopsticks? Never mind—let's see what we can do." He pulled open his desk drawer to rummage and eventually came up with four chopsticks. "There! Knew I had some somewhere." He wiped them on the sleeve of his shirt and handed her a pair. "Dead hygienic now. Hey, this looks a bit of all right. I'll forgive you the missing won ton and sweet and sour. This'll do nicely."

"Where is everyone?" she said as he filled his mouth with hot noodles. "Why are you on your own? Everyone out clue-hunting?"

"I've sent "em home," he said and collected another mouthful. "On call if there's any problems, but I saw no need to keep "em sitting here. There's a uniformed watch on that can manage well enough. And my lads—well, it's Christmas, "n't it? I'll work their butts off next week, but till the New Year's behind us, it pays to be nice to the buggers."

She smiled at him over her own noodles and said jeeringly, "So, go pull the other one three times till it plays 'Yankee Doodle!' You're just a softie, spoiling your guys because you're a—well, a softie!"

He actually looked as though he were about to blush. "Not a bit of it. There's not a lot they can do this time o' night on either of our cases, and by some bleedin' miracle there's nothin' else urgent at present. I'll get the adoption boys back to the grindstone tomorrow, just you see if I don't, and there's the business of that damned car still to sort out."

"Ah," she said and put down her chopsticks. "I might have an answer to the adoption matter." And she looked at him with her brows up and her lips a little pursed, the picture of innocence.

"What did you say?" He spluttered over a particularly hot prawn ball. "You've got what?"

"I've got a list of names and addresses of people who might have some answers for us," she said. "I broke the code, you see." She smiled at him beatifically and reached again for her food and picked up, with considerable expertise, a pile of bean sprouts and chicken.

"Get away!" He was all attention. "So, give me the news! Don't just sit there filling your face!"

She shook her head, smiling sweetly. "I don't like talking with my mouth full," she said indistinctly. "You tell me first what you got out of Goss, then I'll tell you what I've got."

"Like hell I will! You tell me what you—"

"I was first," she said and scooped up more chop suey. He stared at her with his face a picture of chagrin and then threw his hands up in the air and said, "The hell with it. I'll eat too."

They did, in a greedy silence, until they'd cleared the little containers, and then he put down his chopsticks for the last time and quirked his head at her. "Right. Now start talking."

"But I haven't finished," she said sweetly. "And you have. So you start, Gus dear, and then I'll follow."

"You and I are going to have to do some serious talking one of these days," he said. "If it's a fight for supremacy we're going to have, then by God, I'll give as good as I get."

"Goss," said George, making some play with her chopsticks as she chased the last mushroom round the little square dish. "What did he have to say? Could he talk at all?"

Gus gave up. "He talked. A lot, in fact." He opened his notebook on his desk. "Some of it was unrepeatable. Filthy language. We can get him if we want to on any amount of stirring-up-racial-hatred charges. Like this, listen: 'If I have to break a few white heads and get into bed with communists I'll do it for the NHS. Show 'em what'll happen if they don't stop recruiting these black bastards, ruining our hospital. Once they see that black people cause riots and trouble they'll have the wit to stop taking on so many. So yeah, I'll start a race riot if I can. I've done it a few times, working with the blacks, telling them the whites are after them. It always works, frightens the shit out of the Professor, it does.' Lovely stuff, isn't it? There's plenty more like it."

Any hint of laughter had left George now. She put down her chopsticks and stared at Gus. "That's horrible."

"You don't say. Of course it is. But it's what the man's been doing with a few others around here. I've got names and addresses—it's not been a wasted experience, believe me. They were *agents provocateurs*—making it seem they were on the black side as activists while encouraging all the unrest they could. They were very active lately because of Choopani's fundraising, of course."

"And Harry's murder," she said, her eyes bright. "What about that?"

He shook his head, closing his notebook and snapping the rubber band around it. "No joy, George. Sorry about that. Goss and his nasties were at a meeting that night. My lads collected statements from them all. Alibied to their "orrible eyebrows they are, the bleedin' lot of "em. That's a dead end. As dead as mutton. As dead as Harry."

She looked down at her hands. "As dead as Harry," she repeated softly. "Oh, hell!"

"Yeah. I wanted it to be one of them, of course I did, in that I want to find whoever it was. But it wasn't Goss or his mate Prior—there's a nice specimen I don't think. South Africa can have him back any time—nor is it any of his collection of British Patriots, either. We're back at the opening of the same old cul de sac. Got to start again, unless..." He brightened. "Now it's your turn. What have you got?"

"Goodies," she said crisply. "Isn't that what you call it?

She told him, propping her elbows amid the wreckage of their supper, her chin on her hands. Told him about Cherry and the typewriter and the James Bond movie, all of it, and he listened in silence, never taking his eyes from her face.

"So then," she went on, and leaned back to push her hands into the pockets of the baggy jacket she had thrown over her jeans and old shirt. "I went back to the lab and settled to it, picking out the words. It took ages." She grimaced. "Surprising really how long it did take, at first. But I speeded up as I got used to it and saw what it was whoever it was had done."

"So, am I going to be shown whatever it was?" he said. "Or is there more teasing to come? I never thought you'd be that much of a tormentor, George."

For quite unexplained reasons her face flamed and he laughed at that, a soft little sound at the back of his throat.

"Aha! I touch a raw nerve! Bliss. I like "em raw. The more raw the better. OK, ducks, do I get the transcript?"

She pulled her hands out of her pockets and pushed the contents of the right one forward: a couple of folded sheets of paper. He took them with an odd little incline of his head, smoothed them on his desk and bent to look. She studied the way the light touched the rough dark curliness of his hair and wanted to reach out and touch it; but instead she got to her feet and walked round the desk to stand beside him.

"As I see it," she said. "What this is—"

"I can see it too," he said and was clearly absorbed. "Names, addresses, color of hair, weight, DOB—date of birth. It's clearly a description of a baby, that last, isn't it? Another is the babies these people were given? Or the babies they produced themselves?"

"You haven't reached the end of the list yet, Gus," she said and reached forwards and pulled away the top sheet. "Look at that."

The two sheets lay side by side on his desk now and could be read easily.

PAGE ONE
1. Chester
17 Tyndall Close
Hatfield
Bald
Weight 4 kilos 600 grams
DOB 3. 4. 92

2. Flaherty
Market House
Bishop's Stortford
Dark hair short
Weight 5 kilos 10 grams
DOB 7. 7. 92

3. Dickenson
47 Lybrand Street

Blackheath
Bald
Weight 4 kilos 750 grams
DOB 27. 4. 93

4. Cranmer
9 Oxford Terrace
Wapping
Red hair short
Weight 4 kilos 75 grams
DOB 10. 6. 93

5. Irwin
11 Fife Street
Kensington
Black hair long
Weight 5 kilos exact
DOB 17. 8. 93
6. Braham
179 Applecroft Avenue
Denham
Black hair short
Weight 4 Kilos 800 grams DOB 23. 6. 93

PAGE TWO
7. Lennon
Dark hair long
Weight 3 kilos 105 grams
DOB 14. 7. 93

8. Chowdary
Dark hair short
Weight 4 kilos 200 grams
DOB 27. 10. 93

9. Popodopoulos
Dark hair long
Weight 5 kilos 75 grams
DOB 1. 12. 93

"You see?" she said softly. "The first six are names of people who either had or were given babies. The last three, though, we know had babies taken from them."

He frowned. "It's hard to be sure," he said. "Maybe these other six are people who had babies who died?"

"That's my point, Gus. These last three babies didn't die, I'm sure of it. I think they had babies taken from them to give to other people who wanted to adopt. They were stolen, like the old gypsies."

He shook his head. "It doesn't make sense, George. Why have two kinds of people on one list? I mean people who adopt and also people who give birth but their babies die—or whatever it is that happens to them."

She stood there and thought for a moment or two and then slowly went back to her chair on the far side of his desk.

"You're right," she said flatly. "It doesn't make sense, does it? Dammit! And I got so excited—I should have had more sense. Though if we find those other six people lost babies too…"

"Ah, then indeed we might find out the how and why. But until we know just why all these people are together on this list we can't make any judgments."

He looked up then and lifted his brows at her. "Who made the list, by the way? Any idea?"

She bit her lip and then shook her head. "No," she said unwillingly. "There's no hint or clue to that there, is there? We only know that Harry had the original coded lists—the ones we made that one from." She lifted her chin at the two sheets of paper on his desk.

"Then I think we may assume at this stage it was Harry who made it," Gus said briskly. "The pages were in his effects, right? That child Cherry found them?"

"That's right. She did. But…"

"But what?"

"He couldn't type," George said. "Cherry was adamant about that. He was as awkward around machinery as—as—

well, he couldn't cope with a typewriter."

"Oh, come on!" Gus looked sceptical. "Anyone can make a stab at it. There are the letters, you just have to hit them."

"There were no mistakes on that list," George said slowly. "I asked Cherry. She said whoever typed it knew what they were doing, because when you can't see the letters coming up properly, as you can't when you use this PS key, then you're more likely to make errors. There wasn't one." She shook her head. "It wasn't Harry's list. I'm sure of that. I think he found it, and worked out who did make it, and let whoever that was know it. And that was why he was killed, maybe."

He grinned a little crookedly. "Hey, you've replaced young Goss as chief suspect without too much difficulty!"

She grimaced. "Well, there it is. It isn't Goss, so I have to think again. And the more I think about it, the more I think Harry must have died because he found out something someone didn't want known. It sounds corny, I know, but it makes sense, doesn't it?"

Gus was silent for a while and then nodded. "You could be right. But I need more evidence than that. All these—"

"Yeah, I know. All these maybes," George said. "You say that to me all the time."

"Then it's time you learned from what I tell you," he said sententiously, but spoiled the effect by laughing at her expression. "Oh, don't look like that, ducks. You've done a smashin' job! I could never have broken that code in a month of Sundays. It's a fabulous contribution. You've given us a whole lot of new leads we can work on. You're so much a part of the team, we'd be lost without you."

"Oh, goddamn it!" she wailed. "You make me feel a right heel! It wasn't I who worked it out, was it? It was Cherry."

"Without you she'd never have done it," he said. Now it was his turn to get to his feet and come round the desk. "You're the one who pushed and shoved and tweaked to make it happen. I want you to know how much you're appreciated."

She managed a grin. "OK, I realize." He was standing very close now and that made her feel rather odd; like a schoolgirl again, shaky and a little sweaty. Delicious. He seemed unaware of it, for he simply bent his head, kissed her cheek and with one hand squeezed her shoulder. Then he went back to his chair.

"OK," he said from the other side of the desk. "What next? I'll tell you what next. Tomorrow, I send my lads out to see these people to find out what they have in common. They're a mixed bunch in terms of addresses. A couple of locals, but the others are all over the place. Denham and Blackheath and Kensington and Bishop's Stortford..." He frowned. "I'll make you a forecast, though. They'll all turn out to be well heeled. These are pricy addresses. I smell money."

"You could be right. I imagine buying babies for adoption is expensive."

"Still on that? But we agreed that—"

"Yeah," she said. "I know. We agreed that this list couldn't be such people because of the last three names. But I'm still convinced that that's what it was all about. Do you doubt it?"

He was considering. "I can't say," he said after a long pause. "Honestly, I don't know. It's an intriguing hypothesis, but we don't have enough evidence to put in the cat's saucer for her supper, do we? Not a bleedin' smidgeon of it. Just an idea."

"It's a bloody good one," she snapped.

"I don't deny that," he said. "Like I said, I'm very intrigued, I think you might be right. But might won't do for me or the courts. I have to have facts. Nasty things, facts are. Hard and bumpy with rough corners. But I have to have "em. Addicted, you might say." He produced one of his leers, but it was a half-hearted one.

She sighed. "Well, there's not a lot else we can do, I suppose." She tried to sound very casual but wasn't sure she managed it. "Time I headed home, I guess. Ma and Bridget'll be wondering where I am."

"Fine," he said and got to his feet. "I can finish all this in the morning. On our way then."

"Oh," she said, pretending surprise. "You're coming with me?"

"Be your age, ducks. Didn't I tell you before I was comin'? I miss your nice old ladies if I don't see them. Anyway, we got other fish to fry." He slapped her rump as she stood up and then, his jacket now on, reached for his overcoat and for hers, and switched off the light on his desk, plunging them into almost total blackness.

"Just think," he said, and his voice was warm and amused in the darkness. "I could ravish you here and now, and no one'd know."

"I would," she said, trying to keep her voice light and not sure if she managed it.

"I'd see to it you would. But not here, sweetheart. Let's go to your place. It beats here on account of it doesn't smell of disinfectant and the stuff they use to keep the cockroaches out." And he put his arm round her shoulder to lead her out.

She went without any demur. She now knew, to her chagrin and with somewhere deep inside a sort of shame, that she, a strong woman, was so willing that she would go with him anywhere he wanted her to, for any purpose.

30

"I think it would work," George said stubbornly. "It did last time. I mean, if I hadn't done what I did, we'd never have found out who killed Richard Oxford, would we? You were livid then because I didn't tell you I was going to do it, and I suppose it was dangerous too. Well, this time I'm telling you. And how can there be any danger in it? No one'd even know it was me. That's terrible grammar, but you know what I mean."

He was silent, sitting hunched up on the rug, his arms round his knees, staring into the flames of her fire.

"You'd think, wouldn't you," he said almost dreamily after a while, "that seein' they're not actually burnin' anything there'd be a sort of pattern to the flames. But they look just like they're real."

"They are real, dummy," she snapped. "They're burning gas, is all. And stop being so—so—Oh, will you listen to what I'm saying? Why can't I try it? I think it'd work."

"I thought it'd work to come home with you tonight. I thought we'd have a nice cuddle on your nice sofa," he said plaintively. "And what happens? Your old ladies go all sprightly on me and sit up and chatter for hours an' then when we are left alone at last an' the lechery can begin, bugger me if you don't go and start playin' detective all over again! I've got better things for you to think about than solvin' crimes."

"Oh, Gus, do stop it. It's not exactly a turn-on to—You're too premeditated about it," she said, and shook her head more at herself than at him. When he'd brought her home the thought of spending an hour or two rolling on the rug by the gas fire with him had been chokingly exciting, but by the time Vanny and Bridget had at last wandered off to bed, each clutching their cups of malted milk (they'd developed a passion for bedtime Horlicks since coming to London) much of the excitement had gone, converted into a sort of edgy irritation. It was like being desperately hungry but having to wait so long to get food that by the time it arrived any appetite had completely foundered. She had started talking about the murders as a sort of diversionary tactic, thinking it would help her relax, maybe allow the sense of urgent need that had been so very warm in her belly as he drove her home to come back again, but as she talked, so the idea she had had for solving the adoption scam had grown and stretched itself and she had become more and more absorbed in it, the result being that any remnants of sexual feeling had vanished completely.

"I'd hoped I was enough of a turn-on in my own right," he said quietly. "That you were—oh, not the sort of silly woman who needed a special line of chat."

"I don't!" She said it almost despairingly. "But I do need to get my head together. And Ma and Bridget being here and sitting up so late and all, it sort of…"

He turned his head and looked at her. "Turned you off?"

"Mmm."

"Just like your pretty fire," he said. He reached forward and tweaked the tap at the side. The flames sighed and died down and the room darkened a little.

She was silent for a while and then sighed herself. "I suppose so. Does that upset you?"

"Course it does!" He looked at her with wide cow-eyes, mocking his own disappointment. "I was all set for a bit o' nookie. But there it is. You're a captious creature, all woman." Again one of his leers, with which she was becoming familiar. "I'll have to convince myself that it just adds to your feminine charms in my macho eyes."

"Gus, please will you—"

"Concentrate on matters detective," he said briskly, getting to his feet and brushing down his trousers before sitting beside her on the sofa. "I might as well. It's the only bit of concentration I'm likely to get out of you tonight. OK. You want to advertise for would-be adopting parents."

"Yes."

"Because you reckon the people on that list will apply."

"Yes."

"And that'll lead you to the murderer."

"Yes."

"Sounds like going to Marble Arch via Beachy Head, if you ask me." He spoke judiciously, his head on one side as he looked at her.

"Pardon me?"

"A long way round. A trot all round the houses instead of a direct route."

"D'you know of a direct route?" she demanded.

"Sure. Like I said when you first showed me this list. We can go and see them all. We've got their addresses, so it'll be easy enough. Then we can ask them."

"But that won't find us Oberlander, will it?" she said as patiently as she could. "It's Oberlander we want. They're not on the list—but they're the ones we know will have the most information! But it's possible that one of those is the Oberlanders with a false name, the way we originally thought. If they are, then going to see them will alert them. I want the Oberlanders to come to us, ideally using the false name again. Don't you see?"

He looked at her thoughtfully for a long moment. "And suppose Oberlander, whoever he is, murdered his own child? Or hers, of course. Will he—she *still* contact you?"

"It's worth a try," she said, with a return of her original stubbornness. "Anyway, it's a way to get moving, isn't it?"

"I suppose so. I can't think of a better one at the moment."

"Well then?" She was triumphant.

"But that doesn't mean that your idea has to be a good one, just because I don't have a better. You don't always need a yard stick to know something don't measure up."

"Oh, you're full of wise saws and precepts tonight!" she said crossly. "A regular Polonius! What possible harm can it do, Gus? It mightn't work, I grant you, but on the other hand it'll only cost a few quid. I'll pay for it myself if that's what's bothering you, though I would have thought the police budget—"

"Don't use such filthy language in my presence," he said, sounding as shocked as a Victorian Miss. "Budget is a *very* dirty word in my office! Anyway, it isn't that. It just seems..." He shrugged. "But I suppose you've got a point. It can't do any harm."

"And it might do some good."

"Or—hang about a bit. It might warn the murderer, whoever it is, that we're on to him or her." He seemed genuinely interested in the discourse for the first time. "Now will that be a good thing or a bad thing? Let me think." He pondered for a while. "I don't know," he said at length. "I really don't."

"I don't see how it can tip our hand. I shan't sign it with my name or anything! Look, suppose it's something like this." She jumped to her feet, went over to her little desk and began to scribble on some scrap paper. He sat and watched her, seeming happy just to look at her bent head. For all his complaints about her lack of co-operation with his original plans for the evening, he seemed content enough, and she was well aware of that fact even though she was concentrating on her scribbling. It was an awareness that pleased her.

"Look," she said eventually, and pushed the piece of paper at him. "Try that."

He read aloud: "Childless? Do you have a good home to offer to orphaned or abandoned children? All support given to those seeking children from overseas. Contact Box Number blah."

"It's mysterious enough," he said as he gave back the sheet of paper. "I'm not sure you won't have trouble placing it."

"Why?"

"There are laws about baby farming in the UK," he said. "About selling babies for profit. A newspaper might think this contravenes that law and refuse it."

"But there's no mention of money there," she pointed out. "Just an offer of support to caring people who can offer children a home. There can't be anything illegal in that. Let me try, Gus."

He looked at his watch and then stood up. "OK, ducks. Like I say, I can't see any harm in it. Where'll you put it?"

"I'll work that out tomorrow," she said, elated at the thought of doing something positive at last. It seemed suddenly even more important to her to get the case moving faster than it had been. "I suppose there are some specialist magazines for the childless? There's usually one for everything, isn't there? And I could try the local papers in all the areas where people on the list live."

He nodded approvingly at that. "Now that is sensible thinking. Forget the magazines. It takes ages for their ads to appear, I imagine. And take a tip and make them display ads. Otherwise they might miss "em. And make me a promise right now."

He was beside the door that led into her little hallway, pulling on his coat.

"Depends on the promise."

"No rushing off to interview people on your own if you do get an answer that gives a lead."

She considered for a while and then nodded. "That sounds fair enough. I'll let you know, word of honor, if I do flush anyone out."

"Make sure you don't forget." He stood there a moment longer looking at her and then sketched a deep elaborate sigh. "Ah me, the pains suffered by lovers! When, oh when will my beloved surrender unto me? "Night, ducks. See you around."

And he was gone, closing the front door quietly behind him, clearly considerate of the old ladies sleeping in the bedroom. She laughed, but perversely became aware of a stab of regret mixed with a faint rekindling of desire. Damn it all to hell and back, would she never get her hormones sorted out?

The advertisements were accepted without demur by local papers in Hatfield (which also covered Bishop's Stortford), in Hertfordshire, Blackheath, Kensington and Denham to the west of London, as well as the local one that covered the hospital and therefore Wapping too. None of the ad sales people made any comment about the content of the advertisement and she was pleased with herself about that. Gus's doubts about the legality of such adoption offers had alarmed her; but she had the impression that each paper was fighting for every bit of advertising revenue it could find and was unlikely therefore to scrutinize anything too closely.

And then she settled down to wait. The papers were all weeklies and appeared on different days; she did calculations on the backs of old envelopes working out how soon she might be likely to get responses, remembering that any letters had to reach her via the newspapers. Each of them assured her that there would be no delay in sending box-number mail, but she had her doubts, and almost despaired of finding a way of containing her impatience as the next week crept by. She tidied every inch of her own office, caught up with every piece of laboratory work she could, drove her staff almost demented with demands for year's end organizing and generally had a miserable time of it, including going to bed early on New Year's Eve, because there was nowhere she wanted to go to celebrate. Anyway, she told herself gloomily as she pulled the duvet up at eleven p.m. and switched off her light, I'd rather ignore the way time is going by.

It wasn't even as though her private life offered any direction. Vanny and Bridget, due to return home to Buffalo in just two weeks' time, worked themselves into a frenzy of activity, sightseeing with enormous verve and energy. They wanted to cover all the ground they could, "Not least," as Bridget told George privately, "because I'm not sure when if ever we'll get back to Europe. Your Ma's coping better than I'd hoped, but she still wanders in her memory a bit, in case you hadn't noticed."

George had noticed and tried not to. There were more moments when her mother looked at her blankly when she said something commonplace, and needed explanations; more occasions when she lost her way to the bathroom of the tiny flat and was puzzled; more times when she drifted off into a private world of her own in the middle of a conversation and seemed unaware that she had done so. But she was coping well enough, as Bridget repeated over and over again, and having a great time.

"I don't think she knew how much fun it would be coming to Europe," Bridget said. "All she thought about was seeing you, but now she's here she's eaten up with it all. Wants to go to Amsterdam, now—"

"Amsterdam?" George said blankly.

"We thought a longish weekend. You wouldn't mind? We could see the Rijksmuseum and the Van Gogh exhibition and all that. No bulbs, I guess, not in January, but all the same, we could ride the canals and see Anne Frank's house and so forth. If you don't want us to go though, honey, you just say the word."

"Of course you must go if you want to!" George said warmly. "It sounds like a great idea!" She helped them make arrangements, borrowed Hattie's car again to take them to the airport to catch their plane, and returned to the empty flat not as gratefully as she had expected, but actually missing them and their untidiness about the place. It was a lonely business being there.

And there wasn't much sign of Gus either and that was the loneliest part. He had called her briefly the day after she had persuaded him of the value of her plan to tell her a major robbery on the patch was going to absorb a good deal of his time for the next few days, though he had good leads on it, and of course was still using some of his lads to continue the Oberlander and Rajabani investigations.

"But I won't have much time myself to come around, oh misery me. But if there's anything important, you call me and call me fast, you hear? If you get a response from these ads—"

"I'll call you!" she said. "Stop mother-henning again."

"I shouldn't have agreed to such an idea," he said fretfully. "No need for it. We've got enough to get on with the list of addresses and names we've got. I suppose the ads are in already?"

"Of course."

"Yeah, I should have known you wouldn't waste time. Well, be careful. And remember your promise. Nothing stupid."

"I won't forget," she said. "Now go catch robbers. Goodbye." She'd hung up the phone almost pettishly. No chance of seeing him when her Ma and Bridget went away; wasted opportunities there. And she was so angry with her own perversity, considering how she'd been the other evening, that she refused to think about Gus at all for the rest of the week.

She failed, of course.

Her calculations turned out to be right. On the third day after the first two ads appeared, one in Denham and the other in Blackheath, two fat envelopes were delivered to the flat by a complaining postman who had to wait for her to answer the doorbell as they wouldn't go through her letterbox. Denham had produced seventeen responses and Blackheath twenty-three. None of them were from Oberlander, and none of them were from the people listed on the coded sheet as living there.

Two days later another flurry arrived; sixteen from Kensington, thirty-two from Hatfield and Bishop's Stortford and, to her surprise, fifteen from Wapping. Surprise, because somehow she had assumed that the local poverty-struck area wouldn't support that many people with the resources to consider private adoption, and even though her advertisement had said nothing about cost, she knew perfectly well from the other letters she'd received that many people realized that money would have to change hands if they were to get their desires. And then she remembered the well-off who had colonized and gentrified swathes of Docklands, and stopped being surprised.

She was moved by the letters, for they were powerful and eloquent. As she plowed her way through one after another her mood drooped and finally descended into a deep despondency. The desperate hunger for parenthood that jumped off page after page was very affecting and it stirred anxieties in her, too. A woman in her thirties, she thought with some pain, shouldn't expose herself to this sort of stuff if she didn't have definite plans to get herself pregnant. And I haven't, have I? But that was not to be thought of, and she plunged back into the letters, reading every one even though none of them offered her any clues to the whereabouts of the Oberlanders, and surprisingly to her, none of them came from people whose names appeared on the decoded list.

She stopped to think then. Perhaps the people on that list were successful adopters? Perhaps they were there because they had somehow been supplied with babies? Such people wouldn't try again, would they? They'd have their own avenues to explore anyway if they wanted more babies, and wouldn't need any such service as the one she'd advertised. All she had done by her efforts was flush out a lot more distress and perhaps—guilt rose as she thought about it—created hopes for a family in people who would gain nothing from their responses to her lure. She felt worse and worse as she read the letters, wanting to write to them all to apologize for encouraging them to display their sores to a total stranger.

Until she reached a letter signed David Hillman. It was one
of the batch from Kensington and she started to read it with
no great hope. The handwriting was ordinary, not particularly
crabbed and not particularly elegant. There was little to be
gleaned about the personality of the writer from it; the address
was a block of flats in Sloane Street; rather rich then, she
registered. Her sensitivity to the subtleties of class and money
in this country was not well honed but she'd lived here long
enough to know that anyone who had the word "Sloane' in
his address was someone with a high regard for himself, who
enjoyed that of others, too.

The significant part of his letter almost slid by her at
first. There was the usual colorless start, "We are interested
in your advertisement of last week in our local paper..." but
then he went on: "Our reason for wishing to adopt as soon as
possible is one I hope will be regarded with sympathy by your
organization. We have adopted once and, we thought, with
great success, but to our great grief our baby did not thrive. My
wife is, as you can imagine, in a state of deep bereavement.
I know no baby can replace another, but if we could be
considered as a priority because of the pain of the loss we have
already suffered, it would be much appreciated. There would
be no problems about being ready for a child; we have all the
equipment and clothes any little boy would need..."

She sat and thought for a long time, staring at the letter.
The story was the nearest of any to the Oberlander one
that she had seen. Other letters spoke of years of seeking a
pregnancy of their own via IVF and GIFT and other forms of
fertility treatment; of long waits on lists of official adoption
agencies, of the despair of watching the calendar move on and
knowing that they were rapidly approaching the age at which
they would no longer be regarded as eligible to adopt; only
this one said anything about having adopted before. And the
baby, he had written, did not thrive. An odd way of putting it,
she thought; most nonmedical people might say a child had

passed on, or been lost, or some other euphemism, or might despise the use of soft language and say bluntly it had died. But this man had written "did not thrive' which rang strangely in her ears; it was a phrase used by pediatric experts for a child who stopped growing and seemed to be ailing for an unknown reason. Yet this man was not medical. At the start of his letter he'd described himself as a businessman. Why should he use such a phrase? And then he'd made such a point about having all the equipment a little boy would need, so the child who had not thrived for them had been a boy...

It happened yet again. She sat there and stared at the page; blinked and stared again; and then lifted her chin and laughed aloud. The cogs of her mind, that absurd mind of hers that juggled with cut-out bits of information and then slotted them neatly into place like a jigsaw had done the trick again.

"Hillman," she said aloud. "That means the man from the high ground. Oberlander, in German, surely?"

31

She seemed to spend the entire day trying to reach him. She called the police station first of course, only to be told he was out. She left a message asking him to contact her. An hour later and then an hour after that she phoned again and was assured the message had been passed on, they could do no more, and she could hear the faint amusement in the voice of the person at the other end of the phone, which made her blush and slam the phone down angrily, feeling she couldn't ring the police station again. So she called his flat, and all she got was the buzz of an ansaphone and his voice blandly inviting her to leave a message. Again she banged down the receiver; almost taking his absence as a deliberate personal insult.

She sat and glowered at her grimy office window and tried to decide what to do. She'd made him promises, hadn't she, not to go off on her own, not to keep secrets from him? Well, she amended, not precisely *promises*, more undertakings to try not to behave so. Well, hadn't she tried? She'd tried damned hard. Here she was sitting with a direct lead to the man they had been looking for all this time and just because she couldn't reach Gus, he had to be left alone? Why, he could do anything in the time that might elapse before Gus was available! Run off, kill another baby maybe, who could say what he might not do? And she stifled the awareness that this was nonsense. Hillman-cum-Oberlander (and she was completely convinced this was the case) could have no such intent, for if he had he would hardly have responded to a newspaper advertisement.

She jumped to her feet. Half-promise or no half-promise, she wasn't going to sit about here waiting like a dutiful puppy dog for the master to come home. She would go and see Hillman. It could do no harm, surely, and if she came back with the case solved, ready to put in his hands, Gus could hardly object.

She was elated as she arranged with Sheila to hold the fort in her absence. Her gargantuan efforts at tidying over the past few days hadn't been wasted. Now there was no reason whatsoever why she should not be off about police business, and so she told Sheila, who sniffed and grudgingly agreed to keep an eye out and to bleep her if anything urgent came up. The fact that she fervently hoped it would was not lost on George, who had a lively awareness of her staff's views, but she only smiled cheerfully at her and went.

She took the tube for her journey westwards, climbing into a train at Shadwell and joining the District Line at Whitechapel. She sat contentedly as it rocked its way through the dusty tunnels, agreeably daydreaming of Gus's admiration and praise and warm gratitude when she came back to him with the case half solved. It would be marvellous if the killing of Harry turned out to be linked with Hillman-Oberlander as well, she thought, but then was ashamed of herself once more. Harry's death had been a tragedy; she had no right to diminish it to a mere puzzle that she would enjoy solving. Though to deny she would was impossible.

Sloane Square, when she emerged into it, was bustling with people, and the dull January day was lit up with the cheerful glow from shop windows and the remains of Christmas lights, and her spirits lifted even more. She spent far too little time in other parts of London, she thought. I should go to more theaters and concerts, shop here in the smart and witty streets, live a little; even though she was enjoying herself hugely where she was in Shadwell.

As she turned to walk down Sloane Street in search of Manderly Mansions, the address on Hillman's letter, she contemplated that fact. When she had come down from Inverness to take the Old East job—was it just a year ago? Amazing—she'd been very doleful about it. The surroundings had seemed to her drab beyond belief and the hospital itself depressingly shabby. But now she felt so much a part of the place, and so—the word came into her mind and surprised her a little—so fond of it, she had no more complaints. How much Gus was part of the pleasure of course, it was hard to be sure.

She looked down at the letter in her hand and concentrated on the matter she had come here for. No more private thoughts; only detective ones, she scolded herself. Only detective ones.

What sort of businessman was he to live in so elegant a block of flats? was the first detective question that came to her as she looked up at the facade of Manderly Mansions. Smart indeed: each window carefully boxed with glossy ivy; brass name plate glinting in the dull light; windows polished to a rich gleam; and a uniformed man standing on the front step.

He looked suspiciously at her when she asked for Mr. Hillman and told her he could only let her in after he had telephoned Mr. Hillman to be sure he was there.

"Wouldn't you know anyway, if you're here all the time? You'd have seen him go out," George said. He looked at her forbiddingly. "It's my job to call every flat when people come here, to see if they are at home to visitors," he said heavily. "It's no part of my job to make any decision for them."

"Ah," George murmured. "So New York style security has arrived, has it? There's a happy thought for a dreary day."

"Not for me to say, *madam*," said the uniform with insulting emphasis, and went into the building. She followed him, enjoying his hauteur. "Who are you, she says," the man said, one hand over the phone.

George thought for a moment and said, "Tell him—her? the Hillmans, it's about the advertisement."

He spoke into the phone, listened, nodded and hung up.

"Lift's over there," he said sourly, making no effort to show her the way, but she found it and went up to the third floor, noting the number of the flat beside the relevant button. The lift smelled of beeswax polish and flowers and was thickly carpeted, not only all over the floor but on the walls as well. This place breathes money, she thought, and her excitement sharpened and tightened her breathing.

The door of Flat 32 was open as she stepped out of the lift and looked to her left. A middle-aged woman in a blue striped nylon overall stood there looking at her with a face quite expressionless; no welcome, no surprise, nothing.

"Good morning," she said as George came up to her.

"A—Mrs. Hillman?" George ventured.

"What's your name?" the woman demanded.

"I'm Dr. George Barnabas. I've come about the advertisement that appeared in last week's—"

There was a little noise from behind the overalled woman and a voice cried in a high tone, "Doctor—Oh! It's all right, Olive! I'll come, it's all right."

The nylon overall looked at George again, but with some expression now: a faint sneer. George watched her retreating into the flat, leaving her place at the door to be taken by a very thin woman in a dark green dress that even to George's not particularly experienced eye was an expensive one.

"I'll phone David right away," she said breathlessly. "Right away. Doctor, you say? Oh, I'm so glad you came! It's wonderful that you took the time to actually come—David didn't tell me—do sit down, I'll just call him. Olive! Fetch some coffee and so forth, will you? Now, are you comfortable there? I'll just phone…"

She flurried away to the other side of the very large drawing room into which she had taken George, reaching for the gilded and white enamel telephone which had been tricked up to look as a Louis Quinze one might have looked had the France of the period ever heard of Alexander Graham Bell, leaving George to settle herself a little gingerly on a sofa that had been upholstered in so heavy a velvet that it made her feel she was slipping back into the womb.

She looked around the room as the woman murmured and was first amused and then puzzled. The money that had been spent in here had to be staggering and it was that which seemed funny to her. It was so excessive. The curtains were the same thick blue velvet as the sofa, as were four massive armchairs. The gilt tables and a buhl escritoire against one wall were obviously costly antiques and the floor, huge as it was, was completely covered in a heavy Chinese carpet of magnificent depth and design.

Her puzzlement resolved itself into one question: how was it that people who lived as richly as this had appeared at an NHS hospital in an area as shabby as Shadwell? If this woman was the female half of the Oberlanders, as she suspected (and she might have to find out from Prudence Jennings if she recognized her, unless they admitted it to her themselves), why had she taken her ill baby to Old East? Why hadn't she taken him to a private doctor, or even a nearby NHS hospital? It would have been what George would have expected of someone who lived in these conditions.

The woman hurried back from the phone and sat down close beside George to stare at her with wide dark eyes. She looked, George thought, to be about forty or so, maybe a little less; she had one of those bony faces that made it hard to tell. George looked down at the woman's hands, which were clasped nervously on her lap, and saw how thin and fragile they were, and wondered briefly if the woman was anorexic. She could have been. The green dress was not designed to cling to the figure but a soft and draped affair that would disguise the effects of such behaviour.

"David said not to talk about this till he comes. He won't be long, his office is just down the road. But I have to ask some questions, don't I? Like, I mean, are you the same group? Did she send you? And if you're not, how is it that you're able to do anything? We've been trying so hard for, oh, so long, and everyone said it was impossible, the Government had clamped down and there was no hope and we can't go to see for ourselves what we can do because David can't get a visa or something and he won't let me go alone, he's so protective and careful and anyway I don't think I could—"

George tried not to show her bewilderment. "Which group?" she said carefully. "Go where? I'm not sure that—"

"But aren't you working with these countries? Romania and Bosnia and so on? That's what we were told before. Or are you dealing with Brazil? I'd heard about them but I wasn't certain, but then David told me that they were lovely, just as dark eyed and dark haired as us, so I don't mind at all,"

"Perhaps I should wait till your husband comes, Mrs. Hillman," George said, not sure if she was cutting off a source of information, but also concerned that she might be mishandling this strange woman. She certainly had a wild look about her, and was now sweating heavily across her forehead and upper lip with anxiety, even though the room was only pleasantly warm. "It will be easier than explaining twice, don't you think?"

"Oh, yes, that's what David said, but you know how it is… Some coffee? These biscuits are nice, I made them yesterday. I do so love doing things in the kitchen even though it does irritate Olive when I get in her way, but she understands it's so difficult to be busy when there's—when there's not a lot— Oh dear!" Her eyes filled with tears and she rubbed her face with both hands, smearing her eyeshadow a little. She looked deeply unhappy and very vulnerable and for a moment George wanted to reach out and hug the pathos out of her.

The sound of a key in the door lifted the spirits of both of them. George relaxed with relief as the nervous woman leapt to her feet and ran to meet the arrival, and registered the need not to let herself be infected by Mrs. Hillman's tension. It wouldn't be easy, for she couldn't remember ever meeting anyone in such a state of anxiety outside a hospital ward.

The woman came back clinging to her husband's arm. He was a round man in every way; face, eyes, body, glasses even. His surprisingly black hair was ridged on his head like a corrugated iron roof and he shone with cleanliness and comfort and a sense of his own worth.

"I understand from my wife that you are a doctor?" he said as she shook hands. "Are you perhaps from the same people as—I mean, where from?"

"Yes, I'm Dr. Barnabas," George said. "From Old East Hospital. In Shadwell."

The room seemed to become so quiet that even the traffic in the road outside was silenced. He stood and stared at her, her hand still in his, and his wife, clinging to his arm, was transfixed also, her face actually paling as George looked at her.

"Old East," he said, his voice thinner than before. "In Shadwell. I'm not sure that I know it."

"Oh, I think you do," George said, and then somewhere deep inside herself gathered up all her courage and rolled it into a hard ball to throw at him. "You can't have forgotten the place so soon, Mr. Oberlander."

The woman threw back her head and howled. It was a dreadful sound, a deep baying note of utter misery, and George started forward, driven by an instinctive need to hold her, to help her, as her husband pulled on her arm and half dragged, half led her across the room to the sofa, at the same time as the woman in the nylon overall appeared at the drawing-room door, her face now showing more than a hint of expression.

"It's all right, darling. Please, it's all right," the man was murmuring as he made his wife stretch out on the sofa. "Sylvia, sweetie, do stop, please. It won't help. Please, darling, please Sylvie, choochie, please don't cry so."

But the thin woman was now in an ecstasy of tears and George stood there still and silent as he fussed over her, sitting beside her and mopping her streaming eyes. It went on for some time, until at last the loud sobs lessened and slowed and she seemed too exhausted to weep any more.

"Come and look after her, Olive," David Hillman said after a while. "I have to speak to—to this doctor here. You look after Sylvie. We won't be long."

He got to his feet and looked at George. The light from the lamp Olive had switched on behind the sofa glinted on his spectacles and blanked out the lenses, so that he looked anonymous and strange, and George felt a moment of fear herself. What had she walked into here? Was this man intending to do her some harm?

But then her common sense returned to her and that was a comfort. David Hillman was somewhat shorter than she was herself and for all his bulkiness unlikely to be particularly fit. There was no physical threat here, she told herself, and was able to nod politely when he said, "Please come to my study, will you? We can talk quietly there," and followed him to a door on the far side of the drawing room.

She looked back as she reached the door, and saw the woman Olive on her knees beside the sofa, stroking Sylvia Hillman's forehead. She looked resigned and a little angry; but then Olive looked up and, catching her eye, lifted her brows in a sort of "Honestly, some people!" message, friendly and conspiratorial, making of George and herself a pair. How very odd, George thought, and followed the round man into his room.

He sat down at a desk, ensconcing himself behind it, and George recognized what he was doing: putting a guard between himself and her, with some pomp, and the last shreds of her fear vanished. He was as nervous about her as she was about him, clearly. So she smiled at him when he indicated the chair facing him on the other side of the desk and sat down, relaxing without difficulty.

"This is a lovely room," she said conversationally, as if she'd been at a cocktail party. "Leather is so very beautiful, isn't it?" The space was as leathery as a harness store, she thought privately, deep buttoned chairs and sofa, a desk with leather inset into the top, leather-handled paper knives and pens on it; everything that could be covered in dark green skin had been. It looked like a shop window in Tottenham Court Road.

He brushed the comment aside. "Why are you here?" he demanded.

"I told your wife. Didn't she tell you when she phoned? It was about the advertisement I placed. About babies for adoption."

He was silent for a moment and then seemed to stiffen himself. "Why did you address me by—what was it you called me? Is it because…Well, why?"

"Oh, come on! You know perfectly well I called you Oberlander. And it meant something to your wife, didn't it? I'm sorry if I upset her. I didn't want to, believe me. But I do have to find out what happened. The baby's death was—"

"The baby's what?" He was so stiff now that he seemed to George to be made of board. She lifted her brows at him, never taking her eyes from his face, trying to assess the truth of every hint of expression there. His round face served him well, however. There was little to see in it but a sort of blankness.

"The baby's death," she said again. "We—the police and I—have been investigating that death. I am the pathologist at Old East, Mr. Oberlander—or Hillman. Whichever. I did the post-mortem and…"

He was no longer blank. His face too had crumpled and tears had appeared behind the glasses. She watched with horror as, slowly, they began to trickle down his soft cheeks. Behind her, through the door to the drawing room, she could hear his wife still sobbing. What on earth had been done to these two people to have this effect on them?

32

The sky outside the windows that looked down into Sloane Street slid from grey to charcoal to a deep indigo that vanished into blackness when Olive, fetching yet another pot of fresh coffee, switched on more lights. Still Sylvia was sobbing softly. It was as though she had a bottomless pit of tears locked inside her pathetically thin body from which she would never cease to draw.

David sat close beside her on the sofa, holding her hand, and George, watching them as they told their story, felt her belly taut with pity. People shouldn't be like this, so despairing and desperate, so *hungry*. She tried to put herself in their shoes, to feel the need as urgently as they did, and failed, despite the fact that she had herself thought often enough over the past few years of the way time was rolling on and her own chances of parenthood were becoming slimmer with each year that passed. To want children, yes, that made sense; but to ache for them, need and yearn and long for them to the point of utter desolation as these two had for so many years, that couldn't be right. It had become for them a form of obsession. Not a normal wanting, but a pathological despair. And someone had made a lot of money out of it. There was a great deal of anger deep inside George as she listened to the slow building up of the story, sentence by painful sentence.

"We thought it'd just be easy, at first. Well, you always do, don't you?" David Hillman looked down at his wife at his side.

"Twenty years now. It doesn't seem possible, does it? I was twenty-five and my Sylvie here was twenty when we married. The first two, three years we weren't that interested. We even used something so we wouldn't—Do you remember, Sylv?"

She lifted her chin to look at him and the tears still ran down her face as she essayed a smile; it was a gut-wrenching thing to see and George looked back at David quickly.

"But then things got better. I made a few bob, we moved here and it had everything. There's the park and the Square so near, lots of fresh air, and we thought, right, now we'll start our family. Once we have three we'll get a big house in the country..."

His voice trailed away and he looked down at his wife's hand held closely in his. After a moment he patted it with his other hand and then went on. It was clearly not easy.

"We went to ever so many different people. The top specialists. Here and in America too. I can't tell you what we spent. Tried everything. They never could find out what was wrong with us. They said I'm all right, said Sylvie was, but we still never started a baby."

"If I'd even had a miscarriage it wouldn't have been so bad." Sylvia spoke so unexpectedly that George almost jumped. "I mean it would have proved it was possible, you know? But I never even had that." Her voice was thick and rusty, as though she'd forgotten how to use it in the flood of tears that had engulfed the afternoon.

"At first, we didn't want to even think of adoption. It was our own babies we wanted, ones that looked like us. We've got pictures of our grandparents, even our great-grandparents, and it's marvellous to see the way people look like each other and we thought...But after a while that stopped being so important. Just to have a baby of our own to care for..."

"We tried the donor thing, you know," Sylvia said. Her voice was still thick and choked but she seemed a little less tearful. "David wasn't keen but he said, for me, he said it'd be—" She stopped, shook her head and wept again.

"I didn't care by then. I wouldn't have cared if they'd said chop your finger off, we'll grow it into a baby for you." He sounded more weary than determined now. It was as though in telling the story he was reliving the long exhausting years. "But that didn't work either. They told us they couldn't help us, to go away and forget about it, to make the best of nephews and nieces and godchildren and so forth." He went pink suddenly and sat very straight. "Those bastards knew it all, telling us that! Like that'd be any use to us! Like it'd be any use to anyone! When it's your own home you want your own babies in it, not to borrow someone else's for an afternoon. Bloody patronizing bastards!"

There was a silence for a while and George let it stretch as much as it wanted to. She would put no more pressure on them.

It was Sylvia who spoke first. "Then I met this woman at a charity thing. She said she'd met another woman who'd adopted a baby from Romania. No questions asked, beautiful child, she said. So I looked into it. I—er—I didn't tell David at first."

"We'd gone away on a holiday, one we'd planned to do when our children grew up," David said. "Round the world, you know? Over the Pole and everything. We were away four weeks. Stayed in all the best hotels, saw lots, but it made no difference. I know that. We said to each other that from now on we'd live for ourselves and forget all about babies, but I knew she wouldn't rest that easy."

"He's wonderful, isn't he?" Sylvia said and looked appealingly at George. "Isn't he the best husband a woman could have?"

"Yes," George said and smiled at her. She meant it.

"So when Sylvie told me she knew someone who'd get us a baby from Romania, I said all right, go for it. But she said it'd cost."

"I felt bad about that," Sylvia said. "Afterwards. This—The business hasn't been all that wonderful lately. He doesn't tell me, but I know."

David went pink now. "I don't bother you with business things," he said gruffly. "I never have and I never will. You want to spend, you go ahead, it's your money as much as mine."

"I know," Sylvia said. "When you've got it. But it's tighter than it was, you can't deny, and here was I wanting twenty thousand pounds to—"

"Twenty how much?" George said.

"It didn't sound such a lot to me. I thought...Well, to have our own child after so many years, a thousand a year, really, that was what I thought, not a lot, and anyway I thought that'd be all there was. It wasn't, of course."

"What happened?" George ventured, for now they were both silent, looking down at their laps, clearly lost in memory.

"Mmm?" It was David who went on. "Oh yes. Well, it went on and on. This woman kept phoning, saying next week, next week. I thought we'd been conned, to tell you the truth, but there it was. The check had been paid. It was for cash to bearer so I never could find out who it was. There wasn't anything I could do."

He seemed to rouse himself suddenly, to become aware of how much he was saying, and he looked at her sharply, his round eyes shining like ice crystals behind his glasses. "Look, I'm—we're telling you all this, but how do we know you aren't the same people? That you don't know anyway and are up to some trick or other? We've only got your word for it that you're not."

"I showed you that letter to me," George said. "And my credit cards and so forth. It's the only ID I have with me. Please, do believe me. I'm involved only as the police pathologist. No more. Do please go on. Then maybe we can—Well, maybe we can track down these horrible people who treated you so badly and deal with them. Maybe even get some money back. Though I can't promise that, of course," she ended hastily, suddenly hearing Gus expostulating at her for making impossible-to-keep promises.

"Money back?" David said. He laughed, an oddly mirthless little bark of sound. "That'll be the bloody day."

There was another pause, and then George spoke, carefully, needing to move them on but not alarm them. "So then what happened?"

David looked at her. His eyes were still sharp but he seemed to reach a decision. He put up both hands in a helpless gesture. "Then one day she phoned and said he was here."

Sylvia was sitting very upright now and had taken her hand out of David's and was holding it to her cheek as she stared at George.

"Here?" George said.

"In London," Sylvia said. "It was ever so late. About half past nine, it must have been. David was at the office."

"We were up to our eyes in an MBO," David said, as though it explained everything.

"A what?" George was mystified.

"A management buy-out. It worked, too. We're better off now we've done it, though we're still tight for money. Cash flow problems. But it was worth it, we're a bit safer than we were, which these days is something to be grateful for. But it was a hairy few days, believe me." He shook his head. "A very hairy few days. I never thought I'd manage it."

"And I knew I mustn't bother him at the office. He'd said that and I knew when it was really important and Olive had gone home and so I'—she lit up as she remembered the excitement of it all—"so I got my coat and went down and I took a taxi. And all the way there I thought, what will it be like? I didn't even know if it was a boy or girl then, not even that! I don't think I've ever had such a long journey. The traffic wasn't bad, but still…" She shook her head, still lost in reminiscence. "I gave the cab driver a fiver for a tip. He thought I was mad but I was so grateful to be there. I ran in and across that huge space and at first I couldn't find it…"

"Couldn't find what?" George said gently, afraid to break

the spell the woman was weaving as she sat there, her head up and her eyes huge in her thin face, watching herself in the past.

"The right ladies," Sylvia sounded impatient. "She'd said the ladies room, but there are so many there! How could I know which one? But I found it at last and there she was."

"Where?" George said, still not wanting to stem the flow but needing the details. "Whereabouts?"

"In the ladies," Sylvia insisted, flicking a glance at George. "In the—Oh! I see what you mean. It was Heathrow. The airport."

"Ah!" George's face cleared. Of course. The point at which the babies entered the country. She'd been right; the whole thing indeed was an adoption scam, and the babies for adoption were smuggled in from abroad. Romania? So Sylvia had been told. But who could say? Yet smuggled in they were; this was the evidence Gus had wanted. She could have cheered at her own perspicacity but somehow managed to control her excitement.

"And then what?" she said as carefully as she could.

"She told me they needed more money. I was to put cash in an envelope—they'd told me that on the phone. So I opened the safe."

David looked sideways at George then, a sly little glance. "I usually have some spare liquidity here at home," he murmured.

"I'd done all she said on the phone, so all I had to do was give the envelope to the woman in the ladies and she pushed this bundle at me and I took it and I looked…" She was trembling now, her eyes wide, the pupils greatly enlarged, "I looked and I'd never seen—he looked so—I didn't know it was a boy then. I sat down on the loo, right away I did, and I undressed him—such awful clothes he had, awful—and looked and I thought, David will be pleased, a boy."

Her face puckered then. "He was dreadfully thin though, and he lay there not looking right at all, and so thin. He didn't cry or anything, just lay there, his eyes half open. So I wrapped him up again and fetched him home in a taxi and the next day when

David found out, it was all right." She threw a glance at him that was shining, glittering, brilliant with gratitude. "Even about giving her all that extra money, and then we went out and bought half the babies' department at Harrods. Oh, it was the best day of my life. And we looked after him and I fed him, though it took ages and he had such trouble sucking and I thought it was because of being breast fed and not used to bottles—"

"How did you know he'd been breast fed?" George said quickly, and Sylvia looked at her blankly, halted in full flood of memory.

"Eh? Oh, the woman in the ladies, she said so. Told me he was eight months old, he'd been breast fed and to give him SMA, not ordinary milk."

"She was English, then?"

"What? Oh, yes, I mean, she talked just like—Of course she was."

"What did she look like?"

Sylvia's forehead creased. "I'm not sure. Ordinary, you know. Just ordinary. Not very tall—not very big. Just ordinary."

"What color eyes? Hair?"

Sylvia shook her head. "She was wearing a woolly cap," she said. "I never saw her hair. And glasses, yes glasses. Dark ones. Well, tinted, you know? Half tinted at the top. I'd never seen her before so…" She shrugged. "I knew nothing about her. I wasn't interested, you see. Only in the baby. I was only interested in him."

"Yes," George said. "I see. What happened next?"

"Well, we tried ever so hard. I loved him so much, I really did. Right from the start. They say you fall in love and I did! But he was so thin and sad and so—He never cried, or hardly at all, and when he did it was so sweet. Like a kitten mewing." She smiled fondly at the recollection and George felt her spine go cold. Babies who cried like mewing kittens were very ill babies. This poor woman had had the care of a very sick baby and hadn't even realized it.

"I called him Theodore," Sylvia said then, unexpectedly. "The gift of God, Theodore."

"Teddy," said George.

Sylvia smiled fondly again. Her tears had vanished, leaving only stains behind on her cheeks. In talking about the baby she had lost she seemed to find comfort. "That was David's name for him. Our little Teddy."

"He wasn't well. I could see that and I was worried. I told Sylvia we ought to get a doctor to see him, but she wouldn't."

"It was too soon," Sylvia said with sudden passion. "Too soon, don't you see? I was scared they'd ask where he'd come from and—well, I was scared. Another few weeks, I thought, then we can find the right doctor and have all the right checks done but I was scared they'd try to take him away from us if they knew we'd done such a thing. It's not legal, is it, to buy a baby? And we'd spent thirty thousand." She caught George's eye and looked shamefaced. "Yes. That was how much I had to give her from the safe. Another ten thousand. But it was worth it, it was, it was. Wasn't it, David?" she looked up at him appealingly.

He patted her hand, but didn't look at her. "I got more and more worried. I thought, she doesn't realize how ill he is. I must get him to a doctor and then, thank God, the woman phoned."

George sharpened. "Which woman?"

"The one who'd done it all. The one who'd phoned first. Sylvia's friend, you see, had passed on our names to this person—no one was to have the woman's phone number, it was all very cloak and dagger—and she phoned us to start it all. After we'd got the baby I thought, she'll never call again, and I was worried, I can tell you. I didn't know what our situation was, you see. No birth certificate, nothing legal. It was a mess! Sylvia was happy, happier than I had ever seen her, but I was worried sick." He patted Sylvia's hand for she was weeping again, but didn't look at her. "I sent her a letter—the woman—I asked Sylvia's friend to see she got it, but I couldn't be sure she had."

"But then the woman phoned again," George prompted softly, for he had seemed to fall into another little brown study.

"Mmm?" He blinked. "Yes, she rang and I said he was ill and that I wanted to take him to a doctor, and she said on no account was I to do that, they'd take him away. I said but he's ill, he doesn't look right. She said take him to the hospital. He was just failing to thrive, that's what she said, and to take him to hospital. Old East she said it was. Told me the way and everything. I didn't know it was really the Royal Eastern until I got there. Anyway, she said go there and use a false name and address, to prevent anyone from taking him away from us, and take him to Dr. Kydd's ward. So we did and this doctor—a red-headed one she was—very young—"

"Yes," George said. "I know. She's a very good doctor."

"Is she? Well, she didn't make me feel all that good, I can tell you. I'd asked for Dr. Kydd, of course, but she said Dr. Kydd was away and she was in charge, and I was so glad he was being seen by a doctor, I thought even this one'll be better than no one, and then—then—"

"Yes?" George spoke softly.

"She said we had to leave him behind, he was very ill and needed tests. I wasn't keen, but I thought, well, if he's ill— and the woman on the phone had said Old East was the place to take him so..." Again he patted his wife's hand. "Sylvia wasn't happy but the doctor insisted we leave him there for tests. So I took Sylvia away and left him. But the next few hours I couldn't take it," he said simply. "Sylvia nearly went mad without him. I had to take her back. And this time it was a different doctor, a black one, and he said to leave Teddy but I wouldn't—ill as he was, if he was being seen by all different doctors and not this Dr. Kydd..." He shook his head miserably. "Well, we just took him home."

"I thought: he'll get better, I don't care what they say. What do these young doctors know, so young as they are?" Sylvia said, passionate again. "I knew I could get him well. I would have, if they'd let me." She began to weep again. There seemed no stopping her.

"So then what?" George felt the banality of her repeated prompting, but David seemed oblivious of it.

"We fetched him home." He moved uneasily in his place on the sofa. The memories were getting more painful for him too, clearly. "And the woman phoned again. Said why had we taken him home and I told her, loud and strong, I told her that I wasn't satisfied, that I wanted him to be seen by a specialist, not all these different young doctors, and I was going to one and taking my chances on being asked awkward questions. So she said, all right, she'd help us."

George blinked. "She said what?"

"That's what I thought." David sounded grim. "I felt a bit better though. She told us to take him—the baby, you know—to an address she gave us in Harley Street. Here it is." He reached into his pocket for his wallet and pulled out a piece of paper. "See? Harley Street. Said she'd meet us there and introduce us to the doctor. So we took him there and—and—"

"Well?" George said, gently but needing to push the man a little harder for he was balking now. "Well?"

"It was a sort of clinic. Not a private house like a lot of those Harley Street places. And she was there in the hallway when we arrived and said she'd take Teddy to the specialist. She had the birth certificate and all the papers, she said and she'd give them to us later and to wait there for her. She said the doctor'd be suspicious if he saw us, but that she'd be OK because he knew her agency, so we said all right. It sort of made sense. She went up the stairs with Teddy. And never came down."

Sylvia was rocking in her seat now, sodden with her tears again, and George reached out and touched her hand gently. It was hot and dry.

"She just went away somewhere?"

He nodded. "I found out afterwards there was a different way out of the building. I went to look, of course, after half an hour, but I got nowhere. There were no baby specialists in the building. They were all these alternative doctors, acupuncturists and so on."

"So what did you do then?" George was pushing them as hard as she dared, and David reacted with sudden anger.

"What did I do then? What the bloody hell could I do? We'd been duped, hadn't we? Used and abused and—and there wasn't a bloody thing we could do about it. All we knew was there'd been a baby we'd cared about and now—and now they'd taken him back."

He put both hands up to his face and again began to weep. They sat there side by side in an agony of distress like a pair of dolls in a Swiss clockwork toy, somehow ridiculous in their pitiful state, and George felt her own eyes prickle in sympathy.

"And then you come and tell us he's dead. I thought when I saw your advert, maybe it's the same people and I can find Teddy again, or at the very least, maybe we could start again. I want a baby! I thought we could start again!" It was Sylvia who was speaking now, indeed almost shouting, sitting bolt upright and with patches of high color staining her face. "I saw your ad and answered it. I thought we can start again. I pretended I was David and I thought I could start again and when I told him what I'd done he was so—so *good* about it. And then you come and I think, maybe it'll be all right this time and all you tell us is that he died...It's too cruel. How can life be so cruel? What did I ever do to deserve it?"

"Oh, Sylvia," David Hillman said. He turned to her and held her close. "It's not your fault. I keep telling you that." He looked at George then over Sylvia's head. "If I'd realized how ill he was I'd have taken him to a doctor right away. To think I kept him from proper treatment because I was scared of being caught! It's hell and I'll never forgive myself."

George spoke without stopping to think. All she wanted to do was help him. She wanted at least to take away from his existing misery the burden of guilt. It wasn't his fault the child had died and he was entitled to know that. So she said it, and not until she saw his stricken face did she realize how much worse she had made things.

"But it wasn't your fault!" she said. "He was murdered, you see. Smothered. By someone we haven't been able to find. But it wasn't your fault…"

33

"Under the circumstances," Gus said, "you're forgiven." They were sitting in her office; she'd found him there when she'd come pounding back breathlessly from Sloane Street, and was so delighted to have the chance to pour it all out to him that she didn't stop to wonder why he was there.

"Well, thank you for nothing." She was scathing. "After getting you all that, is that the best you can do?"

"We made a deal that you wouldn't—"

"I've explained about that! If I'd been able to get hold of you I would have done, but they said you were out on that robbery and, now I come to think of it, what are you doing here?"

"Taking a break," he said. "The stuff's gone off the patch and it's another force's problem. So I'm off the hook. But even though I was still on it when you called you could have kept your word. I'm not the only one on the team, after all. Just because I was out and about over that bloody heist—three lorryloads o' the best malt whisky Scotland ever produced, vanished like a bunch o' fairies. I ask you!—you didn't have to go off half cocked. You could have talked to Roop. Got him to trot along and question them."

"Oh, yes," she said with all the sarcasm she could muster. "And can you see your precious Rupert getting the story out of them?" She made her voice stiff and nasal at the same time. "I'm Detective Sergeant Dudley, now just you tell me all about what happened to you. Right now, no messing about." Her voice returned to normal. "I ask you, Gus! He'd have frightened the hell out of them and got nothing."

He grinned at her, a wide winning smile. "Fair enough. He'd have gone in like a hippopotamus, I can't deny. All right. You done good, girl. You done real good."

"Thank you," she said, half mollified. "The thing we now have to do, then, is find this woman. The one who arranged the whole deal. The one who took all the money."

"You didn't think to get the name of the friend to whom Sylvia Hillman confided her desperate need for a baby, did you? The woman who put them together?"

She bit her lip with chagrin. "Hell, we did talk about that, but then—"

"I didn't think you had." He was in a high good humor, clearly finding pleasure in having caught her out. "Not to fret. One of my women constables'll be going along there in the morning to sort out the taking of statements. She'll get it and we'll follow up. It shouldn't take long."

"You reckon whoever it was—the agency contact, I mean—was the murderer of the baby?"

"Who else?"

"And what about Harry?"

"That's a puzzle, I agree. But even there I think we should get some answers once we've got whoever was running the adoption business. It's my guess that Harry found out what was happening and let whoever it was know he had, and that was why he was killed."

"It's definitely someone here, then," George said. It wasn't a question and he didn't treat it as one.

"It has to be. The way I see it is this. Tell me if you disagree. Someone here is running an adoption racket, using babies from abroad, smuggling them in."

"Yes, I've been thinking about that. There's a big—" George began.

"Shut up," he said amiably. "Let me sort this out first, then you can join in. OK? Someone here runs a racket, Harry Rajabani gets wind of it, doesn't cover his back and gets killed. The murderer also realizes that one of the babies is sick—it was sick when it arrived, wasn't it? And thinks she'd better do a check. She knows that if this baby turns up in another hospital and is diagnosed as having AIDS which is what she thinks the kid has, I imagine, then questions will be asked, like where did he get it? and she doesn't want that. They might realize the child was fetched in from a country where there's a lot of infantile AIDS."

"Romania," George said.

"Right. OK, so she suspects this child has AIDS—though why she handed it over, thinking that, I can't imagine, but we'll worry about that later. She suspects it, arranges to get the child from the new parents with a tale of taking it to a good doctor and scarpers with it, leaves them high and dry. Then she kills the baby and thinks she's safe enough."

"There're a lot of questions to be asked there, Gus. First, as you say, why hand it over if she knows it's sick? And then the business of getting the baby in. How does she do it? That's the big flaw in the whole thing. Don't babies have to appear on their parents' passports? You can't just tuck a baby under your arm and waltz through immigration and passport control and so forth. People ask questions. That's what worries me about this whole smuggling notion. It's mine, I know, and it has to be a smuggler, or else why hand the baby over at the airport?" She frowned. "But it's all so—Can people just transport babies without passports and no questions asked?"

"No, you're right there," Gus said. "Even if a woman travels while pregnant and then gives birth abroad there has to be some documentation when she travels back with it. The birth certificate maybe, or something. I can't see Immigration just letting babies in ad lib." He scribbled in his notebook, snapping the rubber band that held it in satisfaction when he'd done so. "I'll check with the Immigration people at Heathrow on that. That'll be easy enough."

"I know!" George said as an idea hit her. "The woman who runs the thing isn't the same one as the one who does the fetching and carrying!"

"Eh?"

"It's different people! I mean if the same woman kept bobbing in and out of Heathrow with babies, someone'd be sure to notice, surely? Recognize her? I know it's a busy airport and so forth, but all the same."

He got to his feet. "We can't get any further till I talk to Heathrow, obviously," he said. "No, no need for you to come along. It's too late tonight. I'll go tomorrow first thing. Right now, I've got to clear up the last of the paperwork on this robbery."

"I wasn't going to suggest it," she retorted. "I do actually have some work of my own to do in the morning. A PM on a man they found on the waste ground down by the river. Another homeless one, I'm afraid, but it has to be done. Let me know as soon as you can, then? I'm really very—"

"I know." He was at her office door, looking back at her questioningly. "You do agree it's someone here at Old East who's been running things?"

"I don't see how it can't be, if you see what I mean. There are a lot of things that obviously tie together—the stealing of the babies in maternity, for example. I reckon it's all very obvious—they were taken to sell to adopters—but why steal babies and risk the enormous hoohah that would happen if people found out? And where did the replacement babies come from?"

"They were smuggled babies who died," Gus said. "She had a customer, our mysterious woman, but dead goods. So she helped herself to live ones."

"Oh, God," George said softly. "How horrible it all is."

"Yes." They were both silent for a while, trying to see into the mind of a person who could behave so, and then Gus gave a little shiver. "Horrible, indeed. Listen, you have work to do."

"I know. A PM."

"After that. You said you'd talk to people on Matty, remember? See if you could snoop for me, find out who, what, where. You know the sort of thing."

"Dear me," she said. "I'm really in the force then?"

"As if you didn't know it." He tipped his invisible hat at her. "I'm going to Heathrow. Get me what you can, hmm? Talk to you tomorrow."

All the time she was doing the post-mortem, next morning, which was fortunately a routine affair and not particularly surprising—she rapidly discovered that the man had died of a massive stroke—she thought about the Hillmans. They had gone on talking for a long time, clearly finding relief in pouring everything out, and she had escaped gratefully after another hour of it, feeling herself almost overwhelmed by their obsessive grief.

It was as though over the years their horizons had narrowed until all there was in view was the prospect of a child to care for. Sylvia in particular had banished all other considerations from her life; he at least had had the daily escape hatch of his business. As she had listened, George had realized why the pair were so very rich and lived so very high on the hog. As all Sylvia's energies had been funneled into the search for a child, so his had been shunted into his business. There was no doubt which was the more fortunate—or fortunate up to a point, George thought. The more Sylvia talked about her feelings and her actions the more George realized just how heavy the guilt burden was for David Hillman. Not only did he blame himself for depriving his wife of the one thing she wanted; he also blamed himself for not suffering so much pain; because he had a child of his own. His business. Buried as he was amid the accounts of his clients, he made money for himself and for

Sylvia at a great rate, yet every pound he made compounded his guilt even further. It was a dreadful trap for any man to be in, and George pitied him profoundly.

But she had picked up other facts from their talk as well as the sense of oppression that came from them. That the idea of using the name Oberlander had been his: "John Smith would have been too obvious, wouldn't it? And anyway, I had a friend called that once, long ago. We used to make jokes about how we were really the same person, likes Signor Casanova was really Mr. Newhouse, and Joe Green was Giuseppe Verdi."

There had also been some talk about the friend of Sylvia's who had put her in touch with the so-called adoption agency in the first place. George had made a mental note to remind Sylvia to give her the name and address before she left the flat, but by the time escape had been possible the matter had gone out of her head. Still, she told herself as she finished off the last notes for the old man and consigned him to Danny's casual care, it gave Gus something to feel superior about and he enjoyed that. And perhaps it's as well the police have something concrete to ask the Hillmans when they go to see them this morning, George thought. It will give the Hillmans something else to think about for a little while, too.

Back at her desk, freshly showered and changed, she sent Sheila over to the canteen to fetch her a sandwich for lunch and then settled to thinking about what she had to do in Matty. Find out, Gus had said, about who, what, where—and maybe why? That was her own idea and she considered it for a while. And then shook her head at herself.

The why was obvious. If she (and did it help to have the field narrowed to females? That had to be thought about too), if she had taken from the Hillmans thirty thousand pounds for Teddy, the motive was very obvious. Smuggling babies for sale paid well (and that still gnawed at her; *how*, for heaven's sake, was the smuggling done? Babies weren't watches or drugs that could be hidden in luggage, or disguised as anything else. Another matter to be thought of later). If whoever it was brought in only one a month that added up to three hundred and sixty thousand pounds—more than a third of a million in a year, and the chances were that there were far more than a dozen a year. She remembered the coded list; there had been nine names on that, and even allowing for the fact that three of those had been people whose babies had apparently died, it was still obvious that this scam was a big one. Reasonably carefully run, too; the details of hair color and so on were there almost certainly to enable the babies to be matched, where possible, to the appearance of the would-be adopters. That was, she knew, normal practice with bona fide adoption agencies; why not with a rogue one? There was no need to think more about the motive, however. Vast sums of money like that were ample motive for anyone.

So; who and what and where; those were the questions Gus wanted answered. And George was somehow, she promised herself, going to answer them. Her success in tracking down the Hillman-Oberlanders had gone a little to her head, she could not deny. There was enormous satisfaction in digging out information that Gus and all his policemen had so far failed to find, and she preened a little as she thought about it.

But preening would get her nowhere, and she drained her coffee cup and pushed it aside. Time to do some hard thinking. She took a large sheet of paper and a pen and ruled it into columns. She'd do the corny thing; why not? It had helped before. No reason it shouldn't work this time.

She pondered long before making headings to her columns, twice ripping up the sheet and starting again, and in the end stopped and looked doubtfully at what she ended up with. There were just five columns. The first she had headed "PERSON', the second "TYPEWRITER', the third "BABIES' and the fourth "RAG AND BOTTLE."

She contemplated the paper and then, unable to think at this stage of anything else, merely added the heading "MISC' to the final column, and chewed the end of her pen before starting, hesitantly at first and then more quickly, to write names.

But she hadn't got very far before she realized that there was no way she could work this out sitting here at her desk. She had to go over to Matty and quiz people, and she leaned back in her chair as she contemplated how much she didn't want to do that. She had no business to be in Maternity, that was the trouble. It was one thing to help the police with enquiries, another to be seen by the staff of Old East, colleagues after all, to be doing so. She could think of nothing more likely to make life unpleasant for her here, and even more importantly, to shut doors to her. If she was to be of any use to Gus at all she had to find a logical reason for going over to Maternity and asking her questions.

It was Jerry who gave her the idea she needed. As she sat there still chewing her pen he put his head round her office door. "Dr. B.," he announced. "I have to go off sick," and he beamed at her happily.

"Off sick?" She frowned. "What is it this time?" Jerry was famous for the ingenuity of his excuses for taking time off, and circumventing him was one of the skills she had learned to develop in her year as his boss.

"True bill this time," he said cheerfully and came right into the room. "See?" He held out his right hand. The thumb was clearly swollen; she could see that from halfway across the room. "I've got an old fashioned paronychia! An honest-to-God hangnail. It's discharging nicely, and I thought I ought to take a look at what the infection is." He smirked. "I just checked the result. It's a strep viridans. Very nasty. Now, you wouldn't want me spreading that around, would you? I really think this time you'll have to let me go."

"Like hell I will," George said vigorously. "Get it dressed over at A & E and then come back. I've got work you can do on the histology films where the odd bug won't matter a damn. Yeah, I know, you don't like paperwork, but hard luck, Buster.

It's where you go till you stop being a walking pesthouse. I can't use you anywhere else, and you're not sick enough to go off work! But thanks, Jerry, you've given me a hell of a good idea for something else." She jumped to her feet and reached for a clipboard to which she attached her sheet of ruled columns. "On your way!"

"Oh, well," Jerry said philosophically. "I thought it was worth spreading on the old Petrie dish to see what would grow. Didn't think I'd get far with you! Glad I was of use anyway." And he held the door open for her as she came round her desk at full pelt.

"Oh, you were useful, Jerry," she assured him happily. "You were very useful!"

34

"Well, it could be nasty, Sister," George said. "Strep viridans, you know."

Sister Lichfield looked pained. "Strep viridans? In my department? I don't think so!"

"I hope you're right, indeed I do," George said and smiled at her, making herself look the epitome of hopefulness. "But for all our sakes, a little check-up won't do any harm, hmm?"

"Well, if you insist." She was grudging. "Though checking people's movements hardly seems to me to be a way of—"

"Oh, you know how it is with infection control," George said vaguely. "We have to look into the oddest corners as well as the obvious issues. Let me start with you, if I may. On these dates, can you tell me if you were on duty?"

George handed over the sheet of paper she'd brought with her. She'd scribbled it in the lift on her way to the department; a list of dates, most of them arbitrary but including all the significant ones; the dates the three babies had died; the date Harry Rajabani died; the date the Hillmans brought Teddy into Pediatrics and the date they came and took him away again (as well as the date they took him to Harley Street and he was taken from them). She reasoned that if people were on duty in Maternity on the last four, they could hardly have been involved with the dead babies, so date checking was, she was sure, the quickest way of clearing away obvious non-starters in the suspect stakes.

Sister Lichfield looked at the list, muttered and went across her office to rummage in her bag, which was hanging on the back of the door. "I'll check my diary," she said. "But honestly, I can't see how this'll help you."

"Honey, I'm not sure either," George said with an air of great candor. "But I've been asked by the Department to make these checks and there it is." Please don't let her ask which department, she prayed inside her head. I'll be hard put to it to think of who might talk such nonsense about infection control. But she was safe. Sister Lichfield didn't ask—public health investigation wasn't a subject many people in hospitals understood very well—and came back to George, thumbing through a small diary.

"Here we are. Sing those dates out then."

George did, and Sister agreed that in fact she'd been on duty for all the days on the list. "Which isn't so surprising," she said a little sniffily. "Seeing there's no one else here to carry the ultimate responsibility apart from me. I've been asking for a full time deputy for months and do you think the Clinical Manager'll listen? Not on your bloody—Oh, all right!" A bell was ringing urgently down the corridor and she went hurrying out, leaving George to fill in the columns on her clipboard.

So, Sister Lichfield had had the opportunity to exchange the three babies who had ostensibly died, but she had not been in Pediatrics the night the Hillmans had come in with Teddy, and of course not in the Rag and Bottle pub either. The thought of Sister Lichfield in the Rag and Bottle made George's lips quirk. She'd hate it, she thought and, more to the point, she'd be very visible, the classic sore thumb. People would undoubtedly have noticed someone like Sister Lichfield in the public bar there.

Didier St Cloud came in as she sat contemplating her list, smelling of sweat and the labor ward; he was in his theater greens and looked rumpled and a little tired but she ignored that and launched herself into the same tale she had given Sister Lichfield as he looked around for the coffee tray that was usually in evidence at this time of day. He swallowed it as easily—even more easily in fact—and George sighed inside; bad enough a senior midwife should be so unknowledgeable about public health measures; that a doctor should be too almost embarrassed her for her profession.

"It's the Professor's Rolls to my clapped-out Mini that I was on duty," he said lugubriously, "I usually bloody am," and he too reached into his pocket and hauled out a small diary.

But matters were not as clear with him, George realized as she talked to him in more detail. Being on duty didn't necessarily mean being in the maternity unit. He was sometimes in Accident and Emergency.

"You'd be amazed how often they need an obstetric opinion down there. We get a fair number of pregnant girls drugged to their eyebrows or mashed up in RTAs," he said. "I'm up and down there like the old yo-yo. Pediatrics, too, come to think of it. Sometimes they want me to consult on an infant—but that's no problem to you, is it? I mean, it's only the possibility of there being strep viridans here in Matty that worries you, isn't it? I assume you'll be taking swabs from us all?"

"Oh, yes," George said, her heart sinking. He wasn't as accepting of her tale as she had thought, after all. Now she would indeed have to take swabs from everyone's nose and throat to shore up her story. A lot of work for nothing. Not that it did any harm to do a survey of the reigning organisms in such a department from time to time, but all the same she could have done without the chore right now. "I'm just collecting data, at present. Seeing whom I need to swab."

"Oh, umpteen people," Didier said, finishing his coffee. "Christ, I'm tired! I've got to hang about though. We've got a twin delivery on the boil. Yeah, you'll have to do masses of swabs, won't you? Not just the consultants and me and the houseman among the medicos, and of course all the midder and nursing staff, but the cleaners and the porters and the physios and so forth. It must run to a huge number, hmm?"

"Not necessarily," George said, extemporizing. "I gather it's not every single person who ever comes here they're interested in surveying. It's the full-time regulars, you know?"

"Really? I'd have thought almost anyone could leave a nasty bug here on just one visit. But even if they are leaving the occasional people out, it's still a lot you'll have to deal with," Didier said. "I mean, this office alone, you'd be amazed who comes in and out of here!"

"So tell me!" George said. She settled back in her chair, trying not to look too eager. "It'd be a great help to have some idea of the population in transit, as it were."

"Well, everyone who has anything to do with Maternity, of course—oh, umpteen. Phlebotomists for example, some of your people come up here to take bloods, don't they? And like I said, physios and so forth. But then there are the other departments—"

"Which others?"

"Well, Pediatrics for a start. Every one of the babes is checked by someone from Ped., you know that. Some of them more than once, if the babies are a worry. We see as much of the pediatric staff as we see of each other, here. GPs come in sometimes too, of course, but I doubt you'll have to concern yourself with them. They'll come under the Community Trust, won't they?" He looked at her, bright eyed and knowing, and she hoped her confusion didn't show. He was after all one hell of a lot smarter than she'd given him credit for being.

"Hmm? Oh, yeah. So, Pediatrics." She scribbled something meaningless on her clipboard, and then stopped short as an idea came to her. Pediatrics; the senior consultant was a person who made many trips to Romania. She caught her breath as she considered that. Why on earth hadn't she remembered that sooner? Could Susan Kydd be the person they were looking for?

"Does Dr. Kydd come to see babies here?" she asked as casually as she could.

"Mmm? Oh, sure, of course! They all do, and not just the medical staff. The senior nurses do sometimes, too. It depends on the condition of the baby, you see. We all do all we can to keep the mother and baby together and if that means bringing the Pediatric people here instead of sending the baby to them, that's the way it has to be. It's Fay Buckland's policy, and no one—not even Susan Kydd—argues with our esteemed boss!"

"So," George said, working hard at being matter-of-fact, "Pediatrics people come here. Who else?"

He frowned. "Let me see. Last night we had one of the cardiologists in here. We delivered a girl with severe mitral stenosis and we started to have problems. Oh, and then the Endocrine lot come in a good deal. For our diabetic mums, you know. Fertility, of course, are involved with Endo.—though they're really part of us, aren't they? The Radiology people come in a good deal, and, oh yes, we've been working a lot with Oncology for the last few months. We've got a couple of patients in remission with leukemias, and they monitor their progress very closely. There's a nice piece of research going on." He stood up and made for the door. "So you see, you'll have a lot of people to sort out, won't you? If this investigation's a really necessary one." And he smiled slyly at her and was gone, leaving her discomfited, trying to gather her ideas into some sort of order.

Had he been teasing her? Did he know perfectly well that her story about investigating a possible outbreak of infection in the department was so much hogwash? Had he been trailing his coat as far as his own alibi went, so confident he wouldn't be found out that he wasn't worried about her? She frowned. It was hard to think of Didier St Cloud as a suspect; certainly harder than seeing Susan Kydd in that role. She was now very high on George's suspect list, but that didn't mean she wasn't prepared to consider other possibilities, and Didier was a very real one. And yet he always seemed so straightforward and so genuinely enthusiastic about his job, so good with the mums and babies. She had seen him with them in the corridors and in her dealings around the department, and she couldn't believe it all had been a con trick or mere professional good manners.

Philip Goss conned you, she told herself then. You thought he was a deeply caring nurse and look what he turned out to be. A fascist bastard who manipulated people for his own racist ends, fomenting trouble and deliberately causing fights...But does that stand in the way of his being a good nurse? Certainly as far as those children I saw him with were concerned, he wasn't acting. They trusted him, felt comfortable with him. Maybe Didier isn't acting when he's with his patients either; yet he could still be the man we want.

Except that isn't it a woman we're looking for? The Hillmans, at any rate, said so. Was there any other reason for thinking so? She frowned again, trying to think it through. At the Rag and Bottle the landlord had been quite clear, as she remembered it, that the person Harry had been talking to was a young man. Why had she been so certain they were looking for a woman? And even if they were, there was always the possibility that more than one person was involved. There could be two criminals, one of each.

She looked down at her clipboard again and sighed. Her idea of sorting out the culprit or even culprits simply by means of excluding those who hadn't the opportunity to carry out the various actions that built up this case was so much nonsense. This department was like Victoria Station; the world and his wife went through it. And, she reminded herself, she'd only been thinking of staff. What about the patients and their families? Every time she came here there were women wandering around in the corridor, strolling up and down, chattering in corners; and visitors too were much in evidence, since there were no officially set hours for them. They could and did come with their flowers and sweets and helium-filled balloons and smuggled bottles of booze any time between nine in the morning and eight at night. Couldn't the criminal have come from anywhere and reached the babies, and later the typewriter on which the codes had been typed, at any time? The office door was always open, and as far as she knew there were no locked doors anywhere in the unit.

She got up to go. She'd have to go back to Gus with her head low and admit failure. They would have to find another way to sort it all out. She shoved her clipboard under her arm and scowled as her bleep trilled in her pocket. That was all she needed, she thought; some sort of emergency in her own department. That was the last thing she was in the mood for right now. She hit the off button on her bleep and reached for the phone.

"Oh, Dr. Barnabas!" the girl on the switchboard fluted. "I knew you wouldn't mind me bleeping you—I told her so, though she did say not to. She's holding on."

"Who's holding on?" snapped George, irritated by the smug tone in the girl's voice.

"Your mother, Dr. Barnabas," the girl's voice said smoothly and George's belly lurched. Oh, God, an emergency at home. Ma was ill. She was suddenly very aware of the way she had neglected the old ladies this past few days. She'd hardly seen them, rushing out to the hospital each morning as she had and coming in late and being monosyllabic until they seemed to take the hint and trailed off to bed early. And now...She swallowed as the line clicked in her ear and she heard Vanny's voice say uncertainly, "Hello? Hello?"

"Ma, are you all right?"

"George? Oh, I told her not to bother you, honey, I am so sorry."

"Ma, what's the matter?" She was sharp with anxiety and she almost felt Vanny shrink away at the other end of the phone.

"Why, not a thing, George, not one tiny thing! I'm having a marvellous time, truly I am. Please not to worry."

"I'm not worried. But—I mean, why did you call? You've never called me here before."

"Well, I told Bridget that! I said to her, we have never bothered George when she's at the hospital and it won't be right to do it now but she said it was our last chance and you'd want me to, so I did, but I am so sorry."

George took a deep breath. She was almost giddy with relief; clearly her mother was well. There had been no need for that lurch of fear and she deliberately relaxed her shoulders, making herself breathe more easily.

"Do explain, Ma," she said in as neutral a voice as she could. "What last chance?"

"Well, it's only today, you see, honey." Vanny sounded apologetic. "We have to pack tomorrow. There is no way, and so I told Bridget, no way that I'll be hurried over that. I would rather we sit about for hours with nothing to do than be hustled. So—"

"Pack?" George said blankly and whirled to peer at the calendar on the wall behind Sister's desk. "Ye Gods, Ma, what's the date? Oh, no! I hadn't—Look, Ma, I'm so sorry. I hadn't realized how soon you were supposed to be going home. I'll get back early this evening and we'll—Ma?"

At the other end of the phone she could hear Bridget's voice expostulating and her mother answering her and then there was a rattle as the phone changed hands. Bridget's voice came crackling at her, brisk and cheerful.

"Your ma won't come to the point, but I'm not so scared of you. George, you promised you'd spend this last free day we have with us. We talked about it, remember? We saved the Tate Gallery for today. And I told Vanny she should ask you what time we were to be ready for you and she just shillyshallies round it. So here I am asking you. What time should we be ready? Will we meet you there, or will you come home and we start from here?"

George had, of course, totally forgotten. It had been one of those vague promises people make and she could remember now the conversation a couple of days after Christmas. At that point the departure of the old ladies had seemed eons away; and now it was here. She looked at her watch and did some fast planning at the back of her mind.

"I hadn't forgotten, really," she lied. "I mean, it had sorta slipped my mind just at present, but I've got just a couple of things to deal with here, and I'll be on my way. We'll be at the Tate in plenty of time to see all you could possibly want to. And I'm sorry you had to chase me."

"That's all right, honey," Bridget said serenely. "We know how it is with you, saving lives and all." The phone clicked and George hung up, wondering just for a moment if Bridget had been digging at her. After all, she knew perfectly well that George's job was in no way a life-saving one.

She called Gus then, knowing he wouldn't be there, and left a message saying she needed to talk to him as soon as possible, and the young constable at the other end of the phone showed no surprise, which was one comfort. The last thing she needed was the sniggering she sometimes suspected was going on when she made contact with Gus at his office. Was their relationship the subject of gossip there? She supposed it was possible, even likely, and found the thought uncomfortable.

She came clean with Sheila, telling her directly what had happened, and Sheila nodded and was as nice as she knew how to be.

"It's all right, Dr. B., I can hold the fort here easily. I shan't say a word to anyone about where you really are, and never you think it. Not even the staff'll know. Just you and me. It's not every day you get the chance to be with your mum, is it?" She sighed sumptuously. "Not that I mean to be morbid, but after all, she is an old lady, isn't she? And think how awful you'd feel if you'd missed today and she went home and then Something Happened." Sheila was the only person George knew who could actually speak in capital letters. "You be on your way, Dr. B. Leave it all to me."

So she did; and at half past two the three of them, she and Vanny and Bridget, climbed the steps of the Tate Gallery, where Vanny was to find for George the last piece of the jigsaw puzzle that was presently filling her thoughts.

35

"My dogs," said Bridget with deep feeling, "are barking!" She kicked off a shoe and rubbed her foot with a pained expression on her face.

George, sitting beside her on the long bench, grinned in sympathy and leaned back. They seemed to have been walking through the huge rooms for hours, gazing at canvas after canvas, trailing behind Vanny who was indefatigable. She trotted happily from painting to sculpture and back again, peering at the labels, reading her catalog with absorbed interest and then looking again. George had forgotten now just how much her mother had always enjoyed paintings; had forgotten the long afternoons of her childhood when she would sit curled up on a museum bench with a book while her mother wandered, as she had this afternoon, rapt and happy.

"I hope you're enjoying it, though," she said to Bridget. "It'd be a pity to spend your last day doing something you didn't want to—"

"Oh, don't get me wrong, sweetheart! I adore paintings—those impressionist rooms were darling. It's just that my feet don't have the stamina my eyes do. I don't know where Vanny gets it from—"

She looked across the big space to where Vanny was contemplating a trio of Victorian story paintings by Augustus Egg. "Look at her there. What's that set called? *Past and Present*, isn't it?" She peered at her own catalog. "Yeah, that's

it. I ask you. What could that poor wife have done to have
suffered such a dreadful fate? And why does Vanny care so
much what it was?" She shook her head fondly as Vanny came
back towards them.

"I just love the way these painters could show you a whole
world and way of life in just one little painting," she said as she
came up to them. "The painting itself is so—well, so perfect!
Just look at the wallpaper and the tablecloth in that one, the
first of them." She waved a vague hand towards the Augustus
Eggs she had been looking at. "But it's more than that."

"What more, Ma?" George said a little lazily. It was
difficult to concentrate on the luscious detail of the paintings
that surrounded them in the big airy rooms, but concentrate she
should. Ma would be gone in a day or so and she wouldn't have
the chance to talk to her then about anything.

"Oh, what their lives were really like," Vanny said, her eyes
bright and alert. She looked far more like the mother George
remembered from her more vigorous middle years than she
had at any time since her arrival in London. "What the cities
were like, what the people did and the jobs they had. There's
that marvellous one called *Work* with so many things going
on it, it's like you were living at the time to look at it. It's
not here though. May have it in a different gallery. But the
same painter—Ford Madox Brown, his name was—did my
real favorite. Look here." She reached down and pulled on
George's arm. "It's over here. I've always loved it. This one
and the Richard Dadds are what I wanted most to see. Over
there."

"Richard who?" Bridget said as she replaced her shoes and
stood up too. "Is he someone special?"

"He went mad and killed his pa with an axe," Vanny said
matter-of-factly over her shoulder as she led them to a far
corner of the gallery. "And he painted fairies like no one else
ever did. Take a look at the *Fairy Feller's Master Stroke* if you
want to see how good he was. It's in another room. I'll show

you in a moment or two. But this one's even more of a favorite. I just love it. Here you are!"

She had stopped in front of a small painting which hung almost in the corner. It was oval and simply framed, barely a foot wide and not much longer. It showed two mid-Victorian people, a man and a woman sitting side by side and staring out somberly at the viewer. They were young and neatly dressed, she in a large bonnet and warm, voluminous shawl, he in a round hat and a heavy overcoat buttoned to his neck against the cold. They had a large umbrella keeping the wind off them, for they were shown sitting beside the ropes that served as a rail on a ship. In the background other passengers smoked and laughed and beyond them there was a view of rough seas and white cliffs. The whole mood of the painting was of deep sadness.

"There!" said Vanny in huge satisfaction and with an almost proprietorial air. "Do you see what I mean?"

"Not entirely," Bridget said after a moment, with complete candor. "You tell me the truth, now, Vanny. What meaning am I supposed to see? They seem like nice young people in a picture, is all. What have I missed?"

"Why, the birth of America, that's what!" Vanny said with great vigor. "Or part of it anyway. It's called *The Last of England*. Just look at those two people! They're having to emigrate, right? There's a lot of poverty at home in Britain— that was the time people were emigrating in the most amazing numbers, around 1850 or so. So, they've decided to up stakes and go and seek their fortune in the New World. But they're scared. He's specially miserable, because he feels he's kinda failed her, his pretty little wife, couldn't make a go of it here so he's taking her away from all she's ever known and loved. Oh, he feels bad about that! He doesn't like the company much either—all those noisy revelers in the back of the painting, see? They're not his class at all, so he knows the journey won't be easy. And there'll be problems over food too—see the cabbages they've got tied to the side of the ropes there, on the rail? That's how it was. Fresh food at sea was a real worry. By the time they arrive in New York they'll be a lot sadder than they are now." She shook her head in warm sympathy. "And then the saddest thing of all. See their hands?"

Bridget peered and so did George. The man was holding his wife's gloved right hand in his, protective and caring. The cold had made his own bare fingers a little blue, but at least she was warm, and George said, "You're right, Ma. It does tell a story, doesn't it? I wonder why he had no gloves? Too poor, maybe?"

"Oh, that—maybe." Vanny dismissed glovelessness with an impatient shake of her head. "No, it's her other hand I mean. See?"

The woman's other hand was just visible in the folds of her thick cloak. George frowned in puzzlement and started to speak. "She has no glove on that hand, has she? Maybe it's in her pocket or—"

But it was Bridget who spotted what Vanny wanted her to see, and Vanny crowed with delight as she said so.

"Oh, look! She has a baby's hand there!"

George bent and peered too and there it was; peeping above the closed fingers of the woman were four much smaller fingers.

"Oh, that is so sweet!" Bridget cried. "She has her baby there. Under her cloak to keep him safe from the cold. Oh, those poor dears! How long would they be at sea?"

"About three or four weeks, I think," Vanny said. "Maybe longer. Looking at the ropes in the background it's clear it's a sailing ship, isn't it? Not a fast steamship. I'm not sure when the first steamship took immigrants, but at this time anyway, poor people had to rely on the winds. It could take a long time, and them with a baby too, probably getting sea sick if nothing worse—"

"They'd have needed more than a couple of Valium to keep it quiet on board," Bridget chuckled. "I keep praying there're no babies on the plane day after tomorrow. I'm fresh out of pills and—"

"Oh, my God!" George said loudly. "Oh, my giddy God!"

The two old ladies turned and looked at her in unison, staring anxiously. George would have laughed at the comical effect of their synchrony if she hadn't been so transfixed.

"What is it, honey?" Vanny said. "Are you sick?"

"Sick? Oh, Ma, I'm not sick or anything like it! You've just solved the case that I've been working on all these weeks, that's all! Of course that was how they did it! And getting them shouldn't be all that difficult, now we know what to look for!"

"No, dear," Vanny said peaceably and looked swiftly at Bridget. "If you say so. Um, how about a little cup of tea? I guess maybe you are a bit tired after all."

"They told me you were here having supper," George said, sliding in beside him and reaching for a chip from his plate. "Nice to be some people."

"This is the first proper meal I've had for days," he growled. "Kitty! Fetch the doctor some grub, will you?" Kitty looked up from the other side of the restaurant, waved and flashed a grin at George. "So, what's so urgent? I did get your message and tried to call but I don't have to tell you you weren't available. Found out who done it, hmm? Went to Maternity and got someone to confess, have you?"

"No." She refused to be baited. "I decided that wouldn't work. Too many people marching in and out all the time. There's hardly a department that doesn't overlap with them. You might as well try and sort out alibis for everyone who walks in here in the next week."

"Hmmph," he nodded. "I supposed that was likely. Well, we'll have to get our heads down even harder, won't we? We're looking for the friend Sylvia said put her in touch with the scam in the first place. Not much joy there yet, but the robbery's all sorted, at least. They got them in Manchester, as sweet a collar as you ever heard. I've got the paperwork sewn up and we're clear. Tomorrow we can bring back all the people

I've had working on the robbery to the murder room and we'll see if we can crack this little bugger, however long it takes."

"It mightn't take as long as you think," George said with elaborate casualness. "Seeing I know how it was done."

"Eh?" Gus stared at her with gratifying surprise, but she only smiled at him and leaned back in her chair as Kitty arrived to put a piece of plaice and some chips in front of her.

"Thanks, Kitty. That looks lovely. A glass of water, too, please? Bless you."

Kitty showed a decided tendency to linger and chat but Gus glared at her so she made a face and went to fetch the water. Gus demanded, "What does that mean, then?"

"I've worked out how the scam was operated." She leaned forward, unable to hide her glee any longer. "I can see the whole story. Just you listen and see if you don't agree. No interruptions, now!"

She speared some chips and began to eat, talking with her mouth full. Gus pushed his own plate aside and propped his chin on his fists to listen.

"OK, I am a person—I'm not sure what sort of person—but a person who has access to people who want babies. At this stage I have to say I'm not sure how that access was obtained, but I have a strong suspicion. I'll be working on that. Let's just say for argument's sake now that I am that person.

"Right. I realize that a lot of money can be made by satisfying the wishes of these people who want babies. So I think about how to do it and I find out that there are a whole bunch of babies without parents in a foreign country. White babies, though some of them are dark haired and dark eyed, being of Gypsy origin, but the sort of babies the potential customers want. How to get them, however, from the country where they are, which is of course Romania—all that publicity about Romanian orphans a couple of years back, remember— how do I get them from Romania to the UK?"

"I suppose—" Gus began but she shook her head at him.

"No, not a word till I've done. I know, as this person, that you can't just go and select babies and take them to the airport and say to the officials there, 'Oh, I'm just taking these babies to England!' You have to have them documented. Passports and so forth.

"So, since there is no way I can get them on to passports— not every one of them and it's my intention to bring in one hell of a lot—I need to smuggle them out of Romania into Britain. How? You can't do it by packing them into cases or hiding them in luggage, can you? Babies breathe and move and cry. You can't carry them through in hand luggage on account of all that has to go through security and is checked by X-rays. No good at all.

"So…" She stopped, triumphant. "So, I decide to carry them the way mothers carry babies before they're born."

He laughed at that. "Reverse birth, eh?"

"As near as dammit. From time immemorial, to quote the cliché, mothers have bound their babies to their bodies and carried them that way. Look at this."

She reached into her pocket and pulled out the postcard she'd bought at the souvenir desk at the Tate Gallery. "Can you see it?"

He looked at the copy of "The Last of England' and slowly a smile lifted his face. "I remember this. We had it in a book at school. The history master was keen on it."

"Then you know the details?"

"Emigration in the 1850s," he said. "There was something else…" He looked more closely and then smiled even more widely. "Of course. The baby. He used to talk about the baby." His voice died away and he stared and then looked at her. "Of course! It has to be the only way, doesn't it? Why didn't we think of it sooner?"

"It was Vanny who made me realize. And Bridget who put the lid on it," she said and told him of her time at the Tate that day and he laughed.

"That's my dear old ladies! Going day after tomorrow, are they? Pity. You'll miss "em." His eyes glinted then. "I won't quite so much, as long as I can go on visiting your place to see where they were—being sentimental, like."

"If you leer again, I'll hit you," George said amiably. "So, Gus, what do we do? Stake out the airport? Look for women wrapped in big upper garments, bigger than their faces and legs'd make you think they needed? Because I can't see the scam stopping, can you? Why should it? Not when there's money to be made."

"I'd already decided the airport was significant, of course. I've got men crawling round there, but I think we can be a bit more specific. We need to be sure these children are being brought in from Romania."

"I'm sure of it," she said. "The Oberlander baby, remember."

"Yes," he said and nodded. "AIDS. Not that it doesn't happen in other countries, of course."

"But in Romania it's endemic among babies. Orphaned babies—or rather babies in orphanages. Not all of them actually have dead parents, of course. But yes, I think we can be certain. These babies are brought from Romania—"

"So we stake out flights from there."

"Remember that they needn't all be direct flights."

"I'm well aware of that. Don't teach me my job. OK, we stake it out, and when we get whoever is shipping the babies in—"

"That should lead us to who is behind it all," George ended triumphantly. "I don't imagine the prime mover does the actual fetching and carrying."

"But I suspect he or she did the killing of Harry Rajabani," Gus said. "That's obvious."

"Because Harry had worked out what was going on?" George frowned, and then her face cleared. "I was about to say how, but of course. I know now who it was who—at least, I think I do."

"Who killed Harry?"

"Probably. Certainly who's behind it all," George said. "It has to be! It can't be anyone else. For a moment I wondered about Susan Kydd—the consultant on Pediatrics. She travels to Romania often, but then I realized who it had to be."

"Is this a private conversation, or can anyone join in?" Gus asked plaintively.

"Listen, Gus, don't interrupt!" She was sitting bolt upright, staring at him with her eyes glittering. She was so excited she could hardly get her words out. "She told me herself how much she cared about those childless people. She'll do anything for them—and she also wants money, wants it badly. To improve the service, to make herself independent of the hospital. It all makes perfect sense to me."

"I'm glad to hear it." Gus was acerbic. "Let me know when you're ready to make some sort of sense as far as I'm concerned."

"Julia Arundel," George said. "It has to be! She was the one who knew who the people were who'd be open to the idea of adopting. She knew which of them had money. No one knew them better than she did."

"For Gawd's sake, you daft 'aporth, who is she?" Gus bawled and some of the people at adjoining tables turned to stare and snigger. Kitty, on the other side of the restaurant, called out, "She's the cat's mother!" and giggled too.

George dropped her voice and leaned closer. "Julia Arundel. The consultant in charge of the Fertility Unit. It all fits so perfectly, Gus. It has to be her. She has access to the names of people who want babies. She promises them babies, takes money from them, like she took it in advance from the Hillmans, and then she imports the babies. She gets someone to smuggle them in tucked inside a shawl or a jacket and gets them drugged so that they don't wake up—Valium, like Bridget said, maybe. Then one day one arrives dead, and she has to be really frantic, doesn't she? Money has changed hands and—and then she remembers the Maternity Unit just down the corridor. She takes the dead baby and swaps it for a live one and passes it on."

She lifted her chin then and went on softly, "And Gus, that means if I'm right, those bereaved parents are going to be able to get their babies back, doesn't it? Though God knows what that'll be like for the people who adopted them." She closed her eyes for a moment, all excitement and enjoyment gone. This was a horrible tangle. But she was certain she was right. She opened her eyes and went on talking, eagerly.

"She does that three times—even to one of her own fertility patients, so she has to be a hard bitch, doesn't she? And Harry, who spends a lot of time hanging around Fertility because of his girlfriend Cherry, he finds out. Gets suspicious anyway, and starts to make notes. In code. Using the Matty typewriter where he has to be so often when he sees the neonates. It all fits. He probably got the idea from accidentally shifting the key on the typewriter. People are always making mistakes with keyboards—I've had some awful tangles in my own department because of computer errors caused like that. There was a great fuss over some blood sugars for the Diabetic Clinic. Anyway, Harry gets this information, and Julia Arundel realizes he knows. Maybe he confronted her? Who can say? And she kills him—runs over him. What car she used and where it is we can't know, but maybe if you hunt around for her car in particular, you might get a surprise."

"I'll look," he said tersely. "Go on." He hadn't taken his eyes from her face all through her recital.

"She dresses in anonymous clothes to do it. Woolly hat, jeans, trainers—so they thought she was a guy, the people at the Rag and Bottle." George wrinkled her nose in concentration. "Yeah, that was it. They just assumed it was a man, but it was Julia Arundel. And then she gets a frantic message from one of her clients. The baby she gave them is sick—very sick. She knows she'll have to see him, and arranges for him to be brought here to Old East. Was she planning to kidnap the baby that night and get rid of him? Who can say? Anyway, she couldn't for some reason. But she did manage to get her hands on him later with that tale about seeing the Harley Street consultant. And she killed him because she was afraid what would happen if he was investigated and searches made for the origin of his illness. You can see it all, can't you? Christ, she must be the hardest of women—can you imagine behaving so—"

"We can't be sure," Gus said. "It's a seductive theory, but there's still your Dr. Kydd idea, mind you. But this one's good too." He looked at her with his head on one side. "OK, Detective Barnabas. What next?"

"How do you mean?"

"You've obviously taken my job off my hands. So tell me what to do next."

She reddened. "Stop that damnfool nonsense, Gus Hathaway. If the idea stands up, you know perfectly well what happens next."

He was silent for a while, thinking, and then nodded. "It stands up," he said. "OK. This is no time for me to get the hump over you being so bleedin' clever. Well done. You're a real smart cookie, ain't that the phrase? Ta for your help." He smiled at her a little crookedly. "You're good for a fella's self-esteem, and I don't think! But I'll get over it. Right, we get a picture of Julia Arundel and show the Hillmans. We stake out the flights from Bucharest. We look in the register at Swansea for a car registered to Arundel and see if we can track it that way and check it for evidence of Harry's murder—though it's getting unlikely after all this time that there'll be any traces left. And then—then we see what we have in the way of firm evidence. Because all this is just guesswork, hmm? Good guesswork, but not a shred of proof." And he looked a little happier as he said it.

36

"I'll try to come in the fall, Ma," George said. "I'll be due for a few weeks' holiday by then and I'll be able to stay a while. It won't seem so long, you'll see."

"Of course it won't," Vanny echoed. "Not long at all." But it was clear she didn't believe it.

Bridget, with elephantine tact, had gone wandering off round the shops, leaving them to share a last cup of coffee, and George sat close to her mother looking at her as though she wouldn't ever see her again. It was absurd, she told herself deep inside, to be so melancholy; there was nothing new about the situation, after all. She'd left the States over ten years ago, and had visited back and forth a few times (though this was her mother's first trip to Europe to see her), and never before when they'd parted had she had this keen sense of loss hovering over her. Yet this time she did. She studied her mother's face, the fine lines outlining the eyes, the faint rim of pallor round the irises, the papery cheeks, wondering whether she'd ever see them again, and felt a childish desire to weep. But she controlled it by pushing her attention sideways, making herself aware of the bustle of the coffee shop, the anxious people with their piles of luggage and the noise of the announcer's voice calling messages for lost passengers and details of flights.

"Don't you fret about me, George," Vanny said unexpectedly, reaching up and touching George's cheek. "I know I've been a bit vague and I know Bridget thinks I may be sick. I thought I was, too. But what the hell! You've got to think positive, right? So I do. Maybe I am getting a bit worn out here and there, but that's the way of things. It always has been. Take a look at *Hamlet* again some time—Act One Scene II, lines seventy-two to seventy-three, as I recall. Gertrude's speech to her son."

She laughed, a fat chuckle that was so reminiscent of her younger self that for a moment George was transported to her childhood. "Remember how I used to make you read things by giving you quotes and not telling you what they were so you had to look them up? Here I go again. But like I say, don't fret, honey. I'll be OK for a while yet. I'm better at home, you know. I get a bit bewildered when things are new, that's all." Again she touched George's cheek and then looked over her shoulder at Bridget who was coming towards them with a carrier bag that was bulging cheerfully.

"I know I'm stupid, I should have waited till I got to the duty-free part, but there you are—I could never resist shopping!" she said. "Hey, you two, I hate to rush things, but we oughta be going through to the departure lounge, I reckon. Don't you, George?"

"Yes," George said. She got up and helped Vanny to her feet. She seemed so frail and, despite her cheerful words, so very much in need of care that George ached a little.

"Now, I'll carry that." Bridget was fussing helpfully and together the three of them made their way across the concourse to the entrance to passport control and the departure lounge, and as George stood on her side of the barrier and watched them go, the ache spread through her middle and made her feel heavy and slow and dull; but then, just as they reached the point where they would vanish, Vanny turned back and gave the signal she had used when George had been very small and scared of being left alone somewhere, like at a party full of girls in fancier dresses than hers, or on a carousel. She put her thumbs in her ears and waggled her fingers, and George laughed aloud and made the same gesture back. Vanny was right; there was no need to fret.

Once they had gone she took a deep breath and tried to think about what to do next. Ever since she'd got home last night and listened to the messages on her ansaphone, she'd been worried about it. She'd told Gus, of course, and he'd been interested, but, as he said, couldn't see any need to change his arrangements.

"Tell me again what she said. Exactly," he'd said when she'd begun to protest, and she'd told him he could hear it for himself; and played the tape back at him, listening even more carefully herself, although she'd already listened several times.

"Oh! You're not there!" the breathless little voice had said. Sylvia Hillman. "Oh, dear, not there. I'm not sure—Oh dear." Then there had been just the sound of breathing; and then she had started again, speaking rapidly and clearly in a state of high anxiety.

"We're leaving in half an hour. David said Florida. It'll take my mind off—not that anything will really, but—Well, we're leaving so it'll have to be a message, won't it? And I don't know what to—Oh dear, what shall I—Well, I got a call, you see. My friend Mary, she's the dearest—I mean she really does understand and care and she tries to help and she told me that she'd heard that another woman she knew who she told about the—who she told, just like me, that this woman could get babies, well, she told her, she said, and now she's said that she's getting a baby in the next couple of days, and she thought—Mary thought—that I should know in case I wanted to get in touch and tell her what happened to me and maybe find this woman and make her say what happened to Teddy and—Only David said no. He can't take it any more. And he said I'm not to think about it at all and in Florida there may be babies because of all those Haitians and Puerto Ricans and—and, well, I said I wouldn't tell you but I thought maybe I should because if you can find out who she is you can ask her what happened to Teddy. Oh! and don't call me, will you, or David'll be so—Oh! No, darling, not phoning, just checking the time—" And the tape ended in a clatter as the caller hung up.

"Hardly a clear message, is it?" Gus had said and she had almost shouted at him.

"Clear? Of course it isn't! The woman's half demented by grief and wanting and—I did explain to you, Gus."

"Oh, I know. Well, you've talked to her, so explain all she said to me, too."

"What she's saying is that the same woman who gave them Teddy—and took him away—has made a deal with someone else. And promised that someone else a baby in the next few days. Which means there's someone coming in to Heathrow with a baby any flight now—"

"That's one hell of an assumption," he interrupted. "How can you be sure it's the same woman?"

"Sylvia Hillman said it is," she said. "And don't ask me how I know it's Sylvia Hillman, because I do. It's her voice."

"I never doubted that," he said mildly. "I'm just asking how you can be sure that the other woman she talks about will be getting a baby from the same source."

"I'm not sure! I'm just saying it seems likely. I'm just saying you should be certain to stake out the flights from Romania for the next few days because the likelihood is someone'll be on one with a baby under her sweater."

"But we are," he pointed out, all sweet reasonableness. "We're staking out the Bucharest flights in Terminal Two."

"And the other places they might come from? Frankfurt and Vienna and—"

"All of them," he said patiently. "We'll concentrate on the other flights of course, but we'll keep a particularly close eye on Bucharest. It makes sense, doesn't it? So there's no need to worry. We'll be watching. It helps to be told there's a high chance there'll be someone, of course. I suppose we could send someone to Florida to talk to the Hillmans."

"Oh, no, don't do that. They've suffered enough. You heard

what she said. She doesn't want David—her husband—to know she called me. I don't want to make life harder for her."

"Fair enough. Anyway, I don't really think there's any need. We're doing all we can. Leave it to us, George. I promise you we'll be watching like the proverbials."

And she had had to settle for that. In the fuss of getting Vanny and Bridget off, it had been fairly easy to keep her anxiety at bay; now, however, it all came back. What was happening? Would they spot the courier and the baby or let her slip through? Would they—

She stopped herself. This was silly. There was nothing else she could do. She'd told Gus what Sylvia had said; the rest was up to him. And now she stood and hovered uncertainly in the middle of the concourse at Terminal Three, not sure what to do next. She'd arranged to take the whole day off from the hospital and now it was only just gone eleven-thirty in the morning; how would she fill in the rest of the day? Gus had made it clear that there was little more she could do with the case; all day yesterday he'd been busy about what he called the nuts and bolts of detecting; chasing information about Julia Arundel's car, setting up surveillance here at Heathrow, and today she had had no time to talk to him. She'd wanted, when she woke, to call him again and report her now total conviction that there would be a baby coming in today or the day after, but from the moment they had woken this morning, the old ladies had been in a fever of busyness and had drawn her into it, unpacking cases that had been packed the day before so that they could rearrange them and then starting all over again.

But now she had got them here and safely into the departure lounge for the noon flight to New York, where they'd pick up a connection to Buffalo, there was nothing left she could do but think. And some of the thoughts were not as agreeable as they might be. Dear Ma, she told herself. Dear Ma. She's all right, really. Isn't she?

She made a detor as she crossed the concourse, stopping at the book shop. It was a big one and there was always the possibility that they had a copy, but the girl at the till gaped at her when she asked for the works of Shakespeare, and pointed to the piles of blockbusters and blood-dripping thrillers that were everywhere.

"We only have normal books," she said. "Sorree!" George sighed and went. She'd have to wait till she got home to get Vanny's message.

It wasn't until she was almost outside the building on her way to the underground station and the journey back to town— they had come in a taxi, she and the old ladies, but she saw no need to be so extravagant on the way home—that she saw the sign, and stopped. "Transfers to Terminals One, Two and Four," it was headed and then gave instructions. She bit her lip and thought for a moment and then headed in the direction of Terminal Two. At last she had something to do.

"Do me a favor," Rupert Dudley said. "I got enough on my plate without having you here and all. If you don't mind my saying so."

"It wouldn't make any difference if I did," George said tartly. "Anyway, I'm not asking you to be glad I'm here. I'm only asking if I can be useful. I know the people in the hospital by sight a hell of a lot better than you do. If the courier's one of them then I could identify—"

"This is a police matter," Dudley said. "I don't need a pathologist, thanks all the same. If I do I'll put out a call for you in the normal manner."

"If Gus were here—" George began and then bit back the words, realizing too late how foolish it might be to even mention him, and she was right. Dudley glowered and turned away with some ostentation to speak to one of his men, ignoring her completely.

George seethed inside, but there was nothing she could

do. She had had enough trouble finding them in the first place and then getting in to them. The Customs man leaning near the entrance to the observation room where they were able to overlook the Customs area had needed a good deal of convincing that she had a right to talk to the policemen who were in there, but had given in when she'd caught sight of Rupert behind him and called out, with a familiarity she had never used before, "Hey, Roop! Tell this guy you're expecting me, will you?" Dudley had been so surprised he'd just stared and the man had taken this as acknowledgement and let her in.

Now as she came out of the room he looked at her sideways and she flushed a little, feeling his triumph, and went as fast as she could till she lost herself in the people milling around on the other side of the barriers that had been set up where the Customs Hall exit debouched into the main concourse. And then stopped.

Dammit all to hell and back, she wouldn't be thwarted. So Rupert Dudley didn't want her there? Too goddamn bad. She'd stay out here and watch; even if they saw the courier and identified her as such—supposing of course she was going to be on the flight from Bucharest—they wouldn't be able to stop her there in the Customs Hall, would they? Well, she amended then, they could but they wouldn't. The person who mattered wasn't the courier but the person who employed her, and would therefore meet her. Or him; it was always possible, George reminded herself, that they would use a man. Or was it? Could a man carry a baby strapped to his body through a long journey and not be spotted? She felt it was unlikely, without knowing why. OK, so whoever it was, even Rupert Dudley wouldn't go off half cocked, surely, and try to intervene before contact had been made with whoever was going to meet that courier? So she would stay out here and watch...

Passing the time was a major problem. She bought several newspapers and tried to concentrate on them, but reading standing up, as people pushed past, wasn't easy. She could have gone away to the coffee shop of course and come back nearer the time when the plane was due in—which was, she had found out from the information desk, at three-thirty—but she feared doing that. There were a great many people meeting planes and the majority were forced to the back of the crowd and had to peer over the heads of those in front in order to see passengers emerging from the Customs Hall; she wanted a place here at the very front and was determined to keep it.

She gave up the papers eventually and looked at the clock for the umpteenth time. The daily Bucharest flight was shown at the very bottom of the list of places from which flights were coming and she read them with a sense of awe at first; Vienna and Moscow, Frankfurt and Sofia, Budapest and Istanbul and Athens; it was like the fairy stories of her childhood of Golden Roads to Samarkand; but the glamor wore off very soon as she watched the Bucharest flight information creep up the board as one after another the planes before it arrived, decanted their passengers and let them out of the Customs Hall in squealing knots to be collected by the excited people waiting around her.

She told herself stories about them, tried to forecast the sort of people the waiters were going to greet as their own, and never got it right. The young couple who looked like honeymooners she had marked down for the prosperous middle-aged parental types, half a dozen places along from her own spot, but were greeted boisterously by three small children in the charge of an au pair. The middle-aged couple, on the other hand, made excited welcoming gestures to a tall thin girl with a shaven head wearing outrageously excessive make-up and the shortest and tightest of skirts that even this season's fashions had thrown up. A couple of ill-dressed people bearing several brown paper parcels in their luggage trolley were met by the most expensive-looking of uniformed chauffeurs, and a group of people who seemed, by their clothes, to be very unsophisticated indeed and likely to be thoroughly bewildered by the sheer size of Heathrow's Terminal Two scattered confidently towards the exit, showing no need to be met and shepherded at all. She gave up her attempts at character-reading and wondered guiltily if she'd be as ineffective judging the people who arrived on the Bucharest flight as she had been judging those from Vienna, and decided to give up the exercise, gloomy though the prospect of long hours with nothing to do might be. Not until the clock crept round to three did she begin to cheer up. Only a half hour now; it wouldn't be long.

And then she reminded herself how silly she was being. Why on earth should there be a courier on the Bucharest plane at all? With all the fuss going on, wouldn't Julia Arundel be pulling in her horns, playing safe for a while? To expect someone on this flight was absurd, no matter what Sylvia Hillman had said.

Or was it? Julia Arundel didn't know she'd been identified as the criminal. As far as she was concerned she'd got away with it. She had exchanged three babies, killed one, even killed Harry, and no one had come near identifying her. She must feel safe, George thought, must be sure it's perfectly all right to continue. Oh, yes, there'd be a courier on this flight. No doubt about it in George's mind. Sylvia was right.

At twenty past three the information board coughed and clattered and produced the news that the Bucharest flight was now expected at four p.m. and she cursed. Her feet were cold and aching, and her back was screaming from the long hours of standing. She was also more than a little hungry—she hadn't even thought about lunch—and furthermore her bladder was starting to make itself felt. Another half-hour. She could manage it, couldn't she? Yes, of course she could.

At five minutes to four the board again clattered with a new message about the flight from Bucharest. Four-fifteen, it announced, was the expected time of arrival now, and at this she stamped her cold feet both in anger and in an attempt to warm them a little, and this time her bladder shrieked urgently at the jolt and informed her that there was no way it was prepared to hold on that long.

She used every control trick in the book; tightened her pelvic floor muscles, straightened her back and lifted her shoulders so as to enlarge her abdominal space and give her bladder more room, bit her tongue and thought of music, the best distraction she knew of, and the urgency began to ease; and then someone at the back of the waiting crowd began to whistle and the shrill sound pierced the air and moved straight into her belly. Again her bladder tightened and now she knew she hadn't a hope of holding on any longer.

"Please," she said to the woman beside her in the crush, also leaning on the barrier. "I must go to the ladies room, but if I go away and my friend comes and doesn't see me she'll be so upset. Will you hold my place till I come back? I'd be very grateful."

The woman looked at her wide eyed and startled. "Pliss?" she said.

"Oh, God," George said and asked the man on her other side. He looked over his shoulder and nodded so she flashed a smile at him and began to push her way out of the crowd. It was easier to control the urge now she was moving and once she was out of the thickest press of people she could run, and run she did, scanning the multitude of signs for the nearest women's lavatory.

She located it at last and shot in and found two women waiting and the available doors all showing the red engaged flash.

"Oh, God," she said again. "I'm about to burst. May I go in front of the line?" The waiting women looked at her, one with a glower and the other with a sympathetic nod.

"Of course," the kindly one said just as a door opened, and George gasped her thanks and shot in.

The relief was huge and she sat there with her head down, letting the freedom from pressure roll over her as she caught her breath, for her rush had been a considerable effort. Her pulses slowed at last and she felt ready to stand up and fix her clothes and hurry back to the crowded barrier to wait for the plane from Bucharest.

The other stalls had emptied and been used a couple of times while she'd been there, and as she zipped her trousers and pulled her jacket straight, she became aware of voices coming from further down the line of cubicles. An adult with a child, she thought vaguely, and then stood very still.

There were two voices coming from one stall. They were speaking softly but she could hear them. She was on a line with them and the doors closed off some of the racket from outside, while letting it travel laterally since the inner walls, unlike the doors, ended a couple of feet from the ceiling. She couldn't identify words, but that there was an intense and hurried colloquy going on was beyond doubt.

And neither of the voices was that of a child.

She shot out of the cubicle she was in and over to the wash basin and began to run the water. The mirror in front of her reflected all that was going on behind her and she watched covertly but closely from beneath her lashes as she washed. It didn't seem possible that the person for whom she'd been waiting and watching had somehow eluded her, come on a different flight, walked past her, only to be here now, and yet she was convinced that was what had happened. Those two voices had been too expressive, too tight, too low and too conspiratorial for her to doubt it.

Other women around her washed and dried their hands under the hot-air dryers and prinked with lipstick and powder puffs as she stood there, and still one of the cubicle doors remained closed. The conviction grew in her that there was a deep significance here—yet at the same time she was very aware of the clock creeping on and the need to get back to the crowded barrier in time to watch the arrival of the passengers from Bucharest if she was wrong about what was happening here.

She had washed enough to perform an operation, had dried her hands till they were red with the heat, had primped and tweaked at her hair until she felt like a photographer's model or something before the cubicle door at last opened.

It did not open far; someone slipped out, and George stared through the mirror, fascinated. The person who emerged was a short round girl, quite young but far from youthfully dressed. Her hair was tied up in a scarf and her feet were in heavy boots. George had to crane to see them but the girl stood still for a moment at the door of the lavatory which had now closed again, ostensibly fastening her jacket, a thick one, quilted and lumpy. She had her head down so that her face could not be seen but George had the impression not of roundness like her body but of angularity. The legs in the heavy trousers beneath the thick jacket couldn't be seen; the trousers were ill cut and baggy and showed no sign of the flesh beneath them.

The girl moved away then and headed slowly for the door, and George stood poised, uncertain what to do next. She was as sure as she could be that she was looking at the courier; the clothes, the style, everything about her was as she had imagined the courier would be. The fact that she had clearly not come off the Bucharest flight was beside the point; there had to be other ways of getting into London from Romania than the obvious one, surely?

But if I go after her, then whoever she has left behind in that cubicle will get away, she thought, feverishly pulling at her hair without realizing she was doing it, still trying to pretend she was preening and not watching the woman who had now finished buttoning her coat.

The woman lifted her chin and George managed some how to shift her eyeline so that she was not obviously staring at her, but then couldn't help it. George's eyes flicked back till she was looking at her, and her pulse began to pump thickly in her ears. The girl was staring at her, scared and wide eyed, and her face was exactly as George had suspected it would be;

thin, bony and far from well covered. There was no way that a girl with a face like that was as bulky as her clothes would make a casual looker suspect. Without stopping to think further George whirled and began to move towards her.

It all happened very quickly then. As the girl saw George coming she moved sideways, quite clearly intending to run, but as she did so a woman with four small children in tow came fussing into the lavatory from outside, talking loudly at one of the children who was dragging on her hand and bawling at the top of her voice. The girl in the bulky clothes had to dodge to avoid them, and as she did so, the door of the cubicle she had come from opened again and a woman came out. She was wearing a sensible navy blue coat and a round hat pushed down on to her head so firmly no hair could be seen. Her face was pale and she wore no make-up. She looked vaguely uniformed, and the impression was increased by the sensible bag she had depending from a shoulder strap on her right side and the big oblong carrier bag she was holding in her left hand. George looked at the girl, then at the hatted woman and decided. She made a lunge for the latter, and in that moment the girl in the quilted jacket made her escape, pushing past the woman with the collection of four children, all of whom immediately started wailing loudly as the escaper knocked against them.

But it had been enough for George. She had the woman in the hat and the almost-uniform by the arm and was pulling on it, holding on for grim death.

"Sister!" she said loudly. "Sister Collinson! Not the person I expected to see at all! May I look in your bag, please?"

37

"I don't think," Gus said, "I've ever seen anything funnier."

"If it had been you, you'd be laughing out of the other end of your anatomy," George said, wincing as she moved her right arm. It still ached abominably where the older of the four children had bitten her. She hadn't broken the skin but had made a massive bruise. "That child had jaws like a Rottweiler."

"Yeah, pity about that. Still, if it hadn't been for them…"

"If it hadn't been for *me* your lot would have lost her this time altogether," George said. "Never mind those godawful kids."

"We'd have got her eventually," Gus said. "They've got three more of her couriers since then." He smiled then, a little grimly. "They were very surprised young women when it was one of my PCs they met in the loo."

"Yeah, well," George said. "Maybe. The thing is, I—"

He leaned forward and touched her bruised arm gently. "It's all right, George. I know it was you who broke this case. So will everyone else. That's a promise."

"Oh, God," she said. "You make me sound—" She stopped.

"Competitive? You bet your sweet whatever-it-is." He laughed. "But that's the way I am, too. If I'd had the good luck to be in the right place at the right moment the way you were, I'd be pretty damned pleased with myself too."

"It wasn't *just* luck," she said. "I mean, I had thought about it."

"Who are you kidding, sweetheart? You was waiting for the Bucharest flight, the same as we were. Rupert told me you were there as soon as I turned up, and I saw you for myself! But I thought, who am I to spoil her fun? But then you vanished."

"I was bursting. I had to go."

"I know the feeling." He was richly sympathetic. "And it's never the right time. Only for you, it was."

"I have to admit it was one hell of a coincidence. I'm there for that plane, trying to convince myself the courier'll be on it. And when it comes to the point I have to find a loo, and it turns out to be the loo where the courier is! I ask you! It's stretching credulity a bit."

"Not that much. In real life coincidences like that happen all the time. Read Arthur Koestler if you don't believe me. It's called synchronicity."

"It is?" She searched her memory for Arthur Koestler and couldn't find him there.

"Believe me, you have to trust Nature and this sort of thing is a natural phenomenon." He laughed again, a deep burr of satisfaction. "If you hadn't had a call of Nature you'd have missed her. Let's hear it for Nature."

"Well," she said. "I suppose so." She stretched. "Anyway, I was right, wasn't I?"

"What about? Julia Arundel? Poor Dr. Arundel who is as pure as the driven whatsit and can't believe what's been going on behind her back?"

George had the grace to blush a little. "Well, fair enough, I was wrong there, just like Susan Kydd was a good guess, even if that was wrong too. No, I mean about how it was done."

"Yeah." He went over to the table in the corner to fetch more coffee, and waved through the glass at one of the policemen outside to fetch more when he found it empty. "You got that right. Well done."

She preened. "I'm really pleased about that. It was such a sudden realization."

"Mind you, it was my nice old lady who got it," he said as the coffee arrived, brought by Michael Urquhart. "Ta, Mike. Shut the door on the other side, will you? Yeah. It was all Vanny's doing."

"Aren't I to have any credit?" she said a little plaintively. "I mean, who caught Collinson?"

"Your bladder did," he said promptly, and she made a face at him.

They sat and sipped coffee in silence for a while and then she put her cup down with a little clatter. "What happens now?"

"We've got Collinson's statement to work on. It wasn't hard to get it all out of her. I really think she thought she'd never be caught. She had no plan ready for what she might say if she was, not a hint of an alibi or anything like it. And we got a warrant to check her flat and it's all there, anyway. She kept meticulous records, you know. Very tidy. How Harry Rajabani ever got hold of that stuff from her, I'll never know."

"Did she ever do any of the bookwork involved in her scheme at the hospital?" George asked.

"Oh, sure. She had to. She told me she just went into the Fertility Unit office whenever she had to leave the Pediatric ward and go over to Maternity to see a baby there outside Cherry's normal office hours, and just helped herself to the names and addresses of people she found there. Then all she had to do was contact them and she had her customers all ready and set."

"Um," George said. "Yes, that was the lot we found, wasn't it? Just part of some names she collected from the Fertility office and then typed up in code on Matty's typewriter."

"Yup."

"I have to admit something," George said, not sure why she had to tell him this, but feeling she ought for Cherry's sake. "I wouldn't let Cherry help me decode that list. If I had she'd have seen at once it was a list of her patients—some of them—complete with physical descriptions to make sure of good matches between babies and adopters. She knows all of them, doesn't she? But I thought..." She shrugged. "Silly, I know, but it was police business so I kept her out of it."

He roared with laughter. "It's OK for you, *verboten* for her? You really are a right little madam sometimes, George! Oh, don't look at me like that! You were right to be careful, it just struck me as funny."

"I thought it would," George said sourly.

"You're forgiven." He was very cheerful. "We got Collinson, and that's what matters. She thinks she was doing a public service, you know. Doesn't see any harm in what happened. Except for the babies she had to swap. She admits that was rough on the parents, but says it's all right for them really. They can always have another baby. She's got about as much—oh, I don't know—understanding of what it's like to be a woman as—as a fly. How she ever worked as a nurse I'll never know."

"I should have realized," George said. "I spotted quite early on that she couldn't care less about the job. Not only was she racist—very nasty about Dr. Choopani—she just did the paperwork, stayed at her desk, never did anything with the children unless she had to. Not like Goss, dammit. He might be a fascist pig but he was ten times the caring person she was. Odd, isn't it?"

"Odd? It's crazy!" he said. "Goss reckons to go on with his career, you know. And there's not a lot against him doing it. We can get him on offenses under the Race Relations Act, but as I understand it that needn't damage his chances of staying on the Nurses' Register or whatever it is, or of working. Worries me, that."

"Worries you?" she said feelingly. "How do you suppose hospital staff feel? We try to kid ourselves we're all motivated by the highest of principles and then we find out some of us are the same as everyone else. Greedy, selfish, downright wicked. Like Goss. Only his sort of wickedness he can get away with because of the way the world is, and the Collinson sort..." She shook her head. "She did it just for money."

"It's a hell of a just for," he said. "She told me she's made over a million quid since she started. And I'm not even sure the court can take it away from her even if—or rather when—she's found guilty and sent down. Her overheads were minimal—the price of air tickets for those girls who want to come here anyway—and they come from all sorts of places, not just Romania. The one who got away from you is a Hungarian, apparently. That's why she came in earlier than we expected, on the Budapest flight. As I say, all Collinson had to do was pay their fares and give them a risible cash sum and then she got them jobs as au pairs with families willing to ask no questions in exchange for cheap domestic help. The girls liked it well enough—anywhere's better than Eastern Europe, it seems—and the infertile got their illicit babies, and according to Collinson she's done a public service."

"It's a hell of a public service to kill a baby and a man," George said. "She makes me feel physically sick, you know that?"

"You surprise me." He looked genuinely puzzled. "You cut up bodies and paddle around in guts in a way that makes most people feel really very peculiar indeed—I have to concentrate not to get myself in a state over your PMs—and yet faced with a bit of common-or-garden human greed and selfishness you get all queasy. Odd that."

"Not odd at all," she said passionately. "Bodies aren't ugly and selfish and—human bodies are *beautiful*. Beautifully arranged, beautifully planned, magnificently organized. It's minds that..." She shivered a little. "I think I ought to take an update course in forensic psychology. Maybe I'd feel better about all this then."

"That's all I'm short of," he said. "Jesus! Imagine you going around analysing minds all over the place. It'd be hell."

"You reckon? I'll have to do it then." There was a short

silence and then she said, "How did she kill Harry? I mean which car?"

"I'm embarrassed about that and can't deny it. It was her car. It's been sitting there in the hospital car park in the open all this time. I've given Roop hell over it. It never occurred to me it wouldn't occur to *him* to look there, but he didn't ever think there could be a connection with the hospital, would you believe. He can be bloody stupid sometimes—but that's just between us. It wouldn't do if it got out I'd been slagging him off to you."

She was flattered. "You can trust me."

"I know that. Anyway, that's how we missed checking her car. She used that to run him down, but after the weathering it's had, the chances of there being any evidence left is slim. Not that it matters too much, thank Gawd. She talked willingly enough."

"How did she get him there? To the pub, I mean."

Gus shook his head. "It was Harry himself who did it. He asked her to meet him there. He'd worked out that there was something going on, that some of the people who came into Pediatrics to see Patricia Collinson were not strictly kosher, and he wanted to get it out of her. He'd found the lists, is my guess—she'd typed them, of course, not him. He had broken the code though. So he wanted to talk to her. He chose the place. She dressed in that sort of anonymous stuff that made the landlord think she was a bloke—she wasn't trying to fool anyone. Just wanted to look ordinary, she said—and then ran him over. It was a thing she did on the spur of the moment. No planning at all. He'd rattled her badly telling her he knew and she didn't want to stop her racket. She hit him with the jack from her car, which she keeps on her front seat in case of trouble—I ask you!—and was going to just leave him there. And then after she got in her car she just went for him. Poor bastard. Stupid bastard…"

"And then she went back and parked the car and that was

all?" George was incredulous.

"That's about the size of it."

"Good God!"

"You can say that again. Bloody Roop. Not to have checked the hospital car park…"

"How about the baby she killed?" It seemed politic to change the subject, and George saw no point in nagging about the car. Anyway, it wouldn't have made much difference if they had found it, after all; Collinson could quite easily have said she'd left it unlocked and available to any sneak thief. "She was very careless about that, wasn't she? Leaving the plastic bag over the head. If she hadn't, it could have seemed a cot death like the others, even though it was dumped the way it was."

"She's been careless from the start. She never really thought anything through properly. She had arranged for the Hillmans to bring Teddy in to the Pediatric department so that she could have a look at him and sort out what was going on. But she didn't make sure she was there to meet 'em when they arrived. It would have been all right for her if she'd done that. They never met her, only talked on the phone. So she'd have been safe enough. But when they arrived she wasn't waiting for them at the door as she should have been—she says that herself now—and Prudence Jennings was on duty and took one look at the child and scooped him up. Collinson wouldn't have let a doctor near him if she'd planned it right. She'd have admitted him, killed him quietly—another cot death, it'd have seemed—and that would have been that. She'd have got the Hillmans another baby, she said. As though they were like— like fridges or freezers, things you can swap if the first one isn't up to quality." He grimaced. "It is sickening, at that."

"I'm glad you agree." George was a little sardonic. "Because a woman who can kill a baby and leave the plastic bag over its head when she dumps it has to be some nasty piece of work."

"Yeah, I agree. But for once she did think. Sort of. She left the bag because she said she didn't want to take any chances of any infected material reaching her from its mouth and nose, seeing the child had AIDS. Would you believe it? But there you go, she's all of a piece, I suppose. No surprises about her. Though there would have been, if it had been Julia Arundel, wouldn't there? Agreed?"

George bit her lip. "I suppose so. No doctor who obviously cared as much about her patients as she did could have been quite so—Well, I was wrong, OK? No need to rub it in."

"Would I rub it in?"

"Yup."

"Oh."

There was another silence and then George said, "Has anyone told the Popodopoulos family or the Chowdarys yet?"

"Not yet. We have to track down the babies. And then do something about the adopters. Poor devils are going to be in a terrible state." He stopped. "I wonder if it'd be OK for them to have the baby that came in yesterday with the courier? I gather Dr. Kydd's been looking after him, and he's in reasonable shape. About a fortnight old, and not HIV positive as far as they can tell. The tests will be going on, I suppose. And if not him, there'll be more coming in, I suspect. Interpol are doing what they can to stop the trade but they're not likely to do it just like that. And I can't see the authorities sending the babies back. So, offering them to the people Collinson cheated could help them. Poor sods'll have had a bad time of it. If they've learned to love the babies they got it won't be easy for them to give them up, but—"

"But a new kitten might help," George finished and Gus looked uncomfortable.

"I was afraid it'd sound like that. Anyway, it's out of our hands. Social Services are dealing with that side of the case. I'm glad I don't have to."

"Me too."

"Mmm," he said. "By the way, why did they die? The babies Collinson put in the places of the Chowdary, Popodopoulos and Lennon children?"

It was George's turn to be uncomfortable. "It was Valium. It's not a killer usually, of course. Generally you'd only die from Valium if a lorryload fell on you, but these were fragile babies and the heavy doses they were given to make sure they didn't move or cry during the journey and give away their hiding place flattened them so much they died of—well, they just stopped breathing. So it was a sort of cot death. But I should have found the drug in the PM I did." She brooded. "It's not what you'd look for, that's the thing. And anyway, I'm not even sure I'd have been able to find it."

"The last thing you have to do is feel bad about what you might have missed," he said. "Like the Oxford case, ducks, if you hadn't pressed and pushed we'd never have got anywhere. It's your case, not ours, and you did a good job on it."

"Yes, Gus," she said in a mock cockney voice, and he flicked his fingers at his invisible hat brim and said gruffly, "That's OK, babe," in the broadest Brooklyn twang he could manage.

Much later that night, curled up together in front of the flickering flames of her gas fire, George said sleepily, "Gus?"

"Hmm?"

"I suppose you don't quote Shakespeare much, do you?"

"Try me."

"*Hamlet*, Act One, Scene II. Lines seventy-two to seventy-three."

"Hmm. What about "em?"

"Ma said it to me. Told me it'd make me feel better about her. I meant to look it up as soon as I got home but…"

He laughed softly and she felt the vibration of his chuckle through the bare skin of his chest against her cheek. "All my fault, with my nasty seductive ways. Arf arf, once aboard the sofa and the girl was mine! Popeye's got nothing on me!"

"Sofa?" she said and it was her turn to chuckle. "We weren't on it all that long."

"Complaining?"

"No, I like hearthrugs. So you don't know that bit of *Hamlet*?"

"Who said I didn't?"

"Then what is it?"

He was silent, thinking, and then said softly, "Thou know'st 'tis common; all that lives must die, Passing through nature to eternity."

She was quiet for a long time and then said simply, "Oh."

He held her closer still, if that were possible. "It's all right, George," he said. "I'm here, you know. And I intend to stay."

She took a deep breath and relaxed. "D'you know, Gus, I rather thought you did. And I'm very glad about it. I think Ma will be too." And she sighed again and closed her eyes against the flicker of the flames, and fell asleep.